BOOK II
FALLEN ANGEL

A TRUE CRIME FANTASY

THE WAR
FOR
THE SOUL OF
BROOKLYN

MICHAEL VECCHIONE

Red Penguin
BOOKS

Fallen Angel - A True Crime Fantasy - Book 2

Copyright © 2023 by Michael Vecchione

All rights reserved.

Published by Red Penguin Books

Bellerose Village, New York

ISBN

Print 978-1-63777-479-3

Digital 978-1-63777-478-6

To "Lenny Ristagno".... You know who you are!!
Thank you for all you do. I love you.
~Michael

CONTENTS

PART THREE

PART FOUR

The Devil whispered in my ear, "You're not strong enough to withstand the storm." Today I whispered in the Devil's ear, "I am the storm."
    —*Anonymous*

PART ONE

CHAPTER

ONE

The winter in New York City that year was especially cruel. Snow and bitter cold dominated the weather starting mid-December.

City officials, desperate, and with no hard evidence, attributed the unusual number of fires in the city to an increase in the number of people using electric heaters and leaving their gas stoves and ovens on all day, to keep warm.

No one was buying it.

As the number of injured firefighters and civilians climbed, City Hall went into complete panic. They had no answers.

The city council pressured the mayor and the fire commissioner to act. Demonstrators from neighborhoods across the city where fires had destroyed homes and businesses picketed City Hall every day pleading with their elected officials to protect them. Several demonstrations even resulted in violence, necessitating a call-up of the NYPD to quell the unrest.

The front page of every city newspaper carried dramatic photos of injured firefighters and citizens, burnt-out buildings, businesses and homes. Reporters wrote heart-breaking stories of the suffering, of those rendered homeless, the hardship of small business owners whose livelihood had been utterly destroyed, and the anguish of the families of the injured who were confined to hospital beds for weeks and months while their burns and injuries healed. The editorial pages demanded action in getting to the root of what they called an "epidemic of destructive blazes."

A Christmas Eve fire in the garage/equipment facility attached to the rectory of the Roman Catholic, Church of the Archangels, in the Flatbush section of Brooklyn changed everything. That was because the untimely and tragic death of Firefighter Louis Amato, caught the attention of former United States Attorney General John Caldwell.

Amato, assigned to Brooklyn Rescue Co. 2, had rushed into the structure in an attempt to save someone he was told was inside, when in reality, the building was unoccupied.

His unnecessary death on the eve of Christianity's most joyous holiday devastated the pastor, Father John Keenan, and cast a pall over holiday services and his congregation.

The 'attack' on Christmas Eve, as the fire and death were later characterized by Caldwell, on that particular church, a pro-cathedral in the Brooklyn Diocese, put the priests who lived in the rectory in mortal danger. It was a clear indication to him that an old adversary was responsible.

Once again, Satan was wreaking havoc in Brooklyn.

John Caldwell was the head of a secret organization consisting of lawyers from the United States Department of Justice, which included a Cardinal, and several Catholic priests from the Vatican's Office of Exorcisms.

The group was formed when a priest serving in the Office of Exorcisms in New York City began a research project after he noticed that he and his colleagues throughout the world had been asked to perform exorcisms on criminals who were responsible for horrific crimes.

The priest noticed that the crimes were the type that adversely affected the good order of society and resulted in community upheaval when the criminals responsible failed to be convicted after trial.

The crimes consisted of political corruption, serial killings of society's most vulnerable, child murders, homicides that destroyed families, and the murder of police officers, firefighters and first responders.

Further research revealed that this pattern of horrific crime, social upheaval, acquittal, then chaos, occurred in many countries over decades. And, in those instances, the priest found that exorcisms followed.

Because of his work the priest was familiar with the ways of the Devil. He therefore concluded that Satan was the instigator of those crimes. He had taken over the will of the perpetrators and forced them to commit horrific acts to foment turmoil throughout the world.

The priest was particularly struck by the mayhem in recent years that was occurring in several American cities after criminals responsible for particularly heinous crimes were found not guilty after trial.

It was this pattern that was now playing out in Brooklyn.

The reasons for the prosecution's losses varied from jurisdiction to jurisdiction. However, after closer inspection, it was apparent that the Devil had been able to use *HIS* wiles to influence crucial portions of both the investigation and the trial to bring about the outcome *HE* was looking for.

Because dangerous and guilty people were going free to wreak havoc in US cities due to the influence of the *Evil One*, the priest took his findings to the Cardinal in charge of the Vatican's Office of Exorcisms.

After a close study and much discussion, the Cardinal and his staff agreed with the priest's conclusion. They asked for a meeting with the Pope.

Following that meeting, a decision was made to take the findings to the United States government. The Vatican's Secretary of State reached out to the US Department of Justice and asked for a high-level meeting.

At Justice Department headquarters in Washington, D.C., the priest's research and conclusions were laid out for the US Attorney General.

At first, the AG was skeptical. However, the more they talked and the more evidence the clerics presented explaining how their conclusion was reached, the lawyers and investigators in the Justice Department and finally the Attorney General himself, were convinced.

The president was then consulted.

After a full briefing, he agreed to a plan of attack that had been fashioned by the AG, his people, and the Vatican.

A secret organization within the Justice Department was created. It was dedicated to one mission, war with the Devil.

It was paramount that this group remain secret because knowledge of its existence would cause world-wide panic.

John Caldwell, a seasoned and highly regarded attorney was named as the person in charge.

In view of the fact that the crimes and cases in the US had been, and were expected to remain local, it was decided that an individual local prosecutor, with impeccable qualifications and an exemplary record would be recruited in each jurisdiction where they believed the Devil was operating. That prosecutor would be tasked to handle the investigation and trial of these horrific crimes and would answer only to Caldwell and his group.

Because Brooklyn was now ground zero for the *Evil One*, the group determined that a prosecutor from the Brooklyn District Attorney's office was needed.

For that task they turned to Monsignor Salvatore Romano.

Salvatore Romano was born and raised in Brooklyn. After becoming a priest, he served for many years in several parishes throughout the borough and knew it well.

Following his parish assignments, he was transferred to the Vatican's Office of Exorcisms where he learned to perform the ritual of expelling the Devil from those whose bodies and minds *HE* had taken over. After several years he was named a monsignor. While serving in that office he got to know the clerical members who were now a part of Caldwell's group.

With the *Evil One* operating to undermine the fabric of Brooklyn's diverse, colorful, unique, and generally orderly society, Romano was a natural for Caldwell to bring on as a member.

Because of the many years he spent in Brooklyn and because of the connections he made there, he was the logical choice to identify and recruit a Brooklyn prosecutor capable of handling this sensitive and important assignment.

After taking the monsignor into his confidence and educating him on the group and its mission, Caldwell told Romano that he wanted him to become a part of it. When the monsignor began to say that he was assigned to a parish in upstate New York, Caldwell stopped him and said that the Vatican had given its approval for Romano to join him in this important and sacred work. Romano was honored and anxious to begin.

"When do we start?" he asked.

Caldwell gave the monsignor his first assignment, and added, "When you find that prosecutor you will serve as his liaison to the group, and his confidante."

The monsignor knew exactly who he would approach.

CHAPTER
TWO

Michael Gioca, the Chief of the Brooklyn District Attorney's Rackets Division had been a childhood friend of the monsignor. They were classmates, teammates, shot dice behind the parish house of the church where they both served as altar boys, and even double dated. They were inseparable until Romano chose the priesthood and entered the seminary.

Through the years the monsignor followed his friend's career. He was proud of Michael and was not surprised at the success he achieved in the Brooklyn District Attorney's Office.

Gioca rose from a lowly assistant district attorney first to Chief of the District Attorney's Homicide Bureau, then to Chief of Trials and finally to First Deputy District Attorney and Chief of the DA's Rackets Division. He had become the best trial attorney in the office and was entrusted with some of the most important and high-profile cases in Brooklyn... until his career took an unexpected turn for the worst!

Following a contentious and heartbreaking divorce, Michael fell into a depression that threatened to derail him.

He spent most of his time feeling sorry for himself and missing his two sons who he was very close to.

Unable to concentrate, he would neglect to go into work some days and when he did make it to the office, he left most of his duties to his second-in-command. Then one day a long-time NYPD detective friend of his brought a case to him that Michael felt was his ticket out of the profound state of depression he was in.

The detective received information from a reliable informant that a well-liked and well-respected federal law enforcement agent was on a mobster's payroll and was supplying the mafia captain with intelligence on informants who were providing information about him to the feds. In return the mobster was ratting on his rivals to the dirty fed and being paid very well for it.

Using the fed's information, the mobster murdered four of the informants by shooting them and cutting out their tongues.

With this new information Gioca's detective friend opened an investigation which led to the arrest of the federal agent. He was charged with acting in concert with the mobster in the murder of the informants.

Michael immersed himself in the case and convicted the corrupt Fed after a jury trial. He had achieved his goal. The work and the win brought him out of his funk. However, Michael paid an unforeseen and steep price.

After convicting the popular agent of murder, Michael became a pariah in the law enforcement community.

His boss, the District Attorney, resented him for bringing political heat down on his office.

Jealous of his success, his colleagues despised him for winning the high-profile case.

And many detectives and police officers he had been working with every day in the DA's office, wanted nothing to do with him.

He was at the lowest point of his professional career. He knew that restoring his reputation would not be easy until a case came along that Michael saw as his lifeline.

It was a very high-profile murder case that, with a win, he hoped would resurrect his reputation and salvage his career.

He did win, but things did not improve. Those who had shunned him since he convicted the federal agent, continued to do so.

That case, highlighted by Michael's performance in the court-room, however, became the turning point of his career.

Gioca was Monsignor Romano's choice to be the Brooklyn prose-cutor the group was looking for. Caldwell listened to the monsign-or's pitch and recommendation, but he wanted to see Gioca in action before he extended an offer.

Unbeknownst to Michael, but well known to the group, the high-profile murder case he had taken on had the Devil's fingerprints all over it.

Caldwell and his people followed the investigation and trial of the case and were thoroughly impressed with Michael's talent, courage, his trial acumen, and his success in the courtroom.

Caldwell wanted him.

Romano now needed to convince his friend to come on board.

Because of their history together, and knowing that Michael was loyal, unafraid, a risk taker, and a gambler, Romano was confident that he would deliver. He knew that Michael couldn't turn down what would be the challenge of a lifetime.

He was right.

Once Michael heard Romano's pitch, he accepted the position and began his war with the *Evil One*.

In the months that followed Gioca did battle with the Devil on four occasions, winning each time. However, there was a price to pay for each victory. But Romano had chosen wisely because Michael had the courage, as well as the intellectual and spiritual strength to survive and continue.

That's why, when he got the call from Romano about the fire at Archangel and the death of Louis Amato, he was ready to do battle once again.

CHAPTER

THREE

I t was Christmas Eve, so Michael, his father and two sons were at his sister Pam's home for a family holiday dinner. His sister had prepared a wonderful meal following the Italian custom of the Feast of the Seven Fishes.

Every December 24th, for as long as Michael was alive, the Gioca family had gathered on that night to honor the tradition and to celebrate.

He recalled his maternal grandmother's meticulous preparation for what she considered the most important meal of the year. Soaking cod, or *baccala,* as she called it, for days, then mixing it with calamari, octopus, and shrimp which made up the seafood salad that would be served as part of the meal's *antipasto,* alongside fresh clams on the half shell.

During the day Michael would help his *nonna* by going to the fishmonger to pick up the meal's other sea creatures: eel, smelts, and flounder, that would be fried and served as the main course after his family was done with the spaghetti topped with her special seafood tomato sauce.

His grandmother had passed down the recipes to his mom, who

carried on the tradition. When she died a few years before, his sister picked up the torch. She was faithful to their legacy. Pam would have made her mom and grandmother proud. The Christmas Eve meals she prepared since their passing, were as close to theirs as one could get.

Michael's brother-in-law Artie poured drinks for Michael and his dad as the final minutes of an NFL game they were watching ticked off. His sons were entertaining their new cousin Michelle, the baby Pam and Artie adopted earlier that year, with the many toys she piled in her playpen. Michelle's laughter was infectious and filled the room.

Michael took it all in and smiled.

For months he had been looking forward to this holiday. He knew it would allow him to put the ordeals of the past year aside and relax. His battles with Satan had taken their toll and were the toughest and most pressure packed stretch of his career. Seeing his family enjoying themselves was the tonic he needed.

The call came in just as Michael and his family sat down to dinner.

When Michael looked at his cell phone and saw that it was Monsignor Romano calling, he had the sick feeling that his holiday was about to be spoiled.

"Michael, I'm sorry to disturb you," the monsignor said.

"And Merry Christmas to you too, Sal."

"I know you're at Pam's with the family, but this couldn't wait. *HE's* back."

Michael knew who Romano was referring to.

"Sal, is it something I need to rush out to, or can I have my dinner, and open up presents before I have to descend into the depths of hell again?"

"Mike, there's been another fire in the city earlier tonight, this time in Brooklyn, and someone was killed. The fire marshals are calling it suspicious."

"It was on the grounds of a Catholic church, The Church of the Archangels, in a building attached to the rectory. A firefighter, Louis Amato, died attempting a rescue after being told by a person at the scene that someone was trapped in the burning building."

"Mike, the building was empty!"

"It's Christmas Eve. The church property was set on fire putting priests in mortal danger, and a firefighter died unnecessarily trying to save someone who wasn't there. It all leads Caldwell to believe that this is Satan's work."

"Michael, there is nothing for you to do tonight. The fire is still smoldering, and the fire department hasn't given the okay for investigators to enter what's left of the building. Caldwell will be reaching out to the District Attorney tomorrow to alert him to our taking the case."

"After the holiday Caldwell wants you to meet up with the fire marshal assigned to the investigation. We still don't know who that will be, but sometime tomorrow Caldwell will have a name and I'll call you."

"Sal, it would be helpful when you learn who the lead marshal is, that you also get his cell phone number. Despite the holiday I'd like to at least touch base with him tomorrow. I have the sense that this is going to be a complicated investigation. Speaking to the marshal to find out what he knows at that point will allow me to get started right away."

"You'll have it as soon as I get it."

Romano ended the call with, "Enjoy your night and rest up tomorrow. I have a feeling that you're going to have your work cut out for you with this one. It's shaping up to be a case that the entire city will be watching."

"Merry Christmas, monsignor, and thanks for calling," Michael sarcastically responded.

For the rest of the evening, Michael did his best to celebrate, but the fire and death, likely at the hands of the Devil, preyed on his mind.

Although he didn't know them, he felt for the family of the firefighter. It didn't seem right to him that while he was enjoying the holiday with his loved ones, the family of the firefighter was mourning his death.

He knew that whatever he did he couldn't bring their loved one back. But he made a promise to himself that he would make sure that at the end of the case justice would be done so the Amato family would at least have closure.

On Christmas day, Michael attended the 8 a.m. Mass at St. Charles Borromeo near his office. After Mass, he worked out for two hours at the gym a few blocks from his apartment and by noon he was at his desk in the nearly empty District Attorney's office.

His first order of business was to call his dad, his sons, and his sister to wish them a Merry Christmas. When he spoke to Pam, he thanked her for the delicious dinner and for a great evening.

"Pam, you outdid yourself last night. Everything was perfect. Mom and grandma would have been honored by the way you followed in their footsteps."

"Thanks Mike. I'm pleased that the night went well. I hope that phone call you got last night wasn't a mood dampener. I heard the news this morning. I feel so bad for the firefighter and his family."

Michael was surprised by his sister's comment because the night before he had said nothing about the subject of the call when his father asked him if things were okay.

"Pam, how did you know that my call was about the fire?"

"Michael, I know you, and I know what you do. Your Rackets Division handles the big cases, and it doesn't get much bigger than a fire in a church building on Christmas Eve, where a firefighter is killed. In fact, I'll bet anything that you're at your office right now preparing to begin the investigation. Am I right?"

"Pam, you know me too well. I've called dad and my boys and now I'm just waiting to learn the name of the fire marshal in charge of the case so I can touch base with him. Once I do that, I'm going home to put my feet up and watch "A Christmas Carol," like we did when we were kids. You enjoy your day at Artie's folk's house and give my goddaughter a big hug and kiss for me."

"I love you, Michael. It's Christmas, so don't stay there too long."

He assured his sister he wouldn't and settled in to read the news reports of the fire and the subsequent death at Archangel.

It was 3 p.m. when Romano called.

"Merry Christmas. I hope that despite my call last night you were able to enjoy the rest of the evening?"

"Sal, it was tough, but everyone I care about was there and you could never spoil that."

"That's good to hear. Here are the names and cell numbers of the fire marshals assigned to the investigation, Fire Marshal Kathy Baer and Supervising Fire Marshal Alex Gazis. They both know that you'll be reaching out to them."

"Sal, why do we need two investigators? I know Kathy Baer. She's not only an excellent fire investigator, she's also easy on the eyes." Unsurprisingly, Michael heard what seemed to be a chuckle at the other end of the line.

Romano continued, "When Caldwell spoke to DA Price the DA told him that because of all the eyes on the case, especially the Brooklyn Borough President and several Brooklyn City Council members, the fire commissioner thought it best to have a supervisor assigned. But Michael, I'm not buying it. Something else is at work here."

"Shit! It's not enough that I have to be mindful and watch out for Satan, now I have to be careful of politicians looking over my shoulder?"

"Sal, Caldwell and Price better be ready to run interference for me because I'm not keeping any politicians updated on what I'm doing."

"Michael, just do what you do and don't worry. We'll take care of that. But as I have told you many times before, be careful."

After his phone call with Romano, Michael called both Kathy Baer and Alex Gazis.

Because of the holiday he expected to get only voicemails and he wasn't disappointed.

He left his cell phone number and asked that they meet him the next day in his office.

CHAPTER

FOUR

At 9:30 a.m. the day after Christmas, both fire marshals were at Michael's office.

After he greeted Baer and introduced himself to Gazis, they got down to business.

Because he knew Baer from other cases handled by his rackets division, Michael addressed her.

"Kathy, the only information I have on the case is what I read in the papers. So please fill me in on what you know to this point." Before she could answer, Gazis jumped in.

"Mr. Gioca, because the fire conditions at the site haven't improved enough for us to enter what's left of the building, there isn't much we can tell you right now. We hope that changes by this afternoon and when it does, we'll...no *I'll*, be able to update you. I have your cell number and I'll call you as soon as I can. Okay?"

Having said that, Gazis began to stand as he reached for his coat. Kathy Baer just looked at him knowing what was about to happen.

"Fire Marshal Gazis that's not even close to okay," Michael said without raising his voice but conveying that he was calling the shots.

"Let's get something straight right now," he continued.

"You and Kathy may be assigned by the FDNY as the fire investigators and I respect that. But we," and at that point Michael drew an imaginary circle to include the three of them, "are working together on this investigation."

"However, because I will be the one who takes the case, if there is a case, to the grand jury and then to trial, I will call the shots that need to be called to ensure success in both venues, and I hope you respect that. If that arrangement doesn't suit you then I suggest you reach out to the fire commissioner and have him call me."

Gazis sat back down and said nothing. It was evident to Michael that his little speech did not sit well with him.

Michael looked at Baer who rolled her eyes as she slightly tipped her head toward Gazis. Michael read her perfectly. She was not a fan of his and resented having him tagging along as she went about doing her investigation. She had done hundreds of them and didn't need a supervisor checking on her work.

"Now let's not waste any more time. I want to see the site of the fire and I want to speak to the pastor of the church today. Can we do that?"

Gazis said he'd be happy to drive. The three then left for the ride to Flatbush and the Church of the Archangels.

Flatbush had been founded and settled by the Dutch in 1651. In 1664 it was surrendered to the British along with five other Dutch towns. Under British rule the town of Flatbush became the county seat for the newly formed Kings County. Flatbush played a key role in the American Revolution. It was the site of significant skirmishes and battles including The Battle of Long Island.

Having been founded by the Dutch, who were prominent in the slave trade, historians estimated that between 70 and 80 percent of all Flatbush families had an enslaved person working in their household by 1800. Gradually they were emancipated, and large numbers settled in Manhattan where they would live within communities of free blacks.

In 1894 Flatbush was incorporated into the City of Brooklyn, which became part of the City of New York in 1898.

In the 1920's with the completion of the BMT and Nostrand Avenue lines of the New York Subway System Flatbush was connected to Manhattan and its business centers. In the years that followed, it became a prominent bedroom community for city workers of varied races, ethnicities, and nationalities.

During the 1970's and early 1980's Flatbush experienced an exodus of its traditional, mostly white residents, which was followed by an influx of immigrants from Caribbean countries. By the mid-1980's Flatbush had become a mostly Caribbean-American community which it remains to the present time.

The Church of the Archangels was founded in the early 1920's by Franciscan Friars. Its early congregation was made up of those who were long-time residents of Flatbush and of newly arrived immigrants from western Europe.

However much like the area it served, the church's worshippers began to change in the 1970's and by the mid-1980's its congregation was made up of the Caribbean-Americans who lived within the parish boundaries.

Father John Keenan had been working as a parish priest at the church since 1990. In 1995 he was promoted by the Vatican to pastor and put in charge of the three priests who lived and worked at Archangel.

Fr. Keenan was a kind and generous man who never turned away anyone in need of help. He was beloved by his parishioners and respected and admired by Brooklyn's bishop for his work with the largely poor and immigrant community that his parish served.

As Michael later learned, the kindness of Fr. Keenan played a major role in the fire that led to the death of Louis Amato.

When Michael arrived at Archangel with Kathy Baer and Alex Gazis, their first stop was the church rectory. He wanted to speak to Fr. Keenan to find out what, if anything, the priest knew about the fire.

Unfortunately, the pastor's office assistant told Michael that Fr. Keenan was unavailable because he was officiating at the 12:30 p.m. Mass in the church. She told them to come back at 1:30 when the pastor would be free.

"Mr. Gioca, while we wait, why don't we go talk to the personnel who are at the fire site," Kathy Baer suggested.

Michael was of the same mind.

"Great idea Kathy. But guys, Mr. Gioca is my dad. I'm Michael or Mike."

When both Baer and Gazis nodded that they understood, Michael said, "Now let's go learn something from your colleagues."

CHAPTER

FIVE

The site of the fire was in the church's garage/storage building which was situated behind the rectory. The large garage was constructed a few years before and was connected to the rectory by a short passageway that led into the first floor of the building where the priests lived and conducted parish business. The entrance to the garage faced away from the rectory so anyone entering or leaving the garage would not be visible to someone inside the connected building.

The garage was built to house the church van that was used for various events and for hauling supplies needed for the upkeep of the parish buildings. It also housed the church's maintenance and gardening equipment: tools, ladders, a power lawnmower, power leaf blower, and a gas-powered snow blower.

It was also large enough to hold one or two of the private cars owned by Fr. Keenan and his priests. The short passageway allowing access to the rectory made it a convenient place to park especially if the weather was wet or snowy.

As the group made their way to the area where the building had stood, they were met by Fire Lieutenant James Silecchia, the second-in-command at Brooklyn Rescue Squad 2, where Louis Amato had been assigned.

Kathy Baer, who knew the lieutenant, introduced Michael, after which she introduced Alex Gazis. It struck Michael as strange that Gazis, a supervising fire marshal, did not know the second-in-command of a busy and prominent squad like Rescue 2. He would later learn why.

Once the intros were done, Michael got right down to business.

"Lieutenant, I assume that when you and your squad got here the building had been fully engaged with fire. Am I correct?"

"You're correct, Mr. Gioca. When we pulled up, the ladder company was beginning to apply water to the flames which seemed to be situated around the base of the building's walls and were spreading rapidly. The front door, however, was not on fire."

"When I approached the building to assess whether our rescue company was needed, I saw two men off to the left side of the door. One of them, Patrick Patron, who I believe is the church's caretaker, saw us and waved me over."

"When I got to him, he seemed to be fixated on the flames, so I asked Patrick if they had been inside the building when the fire started. Patron said yes, they had been with another guy, Liam. I asked him if Liam had gotten out, but he didn't answer right away. Then the guy with him leaned over and whispered something after which Patrick said, 'No, Liam is still inside. He couldn't get out.' The person standing next to Patrick, whose name I never got, began nodding in agreement."

"When my guys heard that, they rushed into the burning garage to find the person we were told had been trapped."

"As usual, Louie Amato was the first one in. He took the center area to search, and the others went left and right."

"By that time the fire was roaring. A second alarm was called in because we needed more men to work the fire, which was threatening the church rectory that was attached to the garage."

"About five, no more than seven minutes after the squad went in,

I heard a noise that I recognized immediately. The roof was going to come down. I radioed to my men to get out, but it was too late. The roof collapsed in such a way that the men along the right and left walls were not harmed."

"However, because it crumpled in a 'V' shape, Louie Amato was trapped in the center of the 'V'. It was like he was caught in a vise."

"At first, he seemed to suffer no major injuries, but we didn't know right away that the two sides of the 'V' were compressing his torso and restricting his ability to breathe."

"When my guys saw that, we got the hydraulic rescue tool we use to lift heavy debris off someone trapped beneath it. The device is designed to be slipped below the debris and inflated. This allows us to get to the trapped person and slide them out from under what is pinning them down. We used two devices in that garage because Louie was trapped by sections of the collapsed roof on his left and right."

At this point Lt. Silecchia broke down.

When he composed himself, he continued. "When we finally lifted the sides of the' V' shaped debris and got to Louie, he was barely breathing. He was rushed to Kings County Hospital but never made it. He died in the ambulance."

"Mr. Gioca, he was the best of the best. Louie Amato was the poster boy for first responders. He was unafraid, selfless, and was always the first one into a tough situation. The city lost a hero on Christmas Eve."

Puzzled by what he thought was an incomplete recollection of what happened, Michael asked the lieutenant, "What about the person you were told was trapped inside? Did you find him?"

Before answering the lieutenant paused and took a deep breath. "There was no one trapped inside that building. NO ONE! It was fucking unoccupied! And I lost one of the best people God ever created looking to save a phantom."

"Isn't that why we are here? Aren't we looking to hold people responsible for doing bad things. That SOB Patrick Patron and his whispering buddy sent Louie Amato to his death. We all need to get to the bottom of this. Someone must be held responsible."

While the lieutenant was speaking Kathy Baer walked over to the garage ruins to look around. It was her and Gazis' job to determine the cause of the fire and if a crime was committed. Unfortunately, she couldn't go too far into the ruins, but she did go in far enough to see several things that raised her suspicion.

Among the burnt-out timbers of the walls and roof, she noticed paint cans, tins of paint thinner, and bottles of solvent, all of which were charred from the fire. Scattered about, she also saw several automobile fenders, car license plates, a car bumper, and what appeared to be gas tanks.

In addition, she counted two acetylene torches, three electric power saws, a couple of toolboxes containing wrenches, screwdrivers, heavy-duty pliers, and three automobile jacks, all of which had also been charred.

And despite the strong smell of the burnt remains of the building, the distinct odor of gasoline permeated the ruins.

"What the hell was going on here?" she thought to herself.

When Kathy returned to where Michael and Gazis were still standing with the lieutenant, she told them what she had seen and smelled. She asked Lt. Silecchia if his men had noticed that when they first entered the building.

"Kathy, after we got Louie out, my guys told me about seeing that stuff. One of them worked in an auto body shop before he came into the department, and said he believed the place was being used as a chop shop. I didn't have time to call them, but you should call in the NYPD auto squad to see if they agree. If it was a chop shop that could give you the source of the fire."

"Lieutenant, one more thing, did you see Patrick Patron and his buddy again after you got Louie Amato out of the building?" Michael asked.

"Mr. Gioca, once my guy told me his thoughts about this place being a chop shop, I asked the men to locate Patron and his buddy. I wanted to hold them for either you guys or for the police. They looked all over, but they were gone."

Kathy Baer asked the lieutenant, if he thought he'd be able to identify them in a lineup when they were found?

"Kathy, there is no doubt in my mind. I'll know them when I see them again. In fact, Patron's buddy would be hard to forget because he had this odd-looking mole on his left cheek."

Not shocked by the description, Michael said, "Thanks for the suggestion about auto crimes and for all the info, lieutenant. We'll definitely be in touch."

They shook hands after which Michael and the two fire marshals walked to the rectory. It was time to talk to Fr. Keenan about Patrick Patron and his buddy with the mole.

CHAPTER
SIX

It was 1:35 when Gazis, Baer, and Michael walked up the front steps of the rectory. They were buzzed in by the pastor's clerk and shown to a small conference room. After a few minutes Fr. John Keenan came in and introduced himself.

Michael and the others identified themselves, after which Fr. Keenan asked them if he could get them coffee. They all declined.

"Father, thanks for seeing us," Michael said.

"We would like to talk about the fire, your caretaker Patrick Patron, and another guy he was with at the fire."

Michael's statement seemed to surprise Fr. Keenan.

"Mr. Gioca, are you certain Patrick was at the fire? I haven't seen him for well over a week. He *was* our caretaker but I fired him after one of our priests caught him stealing from the collection boxes in the church."

"Initially he denied the accusation, but when he was also confronted by our parish treasurer with money missing from our weekly collections and from the safe where we keep our funds, he confessed to everything and asked for my forgiveness. I did forgive him, but I couldn't have him working here any longer."

"He gave me his keys and left without making a fuss."

"Father, did Patrick have access to the garage where the fire occurred?" asked Baer.

"Of course, he did. He was the caretaker of the church, and handled all our maintenance equipment, tools, and machines stored there. The priests and I, along with Patrick, all had keys to the garage. We sometimes parked our cars in there when there was room."

"What do you mean by, 'when there was room?'" Michael asked.

"Mr. Gioca, about a month or so after Patrick came to work, he told me he was an auto mechanic. He said he made money on the side fixing cars for friends and friends of friends. He asked me if he could use the garage to do those repairs."

"He assured me that his business would not interfere with his work as caretaker, nor with any church services, because he would only do the auto repairs at night. He even said he'd fix my car and the priests' cars, if needed, for no charge."

"What we paid him for being the caretaker was only what the church could afford, and it wasn't a fortune. I felt that letting him use the garage to make extra money was the charitable thing to do. Which is why I was devastated when he was caught stealing the church's money."

"Father, did you or any of the priests ever see Patrick at work on cars while he was here?" asked Kathy Baer.

"Fire Marshal Baer, the simple answer is no."

"The garage entrance faces away from the rectory so it's impossible to see inside unless you walk around to the front of that building. At the hour he did his work I never had any reason to do that, and I believe that goes for the other priests as well. If we needed to park our cars in the garage, we'd make sure that Patrick knew that so he wouldn't schedule a repair job on those occasions."

"Fr. Keenan, do you have the keys that Patrick returned when he was fired?"

"Ms. Baer, I have them right here in my desk."

Keenen took out a key ring from his desk drawer and held them for all to see. Baer asked, "Father, is the garage key on that ring?"

Keenan went one by one and looked up when he was finished. "The garage key is not here," he said.

Clearly shaken, the pastor put the key ring back into his desk. When he looked up Michael could see that he was embarrassed. In an attempt to rescue him from further embarrassment, Michael changed the subject.

"Father, everything you've told us has been helpful and extremely important to our investigation. Thank you. Now I want to go back to your beginnings with Patrick. When and how did you meet him?"

"Mr. Gioca, one day several months ago our former caretaker, Elian, disappeared."

"Father, could you elaborate ?" Michael asked.

"He didn't show up for work one day. He was with us at Archangel for several years and during that time he never missed a day. He was reliable, hardworking, and cared for our property as if it was his own. So, his absence was troubling to all of us."

"I made several calls to his apartment, where he lived alone, and to his cell phone, but got no answer."

"His family was back in Trinidad from where he emigrated a year before he came to work here. I called and spoke to his mother. She told me that no one in the family had heard from Elian for days."

"I went to his apartment on the second floor of a two-family home owned by a West Indian family. No one had seen Elian, but they were not alarmed. Their work schedules often conflicted so it was not unusual for them to go weeks without seeing him."

"I went back to the rectory hoping that Elian would be there. Of course, he wasn't. The next day, no Elian again."

"Then something strange happened."

"Just after noon, my assistant told me there was a man in the waiting room who wanted to see me about the caretaker job. When I went out to meet him, he told me his name was Patrick

Patron. He said he came to New York from Haiti several months before. When I asked him why he wanted to see me, he said he knew that the church caretaker job was available, and he wanted it."

"I was shocked. In this community news travels fast, but Elian was only gone for one day. I discussed him only with his and his landlord's family. And I only asked if they had seen or heard from Elian, I did not mention that he had not reported for work."

"I thought to myself, *'How could this stranger possibly know that Elian was missing?'*"

"I asked Patrick why he thought that the church might be looking for a caretaker. His answer was, 'A friend of mine told me.' I didn't know what to say so I told him to leave his cell phone number with the clerk and I'd get back to him."

"How long was it before you hired him," Michael asked.

"I was still hoping that Elian would come back to work, but when I didn't hear from him for a few days I called the local precinct to report his disappearance. A detective came and I explained everything. He told me since Elian was a grown man and with no evidence of foul play, there was nothing the police could do."

"I couldn't wait any longer. We are an old parish, and our buildings and the church grounds need constant attention. So, I called Patrick and told him to come into the rectory so we could talk. He was here within the hour."

"I interviewed him, and he had the skills I knew were necessary to do the job. So, I hired him. He was a good worker. He would still be here if he hadn't stolen our money."

Kathy Baer asked, "Father, we were told by Lieutenant Silecchia that when his rescue unit arrived at the fire scene, he saw Patrick standing outside the garage with another man. He described him as having a strange mole on his left cheek. Do you know who that is?"

"Ms. Baer, after working here for a few weeks, as I said, Patrick asked permission to use the garage for his car repair business. When I gave him the okay, he told me he would have a friend Anton helping with the repairs. I told Patrick if Anton was going to be around the church grounds, I wanted to meet him."

"The next day Patrick told me that Anton was out in the garage and asked if I had time to meet him. Actually, I was rather busy, so I told him to bring Anton into the rectory. Patrick's reaction was not what I expected. He dropped his head and, in a voice just above a whisper, he said that Anton wouldn't come into the church building and almost pleaded with me to go out to the garage. So, I did."

"When Patrick introduced me to Anton, I held out my hand to shake his. But the guy would not take it. Instead, he mumbled something, turned to his right and walked away from me. As he did, I noticed a rather large ugly mole on his left cheek. So, Ms. Baer, I would say that it was Anton standing with Patrick outside the garage."

Again, nothing Fr. Keenan conveyed about Anton's reluctance surprised Michael. *"There is no way the Evil One would ever go into that rectory or shake the hand of a man of God,"* he thought, as he and the others thanked Fr. Keenan for his help and walked out of the rectory.

"Kathy, we really need Auto Crimes to tell us if they believe that garage was being used as a chop shop," Michael said as they got into their car. "So please call them as soon as you get back to your office."

"Once we get that answer," he continued, "You guys can go in and hopefully find the cause and origin of the fire. That will tell us if we have a crime, or an accident."

"I'll get on it as soon as we get back," she answered as they pulled away from the rectory.

Gazis, who hadn't said much until then, turned to Kathy and said in a very authoritarian way, "I don't want to wait for an opinion from Auto Crimes, I want you to start looking for Patrick and Anton now. We need to find them to get to the bottom of this."

Kathy, clearly angry at the way she was just spoken to, looked at him and just nodded.

Sitting in the rear seat, Michael took it all in. Although Gazis didn't say it, it was clear to Michael from his tone and attitude that there were important people Gazis had to answer to and to whom he wanted to impress.

Michael chuckled and said to himself, *"Don't worry Alex, we'll find Patrick and make you look good to whomever put you here. But Anton ain't ever going to be found."*

CHAPTER
SEVEN

When Michael got back to his desk, he called Romano. The monsignor answered before the first ring had ended.

"Anxious a bit, Sal?" Michael joked.

"Michael, we've had no news or information about the fire since Christmas Eve. So, YES, I'm on edge," he answered, clearly annoyed at Michael's attempt at humor.

"Sal, there's a lot to tell you but I had no lunch and I'm starving."

"Meet me at *Emilio's* at six and you can fill me in," said the monsignor.

"Perfect." I'll see you in an hour. I can already taste their veal parm. Sal, please don't be late."

Emilio's, a restaurant not far from Romano's office, was his unofficial meeting place for conversations with Michael, particularly when they were getting together near dinnertime.

Caldwell's group had its offices in an old warehouse building near the Brooklyn waterfront in the Red Hook section of the borough. It was chosen because of its remote location and because it looked nothing like a building that would house a government unit of any kind.

Romano had a small office on the first floor of that building. However, when he could, he enjoyed conducting business with Michael at *Emilio's*. The food was excellent and the owner, Emilio, treated the monsignor like Vatican royalty when he ate there.

Emilio learned that he and Romano's father were from the same town, Nola, in Italy. After that, the monsignor never had to wait for a table in the popular, and usually crowded, restaurant. And he never had to pay for a meal. To compensate, Romano always left a generous tip for his waiter.

When Michael arrived, he was greeted by the owner who had gotten to know him because of the frequent dinners he and Romano had enjoyed there over the past year.

Michael was shown to the monsignor's table in a quiet spot in the back of the dining room.

Romano had ordered a bottle of *Lambrusco* and was enjoying his first glass of the slightly effervescent red wine when Michael sat down.

"Monsignor, how are you?" Michael said as he took a sip of the wine. Surprised by the bubbles, he said, "Bubbly? I know I'm good, but it's a little early to celebrate beating that bastard again, we haven't even made an arrest."

"Michael, the wine is not for that kind of a celebration. It is Christmas week and since we had not seen each other for the holiday, I thought a red bubbly was in order. *Salute!* And Merry Christmas."

"*Grazie*, and Merry Christmas to you as well, Sal."

After they clinked glasses, Michael got down to business.

He began by telling Romano that Caldwell was right, the Devil was certainly behind the fire at Archangel. "And in my opinion, *HE's* behind the outbreak of fires across the city. Look at the chaos those fires have caused. We know that's exactly what *HE's* after."

Michael continued, "But I suspect that the earlier ones didn't result in enough chaos and upheaval to satisfy *HIM*. So, *HE* raised the stakes by going after a church and unnecessarily sending a hero firefighter to his death, resulting in heartbreak and discord much more to *HIS* liking."

Romano took this all in, then said, "Michael I agree that on the surface it seems like *HIS* doing, but you don't even know yet if this was a crime or just an accidental fire. And if it is a crime, how can you be so sure *HE* was behind it?"

Michael told Romano about the items that were in the garage, which led one of the firefighters to conclude that it was being used as an illegal chop shop.

"Sal, it was a place ripe for criminal activity. I know in my gut that the fire marshals will find that a crime was committed in that garage which caused it to go up in flames."

"As for the *Evil One* being behind the fire, it's what I learned from Louis Amato's lieutenant and the pastor of the church, that makes me so certain *HE* was responsible."

Michael went on to tell Romano what the lieutenant had said about seeing Patrick Patron, who he believed was the church's caretaker, at the scene of the fire and speaking to him. The lieutenant also said that Patrick was with someone, but he did not get the person's name.

"We found out later that the guy with Patrick was his friend, Anton," Michael added.

"The lieutenant said that Patrick told him that he, Anton, and another guy named Liam were inside the building when the fire broke out."

"Since only Patrick and Anton were standing there, the lieutenant asked Patrick if Liam had gotten out. He said that Patrick hesitated as he was about to respond but didn't answer."

"That's when the lieutenant saw Anton lean over and whisper something to Patrick, which the lieutenant could not hear."

"After the whisper, Patrick finally answered the lieutenant's question. He said that Liam was still in the garage because he couldn't get out."

"Hearing that, the firefighters rushed into the building."

"Sal, I believe that was a trap! When Anton whispered to Patrick, he *told* him to say that Liam couldn't get out, even though the building was unoccupied."

"Anton knew that the firefighters would rush in for a rescue thereby putting themselves in danger. Louis Amato died attempting to save someone who wasn't there."

"There's more. When we asked the lieutenant if he would recognize Patron and Anton again, he said he was certain he could. He added that he would never forget Anton because of the large mole on his left cheek."

Michael went on to tell Romano what Fr. Keenan, the pastor of Archangel, told him and the fire marshals about how Patrick came to him one day wanting to introduce his friend Anton to him. The problem was that Anton had refused to enter the rectory to meet him.

"Patrick then asked the priest to go out to the garage with him so he could introduce Anton. When Fr. Keenan introduced himself, Anton refused to acknowledge him. The pastor offered to shake hands with him, but Anton just turned away. When he did, Fr. Keenan saw the large mole on Anton's left cheek."

"Sal, Anton, refuses to enter a rectory, and doesn't shake hands with a priest, *and* has a mole on his left cheek!

"Anton is the *Evil One!*"

" Remember when *HE* was "Tony" who sent Joey Fanta to rob and kill Lara Winters, *HE* had that distinctive mole on *HIS* left cheek."

"In the Robbie Thomas case, *HE* was the woman who convinced the two jurors to not convict Robbie's killer, hoping the judge would set him free. *She* had the mole on *her* left cheek."

"Now here, Anton befriends Patrick Patron, who just happens to be a church caretaker operating a car repair business out of the church garage and becomes his assistant. That's not a coincidence. *HE* knew that the friendship would give *HIM* access to a building that was attached to the church rectory, where the priests of

Archangel live. Setting a fire in that garage would put the priests, and perhaps even the firefighters who respond to it, in danger, and in *HIS* evil mind, hopefully cause many deaths."

"Sal, but for the quick response of the fire department, *HE* would have succeeded in *HIS* mission to kill the priests. Unfortunately, Louis Amato wasn't so lucky."

"Michael, I hear you," Romano said. "But you have a lot of work to do. There are still unanswered questions: how exactly did that fire start, and who was responsible? Caldwell won't be satisfied and won't rest until you get him the answers."

"Sal, I'm counting on you to keep Caldwell at bay for a while. Tell him that Gioca is confident that at the end of this investigation, Patrick Patron and the *Evil One,* in the person of Patrick's friend Anton, will be the answers to those two questions."

CHAPTER

EIGHT

The Church of the Visitation of the Blessed Virgin Mary in Red Hook was filled on New Year's Eve morning for the 9 a.m. funeral Mass for Louis Amato.

The church had opened its doors at 8 a.m. and 30 minutes later there was not a seat to be had. The people of Red Hook and Louis' colleagues came out in force to honor one of their own.

A large section of the church was reserved for the FDNY, but it could not accommodate all the uniformed personnel who wished to say goodbye to their brother.

Hundreds of firefighters from as far away as Texas and Arizona, as well as the local residents who couldn't get inside, stood in the bitter cold across from the church's front doors on Richards Street, just to be close to Louis' casket as it was carried into Visitation by six members of the FDNY ceremonial unit.

Following the casket was Louis' family, led by his wife of six months, Elena, and his mother Maria and his father Louis Sr.

Michael, the Fire Commissioner, the Chief Fire Marshal, and various chiefs of the fire department were behind the family. Once the Amato family settled into the first row of pews in the old church, Michael and the others sat behind them.

The longtime pastor of Visitation, Fr. Mario Amoroso, a friend of the Amato family since the day he baptized Louis Jr., officiated at the funeral Mass.

Over the years Fr. Amoroso had been a frequent guest at the Amato home for holidays and Sunday dinner, which featured Maria's pasta topped with her legendary red sauce.

Spending lots of time with the family, the priest came to know the young Louis very well and watched him grow into the special man he became.

Six months before, he performed the ceremony when Louis and Elena were married. All of which is why his eulogy for the fallen hero was so meaningful and touching.

"Louie Amato Jr. was a son of Brooklyn," Fr. Amoroso began.

"He jogged the streets of Red Hook, loved sandwiches with eggplant and peppers from our wonderful DeFonte's deli. He worked as a lifeguard at Coney Island, and lived his dream right here in his home borough, becoming a member of the FDNY."

"But on Christmas Eve, hours before he was to spend the holiday with his wife, and his mom and dad, he was killed when the roof of a building on the grounds of The Church of the Archangels, in Flat-bush, came crashing down on him as he searched for someone he was told was inside the burning building. But there was no one to rescue. Tragically, Louie died attempting to save someone who wasn't there."

"It's true what they say- only the good die young."

"Louie was a prince."

"His dad Louis Sr., a former Deputy Commissioner for Labor Affairs for New York City, had been a longshoreman, and now serves as an official of the Longshoremen's Association. His son loved the water, but he dreamed of becoming a firefighter from when he was a young boy. At his wake last night one of his best friends told me that growing up Louie ate, slept, and dreamt that one day he would put on the gear of the FDNY."

"The child who people in his Red Hook neighborhood said would do anything to help his neighbors, grew into a muscular athlete. He was a local little league and sandlot baseball star, played on the best youth football team in Brooklyn, was a strong swimmer which led to him becoming a lifeguard, and later as a member of Engine Company 281, helped their softball team win four FDNY championships."

"Louie's talents were not only in the field of athletics. He graduated magna cum laude from St. Francis College and briefly attended law school. But he had an itch that needed to be scratched. So, after a year studying the law, Louie decided to pursue his dream and joined the Fire Department."

"He personified the Department's slogan. He truly was one of 'The Bravest'. At Engine 281, Louie' job was to enter burning buildings and search for anyone inside. Not satisfied, he became a certified scuba diver in the hope that it would help elevate him to one of the fire department's elite rescue units. He wanted to be involved in the most dangerous and unusual assignments."

"One of the proudest and happiest days of his life, that is until he married Elena, came when he was accepted as a member of Brooklyn's elite Rescue Company 2, located in Crown Heights."

"Louie's lifelong desire to help others was rewarded twice with citations for bravery, when he and one of his colleagues captured a criminal who stole jewelry from a woman, and when he rescued a man from the second floor of a burning building."

"That's why it surprised no one who knew him, that Louie did not hesitate to run into that burning building at Archangel not knowing that there was no one inside to save."

"Elena, Maria, and Louis, in this church and on the street outside, there are hundreds of people who loved your Louie. Their being here, standing in the bitter cold, is a testament to the wonderful man you married, and the son you raised. I pray that when you think of this sendoff, their presence, and what it represents, brings you comfort."

"You lost a husband and son, I lost a great friend, and the city lost a hero."

"I know God has found a comfortable place in heaven for Louie."

"May he rest in peace."

When Fr. Amoroso left the pulpit; there was not a dry eye in the church.

Michael had chills listening to the priest talk about Louis. Through those words he finally got to know Louis Amato Jr., and was thoroughly impressed.

There was another side to that coin, however. The kind of person Louis was, made him the perfect victim for the *Evil One*. Although *HE* failed to kill the priests of Archangel in that fire, Michael was certain that Satan was happy to settle for having taken such an extraordinary life.

After filing out of the church, Michael hung back watching as Louis' casket was loaded into the hearse. Although he had just sat through the funeral Mass, Michael said a silent prayer for Louis and vowed to himself that he would not rest until justice was done for the Amato family.

As he was about to walk to his car, he felt a tap on his shoulder. When he turned to see who it was, Louis Amato Sr. was standing there.

"Mr. Gioca, I'm Louie's father," he said.

"Mr. Amato, I know who you are. I'm very sorry for your loss. I'm Michael Gioca, the prosecutor who's in charge of the investigation into your son's death."

"I know, which is why I wanted to introduce myself," Louis Sr. said.

"I want you to know that you have my and my family's support in getting to the truth of what happened."

"I've kept up with your cases in the newspaper, so I know your reputation. My family and I are happy that you're handling this case. We know you'll do the right thing."

"Anything you need, or any help I can be to you, please reach out to me. You should never be reluctant to call me."

Michael simply thanked Mr. Amato for his support and for the kind words, then handed him his business card.

"Mr. Amato, the same goes with me. Anything you need, or if you just want to talk, call me. My cell number is on that card.

The two men then shook hands. Michael watched as Mr. Amato climbed into the back of the limousine that would take him and his family to say goodbye to his son one final time.

CHAPTER

NINE

On the first workday of the new year, Michael was at his desk bright and early.

His first call of the day was to Kathy Baer for an update on the investigation.

"Happy New Year, Kathy," Michael said when the fire marshal answered her phone.

"Same to you Michael. You're in early for a guy who wears a suit to work," she replied.

Michael laughed, "No bankers' hours on this job, fire marshal."

"Good to hear Mike. I assume you're calling for a progress report on the investigation."

"Yep! What's new and where do we stand?"

"Since we last spoke, NYPD auto crimes went to the scene. They did a thorough examination of what we saw there, and they are sure that the garage was being used as a chop shop. In fact, they had several open stolen car reports from that area, and they think that some of the auto parts that are there belong to the cars reported stolen. I'll know more when they're finished collecting the VINs from the parts and compare them with the VINs of the ones that were stolen."

"That's great news Kathy. Any progress on the cause and origin of the fire?"

"We're getting there but no definitive word yet. Preliminarily, the belief is that the fire may have started in the gasoline that we found on the floor of the garage under the burnt-out hulk of a car we also found. What's holding up the final result is that we haven't yet determined what the ignition source could be."

"Kathy, do you have people out looking for Patron and his buddy Anton?"

"Mike, Alex Gazis is handling that part of the investigation. He stuck me with doing the grunt work at the site and now at the office. Don't get me wrong, it was fortunate that he did because I was able to discover the gasoline and come up with the theory that it was the fuel for the fire."

"Although he outranks me, he's nothing more than an empty suit. He has no field experience."

"Kathy, are you saying he's just a hack who's some politician's stooge?"

"Mike, that's exactly what I'm saying. He's only been here two years. Brooklyn Borough President Tom Pickett had the fire commissioner assign him to us. He went through training because he couldn't avoid it, but he rarely goes out into the field, and he's never been in charge of an investigation."

"Gazis told me that he and the borough president are close," Kathy continued. "He also claims to have established a relationship with the new county clerk in Brooklyn, Alvin Downey, who he says is a big shot in the city's Democrat Party. But there's something strange about that Mike. By Gazis' own admission Downey just got the position, so how could they have gotten so tight in such a short time?"

"And it doesn't end there. Gazis is always bragging about his strong ties to several newly elected progressive members of the city council who he credits with introducing him to the new county clerk."

"The word is that the borough president is going to run for mayor next year, and he needs the support of those city council members. Gazis can deliver that. In return he wants to be named fire commissioner in a new administration."

"Wow! Thanks for the intel. Is Gazis in the office? I want to talk to him. And don't worry, what you just told me will not be repeated."

"Thanks, Mike. I'm sure he's here. As I said he rarely goes out, so I'm sure he has other marshals looking for Patrick and Anton. It also wouldn't surprise me if he also enlisted the help of the NYPD."

"Kathy, the NYPD is not going to do a fire marshal's job. They have plenty of work."

"Mike, I'm telling you, the borough president will call the police commissioner if Gazis asks for police help and meets resistance."

"Kathy, you really think Pickett would lower himself to calling the PC to ask for help for a fire marshal?"

"Yes. He really needs the support from those city council members and Gazis can make sure he gets it."

"Well, I guess for our purposes any help we can get in finding those two will be welcome. I'm going to call Gazis now. Please keep me posted. Talk later."

Before he could make his call, his phone rang.

"Mr. Gioca, Supervising Fire Marshal Gazis here."

"Alex, it's Mike. No need to be so formal. And Happy New Year."

"Sorry, it's just my way. And, Happy New Year to you as well. I'm calling to bring you up to date on the investigation."

Michael did not tell Gazis that he spoke to Kathy Baer. He simply listened as Gazis told him everything he just heard from his colleague. After complimenting him on the swift progress, Michael asked about finding Patron and Anton.

"Mike, I have marshals out in the field looking for both of them. And I was able to enlist the help of the NYPD in that search."

Michael laughed and thought to himself, *"Boy, does Kathy have this guy pegged."*

Gazis continued, "I'm confident that we'll come up with both in a matter of hours."

Michael knew that Anton could never be found, and he doubted Patron would be located anytime soon.

"Okay, Alex. Please keep me posted on all fronts. And if you need me for anything I'll be at my desk all day."

Michael knew he couldn't just sit and wait for Gazis' men to find Patron. He had an idea, but he needed to run it past Romano and Caldwell before he acted on it. So, he called the monsignor.

"Sal, it's your favorite prosecutor calling. Happy New Year!'

"Same to you Michael. What do you need?" Romano coldly said.

"Monsignor, why do you think I have an ulterior motive in calling? Can't a friend call a friend with holiday greetings?"

"Sure, he can, but the holiday was three days ago! And I know you too well. I repeat, what do you need?"

"Sal, I apologize. I should have called you sooner. No excuse. And you're right, I do need something for the case."

Michael went on to give Romano a progress report on the investigation ending with the need to find Patrick Patron quickly.

"Sal, the fire marshals are looking for him and Anton, who they'll never find."

"If I'm going to come up with an answer to whether that fire was an accident or a crime, it's essential that I speak to Patron. He can give me what I need."

"For some reason Alex Gazis relegated Kathy Baer, who is a very good investigator, to desk duty, and assigned the task of finding Patron to himself. Sorry, I misspoke. He assigned it to marshals who reported to him. He hasn't gotten off his ass to do anything so far."

"Being around him at the scene and talking to him about the case and investigations in general, I have no confidence that he or his people will locate Patron, which is why I'm calling. I'd like to use Dina Mitchell and Tim Clark from the DA's office again. I don't have to remind you how successful they were working for me in the Susan Hayes murder case."

"You recall that when the cops in that case needed assistance searching for witnesses in Borough Park, I trusted Dina and Tim to help, and they got the job done. Without them we wouldn't have come up with the two crucial eyewitnesses, Agnes White and Tyrese Smith, and the killer Wilson Knox' prior sex assault victim."

"Sal, I need you to go to Caldwell and ask DA Price to assign Dina and Tim to me so I can send them out to locate Patrick Patron."

Romano listened and when Michael was finished, said, "It seems that there has been considerable progress in the investigation. Caldwell will be pleased. I'm in the office, so as soon as we hang up, I'll go upstairs to see him. I'll call you as soon as I have something to tell you. But I have a feeling he's going to get you what you want."

"And Michael, there was no need for you to apologize about calling me when you did to wish me a happy new year. I know how hard you're working and that *is* a valid excuse."

Michael thanked his friend, and was about to hang up, but Romano wasn't done.

"There's one more thing. We heard about the funeral."

"The enormous turn-out and Monsignor Amoroso's eulogy struck us as evidence beyond any doubt that Louis Amato was a special person. He died way before his time. I want you to know that every member of our group is confident that you will get the answers you need and when you do, you will see that justice is done for Louis and his family."

CHAPTER

TEN

B efore the end of the day, Michael had Dina Mitchell and Tim Clark assigned to him.

Dina and Tim were members of the Brooklyn District Attorney's squad of over 100 in-house investigators. Under New York State law Detective Investigators, or DIs as they are known, working for district attorneys throughout the state, have all the powers of a police officer.

Mitchell and Clark were part of a squad of 15 DIs assigned to Michael's Rackets Division. They worked closely together over the years and Michael trusted them implicitly.

The last time he worked with them was several months before in a case involving the murder of a police officer's wife. The killing was perpetrated by a pawn of the Devil, Wilson Knox. It was a difficult case until Dina and Tim got involved. They were able to find three witnesses whose testimony led to Knox' conviction thus defeating Satan in a case where *HE* was responsible for four murders and multiple injuries to a group of school children.

However, neither Tim nor Dina had any idea that Michael was doing battle with Satan and working for Caldwell's secret government group. As cover for his secret work, the District Attorney had agreed to have Michael remain Chief of the Rackets Division, recognizing that he would be reporting to Caldwell when investigating the cases identified as those instigated by the *Evil One.*

So as far as the investigators knew when they were called into Michael's office late that afternoon, it was to be assigned to a case that the Rackets Division was involved in at the behest of the District Attorney.

Michael began, "Guys thanks for hanging around after hours. I asked you to stay because I have a very important, and so far, difficult assignment that I have confidence you two will successfully handle."

Both thanked him for the kind words and for the expression of confidence in their abilities. Dina asked , "Do you need help in the case involving the fire at Archangel church?"

Tim, seeing the surprised expression on Michael's face added, "We all know that the DA assigned you to handle that case. And the scuttlebutt around the squad is that you're having trouble finding a person of interest and witnesses. How can we help?"

Michael had a big smile on his face when he answered, "You see that's why I want you guys working this with me. You're smart, savvy, and have the guts to get involved in tough cases."

Michael went on to describe all he knew about the fire and the death of Louis Amato.

"The scuttlebutt is correct, Tim. I need to find Patrick Patron. I need to determine if this was a crime or an accident with tragic results."

"Based on what we know now, he was inside that garage when the fire started. Therefore, he can tell me the how, when, and why it started."

Michael did not mention Anton because there was no way Dina and Tim would ever find *HIM* and he didn't want them wasting their time looking.

Dina asked, 'When was the last time Patron was seen?"

"I was told by the lieutenant from Rescue 2 that when they arrived, Patron was standing outside the garage. He lied to the lieutenant, telling him that there was someone trapped inside the burning building which caused Amato and his squad to go looking for a person who didn't exist."

"After the roof collapsed and the firefighters were able to get Amato out, the lieutenant said that one of his squad members told him that he believed the garage was being used as an auto chop shop because of the tools and equipment he had seen inside. The lieutenant then sent his guys out to get Patron but they had no luck. He was gone."

"That belief by one of the Rescue 2 squad guys about a chop shop was confirmed. One of the fire marshals assigned to the case, Kathy Baer, called in the NYPD Auto Crimes Squad to have a look at what was in that garage."

"After examining everything, Auto Crimes is certain that the garage was a chop shop. In fact, they have several open cases of car thefts in the area and are checking the VINs on the parts they found in the garage to see if they match the VINs on their stolen cars."

"Which brings me to you guys," Michael continued.

"I want you to use any information and informants you developed in that car theft ring case you worked with the Feds several months ago, to find Patron."

Six months back the FBI had gone to Michael in his capacity as Chief of Rackets, asking for help in a large mob run auto theft ring they were investigating.

After making sure that the case was not connected to Satan, Michael assigned it to one of his staff attorneys and suggested that Dina and Tim work the case as well. They were skilled in finding missing witnesses and suspects and in developing informants to assist them.

The FBI was looking for individuals who the mob had employed as "spotters." They were street guys from various Brooklyn neighborhoods, usually with criminal records for car related crimes, who were sent out by their mob bosses with a shopping list of cars the mob was looking to steal.

When the spotter found a car on the list, he would notify his mob contact who then sent out thieves to steal the car. Depending on what the mob intended to do with a particular car, it was either shipped overseas to a waiting buyer or it was brought to a local chop shop and cut into parts. The parts were sold to unscrupulous or unsuspecting auto body repair businesses.

Dina and Tim worked the streets and developed informants who led them to several of the spotters. After they were arrested, Dina and Tim were successful in turning a few into confidential informants for the FBI.

Michael remembered from having read the reports about the case, that several of the spotters Dina and Tim found were native to Brooklyn, and others had emigrated to the borough from a variety of countries. All, however, lived in either Flatbush or one of the adjacent neighborhoods.

The reports also indicated that the spotters did their hunting for cars in the neighborhoods where they had grown up or were now living.

Michael was certain that Patron's chop shop was involved with spotters who were locating the cars that were then stolen and brought to him for chopping. He was convinced that finding one or more of them would be the key to locating Patron. So, it was a no-brainer for Michael to put Dina and Tim to work to find what he was looking for.

"Guys," Michael said, "I truly believe that spotters were used to find the cars that Patron was cutting up in that garage. You guys know the players in that business. I'm sure you can use one or two to either locate him or know how to find him."

When Michael was finished, Tim Clark spoke first. "Mike, first of all, I'm sure I speak for Dina as well as myself, when I say that it means a great deal that you asked us to work this case with you. We know how important it is. Bringing justice and closure to a family that lost a loved one under suspicious circumstances, is why we do this job."

"And" said Dina, "Since we ended that case with the Bureau, the informants, and even one or two of the witnesses they used at trial have stayed in touch with me. They're always looking for something, usually money, so they call or bring me info that I turn over to the cops or to the feds, who pay well if it turns out to be worthwhile. So, the informants love me! Mike, don't worry. Tim and I will find your guy."

CHAPTER
ELEVEN

Three days later, two miles into an early morning run, Michael received a call on his cell phone. It was Kathy Baer.

"Good morning, Kathy," Michael said, breathing heavily.

"Counselor, if I didn't know better, I'd think I dialed the wrong number and got some pervert in the middle of whacking off," Kathy said chuckling.

"No, it's just boring old me, trying to catch my breath after running just 2 miles in the streets of Carroll Gardens. Not that long ago I wouldn't have been breathing this way at this point of a run, but as my dad has said to me all too often these days, *a vecchiaia*, old age, is catching up to me."

"Mike, don't even think about that. You have a *few* good years left," Baer responded, now fully laughing.

"Enough of this witty banter fire marshal. I don't think you called this early to just chit chat and make fun of me. And it's freezing out here."

"What's up?" although he had to admit he was enjoying the back and forth.

"Some good news. NYPD Auto Crimes finished looking at the

VINs of the car parts we found in the garage. They've compared them to open cases from that neighborhood and adjacent ones. Mike, they have more than a few matches."

"Kathy, that's great. But while it's evidence that there was criminal activity going on in that garage, we still don't have enough for you to conclude that the fire resulted from that activity. The fire being a pure accident is still a possibility. We need to find Patrick Patron. He'll have the answer. Has Gazis found him yet?"

"I'm glad you brought that up because that was the second reason for me calling. Do you have two DA investigators out looking for Patron?"

"Yes. Why?"

"Gazis got wind of that late yesterday and he exploded. He was screaming to himself in his empty office, about how that 'motherfucker Gioca thinks he's running this case.'"

"He called me in and continued to rant. 'Who the fuck is Gioca to send out investigators to do what me and my people are perfectly capable of doing?' he asked, as if I had a direct line to your thinking."

"When I said nothing, he told me he was calling the DA this morning to complain that you're interfering in his investigation. He went as far as saying that he would ask the DA to remove you from the case. He wants it assigned to someone else but only *after* he makes an arrest. Mike, he's lost his mind!"

"Kathy, none of that will happen."

"Gazis is nothing more than a political lackey who wants and needs the big arrest to give himself credibility. To get that, he must show his people, the borough president, that new county clerk, and the progressives on the city council, that he and he alone solved the case."

"Trust me, if he makes that call, his requests will be dismissed out of hand. There are forces involved in this case that make him and his gang of hacks look like school children."

As soon as the words had left his mouth Michael regretted saying them. He let his anger with Gazis get the best of him.

"Michael, what exactly do you mean by that?"Kathy Baer said with a touch of uncertainty and fear in her voice. "Should I be concerned about something, like my job?"

Of course, he couldn't fully explain what he meant, so he simply said, "Kathy, you have nothing to worry about."

"I'm going to finish my run and calm down. Then I'm going to the office where I'll straighten all this out."

"And, as I have said before, what you told me about Gazis and his intentions, will never be repeated."

"Please keep doing what you're doing and when my people find Patron, which I'm sure will be before Gazis does, you'll be my first call."

"Thanks, Mike. If I learn anything new, you'll be *my* first call."

When Michael got back to his apartment, he called Monsignor Romano. He filled him in regarding what Kathy Baer had said about Gazis calling the district attorney.

"Michael, don't give it another thought. I'll reach out to Caldwell. He'll take care of it."

"Thanks Sal. I don't need that son of a bitch creating problems. If I didn't know better, I'd swear he was working with Satan!"

"Mike stranger things have happened," Romano responded. "You know that better than even I do. Keep your eyes and ears open when you deal with that guy. Stay calm. I'll call Caldwell now and I'll speak to you when I hear back from him."

"Sounds like a plan, monsignor."

"By the way, Sal, we haven't had a glass of wine to toast the new year. How about dinner tonight at *Emilio's*? We can raise a glass and I can fill you in on everything about the investigation. Who knows Dina and Tim may have even found Patron by the time we sit down."

"*Buona fortuna* to them Michael. I'll see you tonight."

Within an hour of receiving their assignment from Michael, Dina and Tim contacted the informants they developed in the mob car theft case.

Everyone they spoke to had heard about the fire and that a chop shop was being run out of that garage. However, none of them heard who, if anyone, were spotting for the cars that wound up there. They told Dina and Tim that they would ask around and keep their ears open for any information about the place.

Disappointed at striking out with the informants, Dina had an idea. She reached out to one of the spotters that she and Tim arrested in the mob case.

Marc Foxx, (not his given name), had emigrated as a young boy from Odessa in the Ukraine with his parents. He now lived alone in an apartment in the Canarsie section of Brooklyn. Canarsie is one of the neighborhoods adjacent to Flatbush, and several miles from the Church of the Archangels.

Foxx was one of Dina and Tim's newly minted confidential informants who called Dina with information about criminal activity when he needed money. His info had been particularly valuable to the NYPD, where Dina sent the intelligence. With the help of Foxx' tips, several detectives were able to close serious cases and take some very bad guys off the street.

Dina told Foxx why she wanted to talk to him. His response was, "I might be able to help you. But I don't want you coming to my neighborhood."

Dina agreed, and a meeting was set for noon the next day at *L&B Spumoni Gardens*, a popular pizza restaurant in the Bensonhurst section of Brooklyn, miles away from where Foxx lived.

It was 12:30 p.m. when Tim looked at his watch. He and Dina had been sitting in *L&B* for an hour because they wanted to be sure they didn't miss Foxx in the unlikely event he got there early.

Disappointed with his apparent no show, they paid their bill and were walking out when Dina spotted Foxx in a half-assed disguise walking toward the restaurant. He was wearing a surgical mask, which wasn't unusual because the covid virus was still stubbornly hanging on in the city. But he had a blonde wig under a ski hat, large sunglasses, and a big shearling jacket, torn at the sleeves and with the manufacturer's logo prominently displayed on its back. To Dina it appeared as if he had rummaged through a Goodwill donation container for his outfit.

Over a slice of *L&B's* famous Sicilian pizza, Foxx told Dina and Tim that he had information about a spotter who he heard had worked with the caretaker of a church in Flatbush who was operating a chop shop out of the church's garage.

"Was it the Church of the Archangels?" Dina asked.

Pretending that he just had his memory refreshed, Foxx answered, "Oh yeah, that's it."

"How did you get this info?" Tim asked.

Foxx didn't answer, which pissed Dina off.

"Listen, Marc, if you ever again want to be paid for info by the PD or any other agency, you better stop with the bullshit and answer my partner's question."

Foxx nodded at Dina, took a bite of his pizza before answering that he had gotten the information directly from the spotter.

"I got to know him when he worked with us in the mob car case. He was spotting for them just like I was. We even went out sometimes. He ain't a bad guy for an Albanian."

"What's his name?" Dina asked.

"Carmelo Giovalin. He came here from some city, Durres, I think it's called, a few years ago on a student visa and never left. He's told me he never wants to go back, so I believe if you need him to help with your case, he'll do it if you say that you won't send him back to Albania."

"Marc, tell us what you know about this guy and the garage at the church," Dina said.

Foxx told them that after the fire Giovalin called him. He told Foxx that he did some spotting for the caretaker and was going underground because he was afraid of getting arrested for being involved with a guy who was responsible for the death of a fire-fighter.

"He said he was afraid he would do jail time, then get deported, even though he had nothing to do with the fire."

Dina asked, "Did he use those exact words about being involved with a guy 'who was responsible for the death of a firefighter?'"

"That's what he said to me before he told me where he was going to hide out."

"Where is he now, Marc?" Tim asked.

Foxx told him that Carmelo said he was going to stay with an old girlfriend who lives in Astoria, Queens.

"He told me that they broke up over a year ago, but he felt that she still had a soft spot for him, so she'd let him stay at her apartment for a while until things cooled down. Her name is Patricia. Don't know her last name. But I do know she works in a Greek restaurant on Astoria Boulevard not far from where she lives."

Foxx said that was all he knew. When Dina and Tim thanked him and began to leave, he passed his lunch check to Dina. She dropped a few dollars on the table to cover it, but Foxx seemed unsatisfied.

"Dina, I gave you gold today. All I get is a slice?"

"We'll see if it's gold. The jury is still out. What do you want?"

Foxx ordered two whole Sicilian pizzas to go, which he told the counterman to add to his check. Uncertain if he should, the counterman gave Dina a look that silently asked, "Is that okay?"

Dina laughed before handing a credit card to the counterman nodding. "Make sure the pies are good and hot," she said, "Because Marc here is going to be carrying them home."

She then waved goodbye to Foxx.

She and Tim got into their car and headed for *"Demetrios Taverna,"* a Greek restaurant where, after a quick Google search, Dina was certain Carmelo's girlfriend worked.

CHAPTER

TWELVE

"**D**emetrios," as it was called by the locals in Astoria, was well known for its authentic Greek food and its great dinner vibe and atmosphere. The clientele ranged from the older Greek Americans who lived in Astoria for decades, to millennials of all nationalities who loved to dress up when having dinner in the place on Friday and Saturday nights.

When Dina and Tim walked into the restaurant it had just opened and the staff was setting up for dinner. After identifying themselves to the young man standing at a maître d' podium just inside the entrance, they were directed to the manager's office located behind the main dining room.

The manager Suzanne, an attractive, pleasant, and professional young woman, confirmed that there was a woman named Patricia working there.

"She's a waitress. She's working tonight and should be here for the beginning of her shift in 30 minutes."

Suzanne then told the investigators that they were welcome to wait in her office. "When Patricia gets here, I'll bring her in so you can talk."

Right on time, Suzanne escorted a young lady into her office. Patricia Thomas, five feet four inches, in her late twenties, with shoulder length brown hair with blonde streaks, and a tattoo on the right side of her neck, looked like she had seen a ghost when Suzanne introduced her to Dina and Tim. The investigators got right to the point.

"We're looking for Carmelo Giovalin, who we believe is staying at your apartment," Dina told her.

Patricia began to shake and then started to cry. "Am I in trouble? Am I going to lose my job?" she asked Suzanne.

Once she was assured that she would not be fired, she calmed down.

She said that she had met Carmelo in a bar in Brooklyn over a year ago, after which they began dating. She broke up with him about seven months ago because she didn't like the bad influence his "shady" friends had on him. She saw him infrequently and when she did it was always in Brooklyn with those "shitheads" around.

"I haven't seen or heard from him since we split until he showed up at my apartment the day after Christmas," she said.

"When he rang my intercom, I didn't want to let him in. But he begged me to open up. He said it was an emergency that he would explain once he was inside. I relented and let him in."

"He told me that some Russian mob guys he had been working for were angry with him and he needed to stay somewhere outside of Brooklyn until things cooled off. He assured me that it was a minor issue and that he would go back to his place by the end of the week."

"Detectives I know that he was probably lying because he's still there, and you're here looking for him. Please tell me, what has he done? Am I in danger?"

Dina and Tim did not tell Patricia why they were looking for Carmelo. All they said was that they needed to ask him some questions. And to put her mind at ease so she wouldn't tip him off before they could get to him, they told her that Carmelo was not in any trouble. They didn't lie, but Carmelo's status could certainly change depending on what he would tell them about his relationship with Patrick Patron.

After spending an hour with Dina and Tim, Patricia became more comfortable. So, when Dina asked, "Is Carmelo at the apartment right now?" Patricia told her that she would be surprised if he wasn't.

"He rarely goes outside, and even orders in all his meals. When I left for work, he was on my couch watching TV."

After thanking her for the help, Dina asked Patricia for her address, which she shared without hesitation. Dina then added, "You're not in any trouble, but if you call or somehow let Carmelo know we're coming to speak to him, that may change. Do you understand?"

"Yes, I do," Patricia answered while vigorously nodding her head.

Tim drove the five blocks to the four-story apartment building, parking around the corner from the entrance. The apartment was on the first floor in the rear of the building, so there were no windows facing the street. The building's main door required a key to enter, however there was an intercom system which the tenants used to let in visitors and delivery people after determining who was there.

Fortunately for Dina and Tim, they didn't have to use the intercom to get into the building. As they were standing in front deciding how to get in without alerting Carmelo, a black guy with a large Doberman opened the front door to leave the building. As Tim went to grab the door before it closed, the dog began to growl and bared its teeth. A startled Dina had just begun to admonish the dog's handler when he said in a soft Caribbean accent , "You're here for Carmelo."

When neither Dina nor Tim answered him, the guy said that they should leave. "Don't waste your time here because Carmelo is not in the apartment."

"A few days ago, he told me that he caught covid but was not going to quarantine. I saw him as he was leaving Patricia's apartment and I haven't seen him since. He looked terrible and could hardly speak without coughing, which he did in my face. The scumbag was not wearing a mask."

"I hope you guys catch that son of a bitch. He abuses Patricia all the time and every time I call the cops, they do nothing."

"Tell me your names because I want to check in with the Queens District Attorney's Office to make sure that you got him. He deserves to be in jail."

Both Dina and Tim were speechless. The guy's rant caught them by surprise.

It was Tim who spoke first. "First of all, what's your name, and who are you?"

"My name is Anton and I'm the building's superintendent," he answered as the dog began to snarl again at Tim, as Anton held the leash tightly.

Tim then asked, "Okay Anton, what makes you so certain we're here for Carmelo?"

Anton didn't answer.

Instead, he loosened his grip on the leash and the dog made a lunge at Tim. With that, Dina unholstered her gun, pointed it at the animal and was about to shoot when Anton and the dog took off running and disappeared into an adjacent alley. When Dina, with Tim right behind her, ran to the entrance of the alley after them, she saw no one. The dog and Anton were gone.

"It's like they disappeared," they later told Michael.

They walked back to the building's entrance and were once again confronted with the problem of getting inside. It was closed and locked.

"We need to get in there. I don't believe that guy Anton. There was something weird about him beside him letting that dog go for you. What was that all about?"

"He claimed to hate Carmelo, and wanted him arrested, yet he seemed to be discouraging us from even checking out the apartment. He wanted us gone. It's really strange," Tim responded.

"Yeah," Dina agreed. "Did you see his face as he was talking about Carmelo? It got all flushed and that weird mole on his left cheek flared up like a candy Red Hot. He sure did seem to hate the guy, but he did everything short of calling the cops to discourage us from going to check out that apartment."

"Dina, Patricia was telling us the truth. Carmelo is in there," Tim said, nodding toward the building.

As Dina and Tim were talking, they got lucky. A young man approached the building and pressed the intercom for Patricia's apartment and was buzzed in. Just as Patricia had mentioned, Carmelo was getting a food delivery.

"We're visiting that apartment, so we'll bring the food in," Tim said to the young man as he showed him his shield. Dina gave the kid a few bucks and followed Tim into the building.

THIRTEEN

Less than 30 seconds after Tim Clark knocked on the apartment door, Carmelo Giovalin answered.

Without looking he held out three dollars to the person at the door thinking it was the delivery kid. When Tim didn't take it, Carmelo finally focused on who was standing there and quickly tried to close the door. Tim had anticipated that and in addition to pressing his full body weight against the door, he had his foot on the door jamb so Carmelo could not slam it shut.

"Carmelo, we just want to talk," Tim said.

Obviously frightened, a stammering Carmelo looked at Tim and then at Dina and asked "Who are you? What the fuck do you want? And how do you know my name?"

Dina told him why they were there. She took the food delivery bag from Tim, and to show Carmelo that they meant no harm, handed it to him.

"Carmelo, you're not in any trouble. Can we come in?"

Handing him his bag of food worked. Carmelo stepped back and told them to come in.

The apartment was small with one bedroom, a living room

which was surprisingly nicely furnished, and a small kitchen and bath. Tim made sure to check the entire apartment before settling down to avoid any surprises..

It was Dina who began the talk with Carmelo, telling him that they were looking for his help. She repeated that he was not in trouble but if he didn't tell them what he knew, and someone else put him in the middle of the case, he'd likely be arrested and perhaps even charged with murder.

"Carmelo, this is your chance to get ahead of whatever may come down. We're going to talk to many others, but if you're first in with the help and information we need, that will be to your benefit."

Dina had gotten his attention. Carmelo listened as he ate his hamburger.

She told him what they knew about the fire, and the business that Patrick Patron was running out of the garage at Archangel Church. She said that they had information that he was working either with, or for, Patron as a spotter for cars that were then stolen as part of a car theft ring. She didn't mention the Russian mob because she wanted Carmelo to either verify or refute their role on his own, without any prompting from her.

"Carmelo, we know you spoke to Patrick after the fire. We want you to tell us everything you know about him and the fire in his garage."

Carmelo finished his burger, wiped his mouth, took a drink from a can of soda he had ordered and said to Dina, "I like you. I'll tell you what I know."

Carmelo began by saying that he met Patron through a gang who was indeed running a stolen car ring in Brooklyn. He said that he believed they were Russian and despite the fact that he was from Albania, they let him work because a Russian friend had vouched for him.

"Was that a guy named Marc Foxx?" Tim asked.

Carmelo didn't answer.

"It's okay Carmelo, you can tell us," Dina assured him. "You won't get this Marc Foxx guy in trouble. We have no evidence that he's connected to this case at all."

After hearing that, Carmelo confirmed that Marc Foxx got him involved with the car theft ring the feds took down.

"My job for them was to look for cars they wanted stolen. Every few weeks they gave me a list of two or three cars, expensive ones usually, and when I spotted one, I called a number and told them where the car was. I never waited around to see the car get broken into and then towed because they didn't want anyone to get suspicious of some guy hanging near a high-end car. They were afraid the cops would be called, or worse, the owner of the car would move it."

"I knew from talking to the guys in the ring that some cars were immediately shipped out of the country, and others were brought to a garage to be cut up for parts. That's how I got to know Patrick."

"One time I went with the tow guys to bring one of the cars to Patrick's garage. I thought they were nuts because it was a garage that was on some church's grounds and attached to a building that said 'Rectory' above the entrance door. I was raised as a Catholic in my country, so I knew what that word meant. It was where the priests lived."

"When I went inside the garage, I saw that this guy Patrick had everything that was needed to cut up cars. He introduced himself and every time I went there with the tow guys to bring a car to be cut up, me and Patrick talked."

"He told me came to the US from Haiti and that he heard about a caretaker job opening at that church and went to speak to the priest in charge about hiring him. He told me that the caretaker before him had just disappeared one day and the priest, who was the boss, was desperate to fill the position, so he got the job."

"Did he tell you how he went from church caretaker to operating a chop shop?" Tim asked.

"Yeah. He said that one of the things that got him the job was his work in Haiti as a car mechanic. This was important to the pastor because the church had maintenance machinery that needed care and sometimes repair."

"After he had been working there for a while, he asked the pastor if he could use the church garage after hours to do car repairs to make some extra money. When the pastor said it was okay, he said he asked him if one of his friends could work with him."

"Tell us about this friend," Dina said.

"Patrick told me that he had met the guy one night in a bar. The guy had been sitting alone and when Patrick sat down near him the guy bought him a drink. Without Patrick even asking him, the guy said he was from Haiti like him. How he knew where Patrick was from was something Patrick thought was strange. They continued to talk, and they hit it off."

"The guy asked him where he was working, and when Patrick told him he was looking for a job, the guy said that he might know of one that was about to open up."

"The guy asked him if he was good with his hands and Patrick told him he had been a mechanic in his hometown. The guy smiled and said that he was sure he'd have something for him. They agreed to meet in a few days."

"Three days later, they met in that same bar. That's when the guy told him about the opening for a caretaker in the church. The guy told him where the church was located, and the next day Patrick went to see the pastor."

"He said that he didn't get the job right then. But a few days later the pastor called him and gave it to him."

"He said that a few weeks after he got the job, the guy who told him about it came to see him. Patrick was working on some snow equipment in the church garage when he heard his name called. He looked up and it was the guy. He asked Patrick how he was doing and when Patrick said he was working hard but the pay was only just okay, the guy suggested that Patrick ask the pastor if he could use the garage to repair cars, as he had done in Haiti to make extra money.

The guy even said that he knew lots of people who he would send to Patrick to repair their cars."

"Patrick liked the idea. He told the guy he would ask the pastor the next day. Then the guy said that he wanted to help him with the repairs because he liked Patrick and wanted him to succeed."

"Patrick asked him if he knew cars and the guy said that he did, but he was not a mechanic. The guy said he would be satisfied with just helping Patrick with heavy lifting and things like that. Patrick told him that if the pastor gave him permission to use the garage for repairs, he'd ask if the guy could be with him."

"Did he get the pastor's permission?" asked Dina.

"Patrick told me the pastor said yes but that he wanted to meet the helper before he would allow him to work with him."

"When Patrick brought the guy around to meet the pastor, he said the guy acted very strangely around him. Despite it, eventually Patrick persuaded the pastor to allow the helper to work with him."

"Did Patrick tell you the guy's name?"

"Yeah, he did. He said his name was Anton"

When Carmelo said the name, Dina turned to Tim and gave him a look that said, "What are the odds?" Tim shrugged and indicated to her that they needed to keep Carmelo talking. Dina nodded and continued with Carmelo.

"Let's get to the chop shop business and how Patrick got in with the Russians," Did he tell you how he came to work for the car theft ring?"

"Yeah. He said that one night, after Anton had been working with him for a couple of weeks, Patrick was working alone changing the spark plugs on a car. Unexpectedly Anton walked into the garage and told Patrick he had a way to make a lot more money than what he was getting for the car repairs."

"Anton told him that he knew some people who he trusted, who were looking for someone who could cut up cars for parts. These people had contacts with auto repair shops across the city that were always in need of car parts and paid well for them."

"Anton said that his people would be buying used and discarded cars from junkyards and auctions and needed them cut up. He said he spoke to them about Patrick, after which they agreed to give him their business."

Carmelo said that Patrick told him that he agreed to do the cutting because he desperately needed the money.

"Over the next few nights, after the pastor and priests went to sleep, Anton and a couple of other guys brought in all the equipment Patrick would need to do the cutting. He told me he was surprised at the quality of the electric saws, the torches, the tools, and the car jacks that he was supplied with. He was not used to such expensive stuff, and he liked having it."

"Two nights later the first car was towed into the garage. Patrick saw that it was a very late model Lexus and was confused. This car was not in the condition he was expecting it to be in. It wasn't old, it was in perfect condition, and it didn't look as if it had been abandoned. So, he confronted Anton and asked what was going on. That's when Anton told him the truth about the car theft ring."

Carmelo said that Patrick was pissed because he didn't want to get arrested and be deported. But when Anton told him how much money he would be making, and that there was no need to worry about getting caught because the local cops had been paid off by the Russians, Patrick agreed to do the cutting for the car theft ring.

"He comes from Haiti, where police corruption is common," Carmelo said. "So, he was used to cops being paid by criminals to look the other way."

"Did he tell you about the fire and how it started," Dina asked.

"Yeah. But before I do anymore talking, I need to use the bathroom. And guys, how about we order some coffee and donuts? On you of course."

After dessert Carmelo told Dina and Tim everything he knew about the fire and Patrick Patron's confession to starting it.

CHAPTER

FOURTEEN

Carmelo said that things were going fairly well for Patrick in the chop shop business, but he was always complaining that he needed more money. Carmelo said that a couple of Patrick's relatives had snuck into the US, and they were living with him. He was feeling the pressure of having to feed and clothe them, which is how he got into trouble with the church and lost his job.

"Patrick told me that on several occasions when he was cleaning inside the church, he saw people who worked in the rectory open the donation boxes that were set up around the church to collect the money that worshippers donated. He said he watched as the boxes were opened and thought that it would be easy for him to get into them and take the cash. So, about a week before Christmas, when Patrick thought he was alone in the church, he pried open several of the boxes and pocketed the money. What he didn't know was there was a priest praying in a remote part of the church who, after hearing the noise Patrick was making, got curious, and went looking for the source. Patrick said the priest caught him with a screwdriver, standing in front of a box that had been broken into, holding a fist full of cash."

Patrick initially denied the accusation. He was confronted with other allegations of having stolen from the church's weekly collection and from the rectory safe, all of which he did."

"After the pastor told him that if he was honest and confessed, the church would not report him to the police. Patrick did confess and the pastor forgave him but fired him."

"Patrick told me that after he was let go, he went out to the garage and told Anton what happened. He said that Anton asked him if he still had the keys to the church buildings. When Patrick said that he went out to the garage to get them so he could turn them over to the pastor, Anton told him to take the garage key off the key ring because they needed to use the garage for a few final cutting jobs."

Patrick told Carmelo that Anton said that sometime that week the Russians were going to be bringing in two high-end cars that needed to have their gas tanks dropped and removed. They had a buyer who would be paying a great deal of money for them, so the Russians would pay Patrick well. Patrick had never done that type of job before, but he wanted and needed the money, so he agreed.

Patrick returned the church keys to the pastor but kept the garage key. Over the next few days, while waiting for the Russians and the gas tank job, he continued to cut up cars at night when he knew the priests were asleep.

Two days before Christmas Anton told him that the Russians would be bringing the cars that night.

"Patrick said that around midnight Anton showed up with two guys and the expensive cars. They drove them into the garage and Patrick went to work with Anton's help."

"He told me that, not having dropped a gas tank before, he messed up. Apparently, the tanks had gasoline in them and when Patrick removed them from the cars, he spilled it on the floor of the garage."

"He panicked, but Anton told him not to worry because the gasoline would dry, and any fumes would go away."

"The problem was that the fumes were still in the air the next day, he said."

"Patrick said that Anton had called him on Christmas eve morning and told him that he had an important, well-paying job that they could do that afternoon. Patrick agreed to do it. So, he and Anton went back to the garage to finish that one last job."

"Patrick said that when he opened the garage door the smell of gasoline was heavy. But when he looked around he saw that the gasoline he had spilled the night before had dried up some, but not completely."

"Anton told him not to be concerned about the gasoline fumes because they were not dangerous. And that even if a fire started they'd be able to get out of the garage quickly."

Patrick relaxed and went to work.

"Wasn't he concerned with the pastor or the priests catching him in the garage where he no longer had the right, or permission, to be?" Dina asked.

"I asked him the same thing. He told me he went at a time when he felt the pastor and priests would be busy preparing for Christmas services and the job he had to do wouldn't take very long to complete."

Tim asked, "Did he tell you what that 'one final job' was?"

"He said that Anton told him that he had set it up some time ago, but it couldn't be done until the Russians had found and stolen a specific car model they wanted him to work on. Apparently, it was an expensive car and they needed him to remove the VIN plate from the engine and replace it with the VIN plate from the same model car that had been junked after a bad collision. He said that Anton had told him that putting the junked car's VIN on the newly stolen car would make the stolen car seem legit. It could then be shipped out of the country with a 'legitimate' VIN."

"It was when he was cutting the VIN plate off the stolen car that the fire started."

Carmelo told Dina and Tim that Patrick said when he began to cut the VIN plate using a rotary power saw, a shower of sparks from the saw cutting the metal rained down to the garage floor.

The sparks ignited the fumes from the gasoline that remained from the spill.

The fire spread quickly but Patrick told Carmelo that he and Anton were able to get out of the garage with no injuries.

"When they got outside the first fire truck arrived," he said. "He told me that he and Anton wanted to run but couldn't because the firefighters asked if anyone was still inside the garage. That's when Patrick said that Anton leaned over to him and told him to tell the firefighters that someone *was* still trapped inside the garage so when they rushed in to save the person, Patrick and him could get out of there."

"Patrick said that's what he did and when the firefighters went into the garage, he and Anton took off. Patrick rushed to my place to tell me what had happened, but he had no idea where Anton went."

"Where did Patrick go after talking to you?" Tim asked.

"Nowhere," Carmelo answered. "He stayed at my place that night because he was too scared to go home. When we heard the news the next day that a firefighter was killed in that fire, both me and Patrick panicked. I told him to find another place to hide out, and I came here."

"Do you know where Patrick is now?" asked Dina.

"No. But if it will help me, I think he'll meet me somewhere, especially if I lie and tell him I've got some cash from the Russians for him. Then when he shows up, you guys can grab him. Will that help me?"

"We'll have to talk to our boss, but I think that will go a long way to maybe you not being charged with anything," Dina answered. "But how do you know you'll be able to reach him?"

"Listen, I'm probably the only friend he has these days. He calls me practically every day to find out what I know. He's scared. But he trusts me. He confessed to me, didn't he? I'm sure that if I tell him I have cash for him, he'll meet."

"So, call your boss and let's do this. I'm tired of being cooped up in here, I'm tired of the shit take-out food, and Patricia will be your friend forever if you get me out of her life."

"Stay right here Carmelo," Dina said, as she and Tim went into the hallway outside the apartment to call Michael.

Carmelo laughed. "Stay here? Where am I going? That's the only way out. Just bring back good news."

After a 30-minute conversation with Michael, which Carmelo later revealed to Dina and Tim felt like several hours, the investigators told him to pack his stuff because he was coming with them.

When he hesitated as if it was bad news, Dina told him their boss wanted to meet him so they could get right into setting up a meeting with Patrick Patron.

CHAPTER
FIFTEEN

An hour after the call, Dina and Tim walked into Michael's office with Carmelo in tow. Sitting with him was Kathy Baer. Since Dina and Tim had never met Kathy, Michael introduced them. They in turn did the honors with Carmelo.

After he heard from Dina that Carmelo agreed to cooperate, and that they were bringing him to his office, Michael phoned Kathy and asked her to be there. He wanted a fire marshal to hear what Carmelo had to say regarding Patron's confession.

He asked only Kathy to attend because he feared that if Alex Gazis was there, with his poor attitude and seeming dislike for Michael, it was likely he would say something negative about Dina and Tim working the case. Michael was concerned that would turn off the now cooperating witness. Over the past several hours Tim and especially Dina had developed a rapport with Carmelo, and if Gazis said anything negative about the two, it would cause Carmelo to clam up.

Michael had another reason for not asking Gazis to his office. He just didn't like the egotistic and pretentious prick, and he wanted

Kathy Baer to get whatever credit the FDNY would be handing out for solving the case and arresting Patrick Patron.

Once all the introductions were completed Dina told Carmelo that Michael was the lead prosecutor on the case, and he had the final say as to whether he would be charged with any crimes resulting from his work with the stolen car ring.

Then, turning to Kathy Baer, Dina told Carmelo that she was the lead investigating fire marshal assigned by the Fire Department. "So, you need to be completely truthful with them like you were with us. They need to hear everything you know about Patrick, how you two met and became friends, about Patrick's buddy Anton, and most importantly, Patrick's confession."

Michael then said, "Can you do that Carmelo? Because if you agree to help us and then bullshit me or hold things back, I promise you we'll find out. And I also promise that you won't like what happens. On the other hand, if you do what Dina suggested and you tell us the truth about everything, I'll become your best friend and you *will* like what happens. Have I made myself clear?"

Carmelo nodded, broke out in a big smile and said, "Loud and clear. 'Mr. G', let's be friends."

Michael laid out what he would need to do. He told him that he first had to set up a meeting with Patrick. "Dina and Tim say that you believe that Patrick will meet with you if you tell him you have money from the Russians. How certain are you of that?"

Carmelo told Michael that when Patrick was fired from the church job and could no longer cut cars for the Russians, he lost all his income. "And since he went into hiding after the fire he would call me to ask if I would stake him some cash. I never did because I went underground too. So, I know he's hurting. He'll definitely meet me after I tell him I have cash for him."

"Okay good. You're going to make the call very soon," Michael said.

He continued with what he expected from Carmelo once Patron

was arrested. "After we get Patrick, you may have to testify in the grand jury, and then if there is a trial I'll need you to be a witness."

Carmelo agreed to it all if Michael promised not to charge him with anything connected to the car theft ring. After Michael agreed, Carmelo had another request.

"'Mr. G,' listen, I worked with some bad dudes in that car ring. Those Russians don't play around. And that dude Anton, Patrick's friend, I only met him once or twice but he's even scarier than those Russkies. I need you to promise that you'll protect me from now until I finish with the trial. And once I'm done testifying I want you to move me out of New York."

"Carmelo, you have my word. We're going to make sure nothing happens to you before the trial. And once you're done, we'll get you out of the city and set you up someplace where you'll be safe."

"'Mr. G,' we have a deal," Carmelo said, reaching out to shake Michael's hand.

Although it was close to 10 p.m., both Michael and Kathy Baer were anxious to hear what Carmelo had to say. Over the next two hours Carmelo told them everything he told Dina and Tim. When he was finished, Michael asked Dina and Tim to step outside the office, leaving Kathy with Carmelo.

"Guys is that everything he said to you? And do you believe him?" Michael asked.

Tim answered. "Mike not only is it everything he even added a few things. He didn't tell us that Patron had described the electric saw he was using to cut the VIN plate off the junked car when the fire started. Potentially that's a nice piece of info. If the fire marshals recovered that saw in the debris, it adds corroboration to the story."

Dina added, "Both Tim and I really believe that this guy is being straight with us, and now you. He was so frightened of the Russians, this guy Anton, and the cops, that he was hiding out in Astoria for God's sake. You can't get culturally more distant from Flatbush than that. And he was driving his old girl-friend nuts because he was camped out in her apartment and wouldn't leave even to eat! What he knows is the straight shit or he wouldn't be so frightened of the people who know he knows."

"Dina, eloquently put." Michael said laughing. "I couldn't have said it better myself."

Back in Michael's office Carmelo had fallen asleep in his chair. When the three came in and saw him, they looked at Kathy Baer who just shrugged. "Long hard day for the kid," she said.

"It has been for all of us," Michael said. "I'm ready to call it a night," he continued, "But I need to speak to Kathy before we leave. Will you guys take Carmelo to the conference room while I do that? I won't be long."

Dina gently woke Carmelo and asked him to go with her and Tim. Groggily he grabbed his bag and followed the two investigators out of Michael's office.

Michael asked Kathy, "Based on your examination of the fire scene up to this point, and the evidence you've looked at, is Carmelo's version of Patron's confession to how the fire started plausible and possible?"

Kathy answered by saying that scientifically the gas fumes in the garage, which she smelled when she entered after the fire, are indeed flammable and could have been ignited with the sparks from a power saw cutting metal. But she hesitated in giving Michael a definitive answer that it was the cause of the fire.

"Michael, before I give you an expert opinion, I want to go back over the scene and check a few things and I also want to re-examine the evidence we've recovered, especially the power saw we found. I want to be certain and not get tripped up on cross-examination by some sharp attorney if this goes to trial. Okay?"

"Kathy we both want to be certain about it all. The last thing we need is to be embarrassed in a case like this with the city, the FDNY, and most importantly, Louis Amato's family all depending on us. But please do what you have to do quickly. We have Carmelo now, but who knows how long he'll stay patient. And we don't want Patron to take off on us. We need to have Carmelo make that call so we can grab him."

"I understand, and you have my word that I'll get to it in the morning." Kathy looked at her watch, saw it was after midnight, and corrected herself, "I mean I'll get to it later this morning when I start my tour. I'm going to have to let Gazis know what I'm doing. He's still my boss and I need my job."

Michael agreed and offered to call Gazis himself.

"Thanks Mike, but it'll be better coming from me."

"One other thing before I go. I want to tell you something about the cause of the roof collapse. I was about to call you with this when you asked me to come over here."

"Michael, I know we've spent a lot of time trying to determine how the fire started, which is obviously task number one. But even when we nail that down we still need to explain how the fire caused the roof to collapse because we've determined, and the firefighters who responded to the garage support this, the roof was never touched by the fire."

This surprised Michael. "So, what's the answer?".

"My office believes that once the fire started it quickly spread across the floor of the garage fueled by gasoline that had been spilt. Now after listening to Patron's confession I know how that gasoline got on the floor. The fire spread to the walls of the garage and heated the steel beams that lined the walls and supported the roof, causing them to bend and twist. Once that was happening they could no longer support the weight of the roof and it collapsed."

"Kathy has the FDNY consulted with a structural engineer as to the viability of that hypothesis?" Michael asked.

"We haven't just yet. This is the opinion and conclusion reached by some of the senior fire marshals in my office based on their experience with fires in structures like that garage. We wanted to wait for the go ahead from you before we reached out to the engineer. If you say it's okay, we'll test our theory with one."

"Kathy, I believe that if we go to trial we'll need the engineer's expert opinion."

"Now go home and get some sleep," Michael said to Kathy. "We've got a few busy days ahead of us."

"I'm going to put Carmelo in a hotel tonight, with Dina and Tim guarding him. Later this morning I'll set up a full protective custody detail to last until Carmelo is finished testifying. I'm going to need the help of your office for bodies to man the custody so perhaps..., on second thought, it might be better if I call Gazis to fill him in on where we are with Carmelo and tell him what you'll be doing. I will then ask him for the manpower for the custody."

Kathy thought about it before saying, "Mike let me talk to him first. I'll get in early like he does and fill him in on everything. Trust me when I say it's better that way. Once I've done that I'll text you, and you can call him to ask for the help with the custody."

"Kathy, that's a plan," said Michael.

With Kathy gone, Michael went to the conference room to speak to Carmelo. He told him his plan for the protective custody arrangement and asked Dina and Tim to work the first 12 hours after which he expected to have reinforcements from the fire marshal's office. As usual the two agreed without a complaint.

This detail being a surprise, neither Dina nor Tim was prepared for it. They needed toiletries and a change of clothes. So, while Dina arranged for the hotel room for the night, Tim rushed home to grab what he needed. When he returned Dina did the same thing while Tim stayed with Carmelo.

By the time they were settled in their room the sun was coming up. Carmelo quickly fell asleep. Dina and Tim on the other hand didn't have that luxury. They took turns napping with one eye open. The last thing they needed was for their prized witness to sneak out and disappear.

CHAPTER
SIXTEEN

I t was 10 a.m. when Kathy Baer's text appeared on Michael's cell phone. He waited 30 minutes then called Alex Gazis.

"Alex, it's Mike Gioca. I assume Kathy Baer told you about the developments last night and early this morning."

Michael could tell by his grunt that he was pissed that Michael and his investigators found Carmelo and were close to getting Patron. Undeterred, Michael was able to extract the assurance from Gazis that he would contribute manpower to guarding Carmelo for as long as necessary.

Knowing he had the financial resources of the federal government behind him, he told Gazis that his office would foot the bill for the hotel where they were housing the witness. In addition, Michael said he would cover the expenses for the food and his guards, and for any overtime incurred by Gazis' people for the duration of the custody.

Of course, Gazis couldn't be gracious. Instead, his reaction was, "Since this is now a 'Gioca production,' I expect nothing less."

Michael let the snide remark pass. Instead he asked Gazis to let him know as soon as Kathy Baer had a definitive opinion about the plausibility of Patron's statement as to how the fire started. Gazis grudgingly said that he would.

Two days later while Michael was on the phone with his dad, he received a text from Kathy Baer. "Call me," was the message.

"Kathy I hope it's good news," Michael said to her when she answered his call.

"Mike, I went back to the scene and reexamined all the evidence, particularly a power saw that was found next to the burnt-out hulk of a high-end car, which I now believe was the one from which Patrick was removing the VIN plate. I checked out the engine compartment and saw the marks that were left by the power saw. And right under that spot there was evidence of gasoline residue that had not completely burned away in the fire."

"Based on everything I saw, it's my considered opinion that Patron's account of how the fire started is more than viable, it's definitive."

"Kathy, that's not good news... It's great news!"

"I'm going to have Carmelo brought to my office so he can make the call to Patron. Kathy, you need to be here so there is no bitching that the fire marshal's office was not represented."

"Just let me know when and I'll be there," she replied.

Michael called the hotel room where Carmelo was being guarded. Luckily, Dina and Tim had the shift. He told them to bring him in.

They arrived with Carmelo 20 minutes later. Michael alerted Kathy, and as soon as she got there, Carmelo made the call to Patron.

The meet was set.

However, Patron never got to see Carmelo.

As soon as he arrived at the agreed upon location, under the Coney Island boardwalk at W. 8th street, he was arrested by a squad of fire marshals led by Alex Gazis.

Patron was brought into the fire marshals' office where he was advised of his Miranda rights, after which he refused to make a statement and asked for an attorney. Only then did Gazis call Michael.

Michael was upset that he hadn't been called when the marshals first brought Patron in, and before they asked if he wanted to make a statement. He wanted to confront and convince him to help himself by talking. That was all now moot because once he asked for an attorney he could no longer be questioned.

"*That was Gazis saying his is bigger than mine,*" Michael said to himself after he hung up the phone.

He cooled down and then called Kathy Baer.

"Kathy, your boss is a prick! He wouldn't give me a shot at Patron because he wants the credit all for himself. Have you guys charged him yet?"

"No," Kathy answered. "Gazis said to me that he didn't want any charges prepared until he got back. Then he left the office."

"Got back? Left the office? Where did he go?"

"He didn't tell me, but if I were betting, I'd put my money on Brooklyn Borough Hall and the borough president's office. He wants to make sure he gets all the credit before the arrest hits the news. That's the way he's wired, Mike."

"Kathy, when he gets back, find out what you can, then call me."

"We're going to need to charge Patron soon. Since I'm the one who draws up the criminal court complaint, Gazis is going to have to consult with me before any charges are drawn."

Kathy Baer would have won her bet. After leaving the office Gazis went directly to meet his buddy, the borough president, and advised him of the arrest. In addition, while driving to Borough Hall, he called the new county clerk and his city council friends and alerted them to Patrick Patron being in custody.

All were pleased when Gazis filled them in on the cause of the fire. He told them that arson, an intentional fire, was not involved.

Being politicians who needed the immigrant vote, Borough President Pickett and the city council members, made it known to Gazis that they didn't want the Haitian to be charged with any serious crimes in connection with the fire. However, they understood that Gazis couldn't just cut Patron loose with no charges filed against him, so they told him that if he charged Patron with simply running a chop shop they would have no issue with his decision. Getting the not-so-subtle hint, he assured them that's how he would proceed.

Under New York State law cutting up stolen cars was not a bail eligible crime. Patron would therefore be released from custody pending a trial. The politicians felt certain that charging him would placate, if not completely satisfy, the law-and-order voters and his release with no bail would satisfy the immigrant community, thereby avoiding a potential revolt at the ballot box that would cost them votes. Once the election had passed, they surely would no longer have any interest in Patrick Patron.

Brooklyn Borough President Tom Pickett knew that his party's bosses would breathe a sigh of relief when he informed them what Gazis told him about the fire and how he intended to handle the matter. His candidacy was therefore safe.

As he left the borough president's office extremely pleased with himself and how the meeting had gone, Gazis spotted the county clerk in the corridor. It appeared to Gazis that Downey had been waiting for him.

"Alex, I know you were in with the borough president," Downey said. "And I can guess what he told you about proceeding with charges against Patron."

"There's no doubt he's very happy that it's not arson, but I'm sure he told you that he knows you can't just let Patron walk away. You have to bring charges of some kind against him. Therefore, he's okay with you charging him with running the chop shop, which is a non-bail eligible crime. Am I right?"

Gazis told him that he was and added that the city council

members were of the same mind. Downey scoffed and told Gazis to ignore them all.

"Listen Alex, Pickett and those city council hacks are playing it safe. Sure, they want Patron released so they can make the most of that decision with the voters, but on the other hand, they're afraid of the backlash if you don't charge him with something. Which is why they'd be happy with the chop shop crimes."

"I'm close to the party leaders, and I'm telling you that if you want to be fire commissioner in Pickett's administration you'd be wise to listen to me and do as I say."

"We need votes to win!" Downey continued. "The large Caribbean community in Flatbush and their relatives and friends, as well as immigrant voters all over the city, will love us if Patrick Patron walks out with one of those Desk Appearance Tickets, the cops call them DATs."

"Alex, this is a nothing case," Downey continued, "A trespass at worst. And the fire, it was an accident. A DAT is like a summons and is appropriate in a case like this. Patrick would be freed from custody immediately and given a date for him to return to court. And, in the end, the worst he'll get is a fine."

Gazis looked shocked by Downey's suggestion.

Undeterred, Downey continued, "Once the facts as you've explained them are laid out in the press, everyone in the city will see that Patron didn't kill that firefighter."

"So, trust me. Do it. Give him a DAT. No one is going to bitch about it. The mayor is done this year, he won't care. And I'll convince Pickett and the city council members to publicly back your decision, which they'll do if they want the party to continue to support them."

"Charge him with something that makes him DAT eligible. And when the press photographs him being released from custody, you'll be our hero, Alex."

"One more thing. If that Gioca guy disagrees and upsets the plan, don't worry. It'll be a few months before a trial starts. And since life is unpredictable, things could take an unexpected turn. Evidence could disappear, an important witness or two could suffer memory loss or have an accident, which would make it impossible for them to testify. There are always things that can be done to ensure that we get what we want."

When the county clerk was finished, Gazis nodded in agreement.

CHAPTER
SEVENTEEN

"A DAT, is he fucking crazy?" Michael screamed into the phone at Kathy Baer. She had just finished talking to Gazis who, upon his return, told her where he was and what he decided to do. He then lied, claiming that giving a DAT to Patron had the backing of 'Borough Hall.'

What he didn't tell her was that the decision was made purely with votes in mind and was solely the idea of County Clerk Downey.

Although he didn't know the full story behind the decision, Michael's sixth sense told him that politics was the motivation for the DAT decision. He said to Kathy, "I don't buy for a second that the DAT decision came from Gazis. I'd stake my life on the fact that it came from some political hack in Borough Hall. And that ambitious son of a bitch didn't have the guts to tell them all to go to hell. He caved to satisfy the politicians. That's bullshit! Because I know a family and an entire department of firefighters who won't be satisfied."

"Kathy you're the arresting officer and it's your responsibility to prepare the arrest papers, not Gazis. I'm asking you to stall. Please don't do anything as far as charging Patron until you hear from me."

"If Gazis gives you a hard time, remind him that the arraignment paperwork and the legal charging documents are prepared by an assistant district attorney, and since I'm the ADA assigned to the case you'll need to speak to me to get them completed."

"I'll be 'unreachable' for a while. That will buy me time to do what I have to do to make sure Patron is charged properly."

Kathy Baer told Michael she would wait for his call.

From the moment he first learned of how the fire started, Michael was thinking about the crime he would charge Patron with. He had an idea but wanted to get the opinion of a few of his district attorney colleagues before he spoke to Monsignor Romano and ultimately John Caldwell.

When he ran the idea he was thinking about past the ADAs he had been working with for many years, they all told him he was crazy. The consensus of opinion was that Michael would never get a grand jury to go along, and if by some miracle they did, the indictment would never survive a defense attorney's motion to dismiss it for being insufficiently based in the law.

Michael heard what they had to say and respected their opinions, but he was not deterred. He was prepared to forge ahead and do what he felt was not only right, but legally sound. He was a 'gambler' after all, and the reward, if he was successful, was worth the risk. It was time for him to speak to the monsignor and John Caldwell.

Because he had Kathy Baer waiting to hear from him, he couldn't go to Red Hook to meet with Romano and Caldwell at their office. He called Romano from his cell then patched in Caldwell, who was expecting a progress report from Michael since Patron was taken into custody.

"Michael, we've been waiting to hear from you," Caldwell said when he got on the line.

"John, I'm sorry it's taken so long but we've had several complications since the fire marshals scooped up Patron. I didn't want to give you guys the story piecemeal, so I've been waiting for things to settle down."

"Have they settled?" Romano asked.

"Not exactly, Sal."

Michael told them how the fire marshals had only alerted him to Patron's arrest after they had gotten him back to their office, *AND* advised him of his Miranda Rights.

"He immediately clammed up and asked for a lawyer. That pissed me off because I wanted a shot at getting him to talk."

"This guy Alex Gazis, the supervising fire marshal, has been nothing but a pain in the ass from when I first met him. In fact, he's the reason why I need to speak to you guys."

Michael went on to tell Caldwell and Romano what Kathy Baer had told him about Gazis' intention to issue a desk appearance ticket to Patron, and why it was wrong to proceed that way.

"To be eligible for a DAT, the defendant can only be charged with a minor crime and must not be a risk to leave the jurisdiction. Once the DAT is issued, he's released from custody and told to appear in court on a date several weeks or months in the future."

"Gentlemen, this guy is not in the country legally, he has family in Haiti, friends in other Caribbean countries, and is therefore clearly a flight risk. And that's in addition to the fact that the fire he's responsible for starting, resulted in the death of a firefighter."

"What do you believe is behind this decision?" asked Caldwell.

"John, the real question is *WHO* is behind that decision. Gazis told Kathy Baer that the decision was his, but I believe it was foisted on him by someone in Borough Hall and is politically motivated."

"Gazis agreed to do it because he knows Pickett is going to run for mayor, and if he's elected Gazis becomes fire commissioner. To win, however, Pickett needs the support of the progressive caucus in the city council. Gazis giving an immigrant like Patron a DAT and releasing him from custody will certainly please the caucus and motivate them to endorse Pickett. That means he'll have their full support and their organizations will work to deliver the votes he needs to win."

Romano, who was listening carefully, spoke up.

"Michael, everything you've said makes sense. But who over at Borough Hall is pulling Gazis' strings?"

'Sal, I have a thought, but I can't give you a definite answer right now. I need more facts. But I promise you that I'll have an answer before this case is over."

"Right now, though, I, no we, have to prevent this DAT from happening. The Amato family deserves justice and every firefighter who runs into a burning building to save a life needs to know that it won't be in vain."

"Michael, what do you want to do?" asked Caldwell.

"John, I want to arrest and indict Patrick Patron for murder."

Michael spent the next hour telling Caldwell and Romano how he would accomplish it.

Because Patron had been fired from his position as caretaker for Archangel Church he no longer had the right nor the pastor's permission to be on church property. In fact, Monsignor Keenan had confiscated Patron's set of keys to all the church buildings believing the garage key was among them. He kept the garage key without permission and used it to enter the garage illegally to commit a crime, auto stripping. The auto stripping led to the ignition of gasoline fumes and the fire was the direct cause of the roof collapse which resulted in Louis Amato's death.

By their silence it was clear to Michael that they didn't understand what he was saying. He needed to simplify it for them.

"Guys I know that on the surface this seems like a trespass case with a tragic result. But it's more than that. Here's why."

"Under New York criminal law when someone, here it's Patron, enters or remains illegally in a premises, the church garage, with intent to commit a crime therein, auto stripping, that person is committing the felony crime of burglary."

"Also under that same New York law, when someone is engaged

in the commission of a felony, here a burglary, and another individual, who is not a participant in the crime, here Louis Amato, dies or is killed, the person committing a felony can be charged with Murder in the Second Degree. This type of murder is commonly called felony murder."

Michael went on to say that it did not matter how the non-participant died, all that was necessary to charge felony murder was the death of the non-participant during the course of or as a result of a felony.

"In sum, Patrick was in the midst of a burglary because he entered and remained unlawfully in the church garage with intent to commit a crime inside, auto stripping, when a fire started, due to his actions, which caused the roof to collapse, killing Louis Amato. Gentlemen, that's why I can arrest, indict, and convict Patrick Patron for murder."

"And when I do, we'll have beaten Satan once again."

CHAPTER

EIGHTEEN

After completing his conversation with Caldwell and Romano, Michael called Kathy Baer and told her that he intended to charge Patrick Patron with murder.

"Don't tell Gazis what I'm doing because you shouldn't have to take any of the heat. I'll explain everything. Just let him know that I'll be over to your office in 30 minutes to discuss things. If he presses you on why I'm coming there, be as vague as possible."

"Michael, he's not going to take this well," Kathy said.

"Kathy, forgive my language- I don't give a fuck how he reacts. What I'm doing is well within the law and I believe it's the right thing to do for so many reasons. I'll see you in a half-hour."

FDNY headquarters, where the fire marshals had their offices, was a five-minute walk from the DA's office. When Michael got there he saw several reporters and news film crews waiting outside the building. After passing through security, he took the elevator to the fire marshals' floor. As he got off he was greeted by Baer who told him that Gazis was waiting for him in his office.

"He's anxious to get the DAT issued so Patron can be released," she said.

"I'll bet he is. Those news crews I saw hanging around down-stairs have deadlines, Gazis doesn't want to miss his 15 minutes of fame when he releases Patron and tells the press 'it's the right thing to do given the evidence we have.'"

"Michael, do you think Gazis alerted them to be here?" Kathy asked.

"If he didn't do it personally one of the political hacks in Borough Hall certainly did. They want to milk this for all the votes they can get out of the Caribbean community."

"Well, they came for a show, and they're going to get one. Just not the one they were expecting."

Just as Michael was saying that Dina Mitchell and Tim Clark stepped off the elevator. Seeing them, Baer gave Michael a look that said, "Why are *they* here?"

Reading her perfectly, Michael said, "They're my insurance policy. If Gazis gives me a hard time and refuses to be a part of charging Patron with murder, Dina and Tim will take custody and bring him to criminal court for his arraignment."

"The necessary paperwork is all done, and I have it right here," Michael said, holding up a manila envelope containing the court papers he prepared before leaving his office. "I either hand this to Gazis or you, or to Dina and Tim. That will be Gazis' choice. Now let's see which way this is going to go."

The group walked to Gazis' office and while Dina and Tim waited outside Kathy and Michael went in to meet with him.

As expected Gazis did not take the news well. Perhaps he saw his shot at becoming fire commissioner in a Pickett administration going up in smoke. And if that was the case he needed to play nicely and go along with what Michael was doing so he wouldn't jeopardize his present position. Accordingly, he told Michael that he would have Kathy Baer and one of her partners escort Patron to criminal court for his arraignment.

Michael handed the court paperwork to Kathy. "I'll meet you

over at the courthouse. I called ahead and they're expecting us. The case will be put on the calendar as soon as you get there."

Kathy left the office and as Michael was getting up from his seat, Gazis stopped him. "Before you leave," he said, "You should know that this decision is going to piss off some people in high places. This DAT idea came from Alvin Downey the new Brooklyn County Clerk. He's got a load of juice with the Brooklyn Dems, and he was counting on this going according to his plan, so Pickett would have an easier road to the mayoralty. You still have to work in this borough, so If I were you, I'd watch my back. I hear that he's a mean SOB who holds a grudge if he doesn't get his way."

"Alex, thanks for the heads-up. If you speak to this guy Downey, tell him that Gioca is a mean SOB as well, and if he fucks with me he's going to lose. Now I have an arraignment to prepare for."

"Michael, just one more thing before you go. After I left Borough Hall, I began to think about the tragedy that this guy Patron is responsible for. And the more I thought about it the more I questioned the decision to simply issue him a DAT. I'm ashamed to say that despite my doubt, I agreed to do it for purely selfish reasons. I now see that what you're doing is the right thing. I hope you can forgive me."

"Alex, it takes a big man to admit when he's wrong. I admire you for that. And as far as I'm concerned, the past is the past. Let's concentrate on convicting this son of a bitch."

With that Michael left the office and with Dina and Tim driving, he headed to Brooklyn Criminal Court.

Apparently, word of Patron's arrest for murder spread quickly. When Michael arrived at the courthouse the same news crews and TV vans that were outside fire department headquarters were now assembled out front.

When Michael got out of his car he was surrounded by reporters and cameras. Refusing to comment on the murder charge, other than to tell the reporters that he would see them inside, he, Dina, and

Tim, went directly to the courtroom where Patrick's arraignment would be held.

True to his word, the judge's arraignment clerk placed the case on the calendar and after about 15 minutes Patrick Patron, represented for the proceeding by an attorney from the Legal Aid Society, was arraigned on the charges of felony murder, burglary, grand larceny, and auto stripping.

When the details of the felony murder charge were read into the court record by the clerk, murmurs were heard from the press. Obviously, they were expecting to hear that arson was the felony that raised this to a murder, not burglary. This would be the subject of much speculation and consternation over the weeks and months that followed. Not only in the press, but with the members of Brooklyn's legal community as well.

Three days after he was arraigned in criminal court, Patrick Patron was indicted by a Brooklyn grand jury for felony murder and related crimes.

The case was transferred to Brooklyn Supreme Court for arraignment on the indictment and trial. Supreme Court Judge Armando Rinaldi would preside.

The morning after the indictment, Michael got a call from two professors from Brooklyn Law School, informing him that they were now representing Patrick Patron. They asked for a meeting later that day to discuss the case. The meeting was set for 4 p.m. in Michael's office.

Having been an adjunct professor of law at the same school for many years, until he took a sabbatical when he began to work for Caldwell, Michael was familiar with Patron's new attorneys. They were not trial attorneys but were legal scholars who taught and did appellate work, so he had a good idea what they wanted to talk about.

Professors Sean Farrell and his wife Alice Farrell were right on time for their meeting with Michael. And just as he suspected they would, they questioned the legality of the felony murder charge, claiming that the burglary component of the charge was not supported by the law.

They argued that it was a specious attempt to fit the facts into the realm of the New York State murder statute and it would never survive a motion to dismiss, which they would bring, unless Michael on his own dismissed the count.

"Michael, you're too good of a lawyer to think that a judge will let this charge stand," Sean Farrell said. "This is clearly an overreach."

"We know you must have had a lot of pressure from the fire department and from the Amato family to hold our client responsible for the death but dressing up this dog of a case just to satisfy them and the public is unethical," argued Alice Farrell.

She continued, "If you do the right thing and dismiss the murder count, we'll get our guy to plead to the car theft charges and you can save yourself the embarrassment of having the case dismissed, once we make our motion before Judge Rinaldi."

"Sean and Alice, I *am* doing the right thing! Your client *is* responsible for the death of Louis Amato, and I believe that when Judge Rinaldi hears my answer to your motion he'll see things my way."

The arraignment for Patron on the indictment, and the hearing on his motion to dismiss it, was set for three weeks after the meeting.

During that time the Farrells launched a campaign in the press and in the Brooklyn legal community denouncing the indictment and Michael personally. They raised the old criticism of Michael being a reckless prosecutor and grandstanding for his own benefit.

None of it worked.

When all was said and done, the Farrells' motion was dismissed by Judge Rinaldi from the bench immediately after it was argued.

To say that the Farrells were surprised and shocked that their arguments were summarily rejected would be an understatement.

The two professors hung their heads as they left the courtroom with not so much as a goodbye to Michael.

Having dispatched the legal scholars, Michael figured that a real trial lawyer would be standing next to Patron when the case was again on the court calendar.

Early the next day, as Michael was finishing up a bagel and coffee at his desk, his office phone rang. When he answered he was surprised at the caller.

"Mr. Gioca, this is Borough President Tom Pickett. We have never met, but I'm calling to congratulate you on the indictment of Patrick Patron. I've read the papers this morning and want to say that I admire your tenacity and your adroitness in coming up with that theory for the felony murder charge. We're all happy that the person responsible for the death of Firefighter Amato will be held accountable. The citizens of Brooklyn are lucky to have you protecting them."

Michael, of course, had no idea that Pickett, although not as radical a thinker as County Clerk Downey, actually wanted Gazis to bring only minor car theft charges against Patron to ensure that he got his fair share of votes out of the Caribbean community in his run for mayor. So, he didn't have a sense as to how disingenuous this call actually was. He therefore thanked the borough president for his kind words.

"Mr. Borough President, thanks for the call. It means a great deal to me. After the smear campaign my legal adversaries subjected me to over these past few weeks it's gratifying to hear your kind words. But without giving up my source, I have to ask if the new Brooklyn County Clerk, Mr. Downey is angry at how this has turned out?"

After a few moments of silence Picket responded.

"Mr. Gioca, I'm not sure what you're saying, and I'm completely baffled. County Clerk Downey? Who is that? The Brooklyn County Clerk is a 75-year-old woman, Anna Simms, and she's been county clerk for the last 30 years. You need to check that so-called source," Pickett said chuckling.

"Good luck with the trial and I hope we have a chance to meet soon."

Michael again thanked Pickett for the call and the support and hung up.

It all now made sense. Although Gazis had said that the idea to issue a DAT had come from someone named Alvin Downey, who, after speaking to Pickett, Michael learned didn't exist, he was certain that Gazis had actually been seduced into that decision, by Satan!

CHAPTER

NINETEEN

Two weeks later the case appeared on Judge Rinaldi's calendar for a status conference and to dispose of any legal matters that would prevent or delay the setting of a trial date.

Patron's new attorney James Kellogg, a veteran Brooklyn trial lawyer, stood before the court and made an oral motion to reopen the matter of dismissing the felony murder count in the indictment.

Judge Rinaldi was having none of it.

"Mr. Kellogg, I appreciate that you're just getting involved with this case, but Mr. Patron's prior attorneys presented me with a legal tome on this issue and argued for over an hour urging me to dismiss that murder count. There is nothing more you can do or say that will change my decision. The issue is preserved for appeal. Should there be a conviction, you can raise it with the appellate court."

After a long session of legal maneuvering and trial planning, the judge set a trial date three months in the future. However, he gave both Michael and Kellogg the right to ask for a calendar date any time during those three months if his intervention was necessary to either clear up a legal matter or resolve a disagreement.

As it turned out the judge was prescient. There were issues with subpoenas the defense wanted to serve on potential witnesses, as well as a series of problems with fire department personnel who Michael needed for his case.

To resolve these, the three-month date for trial had to be pushed back another three months. This brought the trial date into the summer months and because of vacations and the shortage of jurors, the date was pushed back yet again to late September.

Michael put the delay to good use. He was able to thoroughly prepare the NYPD Auto Crimes detective, and the building construction expert he would be calling, both of whom had testified many times in the past. There was also time needed to prepare first time witnesses, Monsignor Keenan, Lt. Silecchia, and Carmelo. And much to his surprise he also needed to use the time to prep two additional novice expert witnesses, Alex Gazis and Kathy Baer.

"I can't believe you two have never testified in court," Michael said when he had them in his office for their first prep session.

"Mike we're so good that when we arrest someone they cave and plead guilty," Kathy said jokingly.

Gazis then added, "It may seem like she's joking, but Patron is the first to take one of our cases to trial since I've been in the office."

When all was said and done, Michael's preparation had gone well. In addition to getting his witnesses ready for battle, he became an expert on the engineering that went into the construction of a building with the type of roof that topped the church garage, as well as the effect of heat on the steel beams used in the building's construction to support the roof. Last but not least, he learned the science of how and why gasoline fumes ignite.

In addition, Michael got to know Louis Amato's family.

Before one scheduled afternoon court date, Louis' mom Maria invited Michael to their home for lunch. Expecting perhaps pizza or sandwiches, Michael was surprised when he went into the dining room and saw a veritable feast laid out.

Mrs. Amato prepared both a cold and hot antipasto. That was followed by a pasta course, rigatoni Bolognese, and the main course, veal piccata and vegetables. Homemade cannoli and espresso for dessert was the crowning touch on the fabulous meal.

"Mrs. Amato I've eaten so much I might fall asleep in the courtroom," Michael said as he finished the last sip of his coffee. "Thank you for a wonderful meal. But you shouldn't have gone through all this trouble. I would have been satisfied with a hero sandwich from *Defonte's*."

"It was our pleasure," Louis Sr. said as his wife cleared the table. "Since we first met, you have shown the utmost respect to our family and to the memory of our son. And we know how hard you're working to see to it that justice is done. This lunch was a small token of our appreciation."

Throughout the prep period, Louis Sr. became a constant source of support, encouragement, and strength for Michael. "If you need anything at all, do not hesitate to call and ask me," he would say whenever he saw or talked to Michael who would later come to experience first-hand that gratitude and generosity.

"Sal, we have a winner despite all the criticism and consternation over the felony murder charge," Michael told Romano the Friday night before jury selection was scheduled to begin on Monday. The two old friends were sharing a meal at their regular haunt *Emilio's*.

"Michael, as I've told you before, it's great to have your confidence, but with our adversary, there are many things that can happen to hurt or even destroy our case. You've overcome them in the past but there is always the possibility that you'll be put in a position by the *Evil One* that you'll have difficulty getting out of, if you get out of it at all. So far, *HE* has done things to distract you, *HIS* next try may be directly at or to you. I'm praying that doesn't happen. Please be careful."

"Sal, as always, thanks for the wake-up call. Never stop doing that. But I'm so hyped about this case that I don't even think *HE* can distract me." With that their antipasto was brought to the table.

Saturday morning Michael decided to go for a run. Exercise was his way of relaxing and clearing his mind. He often used that time to rehearse opening and closing statements and, on the eve of jury selection, to go over in his head questions he intended to ask prospective jurors. It was those questions Michael was thinking about as he ran the streets of Red Hook nestled along the shore of the East River.

When he approached the intersection of Columbia and Union Streets, just several blocks from his apartment, he was suddenly attacked by a swarm of red bees. He became disoriented as he tried to swat the insects away from his face and head and entered a traffic lane designated for bicycle use that ran the length of Columbia Street. With his vision obscured by the insects he didn't see the moped speeding in the bike lane that was bearing down on him. When the moped reached Michael it didn't stop. The rider clipped the back of his legs, and the handlebar caught him on his side near his waist, sending him hurtling into the middle of Columbia Street where he hit his head as he came down hard on the pavement. He landed awkwardly on his left side and passed out.

A witness who was walking her dog called 911 to report the incident. She said that in addition to speeding in the bike lane, the operator of the moped was not wearing a helmet. She said she didn't get a good look at his face because he was moving too fast, but she did notice something weird on the left side of his face.

When the paramedics arrived they first revived Michael and then examined him for broken bones and a concussion. Their initial assessment was that he had indeed suffered a concussion. He had several open wounds on his left leg and hip which were bandaged, and the pain he felt on his left side when he was eventually loaded into the ambulance indicated that he likely had broken his ribs. Before putting him into their ambulance, they also treated him for the numerous bee stings over his face and neck.

On the way to the hospital Michael was in and out of consciousness mumbling words that the paramedic with him had difficulty understanding. Trying to get as much information about the event for the emergency room doctors, the paramedic asked him what happened. Later when questioned by the police the paramedic told them that Michael's answer to his question was "Something about the Devil getting him."

Hours later when he woke up in the emergency room his sons, Michael Jr. and Kevin, along with his dad, were sitting around his bed. When they saw him open his eyes Michael heard a sigh of relief from each of them.

"Thank God," his father said. "Michael, we thought we were going to lose you. The docs didn't know if you had suffered permanent brain injury. From what they told us you smacked your head pretty good. But now they're saying it was a concussion and you'll be good as new after you rest for a while."

A confused Michael asked, "Dad, guys, what are you doing here? Where am I?"

"Dad, don't you remember what happened to you?" Michael Jr. asked.

"You're in the hospital," Kevin chimed in. "You got hit with a moped after getting attacked by a swarm of bees over in Red Hook."

At that point it all started coming back to Michael. "That was this morning, what time is it now?"

"Michael, it's four in the afternoon. You've been out all that time. You must be starving?" said his father. "I'm gonna let the doc and the nurse know you're awake. And I'll make sure they get you something to eat."

When his father left the room Michael asked Michael Jr. to get him some water. When he handed the cup to his dad, Michael felt a gooey substance all over his face when he raised the cup to his lips. "What is this stuff?" he asked.

"Dad, that's the meds they put on your face for all the bee stings you got. Your face is not a pretty sight right now" his son said. "They told us that with those meds the stings should heal in a few days."

As Michael tried to straighten up in bed so he could see both his sons, he winced and let out a yelp. "Dad, let me help," said Kevin. "You have three broken ribs on your left side and your left leg is pretty messed up. You also sprained a ligament behind your knee, and your thigh and calf are all cut up from when you landed on the street. You scraped it badly."

Just then his father returned with a doctor and nurse in tow. "Mr. Gioca, how are you feeling?" asked the doctor.

"I'm pretty groggy, I have a terrible headache, and my left side hurts like hell. Other than that, I'm just great."

"All to be expected. We're going to keep you for a few days to do some tests. We want to make sure you don't have any brain injury that we might have missed when you were examined after the paramedics brought you in this morning."

The doctor then performed a few simple tests to check out Michael's eyesight, and his cognition, all of which he passed.

"Mr. Gioca, my best guess is that you don't have anything seriously wrong with your brain, but one or two days of observation will make it a certainty. Now rest and we'll get you something to eat. By the way, you're a very lucky man. Your injuries from this accident could have been much worse, if not fatal."

After the doctor left, the nurse asked that Michael's father and his sons let him rest. "You guys can come back tomorrow to visit," she said.

His sons kissed Michael goodbye saying that they'd see him tomorrow.

Before his father left Michael motioned for him to come close to the bed. In a whisper, Michael asked for his cell phone. His dad opened the drawer of a side table and handed him the phone.

"Here it is. But I don't think they want you talking on *that* thing."

"Dad, I promise I won't abuse it. I need to make a couple of calls. After that I'll rest. Be careful going home. I'll see you tomorrow." His dad kissed him and left.

Michael's first call was to Monsignor Romano.

CHAPTER
TWENTY

"Michael, thank God you're awake. You gave John and me a real fright. How are you feeling?" the monsignor asked.

"Sal, how do you know what happened? I certainly would never have told anyone to call you."

"The cops who responded to the scene recovered the ID you were carrying in your running shorts and called the DA's office to notify them that you were hurt. When DA Price was told, he let Caldwell know right away. We've stayed away from the hospital for obvious reasons."

Michael went on to tell Romano what he remembered about the incident, adding that he was certain that the Devil was responsible.

"Why are you so sure?" Romano asked.

"Those red bees came out of nowhere and attacked me just as I was about to cross Columbia Street. That's why I was in the bike lane when the moped hit me. I didn't get a look at the operator, but I'll bet everything I have that it was *HIM*.

"Mike, didn't you tell me when we first went to meet Caldwell, that his building was close to another owned by the operator of a maraschino cherry factory which housed a large, secret, marijuana farm in the basement. And didn't I read that red bees helped you crack the case?"

"Sal those bees were harmless honeybees kept by a beekeeper on Governor's Island across the East River from the cherry factory. They were red because back then they were flying across the river and drinking red dye runoff that was being dumped illegally by the cherry business, onto the streets around the factory. We closed that factory down years ago."

"This bee attack was no accident. *HE* was sending a message that I was the intended target. And just to make sure I got that message, *HE* used red bees, because of my connection to them in that old case in Red Hook."

"We're on the eve of jury selection in the Patrick Patron case. *HE* thinks that if *HE* takes me out maybe the case goes away. At the very least there has to be a delay in the start of the trial and anything can happen between now and then."

"Everything you say makes sense, Mike. But to be certain let's wait to hear what the police have to say about the moped operator. Caldwell has been on the phone with his contacts, so we'll have more information shortly. In the meantime, rest and listen to your doctors."

After his call with Romano, a hospital orderly went to Michael's cubicle to move his bed. Although he was thankful that he was getting out of the chaos that was the emergency room, he was curious about where he was being moved to, so he asked the orderly. "I'm moving you to the gold coast," was his reply.

Michael was taken to the top floor of the hospital, to a private room that overlooked the East River.

"Mister, you're now on the gold coast. These are the best rooms in this hospital. You must have friends in high places because we only put celebs and politicians here," said the orderly as he settled the bed into position, so Michael had a view of the river.

For a hospital room it was special. In addition to the view, the room had a couch and several easy chairs for visitors. The bathroom had the usual stand-up shower, but it also had a bathtub that looked like a jacuzzi with water jets along the sides for Massage. The sink was enormous and the medicine cabinet above it was stocked with necessities such as a toothbrush, toothpaste, and roll-on deodorant.

When the orderly left, Michael used the call button to summon a nurse. In seconds one was at his bedside. Michael saw that her name plate said "Kelly."

"Is everything okay, Mr. Gioca? Does something hurt or are you feeling ill?"

"Thanks for asking Kelly. But I didn't call you for that. I'd like to find out how I managed to get this room. It's like a suite in a fine hotel. I'm no big shot so what gives?" Just as he said that he heard someone at the door to the room say "It was me. I did this for you."

Michael looked over to see Louis Amato Sr. standing in the doorway.

"Michael, first, how are you feeling?"

"Mr. Amato, I'm still groggy and my ribs hurt like hell. But, why?"

"Michael, my position with the Longshoremen's Union has its privileges. I'm the health and welfare officer so I have connections in lots of hospitals especially here in south Brooklyn. I had you moved so you'd be comfortable and taken care of by the best doctors they have here."

"Thank you. But how did you even know I was in here?"

"From my days as a Deputy Commissioner I made lots of friends in the NYPD especially at the 76th precinct here in Red Hook. A police friend called me after hearing about the incident. He knew you were on Louie Jr.'s case and thought I should know what happened. He told me you were brought here. The rest, as they say, is history!"

"Mr. Amato...." Michael was interrupted.

"You were obviously raised very well by your parents, but please call me Lou."

"Okay, Lou, this was so kind and generous and I'm very grateful, but it was unnecessary. I'm not staying very long. My plan is to be out in a day or so and then get back to work. I don't want the start of the trial to be delayed for very long." Michael knew that with any delay the danger of witnesses disappearing, or having a sudden case of amnesia, became more realistic everyday with the *Evil One* as his adversary.

As he said that Michael realized that he would have to notify Judge Rinaldi of his injuries and ask for a delay in jury selection. He made a mental note to reach out to Dina Mitchell and Tim Clark. He would have Dina call the judge, Kathy Baer, Alex Gazis, and the expert witness. He wanted Tim to make sure that Carmelo was safe out on Long Island and that he, Patricia Thomas, and Monsignor Keenan were told about the delay in the start of the trial.

"Michael," said Amato, "However long you have to be here I want you to have the best of everything. You are very important to me and my family and whatever I can do to help you, I will. Now get some rest and I'll stop by when I can. Oh! By the way, Maria, my wife, is praying for you. And she said to tell you that when you get out of here she knows you'll need a good meal. So, the first Sunday you're free, you're invited for dinner."

For the next three days Michael was poked and prodded by neurologists, orthopedists, and internal medicine doctors. He was put through a battery of tests, began to walk after one day and was allowed to use the spectacular bathroom on his own the second day he was there. On the fourth day Michael was finally pronounced fit to be released, with the caveat that he would not return to work for two weeks.

While at home he was attended to by his sons, his father, and his sister Pam. They kept him company, helped him do his prescribed exercises and, in the case of his sister, made him enough meals to last him for the time he was in home confinement and beyond. All he had to do was microwave the dishes she prepared, which was easy because the kitchen in his small apartment was just steps away from the couch where he spent most of his time.

Near the end of the two weeks Michael felt well enough to have both Dina and Tim over to his apartment. He wanted to make sure that all he had tasked them with was done.

"Don't worry Michael, it's all done," said Dina.

The judge set a new date for jury selection for the day after Michael returned to work. All the witnesses were notified and ready when needed.

Michael was especially concerned about Carmelo. He worried that being alone out on eastern Long Island, away from his friends and old haunts, would take its toll. He was especially concerned that Carmelo would venture back to Brooklyn to make up for lost time.

Tim assured Michael that Carmelo was not going anywhere. He said that he had made some friends out there and wanted nothing to do with his old neighborhood because he feared the Russians he was working for.

"Mike, he told me that where he was now living and who he was hanging with was the perfect spot for him. He was certain that none of his Russian 'friends' even knew where Long Island was, let alone would be able to find him out on the east end. He said they never left Brooklyn because it's all they knew."

Satisfied that all was well with the case, Michael was anxious to get back into the courtroom. He had one last visit with his doctor scheduled for the last day of the second week of home confinement and he was certain he'd be given the okay to get back into battle.

He was right. His doctor pronounced him fit, with no lingering effects of his head injury. The pain in his ribs had lessened quite a bit and, despite his leg injuries which would take some time to totally heal, he was given permission to return to the courtroom.

Bright and early on Monday morning, Michael was finally back to work and was ready for jury selection to begin the next day. He received permission from Judge Rinaldi to have Dina Mitchell sit with him at the counsel table for the duration of the trial. He explained to the judge in a phone call that he still had some trouble walking and moving around and he needed someone who could help him navigate the courtroom when it was necessary. Judge Rinaldi was happy to accommodate him.

The next day, before he and Dina left for court, Michael received a phone call from the detective who manned the DA's office security desk.

"Mike, some guy just dropped off a few things he said you might need. Can you have someone come out to get them?" the detective asked.

Michael asked Dina to go and when she returned he was surprised by what she was holding. "Crutches and a cane? Where did they come from?" he asked.

There was a note attached to the cane which Dina handed to him.

"Does it say who sent them?" she asked.

"Yes. They're from Mr. Amato. The note reads, 'I hope these help. Good luck today. We're praying for you.'"

"Michael, what a thoughtful gesture. He and his family are the best," said Dina.

"Yup!" Michael said. Then he thought to himself, *'Nothing like adding more pressure. As if I didn't have enough with this case.'* Then he left his office for the courthouse, making good use of the cane.

CHAPTER

TWENTY-ONE

Judge Rinaldi had a reputation for efficiency in conducting trials. After telling Michael and James Kellogg how he would run things and what he expected of the two lawyers, he asked his clerk to bring in the prospective jurors who had assembled in the corridor outside the courtroom.

The judge's reputation was well earned. By the end of the day 12 jurors had been seated. Rinaldi told the lawyers that he expected to select four alternate jurors the next morning, followed by opening statements.

And that's exactly what happened.

Michael began calling witnesses on the trial's third day and by the end of the week he had presented most of his case.

His first witness was Monsignor Keenan who set the stage for the jury by telling them how he came to hire Patron as the church's caretaker. He said that Patron had keys to every church building, including the garage which was attached to the church rectory where he and his priests lived.

He told the jury that after working for a few months Patron asked his permission to use the garage to repair cars so he could make extra money. The monsignor said he was happy to accommodate him. However, several months later, when it was suspected that Patron was stealing church funds from the weekly collection and from the donation boxes situated around the church, an accusation to which Patron confessed, the monsignor told the jury that he dismissed him from his caretaker position. As a result, Patron no longer had permission or the right to enter or remain on church property.

He added that when he fired Patron, he asked him to give back the keys to all the church buildings. Patron did so immediately. After the fire, however, when the monsignor was asked by the investigating fire marshals if the key to the garage was among those Patron returned, he checked and embarrassingly had to tell them that the garage key was missing and had not been returned.

And lest any juror wonder why neither the monsignor, nor his priests, saw Patron in the garage on the day of the fire, he testified that he and the priests were busy all day preparing for the Christmas Eve liturgy and the entrance to the garage, which had no windows, faced away from the rectory. That prevented anyone in the rectory from seeing what was going on in there.

Lt. Silecchia was next. To save the Amato family the trauma of seeing the remains of their son, and to save them from testifying, he went to the morgue and identified the body of firefighter Amato to the medical examiner.

He told the jury about responding to the fire with his squad and seeing Patrick Patron and another person standing outside the garage.

After Patron told the lieutenant he and the other person were inside working and had gotten out when the fire started, the lieutenant asked if anyone else was trapped inside. He testified that Patrick told him there was. It was at that point that his men, including Louis Amato, went in.

He described the collapse which trapped firefighter Amato between two sections of the roof. He concluded his testimony by telling the jury that after his men were able to free Amato, they discovered that Patron lied because the garage was unoccupied. When he went to confront Patron, he told the jury that he was nowhere in sight.

Fire Marshal Alex Gazis testified as an expert witness as to how the fire started. Gazis explained how the use of a power saw on the engine of a burnt-out hulk of a car had ignited gasoline fumes which he was able to smell when he and his team examined the scene after the fire had been extinguished. The fumes came from a pool of gasoline that was under the burnt-out car.

Gazis explained that a power saw was found in the debris next to the burnt-out hulk, and cut marks were visible on the engine block. That saw was ultimately taken to the police property clerk's office for safe keeping, where it still remained.

Michael then called a metallurgist who was summoned to the fire scene by the fire marshals. He was asked to compare the cuts on the engine to the blade of the saw. His conclusion was that the cuts were consistent with having been made by that saw blade.

Following the fire marshal and the metal expert, a detective from the NYPD Auto Squad took the witness stand and told the jury that he was asked by the fire marshals to examine the contents of the garage. He testified that scattered about were car parts that a later investigation revealed came from stolen cars that his squad was investigating. He said that in addition to those parts, the presence of certain tools and machinery, especially the power saw, heavy duty wrenches, sledgehammers, and a portable car lift, led him to conclude that Patrick Patron was running an illegal automobile chop shop.

Marc Foxx followed the auto crimes detective to the stand, and based on his firsthand knowledge of Patron's operation corroborated the detective's conclusion about a chop shop.

Michael ended the trial's first week with the testimony of a building construction engineer who explained in detail why and how the garage roof collapsed inward. He was followed by the medical examiner who testified that Louis Amato died from asphyxia when he was trapped between the two sections of the collapsed roof which restricted his ability to breathe.

His plan for Monday morning was to call Kathy Baer to testify to the actual recovery of the saw. She would be asked to identify it before Michael moved it into evidence. He decided against calling Patricia Thomas as a witness; therefore, Carmelo Giovalin would be the last one. He would testify to Patron's confession.

When Michael and Dina got back to his office, he asked for Tim Clark to join them.

"Guys I'm ready to wrap up the people's case with Carmelo's testimony. I want you to pick him up tomorrow and bring him here so I can do a final prep. It'll take all day, but I'll sign off on the overtime."

"Do you want us to find him a hotel room around here, so he's close by for Monday morning?" Dina asked.

"Great idea. This way we save you guys a lot of driving. But if he's going to be here in Brooklyn, I want you and Tim to stay with him Saturday and Sunday. He's the most important witness I have, and I don't want to take the chance of anything happening to him."

"Mike, don't worry he'll be here tomorrow for prep and in Judge Rinaldi's courtroom Monday morning," Tim said.

But he was wrong.

"He's dead," a badly shaken Dina Mitchell told Michael while standing outside the motel where Carmelo had been staying. She became emotional and was shaking so badly she had difficulty holding her cell phone as she described the horror she and Tim had found when they walked into Carmelo's room.

"Michael I can't help feeling that this is on me," she said.

Dina was a terrific detective. She was smart, hard-nosed when she had to be, and caring and compassionate when she dealt with witnesses and informants. With Carmelo, she had gotten him to believe in her when she told him that he would be able to start a new life if he did what she asked him to do. So, breaking down emotionally, and feeling that she had gotten him killed, was understandable.

"Dina, if anyone is responsible it's me," Michael said. "I should have had him guarded 24/7. Now tell me what happened."

"When Tim and I left your office last night I called Carmelo to tell him to pack his things because we'd be out to pick him up in the morning to bring him back to Brooklyn so he could have one final preparation session before he would testify on Monday morning."

"Carmelo told me he'd be ready by seven and that he was looking forward to getting the testimony behind him so he could begin his new life."

As Tim and Dina left Brooklyn and headed out to eastern Long Island, Dina called Carmelo to let him know that they were on their way. Carmelo was in a good mood. He told her that he was about to take a shower, then pack, so he'd be ready when they arrived.

"While I was talking to him, I heard him giggling, but I didn't think anything of it because I knew he was happy to be so close to moving on."

"But then I heard what sounded like someone whispering in the background, so I asked him if he was alone. Carmelo assured me that he was. I didn't press it. I now wish that I had."

"Dina, first of all how could you have 'pressed it,' you were ninety miles away," Michael said in an attempt to calm her down.

"Michael, I could have called the local cops to check on him. But I accepted what he said because he was always honest with me once he decided to cooperate."

"Instead, I called Carmelo several more times while on the way out to the motel, and each time he answered. He assured me that he had packed his things and was just watching TV waiting for us to arrive. During my last call, which was about an hour before we got there, he told me to hurry up. 'I'm starving. I haven't had breakfast,' he said."

Satisfied that all was well Dina relaxed as Tim sped along the Long Island Expressway heading to Carmelo's motel.

When the two detective investigators arrived, they went directly to Carmelo's room. They knocked on the door, but he didn't answer. They knocked a few more times and when there was no response, they went to the desk clerk, identified themselves, and asked him to open Carmelo's door.

What they saw caused Tim to gag, and he had to summon all his self-control to repress the urge to vomit.

Dina was so stunned she stood in place and did not move.

Carmelo was seated on the small couch which faced the door, headless!

He was holding his head under his right arm, with his tongue pinned to the chest of his shirt.

"Michael this has to be the Russians," Dina said. "How did they find him?"

"Dina, why do you assume it was the Russians who killed him?" Michael asked.

"Because he had his tongue cut out and pinned to his shirt. We all know that's a message from organized crime that Carmelo was killed because he was an informant."

Michael knew that Dina was right in the usual circumstance about OC sending that message. But this case was far from usual. His suspicion was that his adversary was responsible for Carmelo's horrific death. And *HE* was sending a message to Michael.

"Dina you're not wrong. However, we need to wait for the police to conclude their investigation, so we know for sure. I assume the Suffolk cops are on the scene, right?"

"Tim called it in to them as soon as we found the body."

"Okay, hang there until you get some answers. I'll be here trying to figure out how I'm going to finish off this case. Losing Carmelo really hurts in so many ways. Call me when you know something."

Michael had been jolted by the news of Carmelo's murder. He had lost his most important witness, who, because of Patron's confession to him, was the only person who could put an electric saw in Patron's hands. That made him angry, but he was also saddened by Carmelo's death. Michael had grown to like him, admired him even, for recognizing that cooperation was his ticket out of Brooklyn and the beginning of a new life.

Michael knew that it took a lot for a guy like Carmelo to cast aside the only life he had known and become a cooperating witness. That bravery cost him his life and he couldn't shake the feeling of guilt for convincing Carmelo to do just that. One of the most difficult parts of being a prosecutor was turning bad guys into cooperating good guys. It was a necessary evil, however. And no matter how many times Michael had done it, when in the rare instance he'd lost one, it really hurt.

He knew he couldn't wallow in self-pity. He had to shake himself out of it and get the work. He had until Monday to come up with an idea that would make things right, and thus impossible for the jury to do anything other than convict Patrick Patron of murder.

The phone call he received from Dina Mitchell late that afternoon convinced him that he would need help if he was going to clear his head and accomplish that.

"Michael, the Suffolk detectives have come up with a suspect in Carmelo's murder. But don't get your hopes up that they'll find her," Dina said.

"When they canvassed the motel for witnesses, they came upon one of the housekeeping staff who was about to enter the room across the hall from Carmelo's this morning. As she was gathering cleaning supplies from her cart, she saw a woman who was dressed like a hooker come out of his room. Having worked in motels for some time, she had thought nothing of it. The desk clerk, who was working the night before, confirmed that Carmelo went out around midnight and when he returned he was with a woman. The clerk said they went straight to Carmelo's room which didn't surprise him because she was dressed 'Like a working girl.'"

"When the cops asked for a description, they got nothing but general height and weight, Caucasian, with bleached blonde hair. But something the housekeeper remembered may help the cops.

When the woman turned to walk away from Carmelo's room she seemed to be hiding her face, but the housekeeper did notice what she said was an ugly bruise on her left cheek. Not much to go on, however the detectives are going to put the description into the local and state databases of sex workers with a record, maybe they'll get lucky."

Michael knew that no name would pop up. He knew exactly who the mystery woman was, and the police would never find her, unless their database covered hell!

"Okay Dina. If they come up with something they'll let us know. Now you and Tim need to head home. It was a tough day. Get some rest and I'll see you guys Monday morning. I've got a lot of work and a lot of thinking to do."

"Michael, both Tim and I had cleared the weekend to guard Carmelo, so if you need us for anything we're around."

"Thanks Dina. Please drive safely."

When Michael looked at his watch it was 5:15 p.m. He knew that St. Charles Borromeo Church near his office had a 5:30 Mass on Saturday evening. He headed over there in the hope of finding the help he was looking for.

At the Mass, Michael found it.

He was moved by the priest's homily. It was an inspiring talk about not giving up when things in life become difficult or seemingly impossible to overcome. He talked about the power of prayer and urged those in the congregation who were feeling despair or who might feel desperation in the future, to turn to St. Jude for help.

"He is the patron saint of the impossible because Jesus identified him as a saint ready and willing to assist us in our trials," the priest said.

Those words were like manna from heaven. It was as if the priest had prepared his talk mindful of the trouble Michael found himself in and was speaking to him directly.

At the conclusion of his sermon, the priest asked those in the church to say the prayer to Saint Jude with him. Michael did so, passionately. And the words of the prayer that he found particularly pertinent to his plight, "I...humbly beg thee to come to my assistance; help me now in my urgent need...I will never forget thee," he recited with extra enthusiasm.

As he walked back to the DA's garage to get his car with the priest's words still fresh in his mind, an idea came to him that he knew in his heart would be the solution to his problem. He smiled while looking upward and said, "Thank you."

CHAPTER

TWENTY-TWO

"Kathy, I'm sorry to bother you on a Saturday night, but we need to talk," Michael said.

When he arrived home after Mass, he made several calls before he telephoned Kathy Baer who would play a central role in his plan to overcome the death of Carmelo and convict Patrick Patron of murder.

"Mike, you're not bothering me," Kathy answered. "I heard about your witness and I'm sorry. What are you going to do?"

"That's the reason I'm calling. "

Michael then laid out his idea and plan to salvage the case.

He reminded Kathy that Carmelo had been the only witness to put a power saw in Patron's hands. "My plan was to have Carmelo testify to his confession, which would have tied together all the work you, Gazis, and your team did at the garage with your investigative conclusions."

"Now that Carmelo is gone I need another way to put that saw in Patron's hands, which is where you come in."

"I want you to take the power saw that you found next to the burnt-out car with the cut marks on the engine to the police lab. I need you to examine it for what I hope will nail Patron. I've already cleared this with the commanding officer of the lab. Although it's a Saturday night, he'll see to it that the entire facility, and its personnel, are at your disposal."

Dina was puzzled. "That's all great but what am I looking for?"

"Has the saw been dusted for fingerprints or examined for traces of DNA?" Michael asked.

"Mike, we never did either because we had the confession of Carmelo which was rock solid," Kathy answered.

"Well, the rocks have crumbled. So, I want you to go over that saw with the proverbial fine-tooth comb looking for prints or anything from which we can extract DNA. I know, and you know, that Patron was using that saw so there must be something on it that puts it in his hands. If you find it we'll need to have it analyzed very quickly."

"Mike, I have no problem doing any of that. But you need to...."

"Kathy I'm way ahead of you. I've already spoken to Gazis. He told me to tell you 'God speed.'"

"This will take some time. I won't have any answers by Monday," Kathy warned.

"I know. I'll handle the judge. With Carmelo's death I believe Rinaldi will be generous with giving me a continuance in the trial. Just get started as soon as you can."

"Mike, I'll need you to make one more call. The NYPD property clerk's office, where we secured the saw, needs to be told that I'm coming in to retrieve it. Collecting evidence from them on a weekend is unusual, so that office should be alerted."

"By the time you get to the property clerk they'll be waiting with the saw to hand it over to you. If there's a problem I'll call you in your car."

"I'll be out of here in a half-hour."

"Great... And Kathy, good luck."

Just as Michael said, the property clerk's office had the saw ready for Kathy when she arrived and much to her surprise, the commanding officer of the police lab, Captain Peter Escobar, met her at the elevator and escorted her to the section of the lab that she needed for her examination.

"Fire Marshal Baer, my lab and my people are at your disposal," Escobar told her. "If you need anything I'll be here until you conclude your work."

Her first task was to examine the saw for fingerprints. She asked for one of the lab's fingerprint experts to assist her and oversee her work. She wanted to make sure that she followed all the proper protocols so as not to jeopardize any positive results from being admitted into evidence.

With the expert's guidance she dusted the saw with the fingerprint powder and then took a portable lamp which she passed over the length and width of the tool. She could barely contain her excitement when she saw three fingerprints appear in the powder under the light. She used the fingerprint lifting tape to retrieve the prints and handed them to her assistant. He would now examine them more closely and run the prints through all the databases at his disposal.

While she waited for the results of the prints she went back over the saw, using a more powerful lamp, to look for anything that might have been left on it that would carry DNA.

She felt disappointed until she examined one last part of the saw. There, behind the trigger mechanism she spotted a small piece of what she hoped was skin. She carefully took a pair of tweezers and removed the sample which she placed onto a glass microscope slide. She covered that slide with an identical one, sandwiching the sample between the two. The sample was now ready to be examined so it could be identified. If it was skin, the next step would be to hopefully extract DNA.

Kathy went to see Capt. Escobar. "Cap, I think I may have found something," she said, holding up the glass slide. "I think this is skin.

I'll need it tested to confirm it and if I'm right, I'll need it analyzed for DNA."

"Fire Marshal Baer, because I was counting on you I alerted the medical examiner's office that I might need their DNA analysts to work on something in the event you got lucky. I'll call them now to tell them that you'll be taking the slide over. We probably won't have an answer until after the weekend , but from talking to Mike Gioca that doesn't seem to be a problem."

Kathy was getting ready to leave for the ME's office when the lab fingerprint analyst entered Escobar's office. "I have good news," he said. "First, the prints were usable. And when I ran them through our database they came back as belonging to Patrick Patron."

Kathy was ecstatic. Although it was now well after midnight, she immediately called Michael. She filled him in on the fingerprint recovery and identification and told him that she was bringing the item she had recovered from the trigger of the saw to the ME's office so it could be identified and analyzed for DNA.

"The captain here believes it will be a few days before we have any DNA results."

Michael could barely contain his excitement. He congratulated her and thanked Capt. Escobar for his cooperation. Although the DNA analysis was not completed, Michael knew that it was time to prepare for step two of his plan.

"Kathy, I'm going to call Gazis in the morning and fill him in on your great work, and the results so far. I'm going to ask him to come to my office in the afternoon. I know you've been working practically all night, but I'll need you to be there as well."

"Mike, whatever you need. Just give me a time and I'll be there. I'll sleep when all this is over."

Michael set the meeting in his office for noon. He telephoned Gazis at 9 a.m. and filled him in. Without hesitation the fire marshal said he'd see Michael then.

When Gazis and a weary Kathy Baer walked into Michael's office, they were pleasantly surprised by the smoked salmon, cream cheese, bagels and coffee waiting for them.

"This was the least I could do after ruining your Sunday," Michael said when the two fire marshals thanked him for the brunch.

After they had eaten, Michael said "If we get lucky with the DNA results, what I'm asking you to do here will be the clincher."

Over the next hour Michael laid out step two of his plan.

Later that afternoon Michael called Monsignor Romano.

"Sal, I know it's been a while since we talked, so how about we meet for dinner at *Emilio's*. I have a lot to tell you and I'm craving his veal parmigiana."

"What a coincidence," the monsignor said. "I just got off the phone with Caldwell. He asked me if I heard from you. Of course, I covered and told him that we had had a brief talk last week. You owe me," Romano replied jokingly.

"You're right. Dinner's on me. See you at seven. Okay?"

"Wow! What a generous peace offering," the monsignor sarcastically replied. "You know Emilio never charges me!"

"Oh! That's right," Michael, now laughing, said. "Don't worry, I'll leave the tip. See you later."

Right on time Michael walked into *Emilio's*. The place was packed but as always Monsignor Romano was sitting at the best table in the house nursing a glass of *Brunello di Montalcino*.

"I figured since you're paying why not get the best Emilio has to offer," Romano joked as Michael eyed the bottle of wine as he sat down. "It's a 2015, a very good year for *Brunello. Salute.*"

Before Michael could respond, Emilio was at the table. "*Michele*, you must be complimented on your good taste," Emilio said with a big smile knowing that it was Romano who had chosen the wine. He poured a glass for Michael saying "Enjoy gentlemen. Let me know when you're ready to order."

During dinner Michael filled in the monsignor on where he was with the trial. He told him everything he knew about the murder of Carmelo, emphasizing the witness' sighting of the woman with the mole coming out of Carmelo's room shortly before Dina and Tim found the body.

"Sal, I'm not too proud to admit that I thought *HE* had finally bested me. Without Carmelo I had no one to put the power saw in Patrick's hands. My first thought was that without that evidence the judge might not let this case get to the jury. Kellogg would move to dismiss it for lack of sufficiency and Rinaldi was likely to grant his motion. I was out of ideas. I needed help. I knew St. Charles had a 5:30 Mass so I went there hoping to find that help."

Michael told Romano how moved and inspired he was by the priest's homily and the prayer to St. Jude.

"Sal, it turned out to be a lucky coincidence that I chose that Mass. Walking back to my car, reflecting on the message of the homily, an idea came to me that I truly believe will save the day." Michael told the monsignor about his idea and plan.

Romano listened intently then smiled as took a sip of his wine. "Michael," he said, "There was no luck involved. It was no coincidence that you chose that Mass. Yesterday was the feast day of St. Jude. You being there and hearing his message was meant to be."

TWENTY-THREE

On Monday morning an hour before the trial was scheduled to resume, Michael called Judge Rinaldi's chambers. He answered and Michael filled him in on Carmelo's murder.

"Your honor, he was to be my final witness. His death has caused me to make some adjustments in my case and I'll require some additional time to line up the evidence I'll need."

Anticipating the judge asking, Michael told him that he reached out to James Kellogg to alert him to these developments and gave him a heads-up on the request for a continuance in the trial that he would formally make when court convened.

The judge was non-committal as to how he would rule on the request. He just said, "Mr. Gioca, I'll see you in my courtroom in an hour."

At 9:30 sharp, the judge gaveled the court to order. "Mr. Gioca based on a conversation we had an hour ago, I understand that you have a motion to make. Is that correct?"

"Yes it is, your honor."

Michael then laid out the circumstances of Carmelo Giovalin's murder and asked the court for a week's continuance to compile the evidence he needed to overcome the loss of his most important, and what was to be his last witness. He finished his remarks by assuring the court that if he was not ready to proceed after a week he would rest his case.

It was James Kellogg's turn. Not surprisingly he objected strenuously to any delay in the trial. He expressed sympathy for the unfortunate turn of events, but he told the judge that his client had the right to be tried fairly and expeditiously. He argued that this delay would be a violation of those rights and would irreparably harm him.

The judge, who listened carefully to both attorneys, told them that he wanted to give the prosecutor's request some thought before rendering a decision. "Counsel, I'm going to dismiss the jury for the morning. Let's adjourn until after lunch by which time I'll have a decision."

When they resumed at 2 p.m. Judge Rinaldi announced that after careful consideration he was granting the prosecution's request. He brought the jury into the courtroom and simply told them that due to unforeseen circumstances he was delaying the trial for one week. "But don't worry folks," he said, "I've cleared it with my bosses, and you'll be paid for those days. I'll see you back here next Monday at 9:30 a.m. sharp."

Before the jury left the courtroom Kellogg asked the judge for a conference at the bench. He wanted the judge's assurance that, depending on the evidence Michael presented after the delay, he would be given time, if necessary, to prepare a rebuttal. The judge demurred, saying, "If it comes to that we'll deal with it at that time. I'm sending this jury home now."

When Michael got back to his office his first call was to Kathy Baer to fill her in on the judge's ruling.

"Kathy, as soon as you hear from the ME's office on the DNA results please call me immediately. In the meantime, you now have time to do what we talked about. When you have that lined up I want to know."

Three days later Kathy Baer called Michael to tell him that the ME's office had identified the item she brought to them as human skin and their DNA analysis had identified the skin as belonging to Patrick Patron.

"Kathy, what do they have to compare the DNA they recovered from the skin?" Michael asked.

"Apparently when he entered the country from Haiti he had applied for asylum. As such the feds took a sample of his DNA and filed it in their database. The ME's office searched that and several other DNA databases and came up with the match."

"Terrific," Michael said. "Have you and Gazis made any headway in finding what we need to finish this?"

"Michael, we believe we may have finally located one. And if we're lucky and it's there, Alex will be doing what you want tonight. I'll send you the details of where we'll be."

"Kathy, that all sounds promising. But what did you mean when you said you may have 'finally' located one?"

"Mike, let's just say that we've been running into some obstacles, and our search hasn't gone as smoothly as we would have liked. I'll explain in more detail another time."

Sensing Michael's anxiety, Kathy said, "But don't worry. I have a good feeling about this one. It would be great if Tim and Dina were able to join us. We could use the help."

Michael knew that Tim and Dina would have no problem joining Kathy and Gazis. He was also confident that if they were successful the case against Patron would be much easier to win. His concern was that he was certain the Devil knew that as well.

"Kathy, Tim, and Dina will be there. But I can't stress enough that you all need to be careful out there. Get the job done but take no chances."

Kathy thought it was strange for Michael to caution her so emphatically. Where she and the others would be, and what they hoped to do, in her mind, presented no danger at all. Of course, she had no idea what the real adversary in this case was capable of.

"Mike thanks for the concern, but we'll be fine," she responded.

"I know that, but it doesn't hurt to be cautious. Let's hope all goes well. But no matter what happens tonight, I'll need you and Gazis in my office tomorrow morning."

"Mike, I'll see you around 10 a.m. Keep your fingers crossed."

When Michael ended the call with Baer, he did more than cross his fingers. He silently recited the prayer to St. Jude.

Michael received a message from Kathy around 11 p.m. "We just finished. I'll see you in the morning."

When Gazis and Kathy walked into his office the next morning promptly at 10 a.m., they had big smiles on their faces. They were followed in by Dina and Tim who was holding a compact disk in his hand which he placed on the desk in front of Michael. The DA's investigators had apparently accepted Kathy's offer to join her and Gazis in the field.

For the next hour the four provided Michael with a detailed account of what they accomplished the night before. Gazis and Kathy described their roles and Dina and Tim told Michael that the disk on the desk in front of him was the result of their work in the DA's office's tech room which they did when they returned from the field.

Michael asked the four to leave his office and played the disk.

He was ecstatic at what he saw.

The stage was now set for the climax of the people's case against Patrick Patron.

CHAPTER

TWENTY-FOUR

On Monday when the trial resumed, Michael called Kathy Baer as his first witness. She testified to recovering a power saw next to the burn-out car in the garage. Michael showed her the saw, which she identified. He then moved it into evidence.

"Fire Marshal Baer," Michael continued, "Have you ever operated that saw?" Acting as sheepishly as Michael had instructed, she looked down at her hands and answered, "No." To the average courtroom observer asking that question seemed like a mistake because of the answer it elicited. But it was not a mistake at all. It was Michael setting a trap for Kellogg that he hoped to be able to spring on him later in the trial.

Kathy Baer then testified that after the metallurgist did his work comparing the cuts on the car's engine to the saw blade, she vouchered (the law enforcement word for safekeeping) the saw, placing it in the custody of the NYPD property clerk.

She said that one week ago on a Saturday night, at Michael's request, she removed the saw from the property clerk's custody and took it to the NYPD lab to analyze.

She described for the jury her examination of the saw for fingerprints and for anything that might contain DNA. Baer told them her examination revealed three fingerprints, which she removed using fingerprint tape. She stated that during an additional, very close inspection of the saw, she found a piece of what she believed to be human skin near the trigger guard. She described what she used to recover and preserve the skin.

She testified that when she concluded her work with the saw, she handed over the fingerprint tape with the recovered prints to an NYPD expert to examine and hopefully determine whose prints they were. Michael showed her the print tape which she identified before he moved it into evidence.

Baer continued. She said that within a short time of recovering and preserving the skin using the glass slides, she brought it to the medical examiner's office for DNA analysis. Michael handed the slides with the piece of skin to her and asked if she recognized them. Kathy said she did and after she identified them Michael moved them into evidence.

When Michael announced that he had no additional questions for Kathy Baer, Kellogg excitedly jumped to his feet and began a cross-examination that he was sure would lead to his client's acquittal.

Kellogg's enthusiasm was Michael's first clue that, so far, his plan was working.

When Kellogg spent very little time questioning Kathy about her work at the police lab and used the vast majority of his cross examination asking her questions related to the admission that she never operated the power saw, Michael knew he had taken the bait.

"You've never started that saw? Is that right?" Kellogg asked. Kathy answered "Yes, that's right."

"You've never applied the saw to any metal surface? Is that right?" he continued. Once again Kathy's answer was, "Yes, that's right."

Kellogg ended his flurry of questions with, "And you certainly never placed it against the engine of the car near where you say you found it? Is that right?" Kathy, now looking down at her hands once again, said, "Yes, that's right."

After her last answer Kellogg announced with a flourish, "I have no further questions of this witness, Your Honor."

Michael was pleased with Kellogg's performance. It was what he had been counting on. It was obvious that the defense attorney's strategy in concentrating on that aspect of Baer's testimony was to raise doubts in the minds of the jury that the power saw actually worked, and additional doubts that it could produce sufficient ignition to set the gasoline fumes on fire. That strategy would become even more apparent with his questioning of Michael's next two witnesses.

NYPD fingerprint expert Detective Cal Bush was the prosecution's next. Det. Bush testified to his work in assisting Kathy Baer. He told the jury that the three fingerprints Kathy pulled off the saw were examined by him first for their viability. That is, was there enough of each print visible for a computer to read them in a search for a match? His analysis determined that the prints were viable.

Bush said he took the next step and placed them into various law enforcement databases to search for the identity of the person to whom they belonged. The result of that search was that the three prints belonged to Patrick Patron.

Michael showed him the fingerprint tape that was in evidence and Det. Bush identified it as the tape he used in the process he just described.

James Kellogg cross-examined Det. Bush similar to how he went after Kathy Baer. He virtually ignored the detective's findings with regard to the fingerprints and instead asked a series of questions about the power saw and its operation.

"Have you ever operated the saw, from where you say Fire Marshal Baer lifted those prints?" Det. Bush answered that he had not.

"Have you ever seen that saw in operation?" Det. Bush again answered that he had not.

"So, is it accurate to say that you have no clue as to whether or not that power saw is operable?" Bush answered that it was an accurate statement. "You also have no idea of the amount of power that saw puts out, nor of its capabilities?" Det. Bush answered, "That is correct."

So far everything was going according to Michael's plan. He had one more witness to get through before he would spring his trap.

Dr. Marge Saunders, from the New York City Medical Examiner's DNA lab followed Det. Bush to the stand. Once Michael established her credentials as an expert in DNA analysis, Dr. Saunders confirmed that she was the scientist to whom Kathy Baer gave the slides. Michael had her describe for the jury her analysis of the item contained between the slides.

When she finished, Michael asked her for her findings.

"I found that the item between the slides was a fragment of human skin from which I extracted DNA. I ran it through our databases and found that it belonged to Patrick Patron."

Michael asked why Patron's DNA was in a database. Dr. Saunders explained that when he entered the US from Haiti he was required to provide a DNA sample. That sample was then stored in a database kept by the US government which the medical examiner's office had access to.

When it was Kellogg's turn to ask Dr. Saunders questions on cross-examination he spent very little time asking about the doctor's DNA analysis and findings. Instead, he concentrated on the saw, asking the same questions he posed to Det. Bush. The doctor answered the same as Bush, adding, "Sir, I have never seen that saw," before each of her answers.

Pleased with himself, Kellogg giddily announced that he had nothing further for Dr. Saunders.

The trap was now set, and Michael was ready to spring it.

CHAPTER
TWENTY-FIVE

Believing that Michael was about to rest his case, Kellogg was ready to announce that he had no defense witnesses and would therefore rest the defense case. So, when Judge Rinaldi asked Michael if he had any additional witnesses and Michael answered that he had one more, Fire Marshal Alex Gazis, Kellogg angrily reacted.

He demanded that the prosecution make an offer of proof as to the relevancy of this final witness' testimony which, he added, "I believe is nothing more than a repetition to what we have already heard, and therefore, cumulative."

An offer of proof is often asked for by an attorney who questions the necessity or relevancy of what is about to be offered into evidence. The actual offer is a preview of the new evidence so the judge can rule on whether to allow it.

Kellogg's demand for the offer did not trouble Michael because what he intended to introduce through Gazis would require his seeking and getting the judge's permission in any event. So, he told the judge, "Your Honor, I have no problem making the offer of proof."

However, rather than keeping the jury for what might be a long argument, the judge turned to them and said that because he and the attorneys had some work to do that didn't require their presence, he was dismissing them for the day. He admonished them to return on time in the morning.

With the jury no longer in the courtroom, Judge Rinaldi addressed Michael and Kellogg.

"Gentlemen, I have no idea what Mr. Gioca is about to propose but it's been a long day and quite frankly I'm tired. I'd rather you both get here 30 minutes early tomorrow morning when I'll be fresh, and ready to listen to what he has to say and what you, Mr. Kellogg, say in opposition. After you're both done I'll make my ruling and we can then proceed. How does that sound?"

Starting the day with what Michael hoped to do was good with him, and he had no objection to the court's plan.

As for Kellogg, he was fine with the schedule but he wanted a preview so he could be ready with an argument if he was opposed to what Michael would be asking for. The judge agreed with Kellogg, and asked Michael to provide the preview to him.

Michael complied with the judge's request by having a copy of the compact disk delivered to Kellogg's office at 4 a.m., the next morning, five hours before they were to appear in court again.

At 9 a.m. Michael was sitting in Judge Rinaldi's courtroom waiting for Kellogg and the judge. Down the corridor from the courtroom in a witness waiting room, were Dina Mitchell, Tim Clark, Alex Gazis, and a cart containing a DVD player and a large screen TV, waiting for instructions from Michael.

James Kellogg arrived at 9:01 followed by Judge Rinaldi who assumed the bench seconds later. The judge called the court to order and told Michael he had the floor.

Michael then made his offer of proof.

Kellogg was vociferous in his opposition to what Michael was asking for. He was so forceful in delivering the reasons for his objection, that Michael thought he would have a stroke right there at the defense table. He was yelling so loudly that the judge had to admonish him. He reminded Kellogg that he was in a courtroom, and it would be the law, not his screaming, that would persuade him to rule in his favor.

After an hour of back-and-forth arguments, the judge told the attorneys that he would take a short recess to think about what they had said and would return with a decision.

Twenty minutes later Judge Rinaldi sided with Michael, saying "Mr. Kellogg you're objecting, but you opened the door to this evidence being relevant, by your cross-examination of the last three prosecution witnesses." He then ordered his clerk to bring the jury into the courtroom.

Before resuming the testimony, the judge apologized to the jury for keeping them waiting taking sole responsibility for the delay. After which he told Michael to call his next witness.

Fire Marshal Gazis took the witness stand, and after being sworn in, Michael asked him to tell the jury why he was there.

Gazis began by identifying himself, his position in the fire marshal's office, and reciting his credentials as a certified fire investigator. He told of being assigned by the fire commissioner to supervise the investigation that he and Fire Marshal Kathy Baer were ordered to conduct into the Christmas eve fire at Archangel Church in which Firefighter Louis Amato Jr. lost his life.

He detailed the examination and search of the scene that he, Kathy Baer and other members of the FDNY conducted. During that search he told the jury a power saw was recovered by Baer in the garage, next to the hulk of a burnt-out car. Michael showed him the saw in evidence, and Gazis identified it as the one she had recovered at the fire scene.

Gazis described the discovery of the cut marks on the engine of the car and the work and conclusion of the metallurgist.

Michael followed with a general question about gasoline fumes in the garage. Gazis gave a detailed account of the discovery of a pool of gasoline under the car which was still emitting fumes hours after the fire had been extinguished.

He finished this portion of his testimony by telling the jury that based upon everything the investigation had yielded, it was his expert opinion that the fire was started when the power saw recovered at the scene was being used on the metal of the car engine, causing numerous and powerful sparks which ignited the fumes emanating from the pool of gasoline under the car.

Michael then asked if Gazis had anything that would demonstrate to the jury the type and number of sparks that would be caused by the saw cutting into the metal of that car engine.

When Gazis answered that he did, Michael said, "Tell the jury what you have and how you acquired it."

Gazis told the jury that pursuant to a request from Michael, he and Kathy Baer set out about a week ago to find a car of the exact make and model as the burnt-out car they saw in the garage after the fire.

"We began by checking with auto salvage yards and car auction businesses across the metropolitan area. These turned up nothing. I then made a call to the New York City Department of Sanitation police and asked them to check their inventory of abandoned cars they had picked up from the city streets for the car we were looking for. That yielded nothing."

"The next call was made to the NYPD auto pound where cars seized by the police for a variety of reasons, were stored. I spoke to the lieutenant in charge and told him what we were looking for. He agreed to check his inventory. One hour later he called me and said that he had what I wanted but we would have to find it on his rather large lot."

Gazis told the jury that with the help of Tim Clark and Dina Mitchell, he and Kathy Baer located the car in the far corner of the pound.

"Tell the jury what, if anything, you did after finding that car," Michael said.

"Again, pursuant to your request, Kathy Baer retrieved the power saw she had recovered from the NYPD property clerk's office. At the pound, when we found the car we were looking for, she gave the saw to me, then she went back to wait in our car, which was parked at the entrance to the large lot."

"Your instructions were for me to power up the saw and use it, that is, cut the engine of the car in the exact spot where I had seen the cut marks on the burnt-out car the day of the fire."

"Did you do that, Fire Marshal Gazis?" Michael asked.

"I did. And as I was cutting it your detective Tim Clark video-taped it."

"What was the result of the cutting?"

"Mr. Gioca, a river of very powerful sparks rained down through the engine compartment to the ground below."

"If someone had been doing to the burnt-out car in that garage what you had done to the identical car, where would that river of sparks have gone?"

"They would have gone right into the pool of gasoline under the engine compartment."

"And in your opinion what would those sparks have done to the gasoline fumes that you found were still coming from that pool?"

"The sparks would have ignited those fumes and unless someone immediately put out that fire it would have spread, as we saw it had, to the walls of the garage."

Michael then handed the compact disk, on which his cutting was recorded, to Gazis, and asked him to identify it. When he did Michael asked if he had seen what was on it.

"Yes, it's the recording, made by Det. Tim Clark of your office, of my cutting the engine of the car identical to the burn-out one I found in the garage fire."

After Michael had established through Gazis that the disk contained everything that took place and nothing was added or deleted, he offered it into evidence. Kellogg made a half-hearted objection which Judge Rinaldi overruled. The disk was now in evidence.

Dina Mitchell rolled the cart with the disk player and the wide screen TV into the courtroom. As it was being set up Michael looked over at the jury. Each of them had moved up to the edge of their seats.

As the tape was playing the jurors were mesmerized. Michael later recalled that when the 'river of sparks' began he heard several gasps from jury members. He was satisfied that this demonstration would put the finishing touch on the people's case.

With very little to attack about the video, Kellogg spent his cross-examination of Gazis trying to undermine the credibility of Kathy Baer. He asked in every way possible about Kathy's role in the taping and whether she was a witness to the actual cutting depicted on the video. Gazis, who had been prepared by Michael for this attack, calmly answered, "Fire Marshal Baer's role was to help me locate the car, along with the DA's detectives. Once the car was found, she went back to our vehicle which was parked several hundred yards away from where I was on the other side of the pound. She did not witness the cutting."

Kellogg didn't give up, however. He asked a series of questions about the handling of the disk after the filming had been completed, insinuating that Kathy had seen what was on it before she testified and would therefore have known about the 'river of sparks', even though she said she had never seen the saw in action.

Once again having been prepared for these questions, Gazis calmly told Kellogg that Dina and Tim had prepared the disk, and until today when it was played for the jury, only they, him, and Michael had seen it.

Kellogg was beaten. He asked no further questions of Gazis.

Michael's plan had been carried out to perfection.

However, it remained to be seen if it was enough to fill the void in his case created when Carmelo was murdered.

CHAPTER

TWENTY-SIX

A t the close of the evidence late Friday afternoon, having been told by Kellogg that he had several prior engagements on Monday and Tuesday, Judge Rinaldi agreed to set summations for Wednesday.

So as not to disadvantage Kellogg by telling the jury that he was responsible for the extended delay, the judge did him a favor and told them that because it had been a "rather long and sometimes arduous case," *he* was giving the attorneys extra time to prepare their closings. Acknowledging that Wednesday was the eve of the Thanksgiving holiday, he assured them, however, that he would adjourn that day at 3 p.m. so that they could all be home to prepare for and enjoy the holiday. Their deliberations would begin on Friday.

After the jury was sent home and court was adjourned, Michael offered to buy Gazis, Tim, and Dina a drink. When they got to a bar near the courthouse, Michael was surprised to see that Kathy Baer was waiting for them.

"Dina sent me a text to let me know where you all were going," Kathy told Michael.

"Dina always knows the right thing to do," Michael said, as they sat down at a table in the back. When they placed the drink order, Michael realized how happy he was that Kathy was included.

Michael recounted how the video and the questioning of Gazis had gone.

When their drinks arrived Michael said, "I can't thank you all enough," as he toasted his crew.

Then turning to Kathy, he said, "Now that the testimony is over, I'm anxious to hear about the search for the car and what you meant when you said that you 'believed' that you had 'finally' located one."

Kathy went on to recount what she and Gazis had run into while searching for a car to use in the video. Gazis began the search by contacting several salvage yards in Brooklyn and Queens. Each told him they didn't have what he was looking for. Disappointed but undaunted, he tried one in the Bronx. Bingo! The Bronx yard had what they were looking for but because the car was scheduled to be crushed that afternoon, they needed to hurry to get it.

When she and Gazis arrived at the yard the owner said he had no clue as to what they were talking about. When they told him that someone there had told them they had the car they were looking for, he answered that he worked alone and only he answered the phone. "And I never talked to anyone from the FDNY."

"Mike the same thing happened at an auto auction outfit and believe it or not at the Department of Sanitation yard for abandoned cars," Gazis added. "I spoke to someone at each location, was told they had the car, and when we got there, no one had a clue as to what I was talking about. It was bizarre."

Michael listened, thinking to himself, *'Bizarre is one way to characterize it. Diabolical, however, is more accurate. HE was fucking with us!'*

Kathy picked up the story. "When I contacted the NYPD auto pound, I spoke to the commanding officer, Lieutenant Pat Sullivan. He immediately checked his inventory and told me he had one car. Because of all the other bullshit, I hung up the phone and waited 30 minutes before I called him again. I asked him about the car, and he again told me that he had one."

Satisfied that they would find it there, Kathy and Gazis drove out to eastern Brooklyn where the pound was located. They were joined by Tim Clark and Dina Mitchell. They all met Lt. Sullivan who gave them the run of the yard to locate the car.

After searching for two hours and not finding it, they reconvened at Lt. Sullivan's office. He reiterated that his inventory was correct and that the car they were looking for was on the grounds.

He made a joke and told them that as a kid he was an altar boy in his parish church. And whenever he had misplaced or lost something, he said that his mother and grandmother always told him to pray to St. Anthony and it would turn up. They all just nodded and smiled.

Frustrated, Kathy was about to give up the search and call Michael with the bad news, when Dina stopped her. "Kathy before you make that call, let's give it one more shot. Maybe we just missed it." Everyone agreed.

Unbeknownst to them, when the searchers left Sullivan's office to renew their quest, the lieutenant said a silent prayer to St. Anthony.

It began to get dark when they fanned out through the yard. Surprisingly, Dina spotted a section of the pound that she didn't remember seeing on their first pass through the grounds.

In the very rear of the property and off to the left, stood an old brick building. A closer inspection revealed it was a garage where cars from the pound's inventory were readied for police auction. Dina called out to the others who met her there.

On the far side of the building, obscured from view to anyone not knowing was a small yard that held several cars. When the group checked them, they found the car they were looking for.

Gazis, Tim, and Dina waited at the car while Kathy went back to her car to get the power saw. On her way, she stopped into Lt. Sullivan's office to give him the good news. The lieutenant smiled and said to her, "I guess my mom and my grandma were right."

After another round of drinks, the group broke up, each headed off into their weekend.

Before starting , however, Michael met with Monsignor Romano at his Red Hook office. When Michael arrived, the cleric was standing in front of his building dressed in his topcoat. "Michael, I'm starving," he said.

"Okay Sal. Get in the car. I'm sure we can manage to get a table at *Emilio's*," Michael said jokingly.

Over a bottle of *Nero d'Avola*, a Sicilian wine that was one of Michael's favorites, he brought the monsignor up to date on the trial. When he told the story of the frustrating search for the car that ended with Lt. Sullivan's prayer to St. Anthony being answered, Romano, who had been listening intently, simply smiled when the story ended.

"Michael," he said, "You have more allies in this battle than you thought. As I have tried to tell you many times, you are not alone." Michael just nodded and took a sip of his wine.

TWENTY-SEVEN

M ichael decided that he would make good use of the extra time he was given to prepare his summation. He used all day Saturday to clear his head by doing chores around his apartment and running errands. He also spent two hours in the gym and finally ended his day by ordering in his dinner and relaxing in front of his TV watching college football.

Sunday he spent with his dad and his sons. He met them in Queens near their home and took them out for a traditional Italian Sunday dinner. His sons were particularly interested in how the trial was going, while his dad was content to sit back and enjoy the company of the men in his life.

After dropping off his sons at their house, he drove his dad home. Before leaving Michael's car his dad turned to him and said, "Michael, you have no idea how proud I am of you. Today was special. Being able to spend it with you and the boys...I couldn't have asked for a better day."

Michael turned away from his dad to hide a few tears.

After all that his dad had gone through because of Michael's war with Satan, to see him so happy and healthy warmed his heart.

"Dad, it looks like it'll be just you and me on Thursday for Thanksgiving. Pam is going to be with her in-laws and the boys are with their mom."

"Michael, that's just fine with me," his dad answered as he gave his son a kiss on the cheek and left the car.

As Michael was driving home, he began to think about his summation. When he got into his apartment he went straight to his desk and began writing. By midnight he had a first draft. And by late afternoon on Monday, he had put the finishing touches on an address that he was confident would secure a conviction that would bring justice and closure to the Amato family and would drive another stake in the cold heart of his adversary.

On Tuesday afternoon Michael met with Louis' mom, dad, and widow in his office. He asked them there to prepare them for what would surely be a difficult, gut wrenching, and heart-breaking day on Wednesday.

He told them that he would not pull any punches in his summation when it came to describing the events that led up to the agonizing death Louie had suffered.

He also prepared them for what he called "a tugging at the heart-strings" of each juror, when he talked about the enormous loss their family had suffered at the hands of Patrick Patron.

As his wife and daughter-in-law wiped tears from their eyes, when Michael finished, Louis' father told him how grateful he was for all he did for his family. "Tomorrow will be tough but this hour you spent with us will give us the strength to get through it." He shook Michael's hand and enveloped him in a big hug while whispering, "Thank you," into his ear.

When Michael and Dina, who was still with him at the trial even though he had fully recovered from his injuries, arrived at the courtroom on Wednesday morning they were shocked to see the large crowd of uniformed firefighters gathered in the corridor. As they made their way to the door of the courtroom, many in the crowd wished Michael good luck, adding, "We're counting on you."

He was buoyed by the support. Getting a conviction would be tough enough, and Michael didn't need the additional pressure those words put onto his shoulders. He knew they meant well but he wished he had gone into the courtroom via the back door so he didn't have to see all those he would be letting down if he failed.

When they entered, the Amato family was seated in the first row of the courtroom right behind Michael's table. He greeted the group and accepted their good wishes. Louis' dad then got up to shake his hand. "Michael, no matter what happens we'll never forget you. *Buona fortuna"* he said.

Kellogg's summation lasted just over an hour. As expected, he vigorously attacked the work of the fire marshals and the fire experts. He even disparaged the building construction expert by telling the jury his testimony was worthless because he had not been involved in the construction of the garage and had been paid for his testimony by the FDNY.

At the end he reminded the jury that no one had testified to actually seeing Patrick Patron with that power saw in his hands, concluding with, "And, even if that fire had started the way the 'so-called experts' said it did, my client was not responsible."

Michael had been watching the jury as Kellogg spoke but picked up nothing as to what they were thinking . They sat stoically as Kellogg attacked the case, neither nodding in agreement nor shaking their heads in disagreement, with what he had said. *"This is a tough crowd,"* Michael thought to himself as he rose to speak.

After thanking the jurors for their service, Michael got right into tugging at the jurors' heart strings.

"Tomorrow is Thanksgiving Day," he began. "And like each of

you , the Amato family will gather together. However, unlike you, who will gather to celebrate, the Amatos will gather to remember. There can be no celebration for that family, because at their table will be an empty chair. Louis Amato, a son, a husband, a hero, will be missing."

"Louis Amato won't be there because of Patrick Patron's avarice."

"He won't be there because Patrick Patron, using Archangel Church property without permission to illegally cut up stolen cars and car parts, acted with no regard for human life, by engaging in an activity that created a grave risk of death. A risk that became a reality."

"He won't be enjoying Thanksgiving with his family because Patrick Patron lied to the responding firefighters telling them that there was someone trapped inside that burning garage so he could escape from the scene when Louis and his colleagues rushed into the building to rescue someone who wasn't there."

"Because of Patrick Patron, one of New York's true heroes was needlessly taken from his city, from his department, and from his family."

At this point Michael turned to the packed spectator gallery.

He first looked at the Amato family, who were sobbing.

He then scanned the faces of the many firefighters who had filled the courtroom, most of whom Michael encountered earlier. What he saw heartened him and gave him a welcome shot of adrenaline. Those tough, battle-hardened, heroes were not even trying to hold back their tears.

Michael spent the next hour reviewing the evidence for the jury and refuting the lame points Kellogg had made about no one seeing Patron with the saw, and that Patrick, although there at the scene, had nothing to do with starting the fire.

"Mr. Kellogg wants you to believe that someone else must have started that fire. Is there any evidence that Marc Foxx started it? No!"

"Is there any evidence that Monsignor Keenan, or one of his priests started it? No!"

"Or maybe it was Alex Gazis and Kathy Baer, or the building construction expert, the fingerprint expert, the DNA expert or the medical examiner? The answer to all is a resounding No!"

"Patrick Patron did this, and how do you know that? The evidence says so, that's how."

"And when you do what Patron did, under the circumstances that he did them, what's the likely outcome? An innocent person is going to die."

"Ladies and gentlemen, Patrick Patron must be held accountable for what he did."

Michael then finished with, "Folks as I was writing this summation it struck me that the words of a popular Mariah Carey song were startlingly appropriate for what we heard about Louis and his colleagues, *and* for what I'm asking you all to do today.... 'And then a hero comes along with the strength to carry on, and you cast your fears aside and you know you can survive. So, when you feel like hope is gone, look inside you and be strong , you'll finally see the truth that a hero lies in you.'"

"Louis Amato and his fellow firefighters are heroes that come along every day. Heroes with the strength to carry on, despite the danger they face. They cast their fears aside and run into burning buildings when others are running out, so anyone still inside can be saved and survive."

"Ladies and gentlemen, I know how difficult it is to sit in judgment of a fellow human being. It can be frightening. But I'm asking you to be just like Louis and his colleagues and cast aside any fears you may have. I ask you to look inside yourselves and be strong. I'm certain that when you do you'll see the truth mentioned in the words of the song.... That a hero lies in you."

"Be heroes! Return a verdict that will send a message to all those who risk their lives to ensure that we don't lose ours, 'We have your backs.'"

"Find Patrick Patron guilty of the murder of Louis Amato."

"Thank you."

When Michael sat down he was spent. If it were a football game , Michael's coaches would have told the press that, "He left everything out on the field."

The jury returned on Friday to begin deliberations. After Judge Rinaldi had instructed them on the law they were to use in judging the facts of the case, he had his court officer escort them to their jury room to begin working.

As they were escorted out of the courtroom, Michael paid close attention to their body language. He was looking for any telltale sign of the vote going bad. He saw none, so he was confident but wary. Over a year ago, he had tried what he thought was a slam dunk case, only to be thwarted by Satan, who had reached two jurors and convinced them to vote for acquittal. The jury was therefore unable to reach a verdict and a mistrial was declared.

To prevent a recurrence of the problem Michael asked the judge to sequester the jury for the duration of the retrial. Under the watchful eyes of the court officers assigned to protect that jury, they reached a quick verdict, convicting the defendant of the murder of a police officer.

Michael had gotten no hint that jury tampering was underway here, so he didn't ask for sequestration. He was confident that the 12 men and women in that jury room would decide the case on the facts and the law, and nothing else.

The jury deliberated all morning, with the only communication being their lunch order. By 5 p.m. with still no verdict. Michael began to worry. He was sitting in his office for hours waiting to hear *something*. He couldn't sit any longer, so he decided to walk over to the courthouse to burn some energy and to see how the Amato family was doing. When the jury began to deliberate, Louis Sr. told Michael that he and those with him would be there, in the courtroom, until they reached a verdict, or the judge called it a day.

When Michael walked out of the DA's office building, it began to snow. On the way to the courthouse the snow intensified. When he arrived at the entrance, it was like a blizzard.

Michael went straight to Judge Rinaldi's courtroom to look for the Amato family. He found them sitting in the first row where he had left them hours before. They clearly were troubled by the long wait. While Michael did his best to calm and comfort the family, he noticed that the judge had come into the courtroom to talk to his clerk.

Michael walked up to Rinaldi and asked him if the room the jury was using for their deliberations had a window. When Rinaldi answered that it did, Michael gave him a knowing nod, saying, "Your Honor, we're going to have a verdict very soon."

Before sending the jury out to begin their deliberations, Judge Rinaldi had told them that he would be keeping them as late as necessary for them to complete their business. Michael was sure that those words were ringing in their ears as they watched the snowfall through that window. And as it intensified, they would begin to become anxious about getting home. That's why he was sure that a verdict was imminent.

Less than an hour later Patrick Patron was found guilty of murder.

CHAPTER
TWENTY-EIGHT

That night while Michael was having dinner with Monsignor Romano, he received a call on his personal cell phone. He was surprised when the caller identified himself.

"Michael, this is Mayor-elect Pickett. I hope I'm not disturbing your dinner."

"No sir, you're not."

"I heard about the verdict and just wanted to congratulate you on a job well done. Patrick Patron got what he deserved. I always knew he was guilty of murder. Now he can think about what he did to the Amato family while he rots in prison."

Michael rolled his eyes as he listened to Pickett, the guy who Gazis had eventually told him, didn't want Patrick charged with murder when he thought it would guarantee him votes in the immigrant community.

'How things have changed now that he's been elected Mayor and will have to deal with all the uniformed services and their unions,' Michael thought to himself as he listened.

Michael thanked the Mayor-elect for the kind words, finished the call and went back to his pasta.

"Who was that?" Romano asked.

"That was our soon to be new mayor," Michael answered. He told Romano what Pickett had said and reminded the monsignor of Pickett's position on charging Patrick when he was first arrested.

"Well, he's entitled to a change of heart, Michael. You should be pleased by his praise of your work."

Michael shook his head. "Sal, have you ever heard the expression, 'How can you tell when a politician is lying?.... His lips are moving.' That's what I think of Thomas Pickett's praise of my work."

On December 23rd, four weeks after the verdict and one day short of a year from Louis Amato's murder, Judge Rinaldi sentenced Patrick Patron to 25 years to life in prison.

Two weeks into the new year, Louis Amato's father threw a big party to thank Michael, Fire Marshals Gazis and Baer, as well as Tim Clark and Dina Mitchell. He had rented the upstairs room of a popular Italian restaurant near his home and invited dozens of Louie Jr.'s friends and relatives, and many of his colleagues from Rescue Squad 2. He also invited Monsignor Keenan from Archangel Church who began the evening with a prayer blessing the food, everyone in attendance, and remembering Louis Amato Jr. who, the monsignor said, was surely looking down on the festivities from his place in heaven.

Michael had a great time. At the end of the night, Mr. Amato made a point of making sure that he once again expressed his family's gratitude for all he had done for them. Then he surprised Michael by telling him that he had many friends in politics and that he had been speaking to them over the last year about him.

"Michael, it looks like Marty Price is getting bored with being District Attorney. He's told people, who have told me, that he's thinking of running for congress. If he declares, he'll step down from his position. The people I've been speaking to will back you if you want to run for DA. You'll have all the support you need to succeed him. Please keep that in mind if things play out as expected. You would be great in that job."

Michael was shocked. He thanked Mr. Amato, told him he was flattered and said that he'd surely give all he had said a lot of thought. He was non-committal given that he had a very important commitment to complete. Michael could only think about the battle with the *Evil One*, with no idea when it would end.

As he walked back to his apartment he had a chance to reflect on the night's festivities, which made him very happy. But it was more than that...he was deeply moved by Mr. Amato's suggestion that he consider a run for district attorney. And getting a chance to dance with Kathy Baer was the icing on the cake. Almost two months had passed since Patrick Patron's conviction, and no tragedies had occurred.

In Michael's other wins against *HIM*, the *Evil One* had wasted no time in extracting revenge and punishment against people connected to the case or close to him. Each was a message that unless Michael gave up the fight, these tragedies would continue. That none had occurred after this win caused him to think that rather than expecting Michael to give up, Satan had left Brooklyn.

Just before school was to resume after the long summer break, Michael took his sons on a long-planned vacation to the Caribbean.

One afternoon while sitting poolside at the Atlantis Hotel on Paradise Island in the Bahamas watching his boys enjoy themselves, Michael's cell phone rang. When he checked the phone he saw that it was Monsignor Romano. Thinking that his friend was calling to see how the vacation had been going, Michael was animated in his greeting.

"Sal how are you my friend? I hope you're not missing me too much? You should jump on a plane and join us. I'll book you a room. The plane trip is only a few hours, and we still have five days before we have to leave. What do you say?"

When Romano didn't answer right away, even if it was to just laugh or scoff at the idea of "jumping on a plane" to the Bahamas, Michael knew something was very wrong.

"Sal, what's happened?"

"Michael I hate to spoil your holiday, but I have bad news."

Romano went on to tell him that late the night before, a fire broke out on the upper floors of a new high-end hotel, *The Calla,* in midtown Manhattan. The guests in several rooms had succumbed to smoke inhalation.

Because the hotel had been open only two weeks, it was strange that the fire alarms and sprinklers on those floors had failed to function, so the guests who died never had a chance to escape until it was too late.

Puzzled as to why a Manhattan hotel tragedy necessitated a call to him, Michael asked, "Sal, that's all horrible. But why are you calling me?"

"Michael, because of the suspicious circumstances of the failed alarms and sprinklers, the fire marshal's office was called in to investigate. Alex Gazis and Kathy Baer were assigned. This morning they began their investigation by going into a suite on the floor where it's believed the fire started. That floor and the suite had been previously cleared by the responding firefighters and determined to be safe for the fire marshals to enter. When they walked into the front room of the suite, the floor collapsed. They fell to the floor below. I'm sorry to have to tell you that Alex didn't make it and Kathy, although alive, is believed to be paralyzed from the waist down."

Michael was speechless. When he did begin to say something, Romano stopped him.

"Michael, I'm not finished. When the security cameras on the floor were examined, the investigators saw two men they suspect were the arsonists. They were not guests of the hotel but were lurking around the lobby before the fire began. They were then seen getting on an elevator. When they got off on the floor in question, a security camera picked up their faces. One was a notorious arsonist,

Ricky Sabar, who had been arrested by the fire marshals many times in the last few years. The last time was years ago when he somehow beat a case in which a fire he started in Sheepshead Bay in Brooklyn, resulted in the death of six firefighters. The other guy, who was clearly the one in charge, was unknown to the fire authorities, but not to us."

"The highlight of his description given to Caldwell was the large mole on his left cheek."

PART TWO

CHAPTER
TWENTY-NINE

Michael stood next to her hospital bed and was so overcome with emotion that his knees buckled slightly. Guilt and sadness overwhelmed him. But it was anger that kept him upright. Without it he surely would have collapsed at the sight of Kathy Baer lying there in a coma with a machine breathing for her. As difficult as it was, he knew he had to keep it together, not only for himself but for Kathy's mother and father who were seated at her bedside keeping vigil.

When Michael walked into the private room in Mt. Sinai Hospital on Manhattan's east side, he was greeted by Mr. and Mrs. Baer. After introducing himself, Michael told them how proud and fortunate he was to have worked with Kathy on a case that was not only important to the FDNY and the city, but also to a family, much like their own, who had lost a son.

Kathy was instrumental in seeing to it that justice was done, and that the person responsible for the unnecessary and tragic death of a hero firefighter was now spending the rest of his life in prison.

Michael's promise that he would not rest until the person or persons responsible for Kathy's terrible injuries was captured and punished seemed to bring a measure of peace to the couple.

Although the hotel arson occurred in Manhattan, Michael knew, based on what Romano told him about Satan and his pawn Ricky Sabar being responsible, it was just a matter of time before he and Sabar would cross paths in Brooklyn. The *Evil One* was not finished with the borough. The death of Alex Gazis and the paralysis of Kathy Baer long after Patrick Patron was convicted and sentenced, were proof of that. They were also messages to Michael that there was more death and destruction to come.

However, when Sabar did make his way to Brooklyn to commit some horrific crime, Michael vowed that he would be ready.

Before leaving her bedside, Michael said a silent prayer to St. Jude for Kathy's full and complete recovery. He told her parents that with their permission he would continue to visit and if there was anything they needed they should not hesitate to call. The Baers thanked him, took his business card and promised to keep Michael updated on Kathy's condition.

Just before he walked out the door, Michael turned for one last look at Kathy's broken body. He wanted that image seared into his brain as he prepared himself for the inevitable clash that he expected.

He promised himself that when it did, he would make sure Sabar was convicted and would spend the rest of his life in prison. '*I will never give up and Satan will never beat me.*'

When Michael walked out of the hospital, he was at one of the lowest points of his life. Seeing Kathy Baer strapped to all those machines, lying there helplessly, triggered emotions that he hadn't felt about a woman in the longest time. He also couldn't shake an all-consuming feeling of guilt. As he had done many times in the last couple of years, he couldn't help thinking that had he not agreed to Caldwell's and Romano's proposal to take on the greatest evil known to mankind, Kathy wouldn't be where she was, with a ventilator keeping her alive. And Alex Gazis would be home enjoying dinner with his family, instead of lying in a grave.

Walking to his car, he knew that he needed something or someone, a distraction, to get him through the night. But because of the nature of his work he was limited in who he could speak to.

His first thought was to meet up with Monsignor Romano. Michael's longtime friend had always been a good listener and his counsel would invariably shake him out of his doldrums. His comforting and inspirational words served to restore Michael's confidence more times than he could count.

But that night Michael didn't want to discuss his struggle with the *Evil One*. He didn't want to talk about what happened to Kathy Baer and Alex Gazis. He wanted a diversion.

He was so desperate for company he even considered calling his former lover and girlfriend Lenor "Lennie" Ristagno, despite the fact that she made it clear to him months before that she had no interest in seeing him again.

He thought back to the events that led to that decision hoping to find something, anything that might give him an opening if he called her. He knew talking to Lennie would be the perfect distraction from thoughts of the Devil and, more importantly, from thoughts of Kathy Baer in that hospital room.

Michael and Lennie were a serious couple, until they weren't. She had been a criminal defense attorney in Brooklyn when they met in a bar one evening, struck up a conversation, and were inseparable until life reared its ugly head.

Their respective careers did not allow them as much time together as they would have liked, and would need, to grow a relationship. Late nights working, and spending many weekends in their offices, Lennie with her clients, and Michael with detectives and investigations, took a toll on their love life. And since neither wanted to change careers they decided to end the relationship and remain just friends.

After their breakup, Lennie's talents caught the attention of a new Police Commissioner and he appointed her Deputy Commissioner of Trials for the NYPD, the chief judge for the department's disciplinary system.

Michael and Lennie hadn't seen each other for several years until one of his cases against Satan brought them back together.

The case involved an NYPD police sergeant, who Satan recruited as a pawn to help carry out part of HIS evil agenda. The sergeant, while driving drunk one morning, mowed down and killed a pregnant mother and her small child, and injured several young children she was walking to school.

The *Evil One* orchestrated this tragedy and was instrumental in manipulating the evidence so that the sergeant was not charged with a crime. Just as *HE* had planned, that decision spawned demonstrations, mini-riots, and general chaos in Brooklyn for days.

It also led to the murder of a police officer's wife, orchestrated by the *Evil One* and carried out by another of *HIS* pawns. The murder was made to look like a revenge killing done in retaliation for the failure to charge the drunken sergeant. It too was followed by demonstrations, street unrest, and chaos that the *Evil One* craved.

Michael, after convicting the killer of the cop's wife, wanted to make sure that the sergeant was also punished. Because a criminal case against him was rendered impossible by the Devil's manipulation of the evidence, Michael convinced a police department lawyer to bring administrative charges against the sergeant.

A conviction in the NYPD's trial room would cost the sergeant his job and pension. It was not the prison time he deserved, but it was a punishment that would adversely affect him for the rest of life.

When Michael went to police headquarters to watch the sergeant's departmental trial, he saw that the judge assigned to hear the case was Lennie Ristagno.

So as not to subject her to criticism that her former lover's presence and influence were the reasons, if she found the sergeant guilty, Michael left the courtroom before the trial began, but not before Lennie saw him.

After she found the sergeant guilty, Michael called and asked her to have dinner with him so he could explain his presence at the trial and catch up with each other. After initially balking, fearful they might be seen together, Lennie agreed when Michael suggested a restaurant in Astoria, Queens, far away from prying eyes in Manhattan and Brooklyn.

When their dinner was over, Michael walked Lennie to her car. After she rebuffed his offer to see her again, they hugged and said good night.

It turned out that the *Evil One* was at work once again. A reporter who was tipped off to the dinner, had captured a photograph of the hug. The next day the photo and a story questioning Lennie's impartiality in the sergeant's case appeared on the front page of one of the city's tabloids.

To make matters worse, the day the newspaper ran the story, the sergeant was found dead by gunshot in his home. It was made to appear that after seeing the newspaper photo and story, he committed suicide. A copy of the newspaper was found lying next to the body, a gun in his hand.

Lennie was distraught and angry when she called Michael that morning. She told him that she held him responsible for the bad publicity and that she didn't think it was a good idea that they ever see each other again.

Some weeks later Michael got word that the medical examiner declared the death of the sergeant a murder, not a suicide.

When Michael was told that a witness, the sergeant's neighbor, came forward to say she saw someone with a strange mark on his left cheek leaving the sergeant's house just after she heard what she thought was a firecracker, he knew who was responsible for the death.

However, he couldn't tell any of that to Lennie.

Now thinking back to those events, he realized that his thought of Lennie being the diversion he was looking for was nothing more than a creation of his desperate mind.

Instead, he started his car and headed for the Lincoln Tunnel and Atlantic City. Poker was his old reliable when he needed to clear his head.

One day turned into a week, as Michael lost himself in the poker rooms of several of Atlantic City's casinos.

He checked in with his father and his sons, first to alert them to where he was and then periodically to make sure all was well. He also called Kathy Baer's hospital room at Mt. Sinai to get the latest from her parents. Otherwise, he was *incommunicado* with the rest of his world.

His days were spent sleeping, eating, and thinking while jogging on the famous boardwalk. His nights were taken up by the pastime that he was an expert at and was bankrolling this spur of the moment trip.

One evening while Michael was collecting his chips from yet another winning hand in the poker room at the Tropicana Hotel where he was staying, it struck him that the last time he thought about the *Evil One,* Romano or Caldwell was seven days before when he was in his car on the Garden State Parkway heading to AC. The smile on his face as he stacked the chips had nothing to do with the money they represented, it was all about how the games he played during the past week worked their magic. They provided the diversion from the reality of his war in Brooklyn that he so sorely needed.

Right then and there, Michael decided that it was time to go home. He would get some sleep and check out of the hotel after breakfast in the morning.

While he was at the cashier's window exchanging his chips for cash, he heard his name called over the hotel's paging system. Concerned because only his dad and his sons knew where he was staying, he collected his money and immediately went to the front desk to find out why they paged him.

"Mr. Gioca, you have a phone call," the desk clerk told him, handing the phone to Michael. As he brought it to his ear, Michael's hand was shaking.

"Hello?"

"Michael it's me, Sal." Somehow Monsignor Romano had found him.

"Sal, how the hell did you find me? Was it my dad or my kids?"

"Michael, relax. When I found out about your visit to Kathy Baer in Mt. Sinai, and then not hearing from you for over a week, I figured you were repeating a pattern. The last time you hid out in Atlantic City I eventually found you at the Tropicana. That's why this time I started there."

"Sal, you know me too well. I needed to clear my head and poker always does the trick. Now what's up?"

"Michael, there's been a murder on the Coney Island boardwalk that has the *Evil One's* signature all over it. And Caldwell has heard some talk out of police headquarters that Ricky Sabar is a suspect. He may have killed someone again."

"Sal, I was going to check out tomorrow morning and head home. But now I'll leave tonight. Meet you in your office in the morning?"

"Yes Mike. Drive safely."

CHAPTER
THIRTY

Linda Torre was loved by her students. The former nun was teaching Theology at St. Joseph's College in Brooklyn for the five years since she walked away from the vocation and life she lived for over twenty years.

Linda felt the calling to enter religious life when she was 15 years old and in high school. Her close knit, religious, Italian American family couldn't have been more thrilled when Linda announced her vocation and intention to become a Catholic nun.

After her "novitiate," the period of study, training, and preparation a woman undergoes prior to taking vows and entering the religious life, Linda 'took the veil' and became a nun in the order of The Sisters of St. Joseph.

Sister Linda Torre, then 20 years old, began to teach elementary school at St. Teresa of Avila parish in Brooklyn. Sister Linda was popular with her third and fourth graders and was a favorite of their parents.

After several years in the parish, being fluent in several languages, she, along with another parishioner, started a program to teach English to the many immigrants who were part of the St. Teresa community.

It was her unmarried colleague in the program who presented the temptation that Linda eventually succumbed to.

Emanuel Solis was a handsome, well-dressed, soft spoken, well mannered, man of the world who impressed Linda with his patience and kindness toward the folks in their language program.

She often marveled at how easy it was to work with Emanuel and how stress free he made everything he was involved in. Although she wouldn't admit it to herself, and despite the vows she had taken, Linda was smitten with him.

Emanuel was equally impressed and taken with the young, good-looking Linda. He would constantly compliment her on her ability to connect with the adult students in the program, tell her how he admired her confidence, and how well she carried herself when difficult situations arose. He had even taken her out to dinner several times, hoping to impress her with his *bon vivant* manner.

As time went on it became clear to anyone who was paying attention, that Linda and Emanuel had fallen in love. Finally, over an intimate dinner one night in a small Italian restaurant in Manhattan, Emanuel told Linda his feelings and asked her to leave the religious life. Linda began to weep, telling him that she had been holding in those same feelings and had been struggling to come up with a way to let him know.

That night they pledged their love to one another, and Linda promised to speak to the mother superior of her order the next day when she would announce her intention to leave.

Linda's decision broke the hearts of her mom, dad, and sister. They tried to get her to reconsider and go back to the convent but her feelings for Emanuel were too strong for that to happen. Eventually, Linda moved into Emanuel's apartment and the two immediately began talking about marriage.

Unfortunately for Linda, it was all talk. As much as Emanuel said that he wanted her to be his wife, he seemed content with them just living together. The sex was great, but as time went on it appeared to their friends that Emanuel was losing interest in Linda. Although she hated to admit it, she too began to feel Emanuel pulling away from her.

When one of her former colleagues from the convent told her about an opening at St. Joseph's College for a teacher of Theology, Linda applied. Because of her religious background, and after a very successful interview with the dean, Linda was hired.

While teaching was rewarding to Linda and kept her mind on something other than her crumbling relationship with Emanuel, her schedule did not allow for much home time to repair it. It also provided Emanuel with a good deal of time away from Linda, which he spent wining and dining other women.

On what would be their last Saturday together, they shared a simple breakfast in a coffee shop near their apartment. Linda hoped that being out among other people would spark something in Emanuel that would rekindle their love life. Instead, Emanuel spent the time on his phone and greeting neighbors who came into the coffee shop, often leaving Linda alone at their table with her eggs and coffee.

That night Emanuel turned down Linda's suggestion that they see a movie and have dinner out. She was so upset at his decision that she decided to pack a suitcase and go home to her mom and dad. As she was packing she heard Emanuel talking on his phone to someone who Linda had no doubt was his next 'love.'

Her mother and father welcomed her with open arms. The next day, over Sunday dinner, Linda told them all about her trouble with Emanuel.

"Honey, didn't you tell us not that long ago that you were going to get married?" her mom asked.

"Mom, I misread everything. When he couldn't have me, I was his desire, the forbidden fruit. When he finally got me, the intrigue was gone, and he couldn't get rid of me fast enough. I gave up everything for him. I feel like a fool."

Linda then asked her parents if she could move in with them for a while. They agreed. They lived on the southern end of Brooklyn, miles away from St. Joseph's College. It was not a convenient commute, so she knew that finding an apartment of her own was imperative.

As it turned out, finding a place to live was not easy. The more she struggled to find an apartment, the more upset and stressed she became. The sixty-to-ninety-minute commute every morning and night gave her plenty of time to think, stress, and obsess over her plight.

After months of searching, when a promising lead on an apartment turned out to be nothing more than another disappointment, Linda resigned herself to living in the room she grew up in, forever. That wasn't rational thinking but to Linda it was all she had. She couldn't see a way out.

Her troubles all came to a head one night when Linda ran into one of her students from the English program she ran at St. Teresa's. The student saw her on the subway as she made her way home and they began to talk. The conversation was pleasant enough until the student told her that he was invited to Emanuel Solis' wedding in a couple of weeks. He asked if he would see her there because he knew how well she and Emanuel had gotten along before she left the convent.

It was as if she was hit over the head with a sledgehammer. Linda was stunned. She couldn't say another word and got off the train several stops before hers, just to get away from the carrier of such horrendous news. When she arrived home she ignored the dish of spaghetti her mother left for her and went straight to her room after stopping at her father's liquor cabinet to grab a bottle of scotch.

The stress and sadness she was feeling had finally reached a breaking point.

She had been a social drinker after she left the convent, but that night, she finished the bottle that was three-quarters full and cried herself to sleep. When she woke the next morning she stayed in bed, blowing off the early class she taught.

She failed to show up for any of her classes for the next week. She rarely left her room, barely touched food, and raided the liquor cabinet whenever her father was sleeping or not at home.

When the dean at St. Joseph's tried and failed to reach Linda, thinking the worst, he became worried and finally called her sister Antoinette, who was listed in the college's records as her emergency contact. Antoinette told him everything and said that Linda's drinking, on top of her deteriorating mental state, had the family very worried.

"We've tried everything, but we can't seem to get through to her." Their next move, she said, was to have Linda see a psychiatrist, voluntarily or by force.

The dean asked Antoinette to keep him apprised, offering to help in any way he and the college could.

That night, Linda Torre disappeared.

CHAPTER

THIRTY-ONE

She rode the subway all night.

She slept fitfully with one eye open until a cop shook her awake and told her she had to get off the train because it was going out of service. When she checked her watch it was 6 a.m.

She left the subway station not knowing where she was. When she didn't recognize her surroundings, she panicked. However, calling her parents or her sister were the furthest things from her mind.

Instead, she walked to a small park across from the subway and sat on a bench to calm herself and think about what she would do next. She had no plans because leaving her parent's home was a spur of the moment decision fueled by the deep depression she found herself in.

She was very hungry, so she decided to get some breakfast in a diner she spotted down the block from the station and to find out where she was. When she sat down she pretended to be a tourist who lost her way on the subway. To get her bearings, she asked her waitress if she was close to Times Square because she had booked a room reservation in a hotel in that area.

The waitress, spotting Linda's suitcase, bought her story. She told her that she was in Jamaica Queens, and to get to Times Square she directed her back to the same subway station she came from. The waitress advised Linda to take the F train toward Brooklyn which goes through Manhattan. The stop she should look for was 42nd Street-Times Square.

Although familiar with the subway line, eastern Queens was like a foreign country to Linda. But since the waitress had identified the subway line she had been on, when she came to a decision as to where she was going to stay, she would know how to get there.

When she finished her food and went to the cashier to pay the bill, she saw that she only had $50 in cash. Because she had left home so quickly she forgot to take her wallet which contained her credit cards and several hundred dollars. After paying for breakfast all she had left was $42.

Linda was now faced with a dilemma. Go home to retrieve her money and credit cards where she would have to face her parents and her sister who were undoubtedly worried about her, or make the best of the $42 until she could figure out a way to get more money. She knew that whatever decision she made she needed to get back to familiar territory, Brooklyn.

She got back on the subway headed to Brooklyn. On the way, she decided not to go back to her parent's home. Instead, she rode the F train to its last stop, Coney Island.

With its legendary boardwalk, concessions, arcades, and rides, all fronted by a sand beach and the Atlantic Ocean, Coney Island has been one of the most famous amusement areas in America since its opening at the turn of the 20th century.

When the subway was extended to Coney in 1920 its accessibility was greatly enhanced, and its popularity soared. After World War 2, however, the amusement area began to decline. It became a haven for gangs, homeless and displaced people, and had a rising crime rate which made Coney Island more dangerous than fun.

Although the early 21st century brought a revival, parts of Coney

Island remained perilous, especially when the weather began to turn cold, and its underworld denizens did whatever was necessary to survive.

When Linda arrived in Coney Island it was early spring. Although she had nowhere to go when she got there, she was drawn to the beach by the mild weather. On the way she stopped in a liquor store and used some of her $42 to buy a bottle of vodka, which she took to a spot under the boardwalk.

Like waving a red cape in front of a bull, when Linda began to drink from her freshly bought bottle, she drew several of Coney Island's unsavory characters to her side. She quickly made friends with them. One guy, who said his name was Buck, even offered to let her share the hovel he fashioned under the boardwalk several blocks away from where she had been drinking, to which Linda said yes. She had hit rock bottom but at least she found a home.

Linda and Buck became fast friends. He was a scammer and a con man. He fashioned himself as an expert in getting unsuspecting tourists to part with their money which he used to buy liquor and food for himself and Linda. However, living with Buck had a price. He demanded regular sex from Linda. And as long as he kept the vodka coming, and kept her fed, she was more than willing to pay the price.

Then Linda became pregnant, and Buck booted her out.

With nowhere to go, Linda wandered the streets and boardwalk, sleeping on the sand and eating unfinished food left in trash cans by Coney's tourists and visitors. Then one warm afternoon, a few weeks after Buck had kicked her out, while Linda was panhandling and scrounging through the trash cans around Nathan's, Coney Island's landmark hot dog restaurant, someone approached her and offered help.

Christine Miller, a licensed psychologist, began living on the streets when she suffered a mental and emotional breakdown after advice she had given to a domestic violence victim didn't work out and turned her life into a total disaster.

Dr. Miller, as her clients called her, began working in a shelter for battered women after she closed her private office to do 'more good for more people.' She gave that reason to anyone who asked why a well-respected psychologist would suddenly leave a very successful practice.

Miller told friends that she became unsatisfied with her work because she knew there were so many others who needed her help but didn't have the money to pay for it. So, after ensuring that her private patients were referred to colleagues, to continue their treatment, Christine closed the doors to her Brooklyn office and took a position as resident psychologist in a nearby women's shelter.

Her work at the shelter was extremely satisfying. The women she counseled and helped were all victims of domestic violence of one type or another. Some were battered women who were subjected to regular physical violence at the hands of husbands, boyfriends, and baby fathers. Others suffered because the men in their lives were psychologically abusive in a variety of ways. And many of these women were mothers whose children also suffered as a result of living in an abusive home environment.

One afternoon a woman who was new to the shelter asked to see Christine. She told her all about her abusive husband who returned several months before from eight years of active duty in the army.

She said that when they first met he was a kind, caring, and loving man. They eventually married and had a daughter. However, when he returned from the service, she didn't recognize him. Her loving, caring husband had become a mean, violent, abusive man, who, when he wasn't high on drugs, was drunk on booze.

Arguments and fights were regular occurrences. Her trips to hospital emergency rooms were well documented, as were the complaints she filed with the police. However, when it came time for her to see an assistant district attorney to draw up charges, she always refused saying it was all a mistake. She was sure her husband would learn from the arrest and stop his abusive behavior.

The woman told Christine that he didn't. So, she kicked him out of their apartment hoping that he would get the message that she didn't want him around any longer.

That did nothing to stop him. He would constantly show up at her apartment and bang on the front door begging her to forgive him. He would hang around the outside of her apartment building, and each time she went out he would approach her and ask to be let back in because he learned his lesson. When she refused, he would threaten her then run as she reached for her phone to call the police. He had become an everyday threat.

"Dr. Miller, I can't take it anymore. I can't live my life this way. And I can't have my daughter subjected to all this. I came to the shelter because I don't feel safe at home. I desperately need your help," she said.

Christine told her that for the sake of her daughter she needed to leave the shelter and go back home. She promised to help the woman file papers to prevent her husband from coming near her and getting back into the apartment.

With Christine's assistance the woman did secure an order of protection. But that didn't stop the husband. One night he broke into her apartment threatening to kill her. Luckily for the woman he hadn't gotten past the kitchen where she had been painting a cabinet. When he went at her she doused him with paint thinner she had on the counter, lit newspaper on fire and thrust it toward him to stop his advance. She inadvertently touched the fire to his shirt sleeve which was soaked with the thinner and it caught fire.

The husband, now fully engulfed in flames, ran to a neighbor's apartment, followed by the woman who found him in the neighbor's bathtub. She tried to douse the flames, but it was to no avail.

The husband died and the woman was arrested for murder. Ultimately the woman pled guilty to a lesser charge and was sentenced to prison, and her daughter was removed to a foster home.

Christine blamed herself for the tragedy. And though she tried, she could never recover from the complete emotional collapse she suffered as a result.

She left her position at the shelter, abandoned her apartment and her friends and family, and began to live on the streets. Eventually she made her way to Coney Island where she found peace in all the noise and pandemonium, and anonymity among the crowds.

She also found Linda Torre.

CHAPTER
THIRTY-TWO

When Christine saw Linda picking through the trash cans near Nathan's she immediately thought back to the work she abandoned. Here was a woman clearly in need of help. Whether it was her training, muscle memory, or simply her instincts kicking in, she found herself approaching Linda to offer her a helping hand.

At first Linda was naturally cautious when this stranger approached her out of nowhere. But as the two talked, Christine's experience counseling women like Linda kicked in and Linda relaxed. Christine bought her some food from Nathan's and walked her to the boardwalk where they sat and talked while Linda ate. When she learned that Linda was pregnant, Christine took her to her 'home' so she could get some sleep.

Christine lived in an abandoned concession stand at the far end of the boardwalk away from the amusement rides, arcades, and the crowds. It was not ideal, but it was also not the hovel under the boardwalk that Linda shared with Buck. And because it looked like what it was, no one would be interested in breaking in.

Linda spent that first night in peace. When Christine told her that she could stay as long as she'd like, Linda began to cry. She thanked Christine and accepted her kindness.

Now that she had a roommate, Christine decided to alter the space in the concession stand to provide privacy for both her and Linda. She hung a rope down the center of the interior of the space, over which she placed a large piece of drape-like material she found outside of a restaurant that was undergoing renovations, dividing the space in two. She was able to come up with a mattress for Linda from one of the hot sheet motels off the boardwalk and gave her a couple of her many blankets so Linda would be warm when sleeping once the weather turned cold.

The two became fast friends and were inseparable. Christine, who suffered from high blood pressure, a condition she had kept to herself since she was diagnosed when she first arrived in Coney Island, got to know the medical people at a free clinic not far from the concession stand. There she was able to secure the meds she needed to control her condition. Knowing how kind they were to her, she brought Linda there for care during her pregnancy.

Christine also befriended some of Coney's seasonal workers and did odd jobs for small amounts of cash. That money she now used for food for her and Linda.

Linda was grateful for her help. With proper medical care, food, and regular sleep, Linda got stronger. She began looking for work so she could contribute to the household she and Christine established. She found it at one of the food stands on the boardwalk. The job paid little, but she was able to take home the food left after the day's sales.

When she began she worked only during the day. She was fearful of running into Buck and felt that in the daylight he wouldn't cause a scene or worse. But as she became stronger she also grew more confident. So, to make more money she decided that she would work night hours as well. That pleased her boss.

Although Linda was living in an abandoned concession stand, she did her best to look her best. Her natural good looks had not faded because of her troubles. The clinic allowed her to shower every day, and with some of her wages she was able to buy makeup at a nearby discount store. And with renewed confidence, her upbeat personality, which had been missing for so long, began to come through again.

As a result, she became a favorite of the food stand's customers, especially the men. They congregated at the stand when she was working and bought the hero sandwiches and plenty of beer that she was serving.

By late summer, Linda was happy and thriving. The customers were generous with their tips and her boss had even given her a modest increase in wages. She and Christine began to look around for low-income housing, hoping to move out of the concession stand before the winter set in.

However, unbeknownst to Linda, trouble was brewing. One of the men she attracted to the food stand was a treacherous and vicious Coney Island bad guy, who would eventually become a deadly problem for her.

Ricky Sabar was well known to the cops in Coney Island. He didn't live there but his brother had an apartment off the boardwalk on Surf Avenue, one of Coney's main streets. Sabar had a long criminal record. He had been arrested several times in Manhattan, but most of his arrests were in Brooklyn, especially in and around Coney Island and the neighboring areas of Brighton Beach and Sheepshead Bay. He was known to law enforcement as a serial arsonist.

The Brighton Beach area of Brooklyn, otherwise known as 'Little Odessa' because of the thousands of Russian and Ukrainian immigrants who settled there, was home to Russian organized crime in New York City. And like the Black Hand, the predecessor of today's Mafia, who at turn of the 20th century in Manhattan's Little Italy extorted money from immigrant Italian shop keepers to ensure their stores would not be harmed or destroyed, the Russian mobsters did the same to shopkeepers in Brighton Beach.

Over the years, Sabar was hired by the mob to burn out businesses that failed to pay that protection money and by struggling businessmen who wanted to collect fire insurance money to bail themselves out of financial trouble.

Sabar had not served much jail time for these fires because he always started them in the dead of night and almost always after the cold weather had settled in when the streets of Brighton Beach were deserted.

His most notorious arrest came a few years before, as a result of him setting fire to a supermarket as revenge for the manager throwing him out of the store after he had been caught shoplifting. The fire quickly burned out of control, necessitating several fire companies to respond. When a number of firefighters went to the roof of the market to vent the flames, the roof collapsed killing six. The deaths of six heroes was national news, and the city's newspapers carried the story and its aftermath for months.

Because of his reputation Sabar was suspect number one for the fire marshals who were investigating the blaze. Fortunately for him there were no witnesses, and the surveillance cameras positioned in and around the store were all destroyed in the fire. Sabar was questioned but was released because of the lack of evidence tying him to the fire.

It was the recent arson in *The Calla* hotel in Manhattan in late summer that would put him on law enforcement's radar once again.

The death of Supervising Fire Marshal Alex Gazis, and the serious injuries to Fire Marshal Kathy Baer at *The Calla*, set off an intense investigation involving the FDNY, the NYPD, and the Federal Joint Terrorist Task Force. As a result, surveillance evidence from inside the hotel had been quickly gathered and analyzed. It showed Ricky Sabar before any fire was detected, on the floor of the hotel where the experts determined that the fire started. He was with another male who appeared to be the one calling the shots.

The two men were seen leaving the hotel as fire companies responded.

The next day Sabar was picked up for questioning by the fire marshals. He denied knowing anything about the fire. When he was shown the tape of himself in the hotel, he said he was looking for a friend's room and had no idea who the other man with the mole on his cheek was. With no evidence to charge him, Sabar was released.

Not long after that he had his deadly encounter with Linda Torre.

CHAPTER
THIRTY-THREE

Michael packed quickly and left Atlantic City around midnight. He arrived at his apartment at 2:30 a.m., got some sleep, and walked into Monsignor Romano's office with two cappuccinos at 9:30.

"Good morning Michael. It's good to see you. I hope the time away helped. And, thanks for the coffee," the monsignor said as he took his first sip of the steaming liquid.

"Sal, it did. But before we start, tell me, how are things with Kathy Baer?"

"The latest report I received was last evening. She came out of the coma and is breathing on her own. An FDNY Chaplain visited her and told me that she was still in a lot of pain but was able to speak. He said that her parents told him that the doctors who have been treating her are now cautiously optimistic that she will walk again, but she has a long recovery ahead of her."

"Sal, at this point that's good news."

"Now tell me about this scumbag Sabar, and what happened in Coney Island. What do the police have?"

"At first their only witness was the victim's roommate who told them what I'm about to tell you," answered Romano.

"Early yesterday morning, a homeless woman, Christine Miller, who was living in an abandoned concession stand at the far end of the Coney Island boardwalk, came home after spending the night with a friend, to find that her roommate, Linda Torre, was murdered."

Romano described to Michael the story of what brought Linda and Christine to Coney Island. He told him how they met and became friends and began living together in an abandoned concession stand on the boardwalk.

"Christine, a licensed psychologist and social worker who had fallen into bad times, made sure that Linda, who was pregnant, received prenatal care at a free clinic, and was eating regular meals which she provided."

The monsignor told Michael how, when she became stronger, Linda began working at a food stand on the boardwalk.

"Mike, I'm told that Linda was a looker. After she had gotten herself back together, she became a draw for the food stand. Guys hung around, drinking beer that she served along with the food stand's hero sandwiches, just to talk to her."

"In the beginning she only worked days because she did not feel secure enough to venture out after dark. However, as her confidence returned and her need for additional money grew, she began working nights."

"Christine told the cops that one of the guys who had been hanging out at Linda's food stand, almost every night, was a guy she knew as Sabar. She said that he had a bad reputation among the street people, especially the prostitutes who worked around the boardwalk."

"Linda told Christine that Sabar would constantly flirt with her while she worked, telling her how beautiful she was, and how much he wanted to take her out on a date. Christine told the cops that

Linda never said she was fearful of Sabar, just that 'he was annoying' because he interrupted her as she worked."

"Christine said that Linda rejected Sabar's advances several times, especially recently, because of her pregnancy. Apparently, the night before last she relented."

"When Christine returned home yesterday morning, she saw Sabar coming out of Linda's side of the concession stand wearing a tee shirt with blood on it and his pants. He pushed past her and ran down the boardwalk. Concerned, she went in to see if Linda was okay. She saw Linda, who looked to be sleeping, lying on her bed, completely naked. Christine attempted to wake her. When Linda didn't respond she shook her hoping to rouse her. When she got no response, Christine realized that her friend was dead."

"Then looking more closely at Linda's body she saw open wounds on her torso, a good amount of blood, and bruises around her neck and upper body. She also noticed a liquid all over Linda's exposed vaginal area, her inner and outer thighs, and on her buttocks."

"Christine went out onto the boardwalk to see if Sabar was anywhere in sight. But he was long gone."

"When she went back into the concession stand she noticed for the first time an oddly patterned black and white sweater, and a tweed men's jacket, thrown over a chair next to Linda's bed. Christine had never seen them before, so she assumed they belonged to Sabar."

Romano went on to say that a panicked and distraught Christine ran back out of the concession stand and found a uniformed cop who was on patrol just off the boardwalk. After telling him about Linda, the cop called it into the precinct.

"Sal, this is a horrific crime. And I get why you want me to handle it, for Kathy and Alex. But when you called me you said that this murder had the *Evil One's* signature all over it. How? Other than Sabar and *HE* being together at the fire in Manhattan, what more do we have connecting it to Satan?"

"Michael, in every case you've handled so far, Satan has destroyed not only the lives of the victims, but their families as well. Most recently you saw what sending Louis Amato into a burning building to save someone who was not there did to him and to his family. It's *HIS* 'M.O,' as the police would say."

"But Sal, Linda was a homeless person. How does this fit *HIS* 'M.O.'?"

"Linda may have been homeless when she was killed. But she came from a loving and deeply religious Catholic family. Her mother, father, and sister will surely grieve her loss, and miss her deeply. *HE's* destroyed another family. So, it does fit."

"But if that's not enough," Romano continued, "Not so long-ago Linda Torre had been Sister Linda Torre, a nun in the order of the Sisters of St. Joseph."

"Michael, I'm certain, as is Caldwell, that once you get into this case you'll find that it was not a coincidence that Satan, using Sabar as *HIS* pawn, chose Linda Torre to be *HIS* latest victim."

Michael knew the monsignor was right. But he also knew that the evidence so far was not as strong as he would like, which he told to Romano.

"Michael, we know that, but something I hadn't yet told you may help."

Romano went on to say that between the time he spoke to Michael the night before, and early that morning, the police picked up a street skell who they knew was an associate of Sabar's in the past.

"They wanted to question him, but Caldwell was able to get the police brass to order the detectives to hold off until you got there. He's being held at the Coney Island precinct. Caldwell has spoken to the DA; the case is yours. And, Mike, DA Price had a message for you, 'Get that son of a bitch.' Apparently he was the fire commissioner when Sabar set that supermarket fire. He's never forgotten, nor has he forgiven."

It was time for Gioca to get to work.

CHAPTER
THIRTY-FOUR

When Michael left Romano's office he wasted no time heading to Coney Island and the 60th precinct. He identified himself to the desk officer who directed him to the second-floor detective area. Walking into that squad room Michael thought of New York Yankee great Yogi Berra's famous comment when he experienced something in the present that he had also experienced in his past, it was like 'déjà vu all over again.'

As a young assistant district attorney, Michael spent many days and nights in that squad room. As a 'riding' ADA, as they were called, he was on call for a 24-hour period ready to respond to police precincts all over Brooklyn to interview and record witness statements, and confessions from bad guys and gals, accused of murder.

The room hadn't changed even a little in the many years since he was last there. The hustle and bustle of the detectives; the city issued well dented metal desks at which they worked; the half-broken chairs; the dirty walls painted institutional green; and floors so grimy it would take a professional cleaning service weeks to make them somewhat respectable again. But Michael had to admit that it felt good being back.

Before he could even put his briefcase down, he was met by Lieutenant William "Billy" Grimaldi, the commanding officer of the 10th Homicide Zone detectives.

The 10th was one of five zones, as they were called by the NYPD, that comprised the Brooklyn North and Brooklyn South Homicide Squads. These zones contained the full complement of detectives who investigated only homicide cases in Brooklyn. Each zone covered a different geographical area of the borough and the various precincts therein. Any homicide committed in those precincts was investigated by the detectives assigned to the zone. The Coney Island precinct was located in the 10th homicide zone, which was part of Brooklyn South.

Lt. Grimaldi greeted Michael warmly. They had worked together on many cases, first when Michael was a riding ADA and later when he became Chief of the DA's Homicide Bureau. "Mike, it's good to see you. It's been a long time."

"Same here Billy. I'm looking forward to working together again. Who's the lead detective?"

Grimaldi laughed, "Same old Gioca. Cut through the bullshit and get right to it. Don't you want to have a cup of coffee with your old friend before you get into this?"

"Billy I'd love to but how about you let me speak to that skell your guys brought in, then we can skip the coffee and I'll buy us lunch?"

"Deal," said Grimaldi. He picked up the phone, and said , "Come into my office."

To Michael's surprise, Detective Armin Bondor walked in.

Grimaldi said, "I think you guys know each other."

Michael got up from his seat and hugged Bondor who returned the embrace. "Armin, it's great to see you. But what are you doing in Brooklyn South?"

"Michael, after the murder on the bridge case I took the sergeant's exam and right after the trial I got word that I passed. When I got my sergeant's shield I was transferred here."

"Mike, he's my number two," Grimaldi said. And he's going to be working with you again. He's the lead detective on the Torre murder."

"Billy, that's great. Thank you."

Michael and Armin Bondor got to know each other more than a year before when they worked on solving a high-profile case involving the murder of a young Jewish woman who belonged to the strict orthodox Satmar Hasidic sect. She was killed on the Williamsburg Bridge. The bridge connects the heavily Jewish neighborhood of Williamsburg in Brooklyn to Manhattan's lower east side, an area populated by Jewish owned businesses. The devil instigated the murder that struck at the heart of Williamsburg's deeply religious Jewish community. It was committed by a junkie who constantly needed money to support his drug habit.

Satan, in the guise of someone the junkie knew, appeared to him one night in a dream telling him that Jews who walked the Williamsburg Bridge on Sunday mornings all had money and were perfect robbery targets. The devil convinced the junkie to go to the bridge and wait for a victim to rob.

He spotted a young woman walking the bridge for exercise. Believing she had money, as the devil told him, he grabbed and dragged her to a deserted section of the bridge where he intended to rob her. When the woman told him she had no money, he became angry and strangled her to death. He stripped her of her clothes, and sexually assaulted her in an attempt to misdirect the police into thinking that a sexual predator committed the crime.

Later that day, when he confided to a friend as to what he did, the friend told him that he needed to return to the body and burn it in order to ensure that the cops would find no evidence that would lead to him as the killer.

Late that night, the junkie and his friend returned to the bridge with gasoline. After dousing the body and the woman's clothes with it, they set her and her clothes on fire. The burnt remains were found the next day by bridge workers.

After a thorough investigation with Armin Bondor as the lead detective, the junkie was arrested. Michael indicted, tried, and convicted him of the murder. He was sentenced to life in prison; however, he died shortly thereafter under suspicious circumstances. The devil killed him and staged the death to look like a suicide because *HE* feared that the junkie would reveal elements of the crime and their relationship, which could never be told.

Impressed by Bondor's work and professionalism in the bridge case, Michael was delighted to have him as the lead detective in the Torre murder.

From Lt. Grimaldi's office, Bondor took Michael to his small windowless office to fill him in on what they had in the Torre murder.

Most of what Bondor told him, he already knew from his conversation with Romano. What was new, however, was that the liquid found on Linda's naked body had been collected by the medical examiner and sent to the lab for analysis.

Ultimately Michael wanted to speak to Christine Miller, but he was more anxious to talk to the new witness that the Bondor's guys had picked up.

"Jimmy Pope is his name," Bondor said. "Mike, he's a real low life, which makes what he said he can tell us about Sabar something we need to hear. They're both cut from the same cloth. They hang together, and from what we hear, they love to harass and fuck around, by which I mean rape, the Coney Island hookers, who are deathly afraid of them."

"Armin, let's go talk to this piece of shit. Of course, if he gives us what we need to collar Sabar, he'll immediately become an upstanding citizen."

Bondor laughed as he led Michael to Jimmy Pope.

When Michael and Bondor walked into the small interview room, Pope was sound asleep with his head resting on a table that served as the barrier between interviewer and interviewee. Bondor shook him awake.

Michael estimated his age as late twenties to early thirties. Clean shaven, with a slight build, his pale skin, and sunken eyes told Michael he was still or had been a drug user. He was dressed surprisingly well for a street thug, though. His Adidas track jacket and matching pants seemed relatively new, as did the Ralph Lauren polo shirt he wore under the jacket. His white Nike sneakers had not a mark on them, which led Michael to think that Pope was either obsessed with keeping them clean, or he had stolen them just before the cops picked him up.

Bondor asked him if he wanted coffee and something to eat. Pope said yes to both. Bondor told a cop who was sitting outside the room keeping an eye on him to get an egg sandwich and coffee.

"Mr. Pope, my name is Michael Gioca. I'm an assistant district attorney. I'm working with the police on the case involving the murder of the woman on the boardwalk. I understand from Det. Bondor that you have something to tell us about her and Ricky Sabar. Is that right?"

"Mr. Michael, I don't want no trouble. The cops grabbed me up and took me here, telling me that because I know Sabar I must have had something to do with the murder of that lady who lives in the concession stand. I ain't have nothing to do with it. But I do know that Sabar and her knew each other."

"Jimmy, is it ok if I use your first name?"

Pope replied, "Everybody just call me Pope."

"Okay Pope. Let's start at the beginning. How did you come to know Sabar?"

"I met him on the boardwalk one night before the summer. I was looking for some ladies...."

Michael interrupted, "You mean hookers, right?"

"Yeah, but I ain't found none. That's when this guy who I didn't know, Sabar, come up to me and tell me that he knows what I'm looking for and he can help me. He takes me down off the boardwalk and we goes under it. We walks a little and I see this chick giving a guy a blow job. We wait a good ten feet or more away, and when she's finished Sabar walks up to her and tells her she got to do me now. When she said no, he smacks her across her face and tells her to get to it."

"Mr. Michael, I ain't ask him to do that. While the chick is doing me he's standing off to the side watching. When we was finished, I went to pay her. Sabar grabs my hand and says 'let's go.' I didn't know what to do. But the dude was a nasty fuck, so I left with him."

"From that point on, me and him started hanging together."

"C'mon Pope. It can't be that simple. Why did this total stranger begin to hang with you?" asked Michael.

After some hesitation, Pope said, "Because I have money. He saw me with cash that first night and asked me where I got it. I told him I have a job. I work in Manhattan at a clothing factory. It's good money. When he heard that he smiles and then he says 'we got to stay together.'"

"How often would you two hook up?" Michael asked.

"I be out here every weekend. Sabar been taking care of me with the hookers. They are afraid of him so when he tells them to take care of me they do it. I never have to pay. If they complain, Sabar smacks them around. As payback, I buy him food and beers from the stands on the boardwalk. That's how I know that he and the dead lady know each other."

Michael asked Pope to explain.

"The lady worked at one of the food stands where we liked the sandwiches, and they always had cold beer. At the beginning of the summer that lady wasn't serving, it looked like she was just cleaning up. Then one day we go to the place and the lady is now serving food and beers. And she looked great. She always had a nice face, but somehow she cleaned herself up, fixed her hair, and started wearing makeup. She looked hot."

Pope told Michael that Sabar took notice right away.

"From that point on he only wanted to go to her stand for food and beers. Sometime after July 4th, I meet Sabar under the boardwalk and he had one of the girls blow me. After I'm done he tells me that we're going to meet a friend of his before we go to the food stand. We walk a few blocks and outside Nathan's he walks up to this creepy looking light skinned black dude, and they shake hands."

"What did the guy look like?" Michael asked.

"He was tall, skinny, close cropped black hair, clean shaven, with this fucked up mark on the left side of his face."

"Did you catch his name?"

"Yeah. The dude said his name was Jiz."

Michael hoped that Bondor did not notice his reaction to hearing the name. If he did, and asked Michael about it, he'd have to lie. There was no way Michael could tell the detective that he was thoroughly familiar with Jiz because it was the name the *Evil One* used when *HE* instigated the murder of an off-duty police officer, Robbie Thomas ,on July 4th a couple of years back.

Michael now had to find out how Jiz caused the murder of Linda Torre.

THIRTY-FIVE

"What happened after you and Sabar met up with Jiz?" Michael asked.

"We walked over to the food stand where the lady worked. On the way Sabar was telling Jiz all about her. When we got there we got on a line to order food. Sabar was just staring at the lady while he waited. That's when I hear that guy Jiz tell Sabar that he knows her. He doesn't say how, just that the lady used to be a nun. 'She must be horny as hell,' Jiz said. Sabar's eyes lit up when he heard that. Jiz then tells him, 'You need to fuck her, so she's satisfied.'"

"When we get to the front of the line, Sabar started to talk shit to the lady. You know like, 'You look great tonight. You're so beautiful. I love your eyes.' Shit like that. But the lady paid him no mind. She just smiled and asked for the food order."

"But Jiz kept at Sabar all the time we was eating. 'She's so horny, she needs dick,' he kept saying. He had Sabar so worked up that I thought he was gonna do her that night."

Michael then asked, "Pope, back then did she look pregnant to you guys?"

"No."

"Sabar is such a degenerate that if he knew about her being pregnant, he really would have grabbed her that night and fucked her on the sand."

"But as time went on, " Pope continued, "She started to show, and it was clear that she having a kid. That made Sabar crazy. For the rest of the summer and right up to just a few days ago, he be telling everyone that he was gonna fuck her; that he *had* to fuck her. And that piece of shit Jiz, kept pushing him to do it."

"Did he ever tell you if he scored with her?" Michael asked.

"No, but two nights ago I was coming off the boardwalk and I seen him walking on Surf Avenue behind the lady. It was late, and the stand where she works had closed. So, she must have been going home. I watched them and I seen him finally get up to her and say something. She nodded, like 'yes' and he starts walking with her toward where she stays."

"Did you see where they went?"

"No. I went the other way to the train."

Michael told Pope to sit tight, as he and Bondor left the room.

"Armin, this is great. Not only does he give us how Sabar and Linda met, but he also puts them together the night she's murdered. And Sabar's obsession with having sex with Linda gives us the reason why he was on Linda's side of the concession stand from where Christine saw him leaving the morning she found Linda's body."

Michael asked, "Did you guys put together a lineup with Sabar's photo?"

"We did," the detective answered. "We showed it to Christine Miller, and she identified Sabar's picture as the guy she saw coming out of the concession stand."

"Great. Now let's show the photo array to Pope to make sure he's talking about the same guy."

Bondor retrieved the pictures and showed them to Pope. He pointed to the same photo that Christine picked out. "That's Sabar," he said.

After telling Pope that it would be best if he stayed out of Coney Island for a while, and didn't see or contact Sabar, Michael thanked him for his help and told him that either he or Bondor would be in contact in a few days. He gave Pope his business card saying that he could reach him anytime if there was a problem.

Michael then asked to talk to Christine Miller.

Other than adding that the photo she identified was Sabar, Christine repeated everything Michael already learned from Romano.

Once he secured her assurance that she would cooperate fully in the investigation, and that after Sabar was arrested she would testify at the grand jury, and at a trial, Michel told her that for her safety he wanted to move her somewhere away from Coney Island.

At first Christine was hesitant. "I know I live in an old concession stand, but that's my home. I have people who look after me and I, in turn, look out for them. It would be tough to just uproot my life even if it was to move to someplace better," she said to Michael.

Knowing the danger she faced from the *Evil One,* Michael was persistent.

"Christine, the summer's over. Soon it's going to get very cold on that boardwalk. Living in that old shack will not be pleasant and may jeopardize your health. Let me set you up in a place where it'll be warm and where you'll be safe. When the case is over, if you want to move back into that concession stand, that'll be your choice."

Christine told Michael she wanted to make a phone call before she decided. With Michael and Bondor waiting outside the room, Christine called a friend who she had been visiting periodically throughout the summer to ask if she would allow Christine to stay with her. To her this was preferable to staying somewhere unfamiliar.

Christine met Clara Gordon when she worked at the women's shelter. Clara was her assistant, answering her phone and keeping track of her appointments with the clients who Christine was coun-

seling. Because they shared many interests, the two women social-
ized outside of work and became friends.

After Christine left the shelter, she would occasionally call Clara
to talk when she was lonely. As the spring turned to summer, Clara
began to invite Christine to her home miles from Coney Island,
where she would prepare dinner for them. Though she had no idea
where Christine was living, Clara felt compassion for her, and on
more than one occasion, she would have Christine spend the night.

Christine was thankful for Clara's friendship, but she didn't want
to take advantage of it. So, when she called Clara to ask if she could
stay with her, she fully explained the reason for her request.

The phone call went well.

After she hung up Christine told Michael that they had a deal as
long as she could stay with her friend. Michael agreed. He told Christine to give all her contact information to Bondor who would reach
out to her if and when she was needed. He also impressed upon her
the importance of not telling anyone where she was staying. He
repeated his admonition that she stay out of Coney Island.

"Don't worry Mr. Gioca. I hear you. I won't do anything stupid."

After all he'd been through in this war with the *Evil One*, Michael
hoped that Christine would be true to her word.

Satisfied that he now had enough for an arrest, it was time to pick up
Ricky Sabar.

That turned out to be easier said than done. Bondor and his team
hit all the spots in Coney Island where Sabar was known to hang out.
They came up empty.

His photo was issued to every cop on street patrol, with orders to
detain Sabar if and when he was sighted.

After a week with nothing to show for their efforts, Bondor had
his detectives hit the streets themselves in search of any leads to
Sabar's whereabouts.

Now that summer had turned to fall, Coney Island was mostly

deserted except for the street people. But the persistence of Bondor's men finally paid off. They found someone who not only gave them information on where Sabar might be staying, she also told them what she had seen the night Linda Torre was killed.

They now had a new witness in the murder of Linda Torre.

CHAPTER
THIRTY-SIX

Jasmine Liu had been working the Coney Island streets for several years. During that time just about every cop in the 60th precinct arrested "Jade" as she was known on the street, at least once for prostitution or drug possession. So, when one of Bondor's detectives, Tommy Raines, approached her to ask if she knew Sabar he was not surprised by her answer.

"Yeah, I know that scumbag, all us girls know him and hate him. But I ain't seen Sabar for a few days," she told him. When Raines pressed her about the last time she saw him, Jade opened up and gave him more than he could have hoped for.

Recognizing the import of what she told him, the detective asked if she would come into the precinct so he could record her statement. Without hesitating she said, "Yes, but not with you. Too many eyes around here. I know where that precinct is. I'll meet you there."

Raines drove to the station house and waited outside for Jade to show up.

When they walked into the squad room, Bondor was standing just outside his office. He watched as Raines escorted Jade to an interview room, then called him into his office. "Tom, what have you got?" he asked. Raines then filled in Bondor on what Jade had told him.

"Let's go talk to her so we can get all the details down on paper," Bondor said.

When they entered the interview room Bondor introduced himself and thanked Jade for coming in. "I just want you to repeat everything you told Det. Raines, and don't leave anything out." Raines began writing as Jade told her story.

Jade started by telling the detectives that she knew who Linda Torre was. She had seen her around Coney Island for several months, and "I know she lives with another lady in an old concession stand on the boardwalk," she said. "When I heard she was murdered I was upset because she was pregnant."

"How did you hear about the murder?" Bondor asked.

"It was all over Coney Island."

"Then when I heard what everyone was saying about when the lady was killed, I remembered a couple of things that I saw."

Jade explained that on the night of the murder she saw Linda and Sabar walking together on Surf Avenue headed in the direction of the concession stand where Linda lived.

"They seemed friendly. He was talking to her, and she was nodding her head, like saying 'yes.' At one point he even held her hand. Knowing Sabar I figured he was up to no good."

Bondor interrupted and asked her to explain why she had that feeling. "Detective, Sabar is the worst. He's always looking to get with the girls under the boardwalk and if someone says no, he gets physical. And he never pays for what he takes. He even did it to me a few times. We hate his ass. So when I seen him trying to get over on that lady Linda, I knew something bad was gonna happen."

Raines then said, "Tell the sarge what you saw Sabar wearing that night."

"He had on some ugly ass sweater under a suit jacket, which was open. You couldn't miss that sweater cause it looked like someone had copied a checkered tablecloth, made the boxes bigger, colored them black and white, and made it into a sweater."

Jade continued, telling Bondor that the next morning around 9:30 or 10:00 she was on the boardwalk when she saw Sabar again.

"He was running from the direction of the place where Linda lived wearing only a white t-shirt which had blood all over it. He didn't have on the sweater or jacket I seen him wearing the night before." She added, "He had blood on his hands and face, too."

"When he ran past me he slowed down and said, "You didn't see me-you didn't see me."

"At the time I ain't think anything of it because I hadn't heard about the lady. But when I heard she was killed and *when* and *where* it was, I figured that Sabar done it."

When Jade finished Raines showed her the sweater and jacket they had recovered from the concession stand. Without being asked a question Jade identified the clothes as the ones Sabar was wearing the night she saw him walking with Linda.

Bondor asked her if she had any idea where Sabar might be staying. Jade hesitated before telling him that Sabar had a brother who lived in Coney Island and gave him the address. "He's probably staying there," she said.

Bondor thanked her and told Raines to give her a lift home.

Just as she did when Raines wanted to drive her to the station house, she refused the offer. "Sergeant, I ain't going home. I got to get workin'. You know where to find me if you need me."

Raines gave her his card and told her to be careful. He added, "If you see Sabar, call me."

When Jade left, Bondor called Michael and filled him in on the new information. Gioca was elated.

"Great work Armin. I think we have a case. Now arrest Sabar and call me when you have him."

The first place the detectives hit looking for Sabar was his brother's apartment. Before doing so, Bondor ran the brother's name through the NYPD database so he would have an idea of who they would be dealing with when they got there.

Sammy Sabar was indeed known to the NYPD, specifically the narcotics unit. He was a suspected drug dealer but had not been arrested since he was a teenager. When the detectives got to his fifth-floor apartment they found Sammy standing in the hallway outside his door. Clearly someone had tipped him off that the cops were on the way up.

"What can I do for you Sergeant Bondor?" he said while examining the business card Bondor handed to him as he introduced himself.

When Bondor told him they were looking for his brother, Sammy said that he hadn't seen his brother in over a week. "He drops by sometimes, but I never know when he's gonna show up."

"Then you won't mind if we look around your apartment for him?" Bondor asked.

Sammy replied, "Sergeant, no offense to you personally because I don't know you, I don't like cops. And I don't want you or your people anywhere near my crib. I'll tell my brother you all were here if I see him."

"Now have a nice day," he added sarcastically, as he backed into his apartment and slammed the door.

'Looks like I'm going to need a warrant,' Bondor said to himself as he and his detectives walked to the elevator.

Bondor left two of his men in front of the apartment building with instructions to sit in their car and watch the entrance. They were told to grab Sabar if they saw him and to bring him to the precinct.

When Bondor got back to his office he called Michael. After explaining what happened and his need for a warrant, Bondor was surprised at Michael's response.

"Armin, you don't have enough for a warrant. You went to his brother's place on a hunch Sabar might be there, but you had no hard evidence that he was, nor any evidence that he had been hiding out there. No judge will give me a warrant on those facts. I'm sorry. I want this guy as much as you do, but we'll have to be patient and hope your people spot and collar him."

Bondor was disappointed and frustrated, but he knew that Michael was right.

"Mike, we'll keep looking. He's got to turn up sooner or later."

It was 10 o'clock that night when Ricky Sabar and his representative walked into the 60th precinct station house.

CHAPTER
THIRTY-SEVEN

Dressed in clerical garb, a lime green shirt with a white clerical collar, black slacks and a white suit jacket, Sabar, approached the precinct desk officer accompanied by a man who claimed to be his representative.

Answering the desk officer's question as to why they were there, the representative said, "We're here to see Sgt. Bondor."

The desk officer had them escorted upstairs to the detective squad area.

Sabar's representative introduced himself to Bondor when the sergeant came to meet them. "Sergeant, my name is Anton. I'm here with Mr. Sabar because his brother told him that you were looking for him. He's done nothing wrong and has nothing to hide. So here he is."

Puzzled by the outfit Sabar was wearing, as well as by the garb of Anton who was dressed in a black suit, with a black shirt and tie, and wearing a black pandemic surgical mask, Bondor asked Anton, "Who are you and what why are you here with Sabar?"

"Sergeant, I'm Brother Sabar's representative and advisor. He is a very prominent member of a community, of which I am an elder, which is why I'm here. Perhaps I can help straighten out any issues you have with the brother?"

"Are you his attorney?" Bondor asked.

"I'm not his legal counsel, I'm his spiritual counsel. I'm here to ensure that Brother Sabar is not mistreated in any way. Does he need legal counsel?"

"Mr. Anton, that's up to him," Bondor answered. "It is our intention to put him in a line up and if he's identified we're going to place him under arrest for murder. We will then attempt to question him about that. He'll be advised of his rights, and should he choose to remain silent or ask for an attorney, we will stop and get him counsel, unless of course he has one he would like to call."

"Sergeant, first of all my name is simply Anton. And, as I have said, Brother Sabar has done nothing wrong. He certainly hasn't murdered anyone. But if you are going to arrest him he'll have legal counsel in court. Our community will see to that."

Anton turned to Sabar and said, "Until you get to court and have a lawyer present, do not talk to these detectives."

Sabar began to balk at that advice, saying "I ain't got nothing to hide. I ain't done nothing. I ain't".... at which point, an angry Anton held up his hand and gave Sabar a look that stopped him from saying another word. Sabar just dropped his head as Anton turned and left the squad room.

Bondor took Sabar into custody and called Michael.

An hour later Michael was in the squad room as the detectives were setting up a lineup for Christine Miller to view and, if they located her, for Jade to view as well.

While they waited, Bondor filled Michael in on Sabar's surrender.

"What's the deal with that get up he's wearing? And who was the guy he was with?" Michael asked.

"He said his name was Anton." When Bondor said that name Michael stopped listening. He sat there stunned. *'Shit,'* Michael thought to himself. *'Satan right here inside the station house. Sabar must mean a great deal to HIM. For Linda, and Kathy, and Alex, I've got to convict this bastard.'*

Bondor continued. "He said that he was Sabar's representative and his spiritual counsel. *He* claimed to be an elder of some community that he and Sabar belonged to, of which Sabar was a prominent member. Mike this is all bullshit. Sabar is about as religious as fucking Hitler. This is all a set up for a jury down the road. They're gonna try to sell Sabar as some religious figure who would never commit such a heinous act as the murder of a pregnant woman."

When Bondor finished his update, Michael asked, "Armin, what did this Anton look like?"

"Mike he was on the tall side, thin, with short cropped black hair, and from what I could see he was a white guy. And he was dressed all in black."

"What do you mean 'from what I could see'? Did you see his face?"

"No."

"Why not?"

"Mike, he had on one of those black surgical masks, a pandemic mask. I couldn't ask him to take it off because that's not department protocol. We have to respect someone's choice to wear a mask."

"Armin, Let's go do these lineups. We need to nail this guy."

"Mike, it's only going to be one lineup today. Christine Miller is here but we haven't been able to locate Jade. I've got people out looking for her and if we find her they've been instructed to scoop her up and bring her here."

"Armin, no problem. If Christine identifies him you've got the okay to charge Sabar with Linda's murder. We'll deal with Jade later."

One hour later, Christine Miller, without hesitation pointed out Sabar as the person she saw leaving Linda Torre's side of the concession stand, just before she discovered Linda's body.

Unfortunately, the detectives never located Jade that night. That troubled Michael. He couldn't help thinking that Anton may have had a hand in that.

"Armin, keep looking for Jade. "When you find her, call me."

The next morning Michael was in Brooklyn Criminal Court for Sabar's arraignment.

Bondor had told him what Anton had said about 'his community' providing an attorney to represent Sabar, so he was interested to see who would sign the court appearance book for the defendant.

After waiting more than an hour, Michael approached the court clerk and asked if she had heard from Sabar's attorney. The clerk looked at him strangely and said, "Mr. Gioca, do you know something the court doesn't know? What attorney are you talking about? I was expecting that Sabar would be represented by an 18b lawyer. We're just waiting for him or her to arrive."

18b was a section of New York State law which permitted private attorneys of varying experience levels who volunteered their services at reduced rates to represent indigent defendants. In other words, according to the court clerk, Sabar would not be represented by someone hired by 'his community.' He would have a court appointed lawyer, who he could not choose, paid for by the citizens of New York.

Michael thought this was strange. According to Bondor, when Anton was at the station house with Sabar *HE* was very protective of him. Michael was certain *HE* acted that way because Sabar was important to *HIM*. He wasn't disposable like the others who Satan had used to kill and maim in Michael's earlier cases. Sabar has been a useful and very successful pawn who Michael knew Satan would use again. Therefore *HE* needed Sabar to win this case. So why would *HE* leave Sabar's fate in the hands of someone who might never have tried a murder case, or had very little courtroom experience?

The answer was *HE* wouldn't.

Just as Michael was about to approach the court clerk again to ask that the arraignment be postponed until the 18b lawyer got there, into the courtroom walked Monroe Wilkins, one of Brooklyn's most experienced and talented trial attorneys.

Wilkins approached the court clerk's desk, apologized for his lateness and announced that he had been hired to represent Ricky Sabar and was ready to proceed with the arraignment.

Michael and Wilkins had battled in the courtroom not that long ago.

Wilson Knox was used by Satan to viciously stab and murder Susan Hayes, the wife of New York City police officer Brian Hayes. The police officer worked in the same precinct where a drunken police sergeant, behind the wheel of his car, had killed a pregnant woman, her unborn baby, and her young son. He also injured several young children, the woman was walking to school.

The *Evil One* saw to it that the sergeant, who had a drinking problem, had drank all night in a strip club, seduced and encouraged to do so by one of the strippers, another of Satan's pawns. Her seduction was designed to ensure that the sergeant was as drunk as possible when he got into his car. The resultant deaths were all designed to elicit the outrage, unrest, and chaos that followed.

In addition, when the sergeant was not arrested and charged with causing the deaths because the *Evil One* had interfered with the investigation and manipulated the evidence against him, anti-police demonstrations and rioting broke out in front of the precinct station house where Brian Hayes worked.

Then, to make it appear as an act of revenge for the preferential treatment afforded the sergeant, Satan manipulated one of *HIS* patsies, Wilson Knox, into viciously murdering Hayes' wife Susan.

As *HE* had counted on, this murder and the subsequent arrest of Wilson Knox, who his neighbors claimed was only a handyman, not a murderer, set off demonstrations and rioting in the neighborhood where the Hayes' lived.

Much to Satan's delight, the unrest involved both the supporters of the Hayes' family, as well as anti-police demonstrators. To quell the rioting and restore peace, the police in that part of Brooklyn called for reinforcements from all over the city.

The Devil got exactly what *HE* wanted: anarchy, lawlessness, and turmoil. And Wilson Knox was left to answer for the horrific murder of an innocent. Fortunately for him, his sister worked for an attorney who had the talent, experience and smarts to see that he would not only receive a fair trial but would have a great shot at walking out of the courtroom with a not guilty verdict. That attorney was Monroe Wilkins.

Wilkins nearly pulled off a miracle, but a last-minute maneuver by Michael allowed him to 'snatch victory from the jaws of defeat,' as an old colleague from his early days in the DA's office would say when he'd win a particularly difficult case. Wilson Knox was convicted and sentenced to life in prison.

So, when Michael saw Monroe Wilkins walk into court that morning, he was certain that Wilkins hadn't forgotten the Knox case and would surely be looking to even the score.

CHAPTER
THIRTY-EIGHT

Sabar's arraignment was for the most part uneventful.

After entering a plea of not guilty for his client, Wilkins argued that Sabar, who he claimed had roots in the Brooklyn community, should be released on minimal bail. The presiding judge, who had all she could do to keep from laughing because of the absurdity of the request, ordered that Sabar be remanded to the custody of the city department of corrections with no bail. He would therefore remain in the Brooklyn House of Detention until trial.

At the conclusion of the court hearing, Michael expected that he and Wilkins would talk so he could give the attorney a run down on when he would proceed with the next step in the process, the presentation of the evidence against Sabar to a grand jury. But to Michael's surprise, when the judge asked that he and Wilkins clear out of the well of the courtroom so she could call her next case, Wilkins simply turned and walked out.

'I guess he hasn't forgotten the Knox case,' Michael said to himself as he followed behind Wilkins. *'This is going to be quite a ride,'* he thought.

Over the following two days, Michael presented the evidence to a grand jury. And as expected, they returned an indictment against Sabar, charging him with murder, rape and sodomy. The case was assigned to Brooklyn Supreme Court Judge Camille Giordano for hearings and trial.

Three weeks later, at the first appearance before Judge Giordano, Sabar was arraigned on the indictment. Wilkins again entered a not guilty plea for his client after which the judge ordered Sabar held with no bail and set the case down for a preliminary discussion in her courtroom two weeks hence.

The easy part completed, Michael now had to put a case together that would convince a jury of twelve that Sabar was guilty beyond a reasonable doubt of the murder, rape, and sodomy of Linda Torre. But the more he studied the evidence the more he realized that as it was presently constructed, the case was weak.

He had Christine Miller. Although a licensed psychologist, she had left that profession behind and went to live in an abandoned concession stand on the Coney Island boardwalk. His other witnesses were Jade Liu, a Coney Island prostitute who turned tricks under the boardwalk and was among the missing at that moment, and Jimmy Pope, a low life who was a good buddy of Sabar. Not exactly the kind of witnesses that a jury would put its full faith in to convict a man of murder. And only if both women and Pope held up under the expected attack of Monroe Wilkins, was the case even winnable?

That wasn't good enough for Michael. He had to find a way to bolster the testimony of Miller and Liu that would make it difficult, if not impossible, for Wilkins to walk his client out of court a free man.

It was then that he remembered something that Armin Bondor told him when they first talked about the case which could be his trump card. He called him.

"Armin, it's Gioca. We need to talk."

Armin sensing concern in Michael's voice, asked, "Michael, is everything okay? You sound like something's wrong."

"Actually, things aren't okay. With the witnesses we have this is a shitty case. However if things break a certain way we'll be okay. And that's where you come in. Tell me what you know about the fluid found in and around Linda's private parts."

Bondor described it and because of where on Linda's body the fluid was seen, he said he and the crime scene detective, who had collected a sample of it, believed it to be semen. He also said that when the medical examiner's technician arrived he collected the remainder of it, and it went to the ME's office with the body, where it would be tested.

"Armin, have you gotten any results yet?" Michael asked anxiously.

"No. Mike what's going on?"

"Armin, there's a way to make the case against Sabar stronger, but I need to know what that fluid actually is. If it turns out to be semen I'll ask the lab to test it for DNA. If they find DNA material present I'll then get a court order to take a DNA sample from Sabar and have the lab compare it to what they found in the semen. If there is a match we've got the bastard."

"I'll call the ME. Will you be in your office?"

"Yes. Call me as soon as you have an answer."

Although it seemed like hours, thirty minutes later Bondor was on the phone with Michael. "The ME says that the fluid is definitely semen. Do you want me to ask them to test for DNA?"

When he heard Bondor's news Michael could barely hold in his excitement. "Armin, that's great news. Yes, ask the ME to do the test and have them call me as soon as they have results. Until then there's nothing more to worry about. I'll get back to you when I need you."

"By the way, have you had any luck finding Jade?"

"Mike, no luck so far."

"I hope no one has gotten to her," Michael said.

"I've got detectives looking for her, and every patrol cop has her picture. If they spot her, their instructions are to grab her and bring her into the station house. When that happens you'll be my first call."

With the *Evil One* as his adversary, Michael was always concerned when a potential witness could not be found. But he remained hopeful that Jade would turn up.

But right now, anticipating that the lab would find DNA present in the semen, he decided to write a motion in which he would ask Judge Giordano to order Sabar to provide a DNA sample so it could be tested against the semen found on and in Linda. Michael believed there would be a match, but beliefs don't constitute evidence.

Three days later Michael made a successful argument to Judge Giordano without much debate from Wilkins.

And although the hearing went well, when Michael left the courtroom he had a nagging feeling that he couldn't shake. *'That was too easy,'* he thought. *'Why did Wilkins only offer token resistance?',* was the question he asked himself as he walked to the courthouse elevator.

But he couldn't dwell on it because he had things to do. First he had to arrange for Sabar to be brought from the Brooklyn House of Detention, where he was being held, to his office the next morning. Then he had to notify Bondor to be there as well to swab Sabar's mouth for a DNA sample.

Reaching Bondor was easy. However, dealing with the New York City Department of Corrections and arranging for two correction officers to transport Sabar to his office took most of the remainder of Michael's day.

By 10 a.m. the next morning Sabar's DNA sample was taken and on its way to the medical examiner's office for comparison to the DNA in the semen recovered from the body of Linda Torre. All Michael could do now was wait.

A week later he got the answer to the question he had asked himself about Monroe Wilkins' token resistance to his request to collect a sample of Sabar's DNA. When it was compared to the DNA in the semen found at the scene of the murder, it was not a match!

His attempt to make the case stronger had backfired. He outsmarted himself and in doing so had given the defense a strong argument for why a jury should find Sabar not guilty of Linda's murder.

"Damn it! Wilkins knew that would be the result all along," Michael shouted in his empty office as he slammed his hand down on his desk. "This is the second time that SOB has gotten lucky with DNA."

Michael thinking about the Wilson Knox case. In that case when the victim Susan Hayes' dead body was found in the foyer of her home, a bloody handprint was recovered from the wall above where she was laying. When Knox was taken into custody the police printed his hands and quickly determined that the bloody print belonged to him.

To add extra impact to that discovery, Michael went one step further. He applied for and had gotten a court order to take a sample of Knox' blood so his DNA could be extracted from it and compared to the DNA in the blood on the wall. What he hoped to find was Knox' DNA mixed in with the blood of the deceased, thereby making a strong case against him as the murderer, even more compelling.

The test results showed that the blood in the handprint on the wall was indeed that of Susan Hayes. And there *was* another strand of DNA mixed in with hers, however, it didn't belong to Knox. It was the DNA of an unknown individual.

So, in an attempt to strengthen his case, Michael instead gift wrapped to Wilkins a very strong argument that someone other than his client murdered Susan Hayes.

Undeterred, Michael met with a DNA specialist from the medical examiner's office to discuss the situation and hopefully arrive at an explanation or an answer to the problem he created.

As it turned out after learning everything he could about the crime scene and everyone who had been at the scene when the murder occurred, the specialist came up with a potential solution to Michael's problem.

It would require, however, that blood be taken from the young daughter of the deceased who was present when her mother was murdered. She was a two-year-old who, at the time of the murder, had a cold and runny nose and despite her age, was still attached to her baby pacifier.

When Knox was arrested a baby's pacifier was found in his pants pocket.

The DNA specialist opined that if the pacifier found on Knox belonged to the young girl, it is likely that mucus from her runny nose was on it. Mucus contains DNA. So when Knox took it from her that mucus and its DNA would transfer to his hand. Then when he touched the wall leaving the bloody print he suspected that the girl's DNA would also be on the wall.

To test his theory the girl's blood would have to be analyzed to determine if the unknown DNA in the bloody print belonged to her.

A sample of the young girl's blood was taken, and much to Michael's relief and to Wilkin's dismay, the result of the test was that the unknown DNA in the bloody print was her's.

To put the final piece of the specialist's theory in place, Michael showed the pacifier, which had been recovered from Knox, to the girl's father. He identified it without hesitation.

Knox was found guilty of the murder and Wilkins had lost a case that he was convinced he would win when the unknown DNA was discovered in his client's bloody handprint. A print that otherwise would have sealed his fate.

Now more than a year later Michael was back in the same spot he had been in during the Knox case with Wilkins and DNA that did not match his client. Only this time the medical examiner's DNA specialist would be of no help. This was not a case of a mixture of DNA in the semen found on Linda Torre's body, it all belonged to one individual, who was not Sabar. Michael could not rely on science to help him out of this situation.

But like the last time, he was determined to find a solution to his problem. *'I'll find a way to get past this,'* he vowed to himself as he sat at his desk.

THIRTY-NINE

After thinking about his problem for the next few hours, Michael became frustrated with his inability to come up with a way to solve it. With his stomach growling because he hadn't eaten all day, he decided to take a break and eat something. That's when he thought his friend the monsignor could be the path to a possible solution, as he had been many times before.

'He's probably angry with me because I've neglected him, but he won't stay angry for long once I explain how the case has completely dominated my time,' Michael thought to himself as he placed the call.

"Sal, it's me," Michael said when Monsignor Romano answered.

Although the monsignor was not an attorney, Michael had used him as a sounding board and leaned on him for advice for all sorts of problems and issues that he had encountered in his battle with the *Evil One*. Romano was a good listener and his practical advice had proven to be just what Michael needed.

"Michael is that you?" the monsignor joked. "It's been so long I didn't recognize your voice. I was just about to ask Caldwell to file a missing person's report with the NYPD. I thought that maybe those red bees had gotten you again and taken your phone after the attack."

"Very funny. Can we meet at *Emilio's* at six? I really do need to talk. And because you're breaking my balls after I've worked so hard on this case for the last few weeks, dinner is on you... and so is the *Brunello.*"

When Michael walked into *Emilio's* at six on the dot, he saw the monsignor sitting at his favorite table in conversation with Emilio. The restaurateur was holding a bottle of *Brunello di Montalcino* which he was preparing to open as Michael approached.

"Signore Gioca, *come stai?*"

"I'm well Emilio, thanks for asking.'

"Unlike my friend here," Michael said pointing to Romano, "You had no trouble recognizing and remembering me. Perhaps a glass of that expensive wine will help his memory."

Of course Emilio had no idea that Michael was joking, so not wanting to get between two friends, he kept silent as he opened the wine, poured two glasses, gave a little bow and left the table.

Romano couldn't hold in the laughter as he held up his glass and toasted his friend with, "*Salute*, whoever you are."

Michael, however, was not laughing as he took his first sip of the hearty red wine.

The monsignor noticed his friend's mood, and asked, "What's wrong? Is everything okay with your family?"

"Yes. Everyone is fine," Michael answered.

"It's good to see you," he continued. "I know it's only been weeks, but it seems like months ago that we talked in your office when I got back from AC, because so much has happened."

"For however long it's been, Caldwell has asked me for updates every day. Now stop deflecting and tell me what's going on, and what you need to talk about."

Over dinner, for the next two hours, Michael filled in Romano on every aspect of the case against Ricky Sabar, including who was with him, and how he was dressed when he turned himself in to the police.

"Do you believe that?," Michael said. "*HE* was mocking us. *HE* knew it would get back to us."

To complete the picture, Michael told the monsignor what he knew about the backgrounds of Linda Torre, Christine Miller, Jimmy Pope, and Jade Liu.

Romano listened intently and to every question he asked, Michael enthusiastically provided an answer. However, when he got to the semen testing and his request for a comparison to Sabar's DNA, Romano noticed a subtle change in Michael's manner as he described what had happened.

"That is what you wanted to talk to me about, isn't it?" Romano asked.

"Yes Sal, it is."

"It's Wilkins again," Michael said, clearly irritated with his opponent.

"I'm sure you remember the Hayes case and the issue with the DNA in the bloody handprint on the wall." When Romano indicated that he did remember, Michael continued, "Back then I had the DNA specialist who came up with the solution that saved the day. This is different. No specialist or scientist is going to be able to provide a theory that explains away the obvious, how semen belonging to someone other than Sabar found its way onto and into Linda Torre."

"And Sal, based on what Jimmy Pope, Christine, and Jade told me, Sabar is the killer. I know it in my head, in my gut, and in my heart."

Thoroughly frustrated, Michael finished with, "How did this happen, *again*?.... I don't know what to do."

Romano took a sip of his espresso before he answered.

"Michael, the question is not 'How did this happen?' It's 'Who caused it to happen?' Have you forgotten who your real adversary is? It's not Monroe Wilkins... It's Satan."

"I can tell you what I do when faced with a situation where

answers seem impossible to come by. I go back to the beginning and run through everything that's happened and everyone I've spoken to. Nothing is too small or insignificant to be re-examined," Romano said.

"You should try it because when I've done it, I have either found the solution, or a path that has led me to it."

"And I have one more suggestion," said the monsignor. "Given that the *Evil One* is most likely the root of the problem here, it wouldn't hurt for you to take a minute to ask your number one ally in this fight for some help in a prayer."

Michael laid in bed that night and went over in his mind everything that Romano said. Taking the monsignor's advice, he went back to the beginning and thought about what he knew and how he came to know it.

He couldn't sleep so he grabbed the investigation file from his small desk and started to re-read the police reports of every witness in the case.

Jimmy Pope and Christine Miller both provided valuable information putting Sabar and Linda together: Pope on the night of her murder, and Christine the next day when she saw him coming from Linda's side of the concession stand with a bloody shirt. But neither had provided any insight into the mystery of the unidentified semen.

Around 4 a.m. Michael finally completed his review of the police reports. He found nothing to help him. Then he remembered something that he hoped might lead him to the solution to his problem, Jade Liu.

When the police conducted the line-up from which Pope and Christine had identified Sabar, Jade was not there. Michael had asked Bondor about her. Bondor told him that she hadn't been seen for a few days, but he had detectives and patrol officers looking for her.

It was what Bondor said next that gave Michael the glimmer of hope that he might be onto something that could help with his problem. "Don't worry Mike, we'll find her. I definitely want to speak to her again because I got the feeling *that she didn't tell me everything.*"

At 6 a.m. instead of staying in bed Michael, an insomniac now, was out running the streets of his neighborhood which gave him a lot of time to think about what Jade could give him. Never in his wildest dreams did he consider that what she would ultimately tell him would solve the mystery of the unknown semen found on Linda.

At 8 a.m. Michael called Bondor from his desk. "Armin, I know it's early, but I need you to find Jade. I have a hunch that she can help me solve the problem of the unknown semen. I don't know what time of day your guys had been looking for her, but do me a favor, hit her apartment around six tonight. She has to get dressed and ready to hit the streets sometime. Maybe we'll get lucky."

Bondor agreed but was skeptical about her being there. "Mike, don't be disappointed when we come up empty," he said.

When he hung up with Bondor Michael took Romano's advice and said a silent prayer to his ally.

It was around 7:30 that night when Bondor and Tommy Raines walked into Michael's office with Jade Liu dressed for work.

CHAPTER
FORTY

I t was a very pissed off Jade Liu that just stared at Michael who introduced himself and asked if she wanted anything to eat or drink.

"Who the fuck are you and what the fuck am I doing here?" was her response.

"Ms. Liu, my name is Michael Gioca and I'm an assistant district attorney here in Brooklyn. I'm in charge of the case involving Ricky Sabar. As you may know he was charged with the murder of Linda Torre, the lady who lived in the concession stand on the Coney Island boardwalk."

"And you're here because I want to follow-up on what you told Sgt. Bondor about that. I'm sorry to keep you from your job, but I promise I won't be long, and we'll get you back to Coney Island with plenty of the night left for you to work."

Surprisingly Jade began to smile. "What's so funny?"Michael asked.

"My job. My work. When you say what I do in those words it don't seem so bad. I like how that sounds."

"I'm starting to like you," she said. "What was your name again?"

"Gioca, but you can just call me Mike or Michael."

"I bet your mother called you Michael. Am I right?"

Now Michael smiled and said, "Yes she did."

"Okay, *Michael*, what do you want to know?"

He asked her to tell him everything that she knew about Sabar and the murder of the 'lady who lived in the concession stand,' as she had referred to her.

Jade began by repeating everything she told Bondor. When she finished she looked over to where Bondor was sitting and dropped her head. When Michael asked her if anything was wrong, in barely a whisper she answered "Yes. I didn't tell Sgt. Bondor everything I know."

To put her at ease, Michael told her that it was okay. "Just tell us now what you left out."

Jade picked up her story. "The morning after seeing Sabar walking with the lady I was on the boardwalk and I seen Sabar again, only this time he was alone."

"It was sometime between 9:30 and 10:00. He was running from the direction of the place where the lady lived wearing only a white t-shirt that had blood on it. He didn't have on the sweater or jacket I seen him wearing the night before," adding, "He also had blood on his hands and face."

"When he ran past me he slowed down and said, "You didn't see me-you didn't see me.""

"At the time I didn't think anything of it because I hadn't heard yet about the lady. But when I heard she had been killed, and *when* and *where* she was killed, I figured that Sabar done it."

Michael then showed her photos of the sweater and jacket that were recovered from the concession stand. Without being asked a question Jade identified them as those Sabar was wearing the night she saw him walking with Linda.

Thinking she had finished and disappointed that she hadn't

given him anything to help with the semen problem, Michael started to thank her. That's when Jade stopped him, saying, "Michael, there's more."

'Maybe this is where she gives me what I need,' he thought to himself.

But instead, she finished by telling Michael, "Later that day I went to score some dope from Sabar's brother who lives in an apartment building off the boardwalk. When I go into the apartment, who do I see but Sabar, now all cleaned up."

"Did he say anything to you?" Michael asked.

"Oh yeah! That prick threatened me. He said again, 'you ain't seen me this morning. If you say anything you gonna get it like she got.'"

Sabar had confessed to her!

Michael was thrilled but still frustrated with having gotten nothing from her that helped with the semen issue. The disappointment was all over his face. Jade noticed it and immediately got defensive.

"What? You don't believe me? I ain't lying to you," she said, raising her voice. "I know that Sabar raped and killed that lady."

Overreacting to Jade's acrimonious comments, Michael raised his voice and leaned across his desk toward where Jade was sitting and said, "Well if you're so sure he did it how do you explain that the semen on the body was not Sabar's?"

To his surprise Jade answered, "That's easy. I know how he does it."

Michael, excited at the prospect of finding an answer to his mystery, was nonetheless skeptical.

"Okay you've got my attention. How does he do it?'"

"He buys used condoms."

"What!" was Michael's stunned reaction. "Tell me more."

"Sabar is a really bad guy. He thinks us working girls are his for the taking. When Sabar rapes one of us, he always wears a condom. After he finishes he breaks open one of the used condoms he's bought and spreads it all over the girl. This way if she goes to the cops and says that Sabar had raped her, any semen they recover from her won't be his. He told me he got the idea from that piece of shit, his new friend Jiz."

"Jade, how do you know this," Michael asked in disbelief.

"How do I know this? I sell him used condoms!"

"After I blow a john, I take the condom off him and pretend to throw it away. Instead, I tie a knot at the top and slip it into my pocket. Sabar pays me $5.00 for them. He trusts me to keep my mouth shut, and I can make extra cash."

"And I know what he does with them because I seen him rape one of my friends under the boardwalk, and when he was finished he broke open one of them old condoms that I sold to him and spread the shit all over her. I was so pissed that he would do that to one of my girls, I wanted to fuck him up. But he knew I couldn't go to the cops."

Michael just sat at his desk in silence. He now had an answer to the semen found on Linda, but would a jury believe someone like Jade. *I don't know if I believe her,'* he thought to himself.

Jade must have read his mind. "Listen Michael, if you don't believe my story there's someone you can speak to who'll tell you I'm being straight with you."

"One night I'm walking the boardwalk doing my thing," Jade said, "And this Russian guy comes up to me. Before he says anything, I say it's twenty for a blow job and fifty if he wants to fuck. He starts to laugh and says he's not there for any of that. He tells me that Sabar told him about me. That I sell used condoms which he was interested in buying."

"Was this another rapist looking to avoid getting arrested?" Michael asked.

"No. If he was I would have told him to get the fuck out of my face. Me and my girls got enough problems we don't need no more guys fucking us and not paying."

Jade continued, "He tells me that he works over in Manhattan at an underground sex show and to make the sex look real to the pervs who go watch that shit, they want semen dripping off the woman performer's body when the man finishes. My condoms were perfect for what they was looking for. And if there was trouble the cops wouldn't be able to trace the semen to any of their performers. This was great for me because the Russian was paying me double what Sabar was paying."

Bondor asked, "How do we find this Russian?"

Jade told them what she knew, which was a description and his name, Luka. She said that she didn't have his phone number."

"So how do you do your business with him?" Michael asked.

"When I have condoms to sell, I leave word for him in a coffee shop off the boardwalk not far from the Cyclone. The place is owned by one of his relatives and the guy who answers the phone knows my voice. I call and say that I have Luka's product and when he should meet me."

"We meet at the handball courts just off the boardwalk," she continued. "I'm pretending to watch the games, but I'm dressed for work. He comes up next to me and we start talking. We then walk away as if we're going to fuck, and when we get under the boardwalk he pays me for the condoms."

Michael had no choice. He had to check out what Jade told him. If it was true, he scored big time on finding the answer to the problem of explaining away the semen from Linda's body that wasn't Sabar's.

He had Jade make a call to the coffee shop from a secure phone. She left the usual message for Luka, setting a meet for 2 p.m. the next day. He went over with her a plan to grab Luka which would not put her in jeopardy.

The next day, as scheduled, Jade stood just inside the fence surrounding the handball courts and pretended to be very interested in a game between a guy in his early 70's and a kid in his teens. The old guy was whipping the young guy's ass when Luka approached her with a comment about the match. They talked for a few minutes and then, as usual, walked under the boardwalk.

When they got to the spot where they usually exchanged money for condoms, Luka took money out of his jacket pocket and handed it to Jade. Before she could reach into her bag to grab her condoms, several of Bondor's detectives dressed in jeans and hoodies announced that they were under arrest for prostitution and for patronizing a prostitute.

They were driven to the station house in separate cars and were kept apart when they arrived.

Luka was brought into one of the interrogation rooms in the detective squad area, where Michael and Bondor were waiting for him. After he had his handcuffs removed they told him to sit. They asked Luka if he wanted something to drink or eat. When he refused they got started.

"Luka, my name is Michael Gioca and I'm an assistant district attorney. This is Sgt. Armin Bondor. I know you were told by the detectives who brought you in that you were under arrest, let me assure you that you are not. We did what we did, and the way we did it, for your protection. We want to talk to you, and we wanted it to appear as if you had no choice in going with the detectives. There are lots of eyes out there and we don't want you branded a rat."

Luka said nothing as Michael continued. "We're interested in learning about the condoms we know that you buy from Jade Liu who was brought in with you. We know she's a working girl and she'll be answering to a judge tonight in Criminal Court. We want to know how you came to do business with her. Talk to us and you'll be out of here and on the way home within the hour."

For the first time since he was brought in it appeared to Michael that Luka began to relax. He asked for some water and said that he would tell them what they wanted to know.

Luka began by admitting that he did buy used condoms from Jade.

He said that a guy who he knew for a few years told him about Jade and that he was buying used condoms from her.

"The guy, Sabar, is always looking to fuck the prostitutes around here, but he never pays them. So to protect himself from one or more of them claiming he raped them, he spreads the semen from the used condoms on them to throw off the cops."

"Sabar said he got this idea from a friend of his, this guy Jiz."

"Why did Sabar tell you about Jade?" Bondor asked.

"He told me because he knows that I work at a sex show in Manhattan and figured I might be interested in buying them as well, which I was. But he wasn't helping me free of cost. He is a complete pervert and wanted me to get him in to see the shows without having to pay."

"So I checked out Jade and have been buying from her ever since."

"Did Sabar get what he wanted from you?" Michael asked.

"Yeah he did. And a few times he even brought along that guy Jiz. They're fucking pigs."

Michael thanked Luka. But before he told him he could leave he secured Luka's assurance that if Michael needed him to testify at trial he would be there. He also had Bondor get Luka's contact information.

"You're free to go Luka," Michael told him, "But please don't make it difficult for us to find you when we need you." He agreed and quickly left the room and the station house.

Bondor started to laugh as Luka scrambled out, "He's probably thinking back to the old country where they wouldn't have treated him so well. Ah! America is a great country!"

When they were finished with Luka Michael asked that Jade be brought into the room. "You were right on the money," Michael said. "Luka confirmed everything you told us. And he has no idea you were the source of our information."

"I told you I wasn't lying. Sabar is a real bad guy and I hope you get his ass. But Michael, I got to tell you that from what I've seen all summer, his friend Jiz is worse. If there is any way to put his ass in jail too, please do it. Life will be very peaceful for us girls if you do that."

Michael thanked her and told her that he planned on convicting Sabar with her help. As for Jiz, Michael said nothing. Putting the *Evil One* in a cage was impossible. *'The only way to get HIM is to make sure HIS boy Sabar goes down,"|'* he thought to himself.

"Sgt. Bondor will have one of his people take you home, or anywhere else in Coney Island. You're dressed for work, so I guess that's what you're going to do. "I'm going to need you at Sabar's trial, so please be careful. I'll be in touch, and you know how to reach me if you need anything."

Jade nodded to indicate that she understood Michael and then broke out into a big smile. As she got up from her chair she said "'Mr. G', you're truly a gentleman. And I have something for you." With that she turned away from Michael, lifted her very short skirt and mooned him with her naked butt. "See you next time," she said as a detective walked her out of the room.

Michael looked over at Bondor and the two cracked up laughing.

When Michael left Bondor's office he was feeling much better about his chances of putting Sabar away for the rest of his life. He thought of Linda's sister Antoinette and their parents, and how much that would mean to them. It wouldn't bring back Linda or her baby, but based on past experience he knew how important closure was to the loved ones of murder victims.

As he walked to his car with those thoughts whirling around in his head, someone else with a stake in the outcome of the trial came to mind. Kathy Baer.

A murder conviction for the guy responsible for Kathy's horrific injuries and her friend Alex Gazis' death, Michael knew would please her and her family. He hoped that when justice was done Kathy's mood and her outlook on life would brighten and maybe he'd be able to spend more time with her.

To accomplish that, Michael knew he had a lot of work ahead of him, especially with his two main witnesses, Christine Miller and Jade Liu. They were street people and therefore were inherently unreliable in keeping appointments. And with an adversary who in the past had stopped at nothing to undermine the evidence against *HIS* pawn and had made important witnesses disappear, keeping tabs on them would be essential.

CHAPTER

FORTY-ONE

With the trial date that had been set by Judge Giordano fast approaching, Michael began his witness preparation with Christine Miller.

Despite her lifestyle and her mental breakdown because of the tragedy suffered by one of her clients from the woman's shelter, Christine was an articulate, educated woman, and a licensed, practicing, psychologist. And she cared deeply for Linda Torre.

Christine proved to be the model witness for Michael. She was eager to help, had a great memory, and although late for all of her trial prep appointments, she never missed one.

From the time she identified Sabar in a line up, Christine was living at her friend Clara Gordon's apartment for her own safety. However, when they had finished their final prep session and Michael told her that a detective would pick her up when she was needed for trial, Christine informed him that she had left her friend's place and resumed living in the abandoned concession stand.

"I needed my privacy, and I was not getting it at Clara's. Besides, that place on the boardwalk is my home," she said.

Michael was not happy with her decision but there was nothing he could do other than counsel her to be careful and to reach out to him if there was a problem.

"Christine, it will be getting very cold soon, so you might change your mind about staying in the concession stand and move. If you do, please make sure that you tell me where you wind up." Michael said.

She assured him that she would stay in touch.

As for Jade Liu, she became Michael's 'friend,' as his colleagues had come to call her. She had also endeared herself to some of his Rackets Division staff. In fact one female ADA, who was about the same size as Jade, felt sorry for her because of the tough life she endured on the street, and began giving her clothes that the ADA no longer wore. And when the trial got close to its start date, that same ADA took Jade to shop for clothes appropriate for her appearance on the witness stand.

From early in her prep sessions Jade was enthusiastic and extremely cooperative. She never missed a session and unlike Christine Miller, Jade was always on time.

She was street smart, which Michael knew would enhance her testimony, and she was extremely intelligent.

Jade quickly demonstrated to Michael that she would be able to handle herself on the witness stand when he questioned her, and was under cross-examination.

One morning early in the process of preparing her, Jade arrived at the DA's office before Michael. As she sat waiting for him near the security desk on Michael's floor, ADA's and support staff passed her on the way to their offices. Jade was surprised when a guy she knew emerged from one of the elevators. He said hello to the security officer and disappeared into the interior of the DA's office.

When Michael arrived shortly thereafter he brought Jade to his office so they could begin their prep session. When she took off her jacket, Michael saw that she was shaking. When he sat her down and asked what was wrong, she told him about spotting the person she knew and that he had gone into the office where she assumed he worked.

"How do you know him?" Michael asked.

Now shaking even more than when she first sat down, Jade answered, "I know him because he's one of my johns! He's a trick!"

She described the guy, whose name she didn't know. "I call him 'Caddy', because he drives a Cadillac convertible." When he heard the description, Michael knew who she was talking about.

Although he had not been reporting to Marty Price since he began working for Caldwell and Romano, Michael knew that he had to tell the District Attorney about Jade's customer. Price was thankful that Michael had told him.

"Mike, can you please handle this for me?" Price asked him. "No one knows about you working for the feds, so you still have the air of authority around here." Michael told Price that he would.

"Make sure that he knows that whatever he's doing with her has to stop," Price said as Michael headed out of his office.

He went back and asked Jade to wait in a conference room down the hall. "There's something I have to take care of. When I'm done I'll come get you," he told her.

Jade's customer was an assistant district attorney who was working in the office for about a year. Michael knew who he was when Jade described him because he was assigned to a bureau that had its offices adjacent to the Rackets Division.

When Michael called him into his office the guy was shaking worse than Jade had earlier.

Although It was clear that he knew why he was there, Michael nonetheless asked, "Do you know why you're here?"

"Mr. Gioca, I have a good idea," he answered. Obviously he had seen Jade sitting by the security desk when he arrived for work.

"Whatever you have done with her is your business. But it stops today. Am I clear?"

The guy stammered and stumbled with his words telling Michael that he was a lonely guy who often cruised Coney Island. He said that when he saw Jade he struck up a conversation with her, but that was it. He only wanted to spend time with her to talk.

"I pay her for her time, but we have never had sex," he said. "After a while we became friends, and I took her for rides in my convertible and sometimes I even brought her flowers. She's a nice woman and I like spending time with her. I know what she does for a living, but our relationship is purely platonic."

Michael listened and struggled to keep from laughing. There was no reason for Jade to have lied to him about the ADA being one of her johns. There were, however, plenty of reasons for him to lie.

When finished with his story, Michael told the guy that whatever the relationship was, he had to stop seeing her.

"The DA knows all about this. If he finds out that you haven't, you'll lose your job."

Near tears, the ADA told Michael that he understood, and that the relationship was over.

When the guy left his office, Michael shook his head and said to himself, *'Only in Brooklyn....'*

Michael's remaining prep sessions with Jade had gone well.

One day close to the start of the trial, Jade surprised him with some news. She told Michael that she had met a guy and that they had been seeing each other for some time. He was not one of her johns. He was a guy who worked in a real estate office in Brighton Beach. They had met while both were shopping in a local supermarket. They had struck up a conversation, she said, and he asked her out to dinner. Shortly thereafter they started dating.

"Michael, it was love at first sight," an excited and animated Jade told him.

Michael asked her if the guy knew what she did for a living.

"Yes," she answered. "I liked him so much that before we went on our first date I told him." She added that she had also told him that she wanted out of the street life.

Apparently he liked her as much as she liked him. He told her that her honesty was refreshing and promised to help and support her decision to get out of the prostitution racket.

"'Mr. G', I'm out of the game. He loves me and I love him. We're always together. I even moved into his apartment."

Then she dropped the bombshell. "And I'm pregnant!"

When they finished the prep session and Jade left his office, Michael thought about her news. He admitted to himself that he was both shocked and pleased. He had come to like Jade and hoped that one day she would follow through on her desire to quit the streets and get her life together. *'She seems to be in a good place,'* he thought, *'And that's going to make her an even better witness.'*

CHAPTER
FORTY-TWO

The start of the trial was a week away and Michael had not heard from Christine Miller since she was in for her last prep session several weeks before.

Although erratic about showing up on time for their meetings, she had always made it to his office.

Michael asked Armin Bondor to send his detectives out to look for her, and if they found her they were instructed to bring her to him.

Each time Bondor's people went out, they said that the street people told them she was around Coney Island, but they had no luck in finding her.

With jury selection now two days away, a worried and frustrated Michael called Monsignor Romano. He wanted Dina Mitchell and Tim Clark to help him find Christine Miller. Because they were employed by the District Attorney and were not part of Caldwell's federal group, Michael needed the DA's permission to use them.

He explained it all to Romano who told him that he would have Caldwell call the District Attorney right away. Ten minutes later

Michael had the DA's permission. He called Dina and Tim to his office.

Michael had great trust and confidence in them, having used the investigators to locate witnesses in past cases where the *Evil One* was involved. They always came through. *'I really need them now,'* he thought to himself while he waited for their arrival.

When they got to his office Michael filled them in on the case, including the DNA problem with the semen, and explained what he needed.

"Guys, I'm running out of time and Christine Miller is crucial to my case. She saw Sabar leaving the concession stand, with blood on his shirt, seconds before she found Linda's body. She is one of only two witnesses who put Sabar at or near the crime scene. With the DNA problem I have, putting him there is critical to convicting him. We must find Christine. And when we do I'll put her into a custody and have her guarded until I need her to testify."

Wasting no time, Michael, Dina, and Tim set out for Coney Island on a chilly and windy afternoon, to look for, and hopefully find, Christine Miller.

They hit the boardwalk first because that was the last place Bondor's people were told she was seen. They started at the abandoned concession stand.

Although it appeared that she had been living there, with women's clothes strewn about and the remnants of food and empty take-out containers covering a small table, no one was home.

Michael stepped outside into the daylight to write her a note on the back of one of his business cards. He wanted Christine to know that he was there and was looking for her. He made sure to say that she was not in any trouble. He simply wanted her to call him as soon as she saw the note.

When he went back in to leave the card, he saw some items he had not noticed when he had initially gone inside. He called Dina and Tim and pointed out several articles of men's clothing that were lying over a chair near the back of the concession stand.

Without prompting from Michael, Tim photographed the items with his phone, while Dina made a note listing them, along with their color and size. "You never know when or if they'll become important," she said when they left the concession stand.

They started to walk the boardwalk stopping at the few concessions that were open on the brisk, blustery day. At each location, either Tim or Dina showed a photo of Christine to whomever had been working and to any customer who happened to be patronizing the concession.

They had no luck. No one had seen her.

They also talked and showed her photo to anyone who happened to be out and about on the boardwalk and on the adjacent streets . Their thinking was that Christine might have been spotted by one of them, or they may have spent the night with her in the concession stand, or in one of the many Coney Island flop houses.

Again no luck.

Everywhere they went, and to everyone to whom they had spoken, Michael left or handed out his business card along with a message: "I'm looking for Christine Miller. If you spot her, call the number on the card."

After searching for several more frustrating hours, with the wind having picked up and the temperature having dropped, Michael and the investigators decided to call it a day and head back to the DA's office.

On the way they stopped at the 60th precinct station house. Sgt. Bondor was not working, so Michael spoke to the desk officer and told him that he had been out looking for Christine Miller. He left her photo and his business card with the officer and asked him to pass the word to the cops on patrol that if Christine was spotted to please hold her for him.

Michael got a reluctant "Okay," but he had no confidence that his plea would result in good news.

When Michael, Dina, and Tim got back to his office, they ordered some food and hot coffee and began to plot a new strategy for finding Christine.

It was just before 10 p.m. when Michael's phone rang. The desk officer from the 60th precinct was calling. He told Michael that they had Christine in the station house.

Michael thanked him and said that he would have his investigators go out there to pick her up.

When Dina and Tim came back to his office with Christine, Michael asked Tim, "Where did the cops find her?"

His answer surprised Michael. "The cops didn't find her. Some civilian walked into the station house with Christine in tow, brought her to the desk officer and said, pointing to your business card, 'This guy wants her!' Luckily the desk officer remembered our earlier visit and knew exactly what was going on."

It was near midnight when, a now relieved Michael, asked Christine if she was hungry. She said she was starving, so he ordered some food and let her eat and relax.

An hour or so later, Michael sat with Christine and asked where she had been and why no one could find her.

"Ever since I moved out of Clara's place I feel as if I'm being stalked," she said. "I think people know I testified in the grand jury and know that I've been coming here to see you. I'm very frightened. So I've been moving around a lot."

"How did the guy who brought you into the station house find you if you've been hiding?" Michael asked.

"He didn't find me. We've been together for a few weeks. He's been at the concession stand to protect me. He's a good guy. Today, when he saw one of your cards with my name on it in Nathan's, we talked, and he gave me some advice. Then he brought me to the station house."

"I'm confused," Michael said. "Who is this guy? And how did you meet him?"

"He approached me one afternoon on the boardwalk a couple of weeks ago. He said he heard that I was afraid, and he offered to stay with me for my protection. Mr. Gioca, I was scared out of my mind of the stalker, and this guy was nice to me and seemed to care. So I took him up on his offer. We've been living together at my place. He has been good to me, and here I am."

"How did you know that he wasn't your stalker?" Michael asked. "He knew you were scared. How could he have known that if you had never met him before?"

"That's a good point. It never crossed my mind. But he has been too kind to me to be the stalker."

Everything about Christine's story troubled Michael. *'The fact that she testified in the grand jury is secret. Her testimony is secret. And how would anyone know that she had been here with me. I always had her take a car service which picked her up at some spot outside Coney Island,'* he thought.

Michael excused himself and asked Dina and Tim to step out of the office with him. "She's paranoid about this so-called stalker and not thinking straight. And this guy she says she has been living with bothers me. I'm on the eve of trial and she's crucial to my case. I need her at her best, so I've got to get her straightened out. Then I'll find out who this guy is."

"I think some time with us, living in a hotel with investigators guarding her, eating three meals a day, and having a shower at her disposal, will settle her down," Michael said.

"Can you two take the first shift tonight and I'll set it up going forward? If things move along in court the way I expect them to, the custody should last only for a few days."

Dina and Tim were only too happy to once again be working with Michael and agreed to take care of setting up the arrangements for the first night of protection for Christine.

Hotel living did the trick. After a few days Christine was calm and cooperative as Michael put the finishing touches on his preparation of her for trial.

When Michael left his office to head over to the courthouse the first day of trial, he was feeling guardedly confident. '*I feel good, but with the Evil One always lurking you never know. I can't get cocky,*' he thought.

With Christine, Jade, and Jimmy Pope's testimony, along with the physical evidence found at the murder scene, he had a decent case. However, it was not a slam dunk because of the semen problem. But with Jade's testimony about selling condoms to Sabar and seeing him actually employ one after raping her friend, and Luka the Russian ready to testify in rebuttal if the defense attacked her story, he felt good about his chances of winning. All his prep sessions had gone well. And his two crucial witnesses, Christine, and especially Jade, were ready for anything that the defense would throw at them.

FORTY-THREE

Judge Giordano made sure that jury selection moved along quickly and efficiently. By noon on the second day of trial, Michael and Monroe Wilkins had settled on twelve jurors and four alternates who would decide the fate of Ricky Sabar.

Opening statements were to begin after lunch.

During the break Michael called Linda's sister Antoinette, who was waiting for his call at a nearby coffee shop, and told her that the trial would begin at 2 p.m.

Although Antoinette wanted to be in the courtroom for jury selection, Michael told her that because the courtroom would be filled with prospective jurors there would be no room for her to sit, and standing in the back or along the sides of the room was not permitted. He assured her that he would notify her when opening statements began.

Throughout the investigation and then during the trial preparation, Antoinette had been very interested and helpful to the police and to Michael. She loved her sister and told him when Sabar was arrested and indicted, that she intended to be in court from day one of the trial.

When Michael walked into Judge Giordano's courtroom after the break, Antoinette was sitting in the second row of the spectator section right behind the prosecution table. She approached Michael and whispered "Good luck" into his ear, then gave him a hug. It was like a shot of adrenalin. The stomach butterflies that Michael felt before every trial of his career, magically disappeared. He was ready.

Opening statements from both sides took up the balance of the afternoon.

Michael spoke first and laid out his case with cool precision.

He started by telling the jurors about Linda and how she came to be living in, and then dying in, an abandoned concession stand on the Coney Island boardwalk.

He told them all about Ricky Sabar and how they would hear from witnesses that he was a vicious guy, emphasizing Sabar's penchant for raping prostitutes and treating women with disdain.

Michael described the horrific murder scene and the wounds that had been inflicted on the pregnant Linda Torre. He then told them about the substance that was found all over Linda's body, "Which we now know to be semen."

To soften the shock and lessen the surprise when they later heard the testimony, he told them that the semen belonged to an unknown person, "But you will hear evidence that explains it all," he added.

He told the jury that Linda and Sabar were spotted walking toward her concession stand home the night before her body was found. And that the next morning Sabar was seen coming out of Linda's side of it with blood on him and on his shirt, just before Linda's roommate found her dead body.

To finish strong Michael told them that they would hear from a witness who saw Sabar running from the scene of the crime that morning. She will tell you that when Sabar ran past, he said to her, 'You didn't see me, you didn't see me.'

You will hear that later the same day, in his brother's apartment, Sabar *confessed* to her that he murdered Linda Torre. And to make sure that the witness didn't go to the police, Michael said, "Sabar told her he would kill her if she didn't keep quiet."

Wilkins was next and there were no surprises in his opening statement. It was simple and powerful.

"My client didn't kill, rape, or sodomize Linda Torre!"

"The proof that he is innocent won't come from me," Wilkins said, "Or anything the defense does. It will come from the prosecution's own witnesses, as you just heard Mr. Gioca tell you a few minutes ago. They will testify that the semen, which they believe was left on the body of Linda Torre by her killer, did not belong to my client Ricky Sabar."

"And how did these experts arrive at that conclusion? They'll tell you they compared the DNA in that semen to a DNA sample, taken without objection, from my client. The result- NO MATCH!"

"Ladies and gentlemen, my client did not murder or sexually assault Linda Torre."

"Her killer is still out there."

The next day and for the remainder of the week, Michael built his case using technical witnesses to lay a foundation: detectives, emergency medical personnel, technicians from the NYPD Crime Scene Unit, and the medical examiner who performed the autopsy on Linda.

Even Antoinette Torre's testimony about identifying the body of her sister Linda at the city morgue was technical in nature. However, her heartbreaking and poignant description of Linda's tragic life and their fractured relationship, was not.

Through tears she described her sister's life as a Catholic nun. How Linda falling in love with a man from the parish where she was assigned, led her to leave the convent and religious life, only to be devastated when he abandoned her.

Antoinette told a rapt jury that her sister was never the same.

She described how Linda leaving home and finding her way to

living in an abandoned concession stand on the Coney Island board-walk devastated their family. She finished her testimony by telling the jury that when she and the family learned of Linda's murder, an unbelievable sadness had enveloped them, "A sadness my mother, father, and I will never shake."

When she was done, Michael looked over to the jurors. Most had tears in their eyes, and a few were outright sobbing.

Wilkins did the wise thing and had no questions for Antoinette. He knew he had to get her off the witness stand before she convicted his client with just the sympathy she elicited.

The last witness for the week was Jimmy Pope.

Michael wanted to send the jury home for the weekend with the image in their heads of Linda and Sabar walking together toward the concession stand where she had been living, on the night before her body was found.

Pope did a great job doing just that.

Wilkins tried to shake Pope and dirty him up, but he was largely unsuccessful in the attack on his credibility. Pope and Sabar were friends, so Wilkins had to tread lightly in painting Pope as a street hustler, and a piece of garbage.

At the end of the trial in his summation, Michael would refer to them as, "Birds of a feather...."

When Pope concluded his testimony, Judge Giordano adjourned the trial for the weekend. On Monday Michael's intention was to call Christine Miller to the witness stand. She was ready... or so he thought.

On Saturday evening Michael and Monsignor Romano met for dinner at seven at *Emilio's*. Michael hadn't spoken to the monsignor for over a week, and he knew that Caldwell was likely pressing him for information on the progress of the trial.

The two friends were enjoying a glass of *Nero d'Avola*, a Sicilian red, one of Michael's favorites, when his cell phone rang. It was Dina

Mitchell who was working that night guarding Christine at her hotel.

"Michael, I'm sorry to bother you," Dina began. "We have a problem."

Dina told him that unbeknownst to anyone, Christine had been taking what she said was blood pressure medicine and had run out of pills.

"I didn't know she had a condition," Michael said. "What's the problem?"

"Mike, she doesn't have high blood pressure. At least she doesn't now. She told me that she had been diagnosed with it when she first left her job at the women's shelter and had been prescribed meds to control it. She claims that they worked. She said she stopped taking the meds, but when she began prepping with you she became nervous, stressed, and started getting headaches."

"Instead of going to a doctor to get checked out," Dina continued, "The guy who was living with Christine and protecting her, told her he had a source who could get the pills she needed. He did, and she began to take them."

"When I asked her how the new pills made her feel, she told me that she felt great. She was stress free and felt no pain. Mike in my opinion those were not blood pressure pills. I think this guy has been supplying her with opioids."

'Shit, I knew there was something up with that guy,' Michael thought when Dina said that.

"Dina how did this all come to light?" Michael asked.

"About two hours ago she told me all about her so-called 'blood pressure' problem, and that she ran out of pills. Apparently she had a bunch of pills with her when we brought her to the hotel and she's been abusing them, taking them like candy behind our backs."

"She wanted me to get her a refill. I obviously couldn't do that. But I have a doctor friend at Lutheran Hospital who I spoke to, and he did me a solid after I explained what was going on."

"When I described to him how Christine said she felt after taking the pills, his opinion was the same as mine. He said it sounded like she had been taking an opioid because what she described was not the feeling one would get from blood pressure meds. He added that she was most likely addicted to them and was now suffering from withdrawal."

Dina told Michael that the doctor had filled a small prescription bottle with a harmless aspirin-like medication that resembled Christine's 'blood pressure' pills. He told Dina she could give one of those to Christine when she said she 'needed' it. He hoped they would have a placebo effect on her.

"I asked him if the pills would harm her, and he told me that as long as I limited her to one pill or the most, two, per day she would not suffer any harm."

"When I got back to the hotel room I gave her one of the pills and I told her how I would dispense them for the rest of the time she was with us. She went fucking nuts! She started to scream and carry on."

"She began to beg me for the bottle. I refused. That set her off even more."

"Mike she said that if I didn't give her the bottle she would refuse to testify. That's when I called you."

"Dina, let me speak to her," Michael said.

He spent the next ten minutes arguing with the out-of-control Christine. He tried to persuade her to listen to the investigators who had her best interests at heart. She was having none of it.

She kept repeating that her boyfriend, referring to the guy who was living with her said "You'd pull some shit with me. You've been good to me, so I didn't want to believe him. But he was right. This is fucked up."

"I want those pills. If you don't order these people to give me that bottle, you'll be sorry," she warned him.

Of course she had no idea that they were not the opioids she had been taking and wouldn't come close to giving her the feeling she was getting from her boyfriend's pills. And while Michael considered giving in to her for that very reason, he decided against it. He couldn't risk the pills causing her harm if she took more than the maximum two per day as the doctor had cautioned.

Michael finally got her to quiet down when he told her that Dina would give her another pill when they were off the phone and that he would get back to her the next day. He asked her to give the phone back to Dina.

"Dina, I told her you'd give her another pill and that I'd speak to her in the morning. I'm hoping that a night's sleep will calm her down and I can then talk some sense into her. She was okay with that plan."

"Michael, I'll give her the pill when I get off with you. And I'm scheduled to do a double shift, so I'll be here when you call her tomorrow."

On Sunday morning Michael called the hotel room and had a long conversation with Christine. The night's sleep had worked. She had calmed down, and she told him that she would listen to the investigators who were guarding her and not give them a hard time. "Mr. Gioca, don't worry. I'll see you in the morning at the court-house," she said.

When Michael hung up with Christine he breathed a sigh of relief. *'Crisis averted,'* he said to himself. But the exhilaration he was feeling would prove to be short lived.

CHAPTER

FORTY-FOUR

M ichael got to his desk bright and early Monday morning and put the finishing touches on the questions he planned to ask Christine Miller.

As he was packing his briefcase for court, he got a phone call from Dina Mitchell. She was in her office and sounded upset. "I need to see you before you leave for the courthouse," she told him.

When Dina got to Michael's office the look on her face told him that something was very wrong, and it probably had to do with Christine.

"Michael, Maria Cantone, one of the investigators who was with Christine overnight, just called me. When she woke up Christine to get ready for court, she began to act up over the pills again. She told the investigator that she was 'pissed' at you and that she was not going to testify."

"Dina what the hell happened?" Michael asked. "When I talked to her on Sunday she was calm and on board with testifying. And now she's pissed at me? I haven't spoken to her since yesterday."

"Michael it gets worse," Dina said. "Not only is she refusing to testify, but she also told the investigator that she is prepared to tell the judge that she had been coerced by you into testifying against Sabar."

Now angry because of her threat, Michael told Dina to have the investigators bring her to the courthouse. "I'll speak to her there," he said.

When Michael walked off the courthouse elevator he could hear Christine loudly objecting to being "forced" to be there. As he approached her she went wild. She cursed at him and was screeching that he had threatened to kill her if she didn't testify against Sabar.

He tried to calm her and get her to listen to him, but it was all for naught. He then appealed to her fondness for Linda, asking if she wanted to see the murderer of her friend go free.

"I don't give a shit!" she spat back at him.

He made one more attempt to convince her to do the right thing.

"Christine, I'm calling you to the witness stand regardless of your position," he told her. "You'll have to tell those lies to the judge, under oath, which will put you in jeopardy. Perjury is a crime. All you have to do is testify and tell the truth and you can avoid all that trouble."

"Go fuck yourself!" was her response. "I'm ready to see the judge so I can tell her all the shit you've done to me. Let's go."

Michael had no clue as to what had caused this drastic change of heart. He had tried everything in his arsenal to convince her to do the right thing and testify, but he'd been met with such venom that he finally gave up.

The case was called into the court record, and the judge was ready to resume the trial testimony. Michael asked her to hold off bringing the jury into the courtroom. He told her everything that had occurred with Christine, as well as her refusal to testify, and her accusation against him.

Judge Giordano told Michael to have his investigators bring Christine into the courtroom. When she arrived the judge ordered her to take the witness stand.

There were no jurors in the courtroom, but there were spectators and reporters in the gallery. One reporter from the local NBC News affiliate, who had covered Sabar's earlier case involving the death of the six firefighters in the supermarket roof collapse, had been following the case. He had gotten wind of the problem with Christine and asked permission from the judge to have a cameraman in the courtroom to tape the proceeding. Over Michael's objection, Judge Giordano granted his request.

After Christine was sworn in, the judge told Michael to ask her the questions he was going to ask on direct examination. He had gotten one question out before Christine went wild on the stand. Screaming, she called him a "scumbag who threatened me and forced me into testifying."

When the judge told her to calm down, Christine turned toward her and began to scream at her. This prompted the court officers to approach the witness stand ready to take control of the situation in the event that Christine went after the judge.

She told Judge Giordano that Michael had threatened to have her murdered if she didn't testify against Sabar. She said that he had kept her locked up for weeks in horrific conditions, and that he had fed her everything he wanted her to testify to in court.

She finished her tirade by telling the judge that she knew nothing about Linda Torre's murder and had nothing to say about or against Sabar.

After the trial, Michael would tell Monsignor Romano that the spectacle in Judge Giordano's courtroom had been the low point of his career. He had done nothing but care for Christine from when they first met. "She told the grand jury everything she knew about her friend's murder without hesitation," he said.

"Sal, it was humiliating to just sit at my table while that woman tore down my reputation with her lies."

"And to add insult to injury," Michael continued, "It had all been taped by the NBC reporter who used it on the six o'clock news that night. Sal, my father watches that newscast religiously, so of course he saw it. When I walked into my apartment that night he called me. His first words were, 'What did *you* do?' I wanted to crawl into a hole."

When Christine was done the judge asked Michael if he intended to have her arrested. If so, she would order her held without bail. Michael wanted to get to the bottom of the issue as to why she had turned on him and he thought that a night or two in jail might persuade Christine to talk. So he asked the judge to hold her and had Dina Mitchell handle the arrest. Christine was charged with perjury.

Michael's plan was to have Dina speak to Christine the next day while she was preparing the arrest paperwork, hoping she'd get some answers out of her.

Because he had no other witnesses ready to testify, Michael asked the judge to send the jury home. He assured her he would be ready to proceed with a witness the next day.

Not wanting to see any of his DA colleagues after the disaster with Christine, Michael went home directly from the courthouse.

Jade Liu had now become his most important witness.

He spent the better part of the night preparing for her testimony.

He reached out to Jade, and unlike her street walking days when she worked all night and was only reachable in the morning, he knew she'd be home with her fiancé.

She answered his call on the first ring.

He spent several hours with her working on a final prep. He refined her direct examination and put her through a rigorous cross-examination. She was ready for whatever Wilkins would throw at her.

Jade's testimony on both direct and cross-examination went even better than Michael expected. Wilkins tried to tear her apart using her now prior lifestyle, which Jade handled with the poise that Michael had worked on instilling in her during their prep sessions. And when Wilkins ridiculed and mocked her testimony about her practice of selling used condoms, she parried with, "Your client gave me the idea. And if men like him were sick and perverted enough to buy them, then *why not* expand my business, Mr. Wilkins?"

Michael watched the jury during Jade's cross and except for a wince here and there at certain parts, he didn't detect any outright disgust with her, nor did he see any body language that would have indicated that they didn't believe her.

When Jade left the witness stand Michael felt he had a good shot at convicting Sabar, despite losing Christine as a witness.

Before he closed his case Michael tried one more thing to shore it up. He called Luka the Russian as his last witness.

Michael's intent was to have him testify to his interaction with Jade involving used condoms and to testify that he had purchased them from her on a regular basis. He knew it was a long shot because it was a blatant attempt at bolstering Jade's testimony, which technically wasn't allowed.

Wilkins objected and demanded an offer of proof. "Judge, we need to have Mr. Gioca tell us what this Luka person will testify to so you can rule on its admissibility," he argued.

The judge agreed. After Michael outlined what Luka would say, Wilkins objected, and Judge Giordano ruled in his favor.

Disappointed, but with no recourse to appeal the ruling, Michael rested his case.

Wilkins announced that he was not calling any witnesses and rested the defense.

The judge gave the attorneys two days to prepare their closing arguments, and scheduled summations for Friday. Her intent was to charge the jury with the law they would use in their deliberations immediately after the attorneys concluded their addresses, then adjourn the case for the weekend. She explained all this to the jury before sending them home.

To Michael and Wilkins, Judge Giordano said, "I'll see you gentlemen bright and early on Friday morning."

Michael knew that he had his work cut out for him in order to convince the jury to convict Sabar. And as much as he wanted to resolve what he was now calling, 'the Christine Miller issue,' he knew he couldn't let that distract him. He needed to deliver a summation that would leave the jury with no choice but to find Ricky Sabar guilty.

CHAPTER

FORTY-FIVE

As Michael sat at the small desk in his apartment thinking about how he would construct his final argument, he considered how Wilkins was likely to portray Linda. He will say that she was a woman with mental issues, who had walked out of her life as a nun, thereby rejecting her sacred vows. A woman who had abandoned the family that loved her, to live in an old concession stand on the Coney Island boardwalk while pregnant.

'Surely a portrait that will not elicit a ton of sympathy, despite the heartfelt testimony of her sister Antoinette,' Michael said to himself.

Added to that, he thought, 'My only true witness to Sabar having killed Linda was a prostitute who sold used condoms to a rapist and to a guy who repurposed them in sex shows in Manhattan.' Again not a sympathetic witness.

Michael knew he had to impress upon the jury that despite their troubles and their lifestyles, Linda and Jade were women who did the best they could with the cards that had been dealt. And they shouldn't be disrespected or looked down upon because of that.

Therefore, it was essential that he inject a dose of humanity into the proceedings to show the jury that Linda was more than 'the deceased,' as she had been referred to throughout the trial. And Jade was more than 'the witness.'

So, he decided to open his address with a strong tug at the heart-strings of the jurors. He needed their empathy and compassion.

On Friday morning with all jurors present, Judge Giordano gaveled the court to order so summations could begin.

Monroe Wilkins did not surprise Michael with his remarks. He delivered a logical, and forceful argument of how the prosecution had failed to prove his client guilty, beyond a reasonable doubt. Four words that he used at the beginning of his remarks, in the middle of his remarks, and at the end of his remarks. And each time he used them he did so in a way to convey the sanctity of their meaning.

He then asked, "With those DNA results how could anyone not have a reasonable doubt as to Ricky Sabar's guilt?"

He moved on to Linda.

While he spent a good amount of time talking about the choices she made during her life, he stayed away from a blatant critique of her lifestyle. However, he made sure to detail the abandonment of her religious vocation, and the family that loved her. He followed that with a question and comment, "Mental issues? I'll leave that to you folks."

Then came Jade. When he discussed her, Wilkins took the gloves off. He called her, "Unreliable, unbelievable, and not someone whose testimony you can rely on to convict a man of murder."

Taking full advantage of the judge's ruling which prevented Luka the Russian from testifying, Wilkins said that Jade's story about selling condoms had not been corroborated in any way and should therefore be dismissed as "The fantasy of a hustler!"

"And no matter how much she and Mr. Gioca want you to believe that she has reformed and begun a new life, you can't disregard her criminal record and the life she led on the streets of Coney Island, saying and doing anything to survive."

"Don't let her hustle you into believing her story."

Wilkins closed with, "You are all savvy New Yorkers who I'm sure can see through the sham of a case that Mr. Gioca put before you. Will you be able to live with yourselves if you convict Ricky Sabar based on that evidence? If the answer is yes, so be it. But I'm betting that the answer is an overwhelming NO!"

Michael gave Wilkins a few moments to get back to his table, took a deep breath and began a summation upon which his entire case was riding.

"As I was driving home on Wednesday after we concluded the testimony and both the prosecution and defense rested their cases," he began, "I started to think about what I would say to you in these closing remarks. I thought about Linda and the baby she had been carrying. I thought about Jade and where she was now in her life. Suddenly what struck me was how eerily similar their stories were to an episode in my life when I was just a kid. It had been tucked away in my memory and I had no real reason to remember it until right then."

"My maternal grandfather, to whom I was close, had died suddenly. I was devastated. At five years old I didn't understand death. All I knew was that the man who took me to the zoo, to Prospect Park and to Coney Island, wasn't with us anymore."

"My grandmother saw my sadness and sat me down to comfort me. Born and raised in Naples, Italy, Grandma Rachel had the gift of always saying the right thing, at the right time. In her broken English she told me that my grandpa hadn't just left us. She said that he had been taken by God to live in heaven because God needed to make room here on earth for a baby that was surely born or about to be born right after my grandpa left us."

The story had the desired effect on the jury. Michael captured their attention, and some even had tears in their eyes. But he wasn't done.

"I still missed my grandfather, but my grandmother's story was comforting because I now understood that his moving on was for the purpose of making space for new life."

"What we all heard here," he continued, "reminded me of that story, because the heartbreaking and untimely deaths of Linda Torre and her unborn baby ultimately led to the start of a new life for Jade Liu."

"Linda's tragedy got Jade off the streets. Her decision to come into my office to tell what she knew about this murder, to act as any caring and responsible citizen would, was her first step in turning her life around. She is off the streets for good, she is off drugs, and she has found love with the man she will soon marry."

"Jade was first an important witness for the prosecution, then she became an important person to her new love, and soon she will be the most important person in the life of the baby she will be giving birth to. This is my grandma's story come to life!"

At this point Michael had more of the jurors crying, and he felt great.

He then went on to finish summing up his case.

When he sat down after completing his remarks, he later told Monsignor Romano, he knew that he had done everything he could to honor Linda, to bring justice to her memory and closure to her family, especially to Antoinette, who was sobbing in the second row of the spectator gallery.

When Michael left the courtroom Antoinette was waiting for him. She enveloped him in her arms, saying "Thank you." As Michael walked back to his office to await the jury's verdict he could still feel that hug. He thought to himself, *'That's why I do what I do'.*

For five days, the jury, which had been given what was essentially a one witness case, had not returned with a verdict. Because jurors want to get back to their lives as quickly as possible, Michael knew that when they had been given a weak case, a quick verdict of "Not guilty" was the usual result. Because that had not happened here, with each passing day Michael felt better about his chances.

On the sixth day the jury found Ricky Sabar not guilty.

Although not totally unexpected because Christine Miller had ripped the heart out of his case, Michael was devastated. '*HE beat me*,' was the only thought that came to his mind as the jurors filed out of the jury box, their duty having come to an end.

Linda's sister had been in the courtroom for the verdict and saw how disappointed Michael was.

"I'm sorry Antoinette," Michael said to her when she approached him once the jury had left the courtroom.

"You have nothing to apologize for," she replied.

She thanked him again and told him that she and Linda's family were proud of him. She told him that they knew how hard he had worked, and that he had brought honor to the memory of someone who had lost her way and had come to be looked on by society as a nobody.

"Michael, Linda and her baby are smiling down on you from Heaven."

This time Michael hugged Antoinette and told her he had appreciated everything she said. "I can't accept the result, but your words and the sentiments they convey, make it easier to deal with."

Michael excused himself from Antoinette so he could catch the jury as they left the courthouse. He wanted to hear what had kept them out for five days and why they had voted to acquit Sabar. He was standing at the foot of the courthouse steps when he spotted the jury leaving the building. They spotted him as well.

In his experience Michael had found jurors reluctant to talk when the prosecutor in the case they had just heard approached them. This time was different. The jurors all approached him before he made a move toward them. They were all anxious to speak to him.

Before he could say anything, they congratulated Michael. "You were terrific," the foreperson told him. They expressed empathy for him because of the difficult job he had, with Jade as essentially the only witness. They said that they all knew that Sabar was guilty and that they believed Jade!

When they saw the shocked look on his face, before he could ask why they didn't convict, the jurors told him that they wanted, "One more witness."

"With one more witness," they continued, "We would have voted to convict Sabar in an hour."

Michael didn't tell them that he had another witness but lost her under very strange circumstances. He felt there was no reason to make them feel as miserable and angry as he was feeling. He simply thanked them for their jury service, wished them well, and walked away.

He headed to his office to find out what exactly were those strange circumstances that cost him Christine Miller. In his heart of hearts he knew. Now he needed to confirm it.

CHAPTER

FORTY-SIX

When Michael arrived at his office, Dina Mitchell and Tim Clark were waiting for him.

"Wow! Bad news travels fast," Michael said when he saw the look on their faces.

"We're both sorry Michael," Dina said. "We know how hard you worked on this case and how difficult it was."

"We'd like to take you for a drink. I've always found that a single malt or two helps ease the pain," Tim added smiling.

"You're right Tim, it does. I'd be glad to join you. And guys, thanks for the sentiments and for all your help and hard work. But there's something I want to talk about before we leave. Dina, did you talk to Christine when you booked her?"

"Michael, I did. And I went one step further after I talked to her."

"I spoke to one of the guys who was on duty the night before she had her change of heart about testifying. Bondor's people had been helping us guard Christine throughout the custody. He was one of his less experienced detectives, who looked like he was about seventeen years old."

"Did you learn anything?" Michael asked.

"I learned a great deal. And you're not going to like what I found out."

"Let me hear it, Dina," Michael said.

"Before her boyfriend, as she called him, brought Christine into the precinct the day we were out looking for her, they chatted. Christine said he told her not to let you know that she was taking pills and that she had a supply of them with her. He said you'd object and take them from her."

"Ah! That's what she was referring to when she told me that her boyfriend had been right, when she was arguing with me," Michael said.

"There's more, Mike," Dina continued. "The boyfriend told her that if she ran out of the pills or you took them from her, she should somehow find a way to contact him, and he'd bring her a fresh supply."

"She said that when she did run out she was shocked and angry with you because you didn't respect her needs, even after she told you the pills were for her high blood pressure."

"But she didn't need to contact her boyfriend because we were able to get that pill refill, which made her happy. And even though we were only giving her one or two pills, after you spoke to her she calmed down and said she wasn't as angry with you. That's why she told you she'd be in court the next day to testify."

"So what happened between my call with her and Monday morning?" Michael asked.

"Mike, Bondor's detective told me that after she got off the phone with you she seemed okay. But as the day progressed she became more agitated."

"What did she want, more pills?,' Michael asked.

"Mike, here's where she got slick. Most likely she did want pills, but she knew asking for them was futile. So she did something else. She complained that she didn't have clothes with her that were appropriate for court. She said that she didn't want to let you down by showing up in the sweats she was wearing in the hotel room or the old slacks and blouse she had on when the boyfriend brought her into the precinct to surrender. We had arranged to bring her clothes for court the next morning, but the detective didn't know that."

"So she asked him to call her boyfriend and have him bring her more presentable clothes. He made the call, and when the guy answered the detective told him why. The guy asked to speak to Christine so she could tell him exactly what clothes she wanted. They talked but the detective couldn't hear what Christine said."

"About an hour later a guy showed up at the hotel room with a bag of clothes. He asked if he could speak to Christine before he left because he said he missed her. Christine asked as well, and the detective let them have a few minutes to talk. They were never alone but they were whispering."

"Mike, based on what the detective heard Christine say, I believe that this guy was the one who was living with her and supposedly keeping her safe."

"What did he hear her say?" Michael asked.

"The detective said he heard her tell the guy, 'you were right,' and something about 'you' and 'pills.'"

"Michael, I'm convinced that that short conversation, which should never have been allowed to happen, was what caused Christine to go from cooperative to the crazy woman who made all those accusations against you."

Dina continued, "This guy is no good. He got her hooked-on drugs, filled her head with God knows what ideas, then brought her to you so she could sabotage your case."

Then Tim Clark spoke up. "Mike, when Dina told me all this I immediately figured that he must have been connected to Sabar. So Dina and I went out to Coney Island to do some digging. You were finishing up with Jade and getting your summation ready which is why we didn't tell you what we were doing. You had enough on your mind, and we didn't want to bother you."

"I get the feeling that you guys learned some things."

"Mike, we did. Apparently when Christine disappeared and was incommunicado with you, she was seen hanging around with some guy named Jiz. Who, we're told, is a friend of Sabar."

"The word on the street is that he seduced her."

When Michael heard that name he wanted to explode. But because he couldn't let on that he knew who Jiz was, he remained calm and asked Tim to continue.

"It seems that the hanging out turned a lot more serious. He started living with Christine in that old concession stand and was bragging that they were lovers. People started to notice that Christine was high virtually every day and when they asked her about it she told them it was the 'blood pressure' pills Jiz was able to get for her. 'He takes good care of me and makes sure I'm ok', she would say, if anyone asked."

"Mike, it's clear that when Jiz brought her into that stationhouse he wasn't looking to help her or help you. He had set it up so she would do just what she did to you and your case."

"Do you want us to keep going?" Tim asked. "We can do a deep dive into this Jiz guy and if we come up with something you can take it to a grand jury. Nothing more I'd like to do than put him in cuffs."

Michael knew such an effort would result in nothing. It would be a total waste. The *Evil One* had beaten him. All he could do was accept it and wait for what he knew would be a next time.

He couldn't just outright say no because that could raise suspicions. So he hedged. "Tim, let me give it some thought," Michael responded. This would buy some time. He was counting on Tim and Dina getting into another case and looking to nail Jiz would then be forgotten.

"You're the boss Michael. Just know that we're ready if you give us the word."

With that Michael thanked them for all their help, then said, "How about that single malt you offered? I can really use it."

The three were at the bar in the Brooklyn Marriott Hotel, which shared a building with the DA's office, when Michael received a call from Monsignor Romano.

"Michael, Caldwell and I are sorry about the acquittal. We know how upset you must be. We want to buy you dinner."

When Michael started to beg off because he wanted to be alone to deal with his feelings, Romano told him that there was something they needed to tell him. "Mike, you're my friend, so I don't want to order you to be there, but trust me, you're going to want to hear what we have to say."

"*Emilio's* at six, I presume?" Michael asked.

"Yes. We'll see you there," Romano answered.

Michael thanked Dina and Tim for the drinks and said his goodbyes.

"I'll see you guys in the office tomorrow. Don't drink too much. I'm too tired to have to talk some cop out of collaring you for intox-driving tonight," he joked as he grabbed his coat and headed to face who knows what at *Emilio's.*

FORTY-SEVEN

When he arrived at the restaurant, Romano and Caldwell were at the monsignor's usual table, with a very expensive bottle of *Brunello* in front of them. Michael noticed that the bottle was half empty and thought they had been drowning their sorrow in wine..

He sat, and Emilio brought him a glass. While pouring wine for him he leaned down and whispered, "Michael, *si è lasciato alle spalle quello che è successo oggi. Domani e un altro giorno. Salute.*"

When Emilio walked away Romano said, "Michael, you need to do exactly what he said. Put today behind you. Tomorrow is another day."

Michael ignored Romano, took a swallow of his wine and asked, "Okay guys, I'm here, what do you have to tell me?"

Caldwell spoke first.

"You've been talking to Tim Clark and Dina Mitchell, so you know how the *Evil One* affected the outcome," he began. "You couldn't have anticipated that *HE* would get Christine hooked on drugs so *HE* could manipulate her to turn against you. Until *HE* became her 'boyfriend', she was solid and faithful to the memory of her friend Linda."

"Michael, we're both as upset as you are at the verdict. You're being too hard on yourself. But this is not on you."

If Michael heard *everything* Caldwell had said he would have appreciated the kind words. But he stopped listening once Caldwell mentioned that he knew that Tim and Dina had talked to Michael. He was upset and concerned. If he truly was to turn the page, and forget today and look to the future, he needed to know just how Caldwell had learned about their talk.

"Is someone watching me? Are you spying on me?" he asked angrily. "After all this time haven't I proved my loyalty?"

"How could you guys know who I was talking to?" he continued. "And how did you find out what they learned when they went back to Coney Island?"

"Michael, please calm down. Let me explain." Caldwell said.

"After Tim and Dina interviewed the people who told them about Jiz and Christine, they paid a visit to Sgt. Bondor at his office. They were being polite since he played such an important role in the case. They told him what they discovered. When he told his boss, my contacts in the NYPD informed me," answered Caldwell.

"We have the utmost trust in you and your work. We have no need to have anyone watching you. We are not spying on you."

When Caldwell finished, Michael looked over at his friend. Romano nodded in agreement. That was all Michael needed. He accepted Caldwell's explanation, poured himself another glass of wine and asked, "So why am I here? What do you have to tell me?"

Now it was Romano who did the talking. He told Michael that while the trial had been going on the fire marshals handling the investigation into the Manhattan hotel fire that resulted in Alex Gazis' death and Kathy Baer's injuries, had gotten a break. Two hotel workers who were on the fire floor saw Sabar and his companion there as well. They hid because he said the two looked 'shady,' and were up to something.

"Michael, they saw Sabar light the fire, after being encouraged to do so by the other guy who acted as a lookout. They said the two then left via the stairs. The two workers waited before going down the same stairs and out of the building."

Romano said that the workers called in the fire to 911 but left the area fearing that they would be questioned. "They're illegals Mike and were afraid they would be deported if they got involved."

"What made them come forward?" Michael asked.

"They saw Sabar on TV when that reporter from NBC filed reports from your trial. They recognized him from what he did in their hotel. They said to the fire marshals later that they saw what he had done in Brooklyn so they couldn't just let him get away with what happened in Manhattan."

When they saw how well the migrants who were bused from Texas to the city were treated and not deported, they felt it was safe for them to come forward and tell the police what they witnessed."

The monsignor said that the NYPD notified the fire marshals about the two workers. After interviewing them the marshals took the two to the Manhattan DA's office where they gave formal statements.

"They also were shown photos, and both identified Sabar as the fire starter. They of course couldn't identify Jiz because law enforcement has no photos of *him*."

"The DA took the case to a grand jury but kept it quiet because your trial was going on. However, this afternoon when Sabar was released from custody by the corrections department, fire marshals were waiting for him outside the courthouse and placed him under arrest. Michael, Sabar isn't going anywhere except to Rikers Island to await arraignment and trial for the murder of Alex Gazis and the attempted murder of Kathy Baer."

"That is why we asked you here, to tell you."

For one of the few times in his life Michael didn't know what to say. His disappointment for failing to convict Sabar, which he had been feeling when he walked into *Emilio's*, was gone.

But he wasn't feeling happy at the news, because Sabar's arrest would not bring Alex back to his family, or make Kathy's long road to recovery any less difficult.

He could, however, characterize it as satisfaction.

His trial in Brooklyn had directly led to Sabar being behind bars, and once again facing life in prison.

'HE *didn't beat me, after all,*' Michael thought to himself as he walked home after the delicious meal.

On the way, he made up his mind to call Kathy Baer to tell her the news. But when he arrived at his front steps, his thoughts were interrupted by the man who approached him.

"Michael Gioca?" the man asked.

"Yeah, that's me" Michael answered.

He then handed a large manila envelope to him, and said, "You've been served."

PART THREE

CHAPTER
FORTY-EIGHT

"Damn, that didn't take long," Michael said out loud in his empty apartment.

He had opened the envelope he'd been handed and saw that it contained a civil summons and complaint. Michael was being sued in Brooklyn Supreme Court for millions in money damages. The person suing him was Christine Miller.

The *Evil One* had wasted no time after Sabar was charged with murder for the Manhattan hotel fire, to exact revenge against Michael.

'*HE's going to make my life miserable with this lawsuit,*' Michael thought to himself, as he turned to the last page of the complaint to see who was representing Christine. He was not surprised when he saw the signature of Monroe Wilkins.

Overall the claims against him fit into four general categories: he had falsely imprisoned Christine, had threatened her life, had put her physical wellbeing in danger, and caused her extreme emotional distress and psychological harm.

The specific allegations, for the most part, followed those Christine had made to Judge Giordano. However, as written, they were expanded upon, exaggerated, and contained outright lies.

One allegation claimed that Michael and his detectives by looking for her all over Coney Island had put Christine's life in danger by exposing her as a police informant. Of course, there was no mention of the fact that it was her boyfriend who surrendered her to the police so she *could* testify.

Another was that he had denied her the medication she needed to control her high blood pressure, thereby putting her health at risk. Again, the complaint conveniently left out that her boyfriend had been her pill supplier and, if she actually suffered from high blood pressure, which Michael sincerely doubted, she had never told him about her condition.

A third allegation charged that he had personally threatened Christine with bodily harm if she did not give him what he had been looking for, i.e. evidence that Sabar had murdered Linda Torre.

The claim was that Michael had threatened to throw his office coffee table at her if she didn't testify that she had seen Sabar coming out of Linda's side of the concession stand, wearing a bloody shirt, moments before she discovered Linda's body. All of which she swore in the complaint never happened.

When Michael read that allegation he began to laugh because he couldn't have known about Christine seeing Sabar come out of the concession stand unless she had told him.

And, he didn't have a coffee table in his office to threaten her with.

To support her false imprisonment claim, Christine alleged that she had been locked in a hotel room for days against her will, guarded by cops who had forcibly prevented her from leaving and having any contact with her boyfriend.

Of course nowhere in the allegation was it written that she had agreed to the hotel stay, with guards, because she feared she was being stalked. Nor was it written that the cops guarding her had let her first speak by phone to her boyfriend, then meet with him when he had brought her clothes for her court appearance.

Disgusted with everything contained in the papers, Michael threw them across the room. He knew that he had to alert both Caldwell and Romano to this development, but he was in no mood to do it right then. He'd try to get a good night's sleep and call Romano in the morning to set up a meeting.

Before he turned in however, Michael made a call that he had intended to place before he was distracted by Christine's lawsuit.

"Kathy, I hope I didn't disturb you," Michael said when Kathy Baer answered his call.

"Michael, you never disturb me. It's good to hear your voice," Kathy replied. "I saw the news reports about the trial. I'm sorry."

"Thanks Kathy. I wanted to get that bastard Sabar for Linda, as well as for you and Alex. I can't help but feel that I let you all down."

"Mike, I certainly don't feel that way. I didn't know Linda, but I did know Alex. I'm sure he would express the same sentiment. You can't guarantee a result. But your hard work proves that you are a man of honor. I'm grateful for all you have done."

"Now, I have a feeling that you didn't call me just to tell me how sorry you are. What's up?"

"Kathy, you're right. I didn't call *only* to say I'm sorry. I have good news."

Michael told Kathy about Sabar's arrest for the hotel arson and its aftermath. He filled her in on how the case had been solved and told her that the Manhattan District Attorney's Office would be handling it.

"Kathy, I know the ADA who's been assigned to try the case, and you're in good hands. And I'll be available to help in any way that I can."

Kathy said nothing. All Michael could hear was her sobbing. He knew, however, that they were tears of joy and likely would be followed by a big smile.

"That arrest won't bring back Alex," Michael continued, "But I hope the news will provide a measure of closure to his family."

Finally, Kathy spoke. "Michael all I can say is thank you. I'll be thinking about that bastard sitting in a cell on Rikers Island for every second of my rehab. And it will motivate me to be ready to *walk* into the courtroom when I must testify at his trial."

"Have you told Alex's wife Nikki yet?" Kathy asked. When Michael told her that he hadn't yet called her, Kathy asked him to allow her to do it.

"Nikki has been a source of strength for me since I came home. Her bravery has inspired me to work my ass off, so I'll be able to walk again. She calls every day to check on me and has brought me food and comfort ever since my mom and dad went back home. Mike, I need to be the one to tell her that this is the beginning of the end of our nightmare."

"Kathy I understand. Please give her my best and tell her I'm always here if she needs anything. And the same goes for you."

Kathy thanked him and asked him to stop by when he had some time. "It would be great to see you. You can catch me up on all your adventures."

'Yeah, some adventure,' Michael thought to himself. '*A pain in the ass lawsuit, and the likelihood of having to deal with that fucking nut Christine Miller again.*'

"Kathy, it's a date, he said with a smile. Take care of yourself and don't get hurt working your ass off in rehab. I'll see you soon."

When Michael hung up, he had no idea that when would see Kathy again, he'd have plenty to tell her because his next battle with the *Evil One* was about to begin.

CHAPTER

FORTY-NINE

E den Liquors at 110 Tompkins Avenue was located in the heart of Brooklyn's Bedford-Stuyvesant neighborhood.

From its founding before the American Revolution, Bed-Stuy, as it is known, had been populated by people of different nationalities and cultures. First by Dutch and British settlers, then by German immigrants.

In 1907, with the completion of the Williamsburg Bridge, which connected Brooklyn and lower Manhattan, Jews and Italians who were new arrivals to America, settled into Bedford-Stuyvesant.

During the Great Depression migrants from the American South and the Caribbean began moving in. And by the middle of the 1930s when African Americans started to leave an overcrowded Harlem for the increased housing availability in Bedford-Stuyvesant, the neighborhood became the second largest Black community in New York City. Since then the neighborhood has been a major cultural center for Brooklyn's African American population.

Like many of Brooklyn's neighborhoods it has undergone significant gentrification since the early 2000's. This culminated in a dramatic demographic shift, which included a more diverse population with an increased desire to make the neighborhood home, and an escalation in the value of real estate.

As a result, this new Bed-Stuy was the ideal battlefield for the *Evil One's* next campaign in *HIS* war against Brooklyn and the families that called the borough home.

It was in the early-1980s, well before gentrification had hit Bed-Stuy, Min Jun Choi, opened Eden Liquors.

Choi had emigrated to America from South Korea in the mid-1960s in search of a better life and settled in New York City. For sixteen years he worked in sweatshops in the city's garment district, and in restaurants throughout the five boroughs, before he saved enough money to purchase a business of his own.

It was during those years that he met his wife Sooki and began to raise a family.

While Min worked fifteen-hour days to build his business, Sooki stayed home to raise their son Jimmy and his sister Cindy.

Being a Bed-Stuy outsider, Choi knew that to achieve success, it was important for him to be friendly, gracious, and kind to those who were his neighbors and customers.

It worked. After striving for years to establish himself as a good neighbor and businessman, Choi was well-liked, and respected by the community. Eden Liquors had become a thriving business.

Instigated by the *Evil One*, it was Choi's kindness to his killer that would lead directly to his death.

Robert "Bobby" Headley had been an NYPD patrol officer for five unremarkable years.

When he was recruited to the department he seemed to be the ideal person to wear the badge and patrol the city streets based on the Community Policing model the NYPD established. Headley was young and ambitious.

His African American father had met Bobby's Latina mother at a prayer service they attended during the Christmas season in an Episcopal church in the heart of Bed-Stuy. Bobby's dad lived in the neighborhood his entire life, while his mom emigrated to the US from Nicaragua shortly before they met.

It didn't take long for Norman Headley to ask Carmen Lopez to marry him. They had quickly fallen in love and neither saw any reason to delay what both felt was inevitable. They found an apartment in the neighborhood a couple of blocks from Eden Liquors.

Their only child, Bobby, was born two years into their marriage. He attended the local public elementary school, middle school, and then Boys and Girls High School, after which he went to Manhattan Community College for two years, before finishing his education at John Jay College of Criminal Justice.

Bobby wanted to become an attorney, but his parents didn't have the money to put him through law school and, because he only worked sporadically while in college, he had no savings to use for tuition. Disappointed, Bobby decided to become a police officer. To do so he first had to overcome several minor instances of law breaking.

When he attended high school and community college in Manhattan, Headley was issued several summonses for jumping subway turnstiles and not paying the fare to ride the NYC transit system.

Excusing these as mistakes of youth, the NYPD did not reject his application. He spent six successful months training in the Police Academy, then passed the rigorous psychological testing administered by the department, after which he was sworn in as a police officer.

He was assigned to patrol in Brooklyn's 83rd precinct, which was adjacent to the 79th precinct, where Headley lived and where Eden Liquors was located.

In the 83rd, Headley had been a mediocre cop, but was well-liked. He was known to his colleagues as a guy who liked to party, especially at nightclubs. He was not a big drinker and stayed away from drugs. But he loved nice clothes and cars.

When he was off-duty Headley *was* in fact, a different person. It seemed that he was never far from trouble.

Later, after his arrest for the Choi murder one of his cop buddies told the press, "To hear what's being said about Headley, it's like they're talking about a different person from the guy I know."

Early in his police career Headley was identified as being the leader of a group who had accosted and robbed an undocumented Ecuadorian man. The victim was walking to his Bed-Stuy home from his off-the-books job, on pay day. The Ecuadorian was an easy target because Headley knew that he would never report the robbery to the police because he feared being exposed as undocumented which would result in his deportation.

Headley was wrong. The Ecuadorian, incensed that his entire week's salary was stolen, anonymously reported the theft to the police right after it happened. "The guy who robbed me is a cop," the unidentified caller said.

A week later the Ecuadorian was picked up by ICE, and he told the ICE agents about the robbery. They reached out to the 79th precinct, spoke to the detective who was assigned to investigate the robbery, and told him they had his victim.

Along with an assistant district attorney from the Brooklyn DA's office, the detective went to the federal detention facility where the Ecuadorian was being held to interview him.

After speaking to the victim, who told the detective and the ADA that he recognized the leader of the group that robbed him as a cop living in his neighborhood, the detective put together a photo lineup that included Headley's photo. The next day the Ecuadorian identified him.

However, before the DA's office could complete the investigation, the robbery victim was deported to Ecuador.

The robbery and the photo identification were reported to the local Field Internal Affairs Unit (FIAU) assigned to the precinct where Headley worked. But without the witness and having no other evidence tying Headley to the robbery, the FIAU buried the incident in a file.

It would be when Michael began working on the Choi murder that this FIAU file was uncovered.

CHAPTER FIFTY

The robbery of the Ecuadorian would be only the tip of the iceberg as far as Headley's criminal activity while he wore the uniform of the NYPD.

Several months after that robbery, Headley was involved in a shooting by a male cousin of his in a Manhattan nightclub. Although no one was injured, the cops who reported to the scene confiscated the gun. After being tested by the NYPD ballistics section, it was discovered to be Headley's off-duty gun.

Once again, Headley escaped any discipline when the same FIAU that had been involved in the robbery of the Ecuadorian, absolved him of any wrongdoing and arrested his cousin for removing the gun from Headley's holster and firing it inside the nightclub.

The shooting was followed by what was to be the robbery of a Brooklyn check cashing location by Headley and a female cousin. An incident that was eerily similar to the later robbery of Eden Liquors.

When Headley and the cousin entered the check cashing location he told the proprietor that he was a cop and asked him to allow her to use the bathroom which was located behind the locked, plexiglass enclosed check cashing counter.

Skeptical, the proprietor said, "Let's see your badge." When Headley hesitated before taking the badge out of his pocket, the proprietor refused his request. Headley and his cousin then hurried out the door and disappeared. The proprietor called 911 and reported the incident.

The investigating precinct detectives later reported it to the FIAU after the proprietor had given them the shield number of, "The cop who we think was going to rob us."

As with the past incidents, Headley went untouched.

Michael would later be told that nothing was done by the FIAU because there was no crime.

Several weeks after the aborted robbery of the check cashing location, Headley and that same female cousin decided to rob a gas station on the opposite end of Brooklyn from where Headley lived and worked.

They were sitting in Headley's car surveilling the spot, when undercover officers approached and demanded they get out and identify themselves. The owner of the gas station noticed the car and the two people sitting and watching his place. He was suspicious and called the local precinct to report it.

Headley immediately identified himself as a cop, so he was not arrested nor taken into the station house for questioning. His cousin however, had been searched at the scene and was found to be carrying a loaded .357 automatic weapon.

She was arrested when Headley told the arresting cops he had no idea she was carrying a gun and denied that they were planning anything. "She has been having boyfriend trouble," Headley told the cops. "We were just talking. She wanted my advice."

The FIAU was given a full report of the incident, and nothing was done to Headley.

He felt invulnerable, which is what he told a new friend, Deets, he made shortly thereafter.

Headley met Deets one Thursday night in a Manhattan club. Headley was holding court in a corner, talking to a few of his cousins and a few guys from the neighborhood he had been friends with since they were kids.

As usual, Headley was dressed to the nines, but he was only drinking beer. When he went to the bar and ordered another, a guy introduced himself and asked if he could buy him something stronger.

"Someone dressed as sharp as you shouldn't be seen drinking beer. Let me buy you a scotch. Then I'd like to talk," he said, holding out his hand to shake. "I'm Deets."

Headley enjoyed the compliment and began to tell the guy that he preferred beer. However, before he finished his sentence, the bartender poured him a glass of Johnny Walker Blue. Headley appreciated the man's taste and generosity.

"Thanks man," he said, "But you don't even know me. Do you always introduce yourself with $40 scotch?"

"Mr. Headley, I do know you," Deets said. "You're a police officer and I know you sometimes step out of that role with your friends over there to supplement your income. You see, I'm from Brooklyn, Bed-Stuy to be exact, and I've been watching you."

Immediately Headley suspected that Deets was from Internal Affairs, but when Deets told him that he had a job for him, "A job that'll make you a lot of money," Headley relaxed.

Now, full of bravado, Headley said, "If you know me, and have been watching me, then you must have heard that I'm untouchable."

When Deets nodded in agreement, Headley said, "Friend, I like you. Buy me another Johnny Blue and we'll talk."

It was this new friend, Deets, who told Headley that Eden Liquors was the perfect spot for him to rob.

"The score will make us all very happy," Deets said. "You live near there, so I'm sure, you've seen that plexiglass they have separating the customers from the workers. That's there because the place is a front for a big gambling and illegal numbers operation and they always have lots of cash on hand, especially around closing time on Saturday night."

"They think the plexiglass will protect all that cash from being robbed. But I have a way for you to get around it." Then Deets told Headley how to do it.

"I'm in," Headley said, his false sense of invincibility on full display. "Now how about another scotch so we can toast and seal the deal."

When it was far too late, Headley would find out that everything Deets told him about Eden Liquors was a lie.

CHAPTER
FIFTY-ONE

The next day, Friday, was a regular day off for Headley. He wasn't scheduled to be back on duty until 8 a.m. on Monday morning. After his talk with Deets the night before, Headley couldn't wait for his boys to hear the plan to hit Eden Liquors.

So, at noon on Friday, Headley, and his good friends, Jeff Cooper, Mickey Ruiz and Trini Rojas, met up with Deets at a diner in Manhattan. Over eggs, toast, and pancakes, they talked about the robbery.

When Deets told Cooper and Ruiz the lie he told to Headley, that Eden was a gambling and numbers spot, and how Saturday was their big cash night, Cooper raised a concern that Deets dismissed out of hand. "Is that a Kang spot?" Cooper asked.

The Kang Organization, as they were known to Brooklyn law enforcement, was a vicious and powerful Asian organized crime group that controlled drug trafficking, sex trafficking, and illegal gambling, from the Sunset Park section of the borough, in the south, to Bed-Stuy and beyond, in the north. They would not tolerate any of their gambling spots being hit and the repercussions would be fatal.

Deets, who knew that Eden was not a gambling spot, assured them that he had checked out Eden with someone he knew in the

Kang group and was told that the spot was independent and not one of theirs.

Cooper found it hard to believe that the Kang Organization would allow an independent operation in their territory, especially one that was as successful as Deets made Eden out to be. So he pressed him.

"Listen man, I don't know you. So why should we believe that you did what you said you did, checked with Kang? You ain't even gonna be there with us. Our asses are gonna be on the line, so you got to convince me that we ain't gonna die because we hit a Kang spot."

The plan as Deets explained it, was for Headley and Cooper to be the ones who would go into the store to do the robbery, while Ruiz, whose girlfriend Louisa lived across the street from Eden, would remain outside to act as the lookout. They felt that Ruiz hanging out on the street would not raise the suspicion that Cooper, who lived elsewhere, would.

"What about you?" Cooper asked Deets. "What are you gonna be doing, that you ain't gonna be there with us?"

Once again Deets lied. "I'm gonna be listening to the police radio on a scanner in my car a few blocks away. If I hear that the cops are coming, I'll let Headley and Ruiz know over the walkie talkies I'm gonna give them."

"Shit, you got all the answers, don't you?" Cooper said, not happy with the arrangement, and not caring much for Deets. At this point Headley knew he had to calm things down or the entire job was going to fall apart.

"Coop, if it wasn't for Deets we would never have known that Eden is a gambling spot," Headley said. "Me and Ruiz always be around there, and we both thought it was just selling liquor. So we got to give props to Deets for telling us about it, recognizing that we can do this, and bringing it to us. He's the mastermind so he don't have to be on the scene."

Cooper listened but was still skeptical about Deets' role. He asked Headley to go to the bathroom with him so they could have a conversation without Deets.

"Listen Head," Cooper began, "I ain't a pussy but we puttin' a lot of trust in a guy we ain't know for more than a minute. If he's lying about the Kangs we got lots of trouble. And it seems to me that him putting himself away from the scene when we hit the place gives him an out if it is a Kang spot."

Headley shrugged him off. "Coop, I'm doing this," he said. "If you want out, so be it."

"From when I met this guy," Headley continued, "he's given me a good feeling. Something about him says to trust him."

Cooper listened, then reluctantly gave in. "Okay Head, we been doing scores together for a long time and we ain't ever been caught. So I'm in." Then laughing he said, "You a good luck charm, Head."

"Let's go tell him."

But as they started to leave the bathroom, Cooper grabbed Headley. "Hold up a minute. Before we go out there, I got to ask you something about Mr. Deets."

"Okay, what is it?" Headley asked.

"What's the deal with that ugly fucking mark on his left cheek? Is there something wrong with that guy? He got cancer or something?"

Headley had no answer for Cooper. He just shook his head in frustration. "What the fuck does that have to do with robbing Eden Liquors? Let's go."

When they got back to the table, Headley assured Deets that all was well and that they would be ready to hit the liquor store Saturday night at closing time. Before Deets left the club, he spoke to Headley away from the others. "Listen man," he said, "I'm good with your crew, but we don't need that guy Trini. There's something about him I don't trust. Besides, I don't want to have to split the take five ways. Tell him he's out."

Headley spoke to Trini, who argued with him over the slight, but in the end Trini had no recourse and accepted the fact that Deets had cut him out of the job.

For the remainder of Friday, Headley, Cooper and Ruiz collected the guns they'd need, as well as the walkie talkies that Deets said he would use to notify them of police activity while they were inside Eden Liquors.

On Saturday night, just before the store's closing time of midnight, Headley, Cooper and Ruiz walked across Tompkins Avenue headed for Eden Liquors, with Deets allegedly set up well away from the store listening to the police radio.

As the three approached, they stopped in their tracks. The store's security gate, designed to protect the front door and windows, was lowered and locked. Eden Liquors had closed early.

The three, acting disappointed at not being able to make a purchase, all for the benefit of anyone who may have been watching them, walked past the store and continued to Louisa's apartment. There they would regroup and plan to hit the place the next week.

However, before they reached the apartment, Headley walked away from Cooper and Ruiz and called Deets over the walkie talkie. He wanted to let him know what happened. After several unsuccessful attempts to reach him, Headley gave up.

Because he didn't know why Deets was not responding, Headley didn't want the guys to think that Deets had abandoned them. So, when he caught up to Cooper and Ruiz, he lied and told them that Deets would see them during the week to discuss the plan for their next attempt.

Headley decided he would deal with Deets himself the next day.

But a week went by with no contact between them. Undeterred, on Friday afternoon, Headley got together with Cooper and Ruiz and planned to go back to Eden Liquors Saturday night to rob the place.

Not wanting to spook them, Headley lied again and told Cooper and Ruiz that Deets would be set up in his car as planned. He never told them that he had no clue as to Deets' whereabouts because he was confident that they didn't need Deets to pull off this score.

So, on Saturday night, as they had done the previous week,

Headley, Cooper and Ruiz left Louisa's apartment and headed for Eden Liquors.

This time they *would* get inside, and disaster would follow.

Just before midnight, Min Choi and his clerk Ronnie Collins, an elderly gentleman who lived in Bed-Stuy for all of his seventy-nine years, were inside Eden liquors preparing to close for the night, when Bobby Headley walked into the store. He flashed his police shield and asked Choi to use the bathroom.

Deets told him that this was how he would get behind the plexiglass that protected Choi and Collins.

It worked like a charm. Choi, ever respectful of the police, unlocked the plexiglass door and Headley walked behind the counter and made his way to the bathroom.

After a minute or two, Headley emerged gun in hand. He pointed it at Choi as Cooper entered the store. Headley let him behind the counter, and Cooper pulled a gun which he held on Collins.

Headley demanded the "gambling money" from a shaking Min Choi. He had no idea what Headley was asking for and told him all he had in the store was money to make change for customers when he reopened the next day.

Not satisfied with his answer, Headley hit Choi across his face with his gun, knocking him to the floor. Again he demanded the gambling money, and this time both Choi and Collins said that they only had a small sum in the store to be used for customer change.

Now very angry, Headley ordered Choi and Cooper to their knees. While he held his gun on the two men, Cooper searched them and took the few dollars they had in their wallets.

When Cooper said that he recovered "Maybe a hundred bucks," Headley screamed at Choi to turn over the "Fucking gambling and numbers money," which Deets assured him would be there.

"Mister," Choi began, "The money we made today was from liquor sales, and it's been deposited in the bank. There is no gambling here. We only have the small change money in the register. Take it please. Just don't hurt us," he pleaded.

Still not willing to believe that Deets had lied and set him up, Headley fired his gun into the store's ceiling to frighten the men into turning over the big score he was told would be there.

Of course it didn't work. Neither Choi nor Collins could give them something they didn't have and didn't exist.

At this point, having gotten the money from Choi and Collins' wallets, as well as the small amount from the cash register, Cooper had glanced over at Ruiz who was standing outside the store, and saw him tapping his watch. It was the signal for them to get out. "Head, we been in here too long. We got to go." Cooper said.

But when Headley didn't respond, Cooper looked over at him and was about to repeat his plea for them to leave. Before he could, Headley, who had been staring down at Choi, looked up at Cooper as if he was possessed, and said, "They got to go. They saw my face."

Headley put five bullets into Choi, killing him instantly.

Cooper followed Headley's lead and shot Collins several times.

But because Cooper was shaking when he fired the gun, his aim was off. He didn't kill Collins, but seriously wounded him. The seventy-nine-year-old would never walk again because one of Cooper's bullets had severed his spine.

Headley and Cooper walked out of the store as if nothing had happened. Ruiz joined them and they reconvened in Louisa's apartment. There they gave the guns, and the walkie-talkies to her. It was her job to hide them along with the police scanner that she was monitoring.

Headley knew that Deets would not be monitoring the police calls, so he lied to Ruiz and told him, "As a back-up, we should have Louisa listening to the police scanner. She has a walkie-talkie so she can let us know if the cops are coming, in case Deets falls asleep or something." Ruiz bought the story and Louisa agreed to help them.

Before the three thieves went their separate ways, they divided the take from the robbery. They each scored $300.

For that small amount Min Choi lost his life and Sam Collins would be paralyzed and confined to a wheelchair until the day he died.

Two innocent lives destroyed, two families devastated. All carried out by a New York City police officer. And when that fact was later revealed, it shook Brooklyn to its core.

Just as the *Evil One* had planned it.

FIFTY-TWO

"Michael, *HIS* fingerprints are all over this lawsuit," Monsignor Romano said as he looked over the papers that had been handed to him.

"*HE* wants you so distracted and so humiliated that when *HE* strikes again, you'll be unable to concentrate on what needs to be done to defeat *HIM*. You can't let that happen."

The two friends were sitting in Romano's sparsely furnished office on the Red Hook waterfront. Michael set up the meeting to alert the monsignor and Caldwell to the fact that he had been sued by Christine Miller.

Caldwell asked Romano to handle it, and to make sure that Michael knew that he shouldn't worry about it. "Our group will deal with it, and he'll be represented by one of our attorneys," he told the monsignor.

Romano followed orders and filled in Michael on what Caldwell said. But it hardly reassured him. "Who's going to take care of this?" Michael said, tossing that morning's *New York Times, New York Post,* and *New York Daily News* across Romano's desk.

"Look at the shit they're printing. They bought everything that

Miller and Wilkins said about me in those papers, without asking for a comment, or allowing me to refute it," he ranted.

"And since they think that I was working for the DA's office when I tried Sabar, Price must be having a shit fit. Not only were he and his office named in the lawsuit, but he's also being crucified in these stories for allowing the out-of-control Gioca to do as he pleased."

Nevertheless, Michael told the monsignor that neither he nor Caldwell should worry about him doing his job. "I won't be distracted by *HIM* and *HIS* tactics. And I can handle what Price, my colleagues, and the so-called law enforcement community will say about me. I've been through this before, after I convicted that corrupt fed."

"But Sal, my father, my sister, and my kids read these rags. They are who I'm concerned about. How do I explain it all to them? I can't tell them that I'm in a war with Satan and that this is *HIS* way of trying to destroy me so I'll surrender."

"Monsignor, I need your help. You need to talk to them. I'm sure they'll listen to you because of who you are."

Romano understood what Michael was asking of him. They had been friends for a long time, and he knew how protective Michael was about his family. So, he had no hesitation in agreeing to a family meeting with the Gioca clan.

"Michael, set up the meeting, make it at your father's house, and I'll take care of everything. Please don't worry about this. Caldwell will handle the lawsuit and I'll take care of making sure your family hears the truth, or as much of it as I can tell them. When I'm done they'll know that what the newspapers are saying is complete bullshit."

"Wow! Padre, cursing." Michael said laughing, "That tells me you're really into this and that all will be well."

After the meeting Michael went to his office. When he walked in his phone was ringing. He checked the caller ID and saw that it was DA Price. Before Price could say anything, Michael told him he'd be right up to see him.

The DA was not sitting behind his desk when Michael walked into his office, which was his usual place during meetings with his staff. He was in one of his club chairs, which is where he would sit for casual and unofficial get togethers. Seeing this, Michael, who had been ready for a harangue from Price because of the negative publicity, relaxed. '*He must have spoken to Caldwell,*' Michael thought to himself.

"Mike, I had a long talk with John Caldwell. He filled me in on all this shit and he told me, what I'm sure you know by now. The feds will be handling the lawsuit along with the City Corporation Counsel. We'll all be taken care of rather well he assured me. And, this you may not know, he also said that his people have hired a top public relations firm to counter the bad publicity."

"You've been through this bullshit before, so I know you'll be okay," Price added.

'*Yeah, you sure do know what I've been through,*' Michael thought, '*Because you were one of the assholes who put me through it.*'

"Don't let it affect what you're doing," Price continued, "Caldwell told me that they couldn't be more pleased with your work. I'm proud of you."

Michael thanked Price for the kind words and excused himself. It had been a horrible day so far and it was only 10 a.m. When he got back to his office, Dina Mitchell and Tim Clark were waiting for him.

"Don't let the bastards get you down," Dina told him. "We know what happened in that Sabar case, and for what it's worth, we've been spreading the word around here that it's total BS."

"Mike, do you want us to reach out to those reporters and set the record straight since we were there and we know the truth," Tim asked.

Michael would have liked nothing more. But since he knew that a PR firm Caldwell had hired was involved, he didn't want to do anything without first checking with them.

"Guys thanks for the support and for spreading the word around here that this is all a load of crap. You have no idea how much it means to me. And, Tim, if I need you and Dina to speak to those reporters I'll let you know."

"Now, I have work to do and I'm sure you guys do as well," Michael said.

Dina and Tim got the message. As they were walking out of his office, Dina turned and said, "We're here if you need us." Michael silently mouthed '*I know,*' as he reached for his phone which was ringing.

The conversation with his father, Michael thought, was somewhat strained. While the overall tone of the call ultimately turned out to be supportive, Michael was stunned when his dad began with, "Michael, what did you do?"

Over the next twenty minutes, Michael tried to explain everything. And while his dad told him that he understood, Michael had the sense that this man, who lived for the news and his newspapers, was having a difficult time accepting his claim that it was all made up. It was apparent that his idea of Romano speak to his family was even more necessary than he had originally thought.

Michael ended the call by asking his dad for a day and time to have a family meeting so this all could be hashed out and hopefully put to rest.

"That's a good idea because your sister is a mess over this," his dad said. "And Michael Jr. and Kevin called me this morning before they left for school to ask me if it's true."

"After that crazy woman's testimony at the trial was broadcast by that NBC reporter, those boys had to deal with their friends saying or thinking that you're a corrupt monster who threatens women with coffee tables to get what you want. It was easy for them to dismiss it as the ravings of a lunatic, which is what she looked and sounded like on TV. But now *The Times, The Post ,* and *The Daily News,* have it on their front pages. That's going to make it much harder for them to explain it away. Hearing what the truth is will help them deal with all this. I'll have everyone here after dinner on Thursday at 7 o'clock."

"Son, you know how much I, your sister, and your sons love you and look up to you. In our heart of hearts none of us believes this, but we all need to hear *why* we shouldn't."

Michael hung up and felt as if his world had caved in on him.

His reputation taking a hit from his colleagues was a pain he could deal with, but having his family question his integrity was pain on a different level. He spent his entire professional life doing the right thing. He worked hard to set an example that his parents and his sister could be proud of, and that his sons could and would emulate. He wasn't going to let Satan, using Christine Miller and Monroe Wilkins, tear it all down without a fight.

"Sal, Thursday evening, 7 p.m. at my dad's house," Michael said when he called Romano after he hung up with his father. "My family will be there. And after hearing what my dad said about this mess, they *need* to hear from you. And I need it even more."

"Michael, I'm happy to do it. They deserve to hear the truth."

"Thank you Sal."

"Pick me up at the office and we'll go together," the monsignor said. "There's something I want to discuss with you, and during the drive will be a perfect time to do it."

At 6 p.m. on Thursday, Michael was waiting outside Romano's office to take him to the meeting that would be among the most important in the prosecutor's life.

For two full days the New York newspapers and local TV and radio news was dominated by the story of the corrupt and cruel Michael Gioca and his so-called victim Christine Miller.

"Mike, I'm sorry about all the horrible stories," Romano said when he got into the passenger seat of Michael's car. "Caldwell knows that I'm with you tonight. He told me to assure you that things will quiet down once the PR firm and the lawyers settle in and get down to business. He said for you to just hang in."

"Sal, I've been keeping a low profile since we don't have a case for me to be involved in. So, I can't really hear what's being said about me around the office. And Dina Mitchell and Tim Clark have been running interference for me."

"Also, I have to give credit to Marty Price," Michael said. "He's been checking in with me a few times a day and said basically the same as Caldwell, 'Hang in, Mike.'"

Romano smiled. "Well it's interesting you said what you just said about not having a case. That's what I want to talk to you about."

On the way to his dad's home in eastern Queens, Michael listened as Romano told him the story of a horrific murder in Brooklyn that occurred while he was on trial. He added, "It has the *Evil One's* signature all over it."

CHAPTER
FIFTY-THREE

Romano's talk to Michael's family went better than he anticipated. Without mentioning the *Evil One*, the monsignor told them the truth about the Christine Miller situation. As Michael expected, coming from the monsignor that truth carried extra weight. When he was finished, his sons spontaneously went over to Romano and hugged him. "Thank you," they said.

Later, over coffee and Italian pastries that Michael's sister Pam brought, she and her father expressed their gratitude to the monsignor for "Setting the record straight."

"Monsignor, you made my family whole again," said Michael's father. "The newspapers and TV reports have torn us apart, I'm saddened to say. That I ever entertained even the slightest thought that Michael could do what they were saying he did, makes me ashamed. Thank you for coming here and talking to us."

It was getting late, and Michael Jr. and Kevin had to get home. The older brother had taken their mom's car to the meeting, and Michael walked them to it to say goodnight. Both boys grabbed him in a hug and told him that they loved him. Kevin then said, "Dad no matter what the news was saying we never believed it. You're our hero, always."

Holding back tears, Michael said thank you and cautioned them to drive safely. As they drove off, Michael looked skyward, said a silent prayer and, "Thank you."

A few minutes later, after all the goodbye hugs and kisses from his dad and sister, Michael and Romano set out for Brooklyn.

"I don't think I can ever thank you enough for what you did for my family, and for me, tonight," Michael said to Romano as he drove onto the Long Island Expressway.

"You were perfect. Your demeanor was sincere, what you said was spot on, and as I knew they would, my family hung on every word and accepted them as the truth."

"Michael, it needed to be done and I'm happy it went well."

"Now, having said that, can I finish what I started to tell you on the way out here about the Eden Liquors case?" the monsignor asked.

"Of course Sal. I'm sorry. I'm just so pleased with how the night turned out. I can't shut up. But now I will."

"About a week ago I received a call from a former student of mine, Greg Sanders, who's now an NYPD detective, " Romano began. "He had heard through the grapevine in our old parish that I was in New York and said that he needed to speak to me about something that was bothering him."

"Greg was always a good kid and a bright student. When he was in my eighth-grade class, he came to me to discuss his future. Greg said he felt the calling to become a priest. After some long talks with him and his parents, I told them I would do whatever I could to help."

"After he had completed three years of high school he called and told me he was ready. He entered the seminary, and all seemed to be going well for him. However, six months later, Greg reached me at my new parish to let me know that he had left the seminary. He said that religious life was not for him."

"I wished him good luck and told him that he would be in my prayers."

"The next time I heard about Greg was several years later.

" I received a Christmas card from his parents with a note telling me that he was doing well. He graduated from a junior college and became a New York City Police Officer. His parents wrote that when he left the seminary he got the bug to follow a few of his friends who applied to become cops."

"Then, out of the blue, I got his call last week asking me to meet with him."

"We had dinner at Emilio's. Greg told me that he was assigned to the 79th precinct detective squad in Bed-Stuy, where he's been for a few years. He said that he needed advice and had always respected that I never 'bullshitted' him... his word not mine."

Sanders told Romano that all during his time as a patrol officer he received great evaluations from his supervisors. And that those evaluations led to him being promoted to detective third grade.

"He told me that his work as a detective was exemplary, evidenced by the citations he'd received for solving a number of newsworthy cases that were important to the department and the people who live in the 79th precinct."

"However, over the last few years he said that he'd been passed over several times for promotion to detective second grade. When he asked his supervisors why, the answer he received was 'It's not your time.'"

"But as others, who have been detectives for less time than him, were being promoted, Sanders knew he was lied to," Romano said.

"So, he began to reflect on his career hoping to recall something that could be the cause, and if it was repairable he would do just that."

"Did he come up with anything?" Michael asked.

"He did. Greg remembered an off duty arrest he made just after he was promoted to detective."

"He was shopping in a local clothing store when he grabbed a kid for stealing. The thief turned out to be the son of a NYPD captain. The store owner was adamant about pressing charges because he was being hit by thieves every day and it was cutting into his profit margin. Greg processed the arrest and ultimately the thief was allowed to plead guilty to a misdemeanor and was sentenced to do community service."

Sanders told Romano that he had never been directly spoken to about the arrest, but he had the distinct impression that his bosses were not pleased with him because of it. He said he believes that incident is what was holding back his promotion.

"Sal, we're going to be in Red Hook in a few minutes, " Michael said. "What has all this got to do with Eden Liquors and the Devil?"

"Michael, please bear with me. I'm getting there."

"Sanders is the lead investigator in the Eden Liquors case. He told me there was something about the case that was troubling him. Greg knows nothing of our group nor my role in it. He just wanted to talk to me to get my advice as to how he should proceed. I told him that before I could give him advice I needed to hear everything he knew about the incident, which he proceeded to do."

"Greg said that after the incident he received information from a reliable confidential informant, that a cop named Bobby Headley was involved in the murder. And although he strongly believes that pursuing this angle will hold him back even further from promotion, he knows that he has no choice. According to what he learned, Headley was a bad guy."

Romano explained that the informant, who Sanders had worked with for over a year, reached out to Greg a few days after the incident. He told him that a friend of his, a guy named Trini, told him that he was supposed to be part of the crew that did the Eden job but he was cut out of it before it went down. Trini also told the informant that a cop who lived in the neighborhood was involved and that he had done several jobs with him in the past few years.

"When Greg asked the informant if he knew the cop's name, he said that Trini told him it was Bobby Headley."

"To check out the reliability of the claim that Headley was a bad cop, Greg said he dug into his past. What he found surprised him. Apparently, Headley had been involved in several criminal incidents for which police reports were filed."

"However, despite Headley's involvement and his association with the perpetrators of those crimes, who were arrested, Trini being one of them, he was never arrested, or disciplined by the department."

"Sanders told me that after he read those reports he knew that his informant gave him good information. So, Greg asked him to get back with Trini and get more details."

"A few days later the informant told Greg that Trini said he was cut out of the robbery by a guy who he said was the mastermind of the whole thing. His name was Deets."

Romano continued, "Trini said that Deets and Headley met in a club in Manhattan. Trini, Headley, and a few others were partying when Deets, who none of them knew, bought Headley a drink."

"According to Trini, that's when Deets sold Headley on the robbery of Eden Liquors. Deets said it was a front for a gambling and numbers operation, and always had lots of cash on hand at closing time on Saturday night."

"Trini said that the next day Headley and his crew, which he was a part of, met with Deets to go over his plan for the robbery."

"According to what Trini told Greg's informant, it was after this planning meeting that Headley informed Trini that Deets was cutting him out of the job because he wasn't needed."

"The informant told Greg that although Trini was insulted by the slight, he was not really upset because he felt that Deets' plan was 'Way too reckless. With too much risk.'"

"Greg's guy told him that Trini thought that to come up with a plan that was doomed to fail, there had to be something wrong with Deets that affected his brain. 'It's like he's sick and may be dying,' Trini told the informant. 'So, he don't give a shit if something gets fucked up with the job.'"

"Now this is where I became very interested," Romano said to Michael.

"Greg told me that when his informant asked Trini why he thought that Deets was sick or dying, Trini described his appearance. Using Trini's words the informant said, 'The fucking guy had this big, ugly, fucked up, mark, that looks like a tumor, on the left side of his face.'"

They had reached Romano's Red Hook office building just as the monsignor had completed that sentence. Michael jammed on the brakes, turned to the monsignor, and asked, "So what did you tell Sanders to do?"

"I told him to go see you."

"Michael, when I heard about Deets' face my gut told me that *HE* was behind this tragedy."

"However, before I went to Caldwell with my belief, I did some digging to see if this robbery/murder was consistent with what we know to be among *HIS* reasons for coming to Brooklyn. What I learned confirmed it for me. And when I told Caldwell, he agreed."

"*HIS* choice of Eden Liquors was neither a coincidence nor happenstance. *HE* chose Eden because it was a business with family at its core. It was founded by Mr. Choi, and his wife and kids helped out by working there when needed. In addition the store was the sole source of income for that family since the day it was opened. And their employee Sam Collins, is a grandfather who lives with his son and his family."

"The robbery, the murder, and paralyzing Sam Collins devastated those families. Just as the murders of Louis Amato, Linda Torre, and Alex Gazis, did to their families."

"Michael, causing upheaval and chaos by wrecking families and family life, fits right into *HIS* campaign of bringing violence, mayhem, and anarchy to our borough. Eden Liquors was *HIS* latest battlefield."

"After you speak to Greg, if you agree with me about the *Evil One* and the Eden Liquor's slaughter, then Caldwell will speak to the DA and the case will be yours."

CHAPTER
FIFTY-FOUR

The next day when Michael got to his office he had a message on his desk. Sanders had been summoned to another bureau in the DA's office for trial prep on one of his old cases. The note said that he would be finished around 11 a.m. and asked to meet with Michael. He left his cell phone number and the name of the ADA he was meeting with.

Michael called him and the meeting was set.

At 11:10 Sanders walked into his office. Michael motioned for him to sit while he finished a conference call with the attorney who would be handling the lawsuit and a representative from the PR firm that was hired to deal with the press.

Just that morning another story appeared in the city tabloids alleging that Christine Miller was not the first or only witness that Gioca had mishandled and counseled to lie.

The only truth in the report was that Michael had indeed been assigned to the case mentioned, but the allegations that made up the bulk of the story were total fabrications.

It was the opinion of the PR rep that Miller and her attorney, Monroe Wilkins, under the guise of looking for corroboration of

Miller's allegations against Michael, had been spreading money around to get quotes from "anonymous sources," which they then fed to the press.

The advice from his lawyer and the PR rep was the same- go about your business and don't react publicly to anything that appears in the news.

Michael assured them both that he had no intention of doing anything close to that. "Besides, I think I'm about to get very busy," he said as he glanced over at Sanders.

When he hung up Michael reached over his desk and shook hands with the detective. "I'm Gioca. And you must be Greg Sanders."

"Man, I thought the shit I caught out in the street was bad. But after hearing a bit of what you were just talking about, and reading today's papers, my stuff's nothing compared to what you're going through. I don't know you, but I feel for you."

Not wanting to let on that every time one of these stories appeared it was as if he'd been stabbed in the heart, Michael's response to Sanders was, "Thanks Greg. I appreciate it. I have a good team representing me, and my family doesn't buy a word of it. So, I'm good. Now tell me what you've got."

After some preliminary pleasantries and a discussion of how each of them had come to know Romano, they got down to business.

Sanders repeated everything that he told Romano about the robbery and the surrounding circumstances. And even though he heard it all from the monsignor, Michael didn't stop Sanders because he wanted to hear the facts directly from the source.

"The report of the robbery/murder was called into the precinct just after midnight. Normally it would have been handled by "night watch," Sanders said.

Because precinct detective squads go off duty at midnight, the NYPD assigns two detectives, the "night watch," to cover crimes that occur between 12am and 8am Their responsibility is to do preliminary investigative work and then turn the case over to a precinct detective at the start of his or her next shift.

"However, that night because I was still in the precinct doing some paperwork on one of my cases, the boss assigned it to me. When I got to Eden Liquors, the night watch guys were on the scene as well as two detectives from the Brooklyn North Homicide Squad."

"I, along with the night watch detectives, and the homicide guys, canvassed the area for witnesses, while the Crime Scene Unit scoured the store for evidence."

Sanders told Michael that witnesses had not been forthcoming, but the crime scene guys had recovered a .9mm bullet on one of the store shelves, and .9mm shell casings were recovered from the floor.

".9mm bullets were recovered from Choi's body by the medical examiner, who also said that the track of the bullets indicated that the shooter was standing over the victim when he was shot."

"In addition," Sanders said, "A .45 caliber shell casing was found when the crime scene unit examined Collin's clothing. It was caught in the folds of his shirt."

Sanders went on to say that in the days and weeks after the incident he and his colleagues were out on the streets around Eden Liquors hoping to locate witnesses or even someone who might have heard who was responsible.

"Mike, I would have settled for street talk at that point. I was so frustrated," Sanders said. "Then I caught a break. Out of the blue I heard from an informant of mine who told me he knew something about the Eden Liquors job."

"Mookie is a guy I arrested when I was in uniform. He was a street hustler who sold stolen MetroCards, loose cigarettes, a little weed, and anything else he could get his hands on. By the time I got him he had been locked up about fifteen times, but the most jail time he had ever done was five days in the Brooklyn House of Detention. I collared him for snatching a woman's purse."

"The grand larceny charge was his first felony arrest, but with his record he was facing prison time. He begged me to take it easy on him. He told me that he's always out on the street and sees and hears lots of things that would interest me, especially when I became a detective. He told me that if I cut him a break, he'd work with me and pass on what he knew. He also told me he'd work proactively for me and do some digging when I needed him to."

"The woman whose purse was grabbed got it back and had no interest in going to court to testify. So I went to my boss, told him all this, and asked him if I could cut Mookie loose. I promised to keep an eye on him and if he had information on cases that were assigned to other cops, I would pass it along. The boss gave me the okay, and Mookie has been talking to me ever since."

Sanders said that when he met with Mookie about the Eden Liquors case, the informant told him that, according to his friend Trini, a cop named Bobby Headley, was involved in the murder.

"Mike, I know that the monsignor told you about my issue. But since I spoke to him I've given it a lot more thought. It's no longer a problem. If Headley is involved, then fuck it if he's a cop. If he's guilty, he deserves to go down for this. And I would be proud to put his ass in prison for what he did to Choi and Collins, and for the damage he will have done to the reputations of all my hard-working, honest, brothers and sisters on the job."

"Greg, that's good to hear. I truly believe that's the right choice. But if you know anything about me, you know that I took down a dirty fed, and it cost me a lot. So you have to be prepared for what may come your way from those "brothers and sisters on the job" whose reputations you *will* be helping. They might not see it that way."

"Mike, I know all about you, and what you went through."

"When Romano suggested I speak to you, I checked you out. When I read about the case involving that fed, what happened to you after, and how you handled it, I knew that the monsignor had sent me to the right guy. I also checked you out with Armin Bondor who's a friend of mine. He said you are the best."

"I promise that if I lock up Headley, I'll be ready for whatever comes at me."

"Will you work with me on this?" Sanders finally asked.

Michael didn't answer him. Instead he asked the detective to tell him about Headley's background with as much detail as he had.

When Sanders finished, Michael thought to himself, '*Headley is the type of guy who would make a perfect puppet for the Evil One. He's a bad guy, who would do anything, but had the luck, so far, to never get caught.*'

Michael asked to hear everything Sanders had on Deets. Sanders paused before answering. "All I have is what Trini told Mookie about him. Mike, this guy must be a ghost. There is nothing in our computer about him, nor is there anything in any of the state and federal databases that I've looked at."

Michael was not surprised, in fact he expected that answer. But he needed to hear from Trini directly, before he could give both Sanders and Romano what they were looking for.

"Greg, before I give you an answer about getting involved in the case, I need to talk to Trini. I want to hear everything he knows about Deets."

To cover the real reason that he wanted to learn more about Deets, Michael told Greg a little lie. "You know that I run the DA's Rackets Division. And a straight murder/robbery is usually handled by the homicide bureau," he said. "So, I'll need a rackets angle which will allow me to get involved. And depending on the quality of Trini's info about Deets, that could be my way in."

Sanders told Michael that he understood and asked for a few days. "Mookie will help me get Trini for you. I'll be in touch."

CHAPTER
FIFTY-FIVE

Three days later, Greg Sanders, with Trini in tow, was waiting for Michael when he arrived at his office.

Surprised, Michael asked Sanders to have Trini wait outside while he spoke to him. "Wow, that was fast," he said. "Mookie must have something on this guy to persuade him to come in to see me that quickly."

"Actually, he doesn't. All he had to do was tell him that the DA's office was looking to get Deets. Trini's reaction was that he'd be happy to 'Dime that motherfucker.'"

Michael started to laugh, "Do they still use that expression, 'drop a dime' on someone, when intending to inform on him, even though a call from a phone booth was a quarter before every public phone in this city disappeared?"

"This guy Trini must be hanging in the streets for a long time."

Now Sanders started laughing. "Yeah Mike, he's been around. Detectives in my squad, who've been in the precinct for years, all know Trini. And many of them have locked him up."

"He hates Deets for humiliating him in front of his boys when he cut him out of the Eden job. When I picked him up to bring him here this morning he was standing on the corner we agreed to, and he told me he had been waiting for twenty minutes because he was so anxious to talk to you. I hope he gives you what you need," Sanders said.

"Well, let's see. Bring him in."

For the next ninety minutes Trini told Michael everything he knew and had heard about Deets, and how he came to be hooked up with Headley. When he was done, Michael was certain that it *was* the *Evil One,* using the name "Deets," when he recruited Bobby Headley to *HIS* army of hate and destruction.

Trini told Michael that Deets didn't know Headley before he bought him a drink in that Manhattan night club. Yet he called him by his name, and told him he knew that he was a cop. He also told Headley that he'd been watching him for a while, and he knew that he had been pulling off jobs and was never caught.

Michael knew that it was essential for *HIM* to learn everything *HE* could about *HIS* stooge, especially his penchant for committing crimes. That was part of Satan's method in scouting for, settling on, then grooming a patsy to do *HIS* dirty work.

Also, giving Headley the idea to flash his police shield to get into the secure area of the store was a classic move for the *Evil One. HE* is the master of deceit and deception.

Another thing Trini told him was right in line with what *HE* would do. Trini said that after the robbery Headley told him that Deets abandoned the crew during the first attempt at the robbery, leaving them with no one monitoring the police radio. When Headley tried to raise him on the walkie talkie to let him know that the store had closed early and they were aborting the robbery, Deets never acknowledged him. "Head told me he never heard from Deets again," Trini said.

Michael thought to himself, *'Just what Satan would do. Set the stage for the tragedy then leave HIS stooges to deal with the fallout.'*

But it was the last two things that Trini said that positively proved to Michael that Satan was behind the robbery/murder.

The first was, after the murder Headley told Cooper and Ruiz, who then told Trini, that just before he shot Choi, he heard Deets' voice in his head *telling* him to kill Choi and Collins. "They saw your face," is what the voice said.

'Barbaric and typical of the devil,' Michael thought when he heard it.

But the last thing Trini told him was the icing on the cake.

"Mr. G," Trini said, "Deets' plan was to rob Eden Liquors because he said it's a gambling spot, which none of us from the neighborhood ever heard of. I thought the guy was crazy. Then when he told Headley to use his police badge to get into the store and behind the plexiglass, I thought that the motherfucker was reckless."

"But at the end of the meeting when I got a good look at Deets' face and I saw that fucked up mark, like a tumor, I says to myself, *'This dude is real sick and dying, so he don't give a fuck if Head and the others get caught.'*"

Trini had been right. The plan was crazy and reckless. But Michael didn't care about any of that. It was the mark of the Devil that told him all he needed to know.

Michael asked Trini a few superfluous questions to disguise that he had gotten everything he needed from him, thanked him for his help, and asked him to wait outside the office while he talked to Sanders.

Trini gave him enough. Confident in how Romano and Caldwell would react when he told them that he agreed with them, he let Sanders know that he would be getting into the case by once again telling a little white lie.

"I have all I need for me to take the case," Michael said. "The Rackets Division has a unit that prosecutes crimes committed by law enforcement personnel. Trini has convinced me that it was a police officer and his buddies, recruited by Deets, who did the robbery, who murdered Choi, and attempted to murder Collins. So, I'm in."

Sanders was thrilled. "Thank you Mike. We're gonna get this crew. And you're gonna convict them."

"I'll bring you a copy of my file tomorrow," he said. "And we can get started, *together*, when you're up to speed."

After Sanders left his office, Michael got himself a cup of coffee and called Romano.

"We're back in business," he said.

"You were right Sal. There is no doubt that the *Evil One* is responsible for Eden Liquors. Now get the okay from the DA because Greg Sanders will be here tomorrow with the police file and we're going to get right into it."

"Michael, that's great. I'll have Caldwell call him as soon as I get off with you. By the way, Greg was elated."

"How do you know that?" Michael asked.

Romano chuckled and said, "He called right after he left your office and told me the news. Of course he has no clue as to what he's up against. He's just happy he's working with 'the best', his exact words. I'll let you know when I hear from Caldwell."

It didn't take long for Romano to get back to Michael.

"Caldwell spoke to DA Price. The case is yours. Price also told him that if you need Dina Mitchell and Tim Clark, we don't have to call him for permission, you can have them."

"Sal, that's great. I can't wait to get started with Sanders. We have a lot of work ahead of us. We don't have a case except for Trini's hearsay, which is hardly enough for an arrest, let alone enough for a conviction."

Then switching from the serious to a more playful tone, Michael said, "I'm going to need all my strength to bring this one home, Monsignor. So how about you buy me dinner tonight, so I'll be sufficiently fortified," Michael asked, barely able to stifle his laughter.

Romano took the joke very well and laughing told Michael, "I'll call ahead to make sure that Emilio has a sufficient amount of protein on the menu for you."

"Thanks," Michael answered. "I'll see you there at seven."

CHAPTER

FIFTY-SIX

As usual, the meal that Emilio served the monsignor and Michael was delicious.

During dinner Michael filled Romano in on all that he learned from Sanders and Trini about the Eden case. "This is going to be a tough one, Sal," Michael said.

Romano listened carefully and though he agreed that it was a difficult case, he said to Michael, "Have faith. You're just at the beginning. We have all the confidence in the world in you."

Romano continued, "From what I hear, Sanders is a dogged detective. You and him will make a very formidable team. He'll work until he drops, and he'll be invaluable to you."

Michael also brought Romano up to speed on the status of the civil case against him. He told the monsignor about the advice given to him by the lawyer and the PR rep and assured Romano that "As much as it kills me to say this, I'll abide by it. So please tell Caldwell that he doesn't have to worry about me."

Over dessert, Michael asked Romano to fill him in, a bit more, on Sanders. "You told me a little about his work reputation, but I want to know more about him as a person."

This was important for Michael to know because he would be working with Sanders for the foreseeable future and any opinion and insight Romano had into the detective's personality would help to ensure that things would go smoothly between them.

Romano gave Michael everything he could about Sanders. He now had a very good idea of who Detective Greg Sanders was, both on the job and off.

When they were finished with their meal, as usual no check was forthcoming. As was his practice, Romano reached for his wallet to leave a generous tip for the waiter. However, Michael surprised him when *he* laid down five twenty-dollar bills to cover the tip.

Seeing the look on Romano's face, Michael said to him, "Did you really think I was serious about you buying me dinner?"

When Romano nodded, Michael pretended to be insulted. "After all you did for me and my family the other night," he said, "How could you think I would take advantage of you like that? What kind of person do think I've become?"

Initially the monsignor bought Gioca's act. But when Michael burst out laughing, because he couldn't hold it in any longer, Romano smiled and began to shake his head. "You got me," he said.

The next day, Sanders was in Michael's office bright and early with a copy of the police file for the Eden Liquors case. In addition, he had the medical examiner's full file and report, as well as the crime scene reports and photographs.

It took Michael two days to digest the material.

After having spent the weekend visiting with his dad and his sons, he was ready to sit with Sanders on Monday morning to plan their strategy.

Their meeting, however, was only mildly productive. Although Michael's questions about Eden Liquors, Min Jun Choi, Sam Collins, Bobby Headley, and the robbery crew, were answered to the best of Sanders' ability, the problem was that his knowledge was limited.

Nevertheless, the two settled on a strategy, the success of which was dependent on finding witnesses. To increase that likelihood, Michael enlisted Dina and Tim to join him and Sanders on the team.

Sanders, Dina, and Tim got to work the next day. But after weeks on the streets interviewing people and working their informants, they had nothing to show for it.

Doing his part, Michael spread the word among the assistant DAs in Rackets that any case that was even remotely connected to Bed-Stuy was to be brought to his attention. And to widen the net, he asked the same of ADAs who worked in other bureaus. His hope was to pry information, or an informant, loose from one of those cases.

However, it was all to no avail. The witness drought, as he called it, rolled on.

Having made no progress in the seven months since the incident, it became clearer to Michael that the *Evil One* did a great job in choosing the location of the crime, the time of day and the time year for the crime, and the perpetrators, to ensure that *HE* would get away with this one.

Tompkins Avenue, at midnight, in the dead of winter, was deserted. And even if there happened to be someone out at that time, they would likely be the type of witness who a jury would find less than credible, even if they had the balls to rat out a cop.

The first real break in the case came just past the one-year anniversary of the robbery/murder.

Sam Collins recovered enough from his injuries to speak to Sanders, Dina and Tim.

The three met him in the Westchester County facility where he was completing a long rehabilitation process. When they entered his room, Collins, who was told to expect them, was sitting up in his bed reading a novel entitled "Crooked Brooklyn," that one of his grand-children gave him on his family's last visit.

Collins greeted the investigators with a big hello and a smile. After introducing himself, Dina and Tim, Sanders apologized to Collins for disturbing him.

"'Mr. Detective,'" the seventy-nine-year-old said, "No need to be sorry. I don't get many visitors because my people don't live up near here. This place is a long way from Bed-Stuy, so I have to wait for the weekend for someone to come see me. So, I'm happy as can be that I got three visitors right now."

Sanders told him why they were there, saying, "I know this is difficult, but we need your help if we're going to catch the guys who did this to you and killed Mr. Choi."

Collins told him he'd do his best.

He began by confirming Trini's information that one of the robbers used a police shield to gain entry to the area of Eden Liquors behind the plexiglass. He told them that when the guy flashed the shield "He asked us if he could use the store's bathroom."

He went on to tell the story of what had occurred inside Eden, which corroborated much of what Sanders and Michael had learned from Trini.

When Collins was finished, Greg asked him if he knew either of the robbers or had ever seen them before that night. Collins' answer to both questions was, "No."

Before leaving, Sanders asked Collins if it would be okay to come back to show him photos. "If you recognize either or both of the robbers whose photos may be among those I show you, we'd like you to identify them. Do you think you can do that?"

Collins answered with a shrug. "You come back with them pictures and we'll see what we'll see."

Three days later Sanders went back to Collins with two photo arrays. Each contained six photos. One array had Headley's photograph and the other contained Cooper's. Sam Collins took his time and examined each array for a few minutes, before saying, "I can't say that they're in these pictures or they ain't. I'm sorry."

Sanders didn't let his disappointment show when he said, "Mr.

Collins, it's okay. You take care now and do what the doctors and nurses tell you to do. I'll see you down the road."

Before Sanders left, Collins struggled to lift his hand which he offered to Sanders. This surprised and impressed Greg, who had assumed that Collins had lost the use of his legs *and* arms. Sanders took it, and smiling so he wouldn't tear up, said, "Mr. Collins I'm gonna get the guys who did this to you."

CHAPTER
FIFTY-SEVEN

A disappointed Sanders met with Michael, Dina and Tim the next day. The group, though disheartened over Collins' inability to identify anyone from the photos, was not thinking about giving up. They discussed doing a re-canvass of the area around Eden Liquors hoping that because of all the time that had passed since the robbery someone would feel secure enough to speak up.

They also talked about surveilling Headley when he was off duty. "If he meets up with Cooper or Ruiz at least we'll have independent proof that they know one another," said Dina.

"Great idea," Sanders said. "And I'll put a flag on their names in our computer. So if Cooper or Ruiz is arrested, having been seen with Headley will give us leverage to question them about him. Who knows one or both may give him up hoping to save their own asses."

Michael didn't want to discourage the team from coming up with ideas, so he kept the feeling that they were 'grasping at straws', to himself. He, too, was frustrated at the lack of progress, and hated to admit defeat. However, things seemed hopeless.

'Where do I turn for help?' he asked himself. And then it hit him.

The last time he had this hopeless and helpless feeling about a case with no idea where to turn, he decided, out of desperation, to attend the Saturday evening Mass at the church near his office to pray for guidance. That night the service at St. Charles Borromeo had been conducted by a visiting priest who delivered a sermon about St. Jude, the patron saint of lost causes. His message was, "When things seem hopeless, don't give up."

After Mass that night, as he walked to his car, he thought about the sermon, and his problem. He said a silent prayer to St. Jude asking for help. By the time he arrived at his car he had come up with a solution to his problem. One that would save his case and push back hard against the *Evil One*.

He learned a valuable lesson that night, helped along by Monsignor Romano's constant reminder "You're not alone in this war. And you should trust in your strongest ally," as he pointed to the heavens.

Michael had come a long way from the day he was recruited by Romano when he had serious doubts about his faith. But the battles he had since fought against the ultimate evil, made him a believer again.

Michael checked his watch and saw that it was 12:15, just enough time to get to St. Charles for the 12:30 midday Mass. "Guys," he said, "take a break, get some lunch, take a walk, do something to clear your heads and let's meet back here at 2 o'clock when we can pick this up again. You never know, the break may do us some good."

When Michael walked back into his office after Mass, and saw the faces of Sanders, Dina and Tim, he knew that his visit to St. Charles, and his prayer to St. Jude, had worked.

His ally had come through again.

"Mike," Sanders said, "Just as we were walking back here after lunch, I got a call from my boss. He told me that two hours ago Brooklyn North Narcotics made an arrest of a drug dealer they had been looking for. The guy's name is Frankie Estevez. When they brought him into the precinct he told the narco guys that he knew who did the Eden Liquors job and was looking for a deal."

"He said he was out on the street that night, down the block from Eden, when he heard shots and saw two guys running out of the store. He said he knew them. He named Headley 'the cop,' and Cooper."

"I'm gonna head down to the precinct and talk to him. I'd like Dina and Tim to go with me. If he's worth it, I'll let you know. Then you can come down there and take a recorded statement. If he wants a deal, you're the guy who can do it for him," Sanders said.

"No problem," Michael answered. "Keep me posted and let me know if you need me."

After the three left his office, Michael looked up and whispered, "Thank you."

Four hours later Michael got the call. It was Dina. "Mike we need you and a stenographer down here at the 79. Not only is Estevez talking, but he told us about a woman who was scoring drugs from him when they heard the shots coming from Eden Liquors. Her name is Carmen Sisto. When the detectives picked her up she told them that she had a couple of warrants she wanted to clear up, so she would tell what she knows."

"Sanders has spoken to both Estevez and Sisto and their stories match."

"Sisto said that she knows the two guys who ran out of the store. One is 'the cop who lives in the neighborhood,' and the other is Cooper. She added that she saw Ruiz in front of the store, and he joined the others as they ran. Sisto said that the three disappeared into the Thompkins projects, which is where Ruiz' girlfriend, Louisa, lives."

When Michael got to the precinct, the stenographer who was with him set up in an interview room to take statements from Estevez and Sisto.

They began with Estevez. After advising him of his Miranda warnings because he would be incriminating himself in the drug dealing he was engaged in when he heard and saw what happened, Michael asked him if he understood his rights. Estevez said that he did, but he didn't trust DAs. "I already told Det. Sanders what I know, why I got to repeat it for you?"

Michael explained that he needed a record of the statement because he was required to turn over what Estevez had said to a defense attorney should there be a trial. "And, just in case you don't remember everything when I prepare you for trial, I'll be able to read this to you to refresh your memory."

Estevez still balked at giving the statement to Michael. "'Mr. DA, get Sanders in here. I trust him. I needs to talk to him again, without you around."

Michael did what Estevez asked. He stepped out of the room and had Sanders and Tim Clark, who Sanders said was with him when he first spoke to Estevez, talk to him. After ten minutes or so, Sanders came out and told Michael, "He'll talk to you. But he wants me and Tim in the room when he does."

Michael agreed and proceeded to take a witness statement from Estevez.

Next it was Sisto's turn. And although she openly flirted with Michael as he advised her of her rights, when it came time to answer that final question about talking without an attorney, Sisto hardened.

"Listen 'Mr. DA'," she said, "I don't care about no lawyer, but if you don't promise me a deal on my warrants, and put it in writing and on that tape, I ain't speaking to you. That lady detective Dina told me that you was the big boss, and I could trust you. But I'm from the streets and I need more than someone tellin' me you gonna take care of me."

Michael would ultimately be required to turn over the existence of any deal he made with Sisto, and for that matter, with Estevez too, but he didn't want the steno statement to be cluttered with it. So he needed to convince Sisto to talk with the promise that he'd later put whatever deal they arrived at, in writing. When he presented that arrangement to her, she continued to refuse to be questioned.

He left the room and this time sought out Dina. "Did you have any trouble with Sisto when she was brought in?" Michael asked.

"No, why?" Dina replied.

"She's refusing to cooperate until I agree to put her deal on the record. I tried to get her to trust me, but she's insistent on getting what she wants."

Dina smiled and said, "When Sanders talked to her, she openly flirted with him. I was sitting right next to him, but she only had eyes for Greg. So, let us go talk to her. She might soften with him asking."

"Dina, be my guest," Michael replied. "But you should know that she was flirting with me as well, and it did me no good."

"Well," Dina said now with an even bigger smile, "Greg's younger than you. That might make a difference."

Michael started to laugh. "Just get her to talk. I'll deal with that age crack when we're done."

Sanders turned out to be Michael's good luck charm that day. First he had gotten Estevez to go on the record with Michael and then he sweet talked Sisto into doing the same.

After he finished with the statements, Michael sat with Dina and Tim while Sanders dealt with the paperwork to get Estevez and Sisto released from custody with desk appearance tickets for the drug deal they had admitted to engaging in.

The DATs required them to appear in court down the road. By then, Michael felt certain that by using their testimony he would get an indictment against Headley, Cooper, and Ruiz. And Estevez and Sisto would get their deals after the trial.

While they waited for Sanders, both Dina and Tim said that agreeing to have him talk to the recalcitrant witnesses was a smart move.

"There is no doubt that Greg is the reason they both ultimately agreed to go on record with you. He relaxed them and got them to buy into his assurance that they could trust you," Tim said.

Dina added, "Michael, I totally agree. Greg was invaluable. And given the lifestyle of those two, by the time we go to trial, we may need him again."

Michael was in total agreement. "Everything I had heard about his personality and ability was right on the money."

Just then Sanders walked into the room having finished his paperwork. "Those two are all set Mike. They assured me that they would stay in touch, so you won't have a problem getting them into the grand jury and on the stand at trial."

"Greg, I can't thank you enough," Michael said. "Without you I would have been shit out of luck with them. You were great. Now, I'm starving, as you all must be as well. Let's go eat. Dinner's on me."

CHAPTER
FIFTY-EIGHT

Over dinner, the group discussed the next steps they needed to take in the investigation.

"Technically we have enough to make an arrest right now," Michael said, "But I'd rather not have to go to trial with Estevez, Sisto, and Sam Collins as my only witnesses. A good defense attorney could tear them apart. I'm not greedy. I'd be happy with just one more thing, anything, to corroborate what we now have."

The next day Michael got his 'something.' And that 'something' would lead him to the corroboration he was looking for.

Midway through an early morning run, Michael received a call from Sanders. "Mickey Ruiz was arrested sometime after midnight by detectives from the 88th precinct," Sanders told him. The 88th precinct was adjacent to the 79th, where Sanders was assigned.

"Mike, they got him for a robbery. He was the lookout while two guys held up a check cashing location on Flushing Avenue near the Brooklyn Navy Yard a few days ago. The owner of the spot didn't know the guys who came into the store and held him up. But he recognized Ruiz, who was a past customer, when he joined them as they ran away from the store. The owner reported it to the 88 and they picked up Ruiz at his girlfriend's apartment in the Thompkins Houses."

Sanders told Michael that Ruiz had an extensive criminal record, and he told the 88 detectives that another conviction would lead to him doing a long stretch in prison. "So he started talking," Sanders said.

"He gave up his two accomplices from the robbery of the check cashing spot. And when he told them that he had information on the Eden Liquors case, the 88 guys called me."

"I got dressed and went to speak to Ruiz."

"Mike, he gave it all up. He admitted to being in on the planning, supplying the guns and walkie-talkies, and acting as the lookout for Headley, 'the cop,' and Jeffrey Cooper. He said they were the shooters. He even gave up his girlfriend Louisa Pena, who had hidden the guns and the walkie-talkies after the robbery."

"And there's more. Ruiz told me that Jeffrey Cooper has a brother, Mack is his name. Sometime after the robbery, Ruiz said that he, Mack Cooper, and Headley were 'bullshitting' on the street, and Headley bragged about doing the Eden Liquors job."

"Headley told Mack that he had to waste the owner because he saw my face. But your brother fucked up. He was supposed to kill the worker, but he only paralyzed him. I hope that don't come back to bite us on the ass.'"

"What about Deets?" Michael asked. "Did he mention him?"

"He did, but he claimed that he really didn't know him. He said Deets was Headley's guy who set the whole thing up."

"Greg, that's great! It's just what we needed. Having an inside guy testify along with Estevez, Sisto, and Sam Collins gives me more than enough to go to the grand jury. What kind of deal is Ruiz looking for?" Michael asked.

"I didn't get into that with him. I told him you would be the one to negotiate with. I think you should get down here. We haven't moved him from the 88. Come up to the detective squad room which is where we have him."

Michael told Sanders that he'd be there in an hour with a videographer to record Ruiz' statement.

When Michael arrived he was briefed on the check cashing location robbery by Derrick Barker, the 88th precinct detective who had arrested Ruiz. After which he spoke to Sanders again to make sure he had everything that Ruiz told Greg.

Now fully informed, he, Sanders, and Barker went to speak to Ruiz.

Michael introduced himself and fully advised him of his Miranda rights.

Ruiz told Michael that he was willing to give him everything about the Eden Liquors case, "On the record, and without a lawyer," but he first wanted to hear what kind of deal Michael was offering.

Normally, Michael wouldn't have discussed a deal with a defendant/witness without first hearing what evidence he had to offer. But Ruiz had told Sanders everything he knew, and Michael was satisfied that his testimony would be devastating to Headley and Jeffrey Cooper. And despite his criminal record, Ruiz would play well before a jury because Michael had witnesses to corroborate his story.

"Ruiz, you're a predicate felon, so jail time is mandatory," Michael told him. "But because you were only a lookout, and you're willing to cooperate with us now, and at trial, I will recommend that the judge give you a minimum sentence. I'll also ask the judge to order the Department of Corrections to house you in a protective witness unit in whatever prison you're sent to. This way you don't have to constantly look over your shoulder for someone who may not like that you're an informant. If things go well, I can see you getting out in a few years."

Ruiz didn't answer right away. He asked if he could make a phone call to his wife to discuss the offer. Surprised to hear about a wife, Michael asked him if she was aware of his latest arrest, the Eden Liquors job, and "That spot in the Thompkins Houses."

Ruiz began to laugh. "Mr. DA I ain't stupid. I know what you're asking. My wife don't know nothin' about nothin', especially Louisa

Pena. We live out on Long Island and all she knows is when I come to Bed-Stuy it's to hang with my boys. You ain't gotta tell her about Louisa do you?"

Michael assured Ruiz that his personal life was his to discuss with his wife and he had no intention of letting her know anything about his relationship with Louisa.

"Of course Louisa isn't going to be very happy with you when she finds out that you told us about her hiding the guns and walkie-talkies, so who knows what *she'll* do. I can't protect you from her going to your wife and blowing the whistle on you," Michael told him.

"I ain't worried about Lou. She'll be mad but she's good people. She won't say a word to my wife."

Michael told Sanders to let Ruiz have his call.

After more than an hour talking to his wife, Ruiz told Michael, "I ain't talking no more. And I ain't gonna cooperate with you all. I want to go to trial."

Shocked, Michael tried to get Ruiz to reconsider. "Ruiz, let me remind you that you've already confessed to the felony murder at Eden Liquors and to the robbery of that check cashing place. The only way I don't use those statements against you is if you cooperate with us. And I have witnesses who put you outside the liquor store as the lookout, and after the murder saw you run with Headley and Cooper into the Thompkins Houses where your girlfriend lives. Do you understand all of that?"

"And" Michael continued, "I'm going to take the information you gave us about Louisa and bring her in and confront her with it. And I'll bet she takes the deal I'll offer her. Do you understand all of *that*?"

In response Ruiz said, "Do what you gotta do. I ain't talking no more. I want a lawyer."

Michael just shook his head in disbelief. He told Det. Barker to book him for the check cashing spot robbery only. He would wait for an indictment before he authorized Sanders to arrest Ruiz for the Eden Liquors murder.

"Greg," Michael said, "Let's talk to Louisa Pena, and find Jeffrey Cooper. I'd like to talk to both of them. Let's see if they're interested in doing what Mr. Ruiz was not."

Wasting no time, Sanders, with Dina and Tim, picked up Louisa Pena at her apartment and brought her to the 79th precinct for a chat.

Michael had gone back to his office but instructed them to call him if she was willing to talk.

It didn't take long for Louisa to agree to work with the prosecution.

"That motherfucker Ruiz, I'm gonna make sure you all fry his ass," was her angry reaction to Sanders telling her that she was there because Ruiz had given her up.

Dina asked her if she was willing to speak to an assistant district attorney and tell him everything she knew about the Eden Liquors case. Dina added, "And depending on what you tell the ADA, you might even avoid being arrested."

"What do I have to do? I'll do anything so I don't go to jail," was Louisa's response.

That afternoon, Louisa told Michael, on the record, with a stenographer taking down every word, everything she knew about the Eden Liquors robbery/murder. In return she was not arrested. She agreed in writing to continue her cooperation, and to testify in the grand jury, as well as at any trial related to Eden Liquors.

When Michael came out of the room after the agreement was signed, he was happy, but not satisfied. He turned to Sanders and asked, "Have you found Jeffrey Cooper yet?"

Sanders tried to look disappointed, but he was unable to hold back a smile, "Yes. He was easy to find," he answered. "He's in jail."

CHAPTER
FIFTY-NINE

Months after the Eden Liquors incident, Cooper was shot by a retired NYPD officer who was working security at a Brooklyn bank that he robbed. The security guard shot him as he ran from the bank brandishing a gun.

Ironically, Cooper was paralyzed as a result of the shooting and was permanently confined to a wheelchair. When Michael heard that, Sam Collins, who Copper had shot and paralyzed, came to mind. '*Karma's a bitch,*' he said to himself.

Sanders was able to locate Cooper simply by putting his name in the NYPD database. Although bank robbery is a federal crime, Cooper was confined to the New York City jail on Rikers Island because the FBI chose to let the Brooklyn DA's office handle his prosecution. Because the feds were not involved it would be much easier for Michael to offer Cooper a deal in return for his cooperation if he was interested.

And boy was he interested. When they spoke, he told Michael that all he was looking for was a way to "Save my ass." He wanted a deal that covered the bank robbery, as well as the Eden Liquors case.

Michael found him to be a practical man in that he was not

expecting to be released with no prison time. Cooper knew he would be going to state prison. He just wanted to minimize the amount of time he had to serve as much as he could.

The two men arrived at a place where they were satisfied.

To cover both cases, Michael would recommend a concurrent sentence of fifteen years to life. That would give the thirty-year-old Cooper a chance to have a life outside of his cage, if he was paroled after serving the minimum sentence.

In return, Cooper would tell Michael the entire story of the Eden Liquors robbery/murder and would agree to testify against Headley and Ruiz.

As a bonus, Cooper told Michael where he could find his brother Mack.

"'Mr. G', my brother was with Headley and Ruiz when Headley was bragging about shooting the liquor store owner. You bring Mack in and let me talk to him. I'm certain he'll cooperate to help both of us."

Jeffrey Cooper was right. Sanders located Mack and brought him into Michael's office to talk. His initial reaction to the request that he cooperate, was "I ain't a rat." But once Dina and Tim wheeled his brother into the office to talk to him, his attitude took a turn for the better.

Mack was out on bail for grand larceny. He had snatched a woman's purse on Tompkins Avenue and was nabbed by a cop who was coming out of a coffee shop after buying a sandwich. The purse was recovered, and despite New York's lax bail laws, bail was set. Fortunately for Mack it was an amount which his wife could afford to post. However, because he had a long criminal record, a conviction for the purse snatch would mean a mandatory state prison sentence.

After talking alone with Jeffrey, Mack agreed to cooperate. He told Michael everything he knew about Headley and Ruiz, and about Headley's street confession.

When Michael asked him what convinced him to change his

mind, Mack told him, "I want to save my ass of course, *and* I don't want my brother to take all the weight for that Eden Liquors job."

"I heard on the street that Ruiz had given up everyone to you but was now saying that he ain't have nothing to do with that robbery. He's saying it was all my brother and Headley. I can't let that happen."

Michael prepared cooperation agreements for Mack and Jeffrey that both men signed that day.

When Mack Cooper left the office and Jeffrey Cooper was on his way back to Rikers Island, Michael sat back and couldn't help but smile. He told Greg, Dina, and Tim, "We now have more than enough to arrest and indict Headley and Ruiz for felony murder. Let's go find these bastards and lock their asses up."

Bobby Headley no longer lived in the Brooklyn apartment near Eden Liquors. He had moved into the second-floor apartment of a two-family home in Queens.

More than a year after he murdered Min Jun Choi, he was arrested in front of that home as he set out to walk his dog.

He was brought to the 79th precinct and charged with the murder of Choi, the shooting of Collins, and the robbery of Eden Liquors. Michael drove to the precinct hoping to take a statement from Headley but was not surprised when Headley asked for a lawyer.

After all the NYPD paperwork on the arrest had been completed, Sanders, Dina, and Tim, took him out to their car for transport to Brooklyn Criminal Court for arraignment.

The press was alerted. The arrest of an NYPD officer charged with murder was big news, so they were out in force. Both still and TV cameras recorded Headley's walk to the car.

That 'perp walk' would later prove to be a significant event for PO Robert "Bobby" Headley.

Mickey Ruiz, in jail for the check cashing location robbery, was rearrested and charged with the murder of Choi, the shooting of Collins, and the robbery of Eden Liquors.

Three days after both men were arraigned in criminal court, and held without bail, a Brooklyn grand jury returned an indictment against Headley and Ruiz for the Eden Liquors crimes, and an additional indictment against Ruiz for the check cashing location robbery. The matters were sent to Brooklyn Supreme Court Judge Ronald Cavallo for trial.

Because Ruiz had confessed to the Eden Liquors incident and inculpated Headley in that statement, under New York law they were required to be tried for those crimes by two separate juries. The law would not allow a jury sitting in judgment of Headley to hear what Ruiz, his co-defendant, told Sanders and Barker that he did.

So, when the case first appeared before Judge Cavallo, he told Michael and the lawyers for Headley and Ruiz, Stuart Lieberman and Deirdre Hart, that he would empanel two juries to hear the evidence simultaneously. He would remove the Headley jury from the courtroom when the prosecution was ready to offer Ruiz' confession into evidence. Employing that procedure would eliminate the need to try the case twice.

Neither Michael nor the defense attorneys objected to Judge Cavallo's plan, and a schedule to handle all the pre-trial matters was set. The judge adjourned the case for one month, after which, he told the attorneys, he would schedule a trial date.

Michael's job was to prepare what's called, 'discovery,' for the defense attorneys. Under the law the prosecution is required to turn over copies of the evidence it intends to use against a defendant at trial. This is to avoid 'trial by ambush.'

In a case such as this one, with the investigation taking over a year to complete, there could be hundreds of documents, photos, and tape recordings to copy in order to comply with the legal requirements of the discovery law. To ensure that he got the material to the defense attorneys in the time required by the criminal law statutes, Michael enlisted both Dina and Tim to assist him.

After working diligently for what seemed to be a month, the material was hand delivered by Dina and Tim to the defense attorney seven days after that first appearance before Judge Cavallo.

It was time for Michael to prepare his case for trial.

The place to start that prep work was Eden Liquors. Although he had been handling the case for over a year, Michael had never actually been to the store to see the layout. Immediately after Min Choi was murdered, and after the police crime scene unit concluded their investigation there, out of respect for their husband and father, and for Sam Collins, the Choi Family closed the store. They would take their time to come to a decision on re-opening or shutting the business down permanently.

Fortunately for Michael and his need to familiarize himself with the scene of the crime, the Choi's decided to re-open and resumed doing business, as they believed Min Choi would have wanted them to do.

Michael heard that the store was opened, so he, Sanders, Dina, and Tim took a trip to Bed-Stuy so he could look around inside Eden Liquors.

When the group walked into the store, they saw a young man and woman, who Michael later learned were Choi's, son and daughter, Jimmy and Cindy, behind the plexiglass barrier. The Choi children had a look of terror on their faces.

Michael thought he would alleviate their fear by identifying himself and holding up his DA's office shield, which looked exactly the same as an NYPD detective shield. Sanders, Dina, and Tim did the same. This seemed to make matters worse as the Choi's began to shake with fear.

Michael finally realized that *deja vu* had kicked in. Flashing his police shield was the way Headley had gotten behind that same plexiglass barrier and murdered their father.

Michael asked Sanders, Dina. and Tim to wait outside while he spoke to Jimmy and Cindy. He re-introduced himself and repeated why he was there. He also called their mother, who Michael had met during the early trial prep, to explain to the kids that he was there to help their family, not harm them. After that phone call, Jimmy and Cindy visibly relaxed and finally let Michael and the others behind the plexiglass to do what they had gone there to do.

When he was finished, Michael thanked the Choi's and left the store. On the drive back to the office, he was strangely silent. The visit to Eden Liquors, and seeing Jimmy and Cindy Choi, had a profound effect on him. Dina and Tim tried to engage him in conversation, but it was to no avail. All Michael could think of was his father, and the unbearable sadness he and his family would feel if they suddenly lost their dad as Jimmy and Cindy lost theirs.

Michael said a silent prayer for the Choi family. He asked St. Michael for the strength to convict Headley and Ruiz, *'Who deserve to spend the rest of their lives in prison, like the Evil One in HIS eternal hell.'*

CHAPTER

SIXTY

The remainder of Michael's trial prep went well until it was interrupted by having to sit for a deposition in the Christine Miller civil case.

He and his attorney spent several days preparing for the questioning and Michael hated every second of it. That was not because he couldn't handle the questioning, but because it shortened his preparation time for the Hedley/Ruiz trial.

"This is precisely what *HE* had in mind when *HE* goaded Miller into filing the lawsuit," Michael said to Monsignor Romano the night before the deposition. The monsignor had called Michael to wish him luck but spent the entire phone call trying to calm him. "Mike, I know that you're angry because of the distraction, but as you just said, that's how *HE* wants you to react. *HE* wants to force you into a mistake that you'll regret. You're prepared and have nothing to hide. So stay calm. It'll be over before you know it."

Michael knew that Romano was right, '*A mistake tomorrow could cost me big time,*' he thought to himself as he tried to sleep. He promised that when he walked into that deposition room he'd be cool and focused.

When he woke up the next morning that all went out the window. His cell phone was exploding with texts and emails from his attorney, the PR rep, and Romano. The front pages of the morning tabloids screamed with headlines that accused him of jury tampering.

Before returning any of the messages, he sat as calmly as he could and read the stories. The allegation, from an anonymous source, was that during a trial that Michael handled several years before he signed on with Caldwell and Romano, he carried on a romantic relationship with the foreperson of the jury.

The stories said that the juror, a young, attractive woman from the Bay Ridge section of Brooklyn, flirted with Michael, "From the first day of jury selection." And that "He returned the attention and began dating the juror after the verdict."

Michael remembered the case and the juror. The truth, however, was that the juror would smile, nod, and say good morning to him when the jury was brought into the courtroom for the day's testimony. The greetings were not returned, nor acknowledged by him.

At the end of the trial the jury returned a verdict of acquittal. Michael lost the case. On his way out of the courthouse he encountered some of the jurors who were waiting for him. They stopped him to say that he did a fine job but it was the smiling, nodding juror who "Led the charge against you." Michael remembered shaking his head and saying to himself, '*You can't make this shit up,*' as he walked back to his office.

He never saw that juror again.

The newspaper stories went on to imply that the relationship went as far as Michael introducing the juror to his young sons and his father. And, they said, "Only after his father learned that the woman had been a juror, did he counsel Michael to end it because of the way it looked."

Each of the stories reported that DA Price was unaware of any such relationship. "If the stories are true," he reportedly said, "Mr.

Gioca's conduct would not only be an ethical violation, but it may also be a crime."

Michael was scheduled to be at the headquarters of the Association of the Bar of the City of New York, where the deposition was to take place, at 10 a.m. Therefore, he had little time to deal with the horrendous and totally false accusations printed in the city's daily newspapers. But before he began to get ready for the day, he called his sons.

"Guys don't believe...." Before he could finish his sentence both of his boys, who were on speakerphone, said, "Dad we know it's all a bunch of crap. We never met any such woman and we're sure grandpa will say the same thing. Someone is f—ing with you. You got that thing today, so don't worry about us. Go do what you have to do."

Michael almost began to cry; he was so moved by their support. "You guys are the best. Thanks for being so smart and so savvy. I'll call you tonight."

As soon as the call was disconnected Michael's father called. He spoke similarly as his grandsons' did, but added, "No matter how hard they try, they can't take you down. That's because you've listened each time I've told you to always do the right thing. I love you Michael and I'm in your corner. And, by the way, Pam, who knew I would be calling you, said to tell you not to let the bastards get you down."

With those two calls and those three messages, Michael's day had brightened considerably. But he had one more person to speak to before he jumped into the shower.

"Sal, none of it is true," Michael said before the monsignor even said hello. "It's more of the same from *HIM*. And it's no coincidence that this bullshit story hit the papers on the day of my deposition."

"Michael, both Caldwell and I know exactly what happened. And, Caldwell has already called Price, who claimed that he never said anything to the press, for the simple reason that he was never contacted by the press."

"He too knows it's a hit job, he just doesn't know that the *Evil One* is behind it. Don't worry about us. Go do your thing and break a leg."

Michael couldn't help but laugh at Romano's misplaced comment. "That's for the theater Sal."

"I know, but what could be more theatrical than a totally made-up story that was played out on a different kind of stage, for all of New York to see," Romano replied.

"Now call your lawyer and tell him not to worry. Mike Gioca is going to be fine."

At 5 p.m. Michael was finally done with the tedious and repetitious questions of Monroe Wilkins. Try as he did, Wilkins couldn't shake Michael. He answered every question that he could, truthfully. For those he couldn't answer, he politely told that to Wilkins. And for the few questions that he couldn't remember the answer, he simply said, "I don't recall."

When he and his lawyer left the deposition, neither could contain their happiness with how the questioning went. Over a drink at a restaurant around the corner from the Bar Association, Michael's lawyer confessed something to him. "Mike," he began, "If someone had offered to bet me that you would have handled Wilkins the way you just did, after all those horrific stories in the morning papers, I would have wagered my house that you wouldn't. And right now I'd be homeless. Well done my friend."

"I have a feeling," the lawyer continued, "That when Wilkins and Miller sit down to discuss the future of this case, it will be a very short discussion."

Michael thanked him for the kind words and for his optimism. However, he knew that the quarterback for the rest of this game wouldn't be Wilkins or Miller. The *Evil One* was not done. Michael was certain *HE* had more in store for him.

CHAPTER
SIXTY-ONE

With the deposition completed, Michael used the next few days to put the finishing touches on his trial preparation.

He interviewed and prepared all the witnesses he intended to call, with two exceptions.

Because of their combative attitude toward him, Michael decided to leave Frankie Estevez and Carmen Sisto alone until right before they were needed to testify. He didn't want to risk antagonizing them to the point where they would refuse to be prepped or take the witness stand despite the fact that their deals were dependent on them testifying.

He was confident that he would have enough quality time with them to ensure that they would be ready to withstand what was likely to be a rigorous cross-examination. His confidence was based on having cleared with the NYPD to have Greg Sanders assigned to him for the prep of Estevez and Sisto, and for the duration of their testimony. Those two trusted Greg, so having him part of the team when it came time to work with them would make things go smoothly.

The trial began on a Thursday morning and from that first day of trial until the last day, Judge Cavallo's reputation for running an efficient and no-nonsense courtroom was on full display.

Jury selection took a day and a half to complete, despite the fact that it was necessary to empanel two juries to hear the cases against Headley and Ruiz. He arranged with the administrative judge to move the trials into a courtroom larger than his own to accommodate the twenty-four regular jurors and eight alternates.

It was of no concern to the Judge that it was noon on Friday when he finally swore in both juries. He ordered the attorneys to deliver their opening statements that afternoon.

At their conclusion, the judge wished everyone a good weekend before reminding the attorneys that testimony would begin at 9:30 a.m. Monday morning.

Michael's plan was to use the weekend to prep Estevez and Sisto who were expected to be his second and third witness. He would lead off with Sam Collins.

When he returned from court on Friday, Michael telephoned Sanders and asked him to pick up Estevez and Sisto on Saturday morning and bring them to his office so he could begin to prepare their testimony. Sanders told Michael he had already alerted both and he would have them there at 10 a.m.

Michael also notified Dina Mitchell and Tim Clark to be there.

When he later thought back to what motivated him to ask for them to be present, since it was Sanders who had been the key to securing Estevez' and Sisto's cooperation, Michael recalled Romano's constant reminder, "You're not alone. You have an ally in this war."

It was 10:30 when Michael checked his watch. Dina and Tim had been in his office for thirty minutes but Sanders had yet to arrive with the witnesses. It was unusual for him to be late. From the time Michael met him, Sanders impressed him with his attention to detail and the seriousness with which he took his job.

Dina told Michael that she would go to her desk where she had

Sanders' cell phone number and call him. She made several attempts to reach him but got no answer. Now concerned, she called the 79 detective squad.

When she returned to Michael's office she had tears streaming down her face.

"Greg's been murdered," she said.

Before jury selection began, Michael discussed with Greg his idea of having him assigned to help with Estevez and Sisto. Before he went to the NYPD brass with his request, he wanted to make sure that the detective had no objections. Greg was fine with it.

Later when Michael called to tell him that everything was approved, he took the opportunity to let Greg know that it was likely he would be testifying sometime during the first week of the trial.

After getting Michael's Friday afternoon call asking him to bring Estevez and Sisto to his office Saturday morning, Greg decided to stop at his neighborhood clothing store to buy a new shirt and tie to wear to court when he testified.

According to the reports Michael received after the murder, while Greg was looking at ties and matching them to dress shirts, a young man entered the store and called out Greg's name. When Sanders looked in his direction the young man said, "Remember me?" He then shot Greg several times before turning the gun on himself. Both Sanders and the young man were later pronounced dead at the scene by emergency medical personnel.

The shooter's name was Justin Turner. He was the young man that Sanders arrested for shoplifting in that same clothing store just after he became a detective.

Justin's father William, the retired NYPD captain, was interviewed by investigating detectives after the murder/suicide. He told them that for the past few months, Justin was "struggling with life," and was "glued to his computer." His father said that when he tried to talk to Justin about getting out and looking for a job, all his son would say is that he had something he needed to do.

When detectives had the NYPD cyber experts go through Justin's computer hoping to find an answer to what that "something" was, they discovered that Justin spent a lot of time on the dark web, in a chat room, texting with someone named Deets.

The chats revealed that Justin told Deets that he harbored a great amount of hate for someone who "Ruined my life a few years back." At first Deets seemed to just listen to Justin's problem, but as time went on Deets began to suggest that violence was the path out of Justin's troubles.

One text from Deets read, "Revenge on the one who ruined your life is the answer. It's the only way you'll find peace."

When Justin answered that he agreed, Deets followed it up with a date, time and place for them to meet so "I can give you what you need to take care of your problem," the text read.

The detectives assigned to the case went to the location of the meeting to look for surveillance or security cameras. They found several. The footage they recovered showed that at the appointed time, Justin was approached by a figure who was dressed in black and was wearing a baseball cap. According to the detectives' report, although the stranger's face was partially obscured by the hat and the shadow it cast, there was enough light to see a strange looking mark on his left cheek.

The stranger, who the detectives believed was Deets, based on Justin's texts, clearly could be seen handing a gun to him as he leaned in and said something to the kid.

A text on Justin's computer from Deets, dated after the gun exchange, made it clear that Deets was the moving force behind the murder of Greg Sanders and the suicide of Justin Turner. It read, "You have what you need. After you take care of your problem, you must make sure that you don't spend one day in prison for doing what is right for you. Don't let THEM put you in a cage."

The last report Michael read indicated that the investigation remained open and named Deets as a 'person of interest.' He shook his head as he read that because he knew that investigating further would be an exercise in futility. Deets could never be found.

Dina's news about Greg devastated Michael. Over the course of the investigation, he and Sanders became more than colleagues, they were friends. As he sat at his desk trying to process the loss, carrying on with what he had intended to do that day was the furthest thing from his mind, because it was nearly impossible for him to concentrate.

Dina and Tim said nothing as Michael was lost in thought. Much as he hated to push forward without having some time to grieve, he steeled himself to do just that. *'Anything less would dishonor Greg's memory,'* he thought. But now he was faced with the potential problem he tried to avoid by having Greg with him when he prepared Estevez and Sisto.

It was as if Dina had been reading his mind.

"Don't worry Michael, Tim and I will go pick up the witnesses," she said. "They like us and trust us. You certainly made sure of that when you had us sit with Greg when he convinced them to trust you. They'll be upset because of his murder, but I'm confident that, if necessary, we'll be able to do with them what you knew Greg would do. It'll be okay."

Listening to Dina, Michael thought to himself, *'I don't know what I would do without you and Tim.'*

"Guys, thank you. While you're gone I'm going to try to find out more about Greg's killing. I'll fill you in when you get back." And as Dina and Tim were getting up to leave, Michael said, "Please be careful."

Now alone, Michael called Romano and filled him in on the Sanders' murder. "Sal, this is *HIM*," he said. "Estevez and Sisto, who don't like me, are my key witnesses. They provide corroboration for the testimony of the Cooper brothers. By eliminating Sanders *HE* thinks the witnesses will balk at testifying and I'll have no way to bring them around."

"Michael, I'm so sorry about Greg," Romano said. "What will you do if they don't cooperate?"

"Yesterday afternoon when I called Sanders and asked him to bring the witnesses here this morning, something told me to ask Dina and Tim to be here as well. Turns out that request proved to be a lifesaver. Because what the *Evil One* doesn't know is that both of them had been cultivating Estevez and Sisto from the day they both agreed to cooperate. So if I do have trouble with them, I'm confident that with Dina and Tim's help and support, the witnesses will be fine."

"Sal, I just sent Dina and Tim to pick up the witnesses. Please pray that no harm comes to them."

"Michael, I will. That ally I've spoken of; he saw to it that Dina and Tim were with you today. He won't let you down."

The monsignor's words left Michael speechless.

An hour later the investigators walked into his office with Estevez and Sisto.

It was apparent to Michael that they took the news of Greg's murder very hard. Michael thought to himself that it was going to be a long, difficult road ahead to get them to cooperate.

However, their reaction to the tragedy was totally unexpected.

"Mr. G," Estevez said, "Me and Sisto are on the team. You ain't gotta worry about us. We'll do what we promised. And we'll do it for Greg. "

CHAPTER

SIXTY-TWO

The prosecution's case began on a high note and only got better from there.

Michael's first witness was Sam Collins.

Because he was confined to a hospital bed, he had to be wheeled into the courtroom for his testimony. Collins began by telling the jury the story of his life. He also talked about his family, most of whom were in the spectator gallery of the courtroom, and how he had come to work with Mr. Choi at Eden Liquors.

He went on to describe Choi as a decent, kind, hardworking family man who Collins came to know and admire.

At this point Michael brought him to the night of the robbery/murder. Collins told the story of the cop who "used his badge" to get into the restricted area of the store. How the cop and his partner had demanded money that "We didn't have," which made the cop angry. "So he fired some shots into the ceiling before taking the little money me and Choi had on us."

Collins, filled with emotion and with his voice breaking, told the jury that the cop said, "'They saw my face, they got to go' before he shot Choi and his partner shot me."

As Collins was speaking, Michael looked over to the jury and saw that they were totally absorbed in the testimony.

Sam Collins did just what Michael hoped. He set a tone for the trial that he felt confident would lead to conviction.

Neither defense attorney cross-examined Collins.

Michael watched the jury as Collins was wheeled out of the courtroom. Every one of them followed the bed until it disappeared through the courtroom door, most with tears in their eyes.

Next up were Estevez and Sisto. When they were done, Michael thought to himself that Greg would have been proud of them.

On direct examination they were clear and precise in communicating what they had seen and heard. On cross-examination they didn't try to minimize who they were, or their criminal records, or what they were doing out on Tompkins Ave that night.

And they were candid when asked about testifying for the prosecution with deals. "Yes, I have a deal with the DA," they each said. "But he made me no promises. All he told me was to tell the truth. Which is what I'm doing."

The remainder of the prosecution's case went on without a hitch.

Although the jury clearly did not like Jeffrey Cooper, Michael felt that they did believe him. And when his brother Mack told them about Headley bragging how he shot Mr. Choi, and how his brother was supposed to kill Collins but only paralyzed him, it totally corroborated Jeffrey's testimony of what went down in the store that night.

And when Mack told the jury that Ruiz was standing next to Headley while he bragged, and said nothing, the body language of the jurors told Michael that the Cooper brothers had hit home runs with their testimony.

Michael next called Det. Derrick Barker.

Before Barker took the witness stand Judge Cavallo had the court officers remove the Headley jury from the courtroom so they would not be present to hear Ruiz' confession and how he had implicated Headley in the robbery/murder.

Deirdre Hart cross-examined Barker vigorously but there was

little she could attack him with. When her questions became a personal attack on the detective, Michael could see that the jury had enough of Ms. Hart. When she completed her examination, and Det. Barker left the witness stand, several jurors nodded to him, a silent acknowledgement of a job well done.

After the technical witnesses testified with both juries in the courtroom, Michael closed his case with Sooki Choi.

She told the jurors how she and her husband met, and how they built a life together in America with their two children. She described the hard work her husband put in to build Eden Liquors, which was the family's sole source of support. She told the jury that Choi worked six days a week, twelve hours a day to keep the thriving business going.

She then broke down in tears.

What followed was her heartbreaking recollection of identifying her husband's body "on that cold slab of metal," at the medical examiner's office, "Knowing that I would never see him or hold him ever again."

It was the perfect ending to a case that Michael was convinced was a winner.

As for the defense, Stuart Lieberman went first. His only witness was Bobby Headley.

As Headley walked to the witness stand, Michael smiled to himself. He was happy that the defendant decided to testify on his own behalf. Michael had done his research on Headley.

He anticipated this strategy, so he had Dina and Tim speak to Headley's colleagues and bosses at the 79 to get a read on his personality.

What they learned was that Headley was a smug, cocky individual who always considered himself to be "The smartest guy in the room."

Based on that, Michael figured that Headley would attempt to charm the jury, especially the female jurors, and get over on the asshole prosecutor who had the temerity to put him on trial.

As it turned out, Headley did not do himself any favors.

His defense was "I didn't do it." That's it!

And his attitude when he told that to the jury was filled with all the smugness and cockiness that Michael was told about.

To support his position he testified that while walking his dog on the night of the incident, he saw cops in and around the liquor store and stopped to chat with a detective he knew. He then went on his way.

That was Headley's story and his entire defense!

Michael tore into him on cross-examination. "Isn't it a fact Mr. Headley that at the time this crime was committed, you lived right around the corner from Eden Liquors?" Michael asked. When Headley answered that it was, Michael followed with, "So you had plenty of time to do the murder, go to Ruiz' girlfriend's apartment a block away to dump the guns and walkie-talkies, and get back to your apartment and take your dog for his walk. Isn't that right?" Headley had no response. He just sat and stared at Michael.

He then confronted Headley with what he learned about the cop's financial troubles, to establish in the minds of the jury a motive for the robbery of a location he believed would be flush with illegal gambling money.

When Dina and Tim spoke to Headley's fellow cops about him, one told them that Headley was "Always hurting for money." Michael had them dig into that and it bore fruit.

Michael asked him if he owned a luxury car. Headley answered that he did. "And you love that car, don't you?" Michael had asked. When Headley answered that he did, Michael asked "So, when it was repossessed for failing to keep up with the payments, you were angry and frustrated, right?" Headley grudgingly answered, "Yes."

Michael pressed on. "But that's not all you failed to pay when you owned that car, is it?" Headley shrugged as if to say, "I don't know what you're referring to."

"You let the car insurance lapse, didn't you?" Headley's answer was a whispered "Yes." "And as a police officer you know that driving a car in this state without insurance is against the law." Headley nodded in response.

But Michael didn't stop there. "So you were a New York City police officer who broke the law every time you got behind the wheel of that car and drove it with no insurance. Isn't that right, Mr. Headley?"" He ignored the question and again just stared at Michael.

Michael then asked Headley about his apartment and whether he was behind on his rent. He answered that he was, then volunteered, "But I'm a cop who worked overtime, so I had no reason to rob a liquor store."

Michael didn't expect Headley to mention he worked overtime at that point in the cross, but he was ready for it. He moved a folder of documents into evidence, and asked, "Mr. Headley, do you know what those documents are?"

Headley answered that they were his time sheets.

"And they reflect the days and hours you worked in the months leading up to the day Eden Liquors was robbed, right?"

Knowing he walked into a trap of his own making, Headley hesitated before he began to examine the records. When he finished reading, he looked up and answered, "Yes they do."

"Mr. Headley, how many hours of overtime do those records reflect that you performed during those months?"

In barely a whisper, Headley answered , "None."

Michael sat down. The damage was done.

In an attempt to minimize it and rehabilitate his client, Lieberman stood and began to ask Headley questions on redirect examination in an attempt to convince the jury that Headley was in reality a good guy and a good cop but was "merely misunderstood." Those were words he later repeated in his closing argument. The redirect examination, however, proved to be a fatal mistake.

Lieberman had opened the door to allow Michael to now ask Headley about the prior bad acts for which he was neither arrested, nor disciplined. Headley's character had been put in question and he was about to be hanged for it.

Michael stood and asked Headley about his NYPD suspension for the incident in the Manhattan nightclub where his cousin shot up the place using Headley's gun. Headley had no choice but to admit that the incident took place and as a result, he was suspended from duty.

Michael asked Headley about the incident involving the Ecuadorian man who he and several accomplices robbed on the man's payday. When Michael asked if he recalled being arrested for that robbery and escaping justice because the victim was deported before he could testify, Headley merely shrugged his shoulders.

"Do you remember being stopped and questioned by undercover cops at a Brooklyn gas station, which you and your cousin intended to rob?"

Headley answered "Yes, but we weren't there to rob it. The owner asked me to check out the place because he wanted me to help him identify the best locations in the station to install security cameras. And I told that to the cops."

"Isn't it a fact, Mr. Headley, that it was the owner of the gas station who called the police to report seeing you and your cousin casing the place, because he was nervous that he was about to be robbed?"

Headley didn't answer.

"And despite the fact that your cousin was arrested for the gun she was carrying that day, which you later took responsibility for owning, you weren't arrested because you identified yourself as a police officer?"

Headley answered with another shrug.

Michael saved the best for last.

"Mr. Headley, isn't it a fact that months after the Eden Liquors incident, you and your female cousin entered a check cashing location in Bed-Stuy, and you displayed your police shield and asked the owner to allow your cousin to use the bathroom? A bathroom that was located in the store behind the service counter which was protected by a plexiglass barrier?"

Headley nodded and answered, "Yeah, so what?"

"You were going to rob the place, weren't you?"

"No, my cousin had to pee."

"You mean just like you had to pee when you showed your shield to Mr. Choi and asked to use his bathroom?"

Before Headley could answer, Lieberman jumped to his feet and strenuously objected. Although Judge Cavallo sustained the objection, Michael made his point.

It was now Mickey Ruiz' turn to offer a defense.

CHAPTER
SIXTY-THREE

Like Headley, Ruiz' defense was that he didn't do it.

However unlike Headley, who had depended on the jury believing him and only him, Ruiz counted on the jury believing someone other than himself.

He had an alibi and an alibi witness.

Several weeks before the start of the trial, Deirdre Hart, as required by the law, served a notice of alibi on Michael. Ruiz' defense was that he wasn't guilty of the Eden Liquors robbery/murder because he wasn't there. The notice said that Ruiz was home with his father when the crime was committed, and his father would testify to that.

The purpose of notifying the prosecution of an alibi is to give the state an opportunity to investigate it.

Michael gave the notice to Dina and Tim to look into the veracity of the alibi, rather than Sanders, because Greg had a full caseload of his own and couldn't spare any time to help with it.

Dina and Tim hit the streets but were not having any luck disproving the alibi. They spread their business cards around the elder Ruiz' neighborhood hoping that someone would come forward with information that would help them.

One afternoon just before jury selection was scheduled to begin, a man named Jackson Preacher appeared at the security desk in the DA's office with Tim Clark's card in hand and asked to see him. He told the security officer that he had information about Mickey Ruiz.

Tim and Dina interviewed Preacher who told them that he had been in jail with Ruiz and that they became friends. Ruiz said that he was in jail on a warrant from an old case.

He went on to say that during a previous prison sentence for burglary he studied to become a paralegal and hoped to get a job when the warrant was straightened out, which his legal aid lawyer said would be soon.

He told that to Ruiz, who said he'd speak to his lawyer, Ms. Hart, about giving Preacher a position in her firm. Preacher was grateful and told Ruiz that if he needed any help with the Eden Liquors case, or the check cashing location robbery, he should not hesitate to ask him.

Preacher was considered a 'jailhouse lawyer' by the other inmates so Ruiz didn't hesitate to cash in on Preacher's offer to help him.

A week before Preacher was released, he was approached by Ruiz and another inmate, Isaiah Engels, "We knew him as Ike," Preacher told them.

"It was Ruiz who needed help, but it was Ike who did all of the talking," Preacher said. He wanted him to help prepare Ruiz' father to testify at the Eden Liquors trial.

"Preach, Ruiz needs your help," Ike told him, when they were all in the jail's law library. "I made up this 'bullshit' alibi," Preacher said, "That Ruiz is gonna get his father to testify at trial. His dad needs someone to prepare him for the testimony. You know, so he don't fuck it up when his lawyer asks him questions and especially when that prick ADA cross-examines him. When you get out, go to Ruiz' lawyer's office. You can work there, and his father will come to see you."

Preacher was released and as instructed went to Deirdre Hart's office where he was given a temporary paralegal position. That didn't sit right with Preacher because he was led to believe by Ruiz that Hart would give him a permanent job. He confronted Hart and she told him that she wanted to see how he did prepping Ruiz' father before she did that.

Tim asked Preacher if Hart knew that Ruiz' father was coached to lie. "Mister, I don't think so. That woman seemed as straight as an arrow to me. I doubt she had any idea. And I didn't want to fuck things up, so I said nothing."

Preacher went on to tell them that he did work with Ruiz' father, but "It took a long time for me to get him right. He was a dumb ass."

When Dina asked him why he had come forward to tell them about all this, Preacher said "I did what Ruiz and his buddy asked me to do and then I was booted out of the office by that lawyer. I felt used."

Dina's gut told her there was more to Preacher's motivation than what he told them.

"That's it?" she asked. "You didn't get the job, so you're going to get on the witness stand and blow his entire defense up, and be branded a rat forever?"

Preacher dropped his head and said, "Miss, I want the DA to help me with that warrant case I got. I can't go back to the joint. I won't make it."

Tim told Preacher that they would bring all of this to Michael, and they would be in touch. Preacher told them he'd contact them because there was no way for Tim or Dina to reach him. "I ain't got no phone," he said.

After Dina and Tim spoke to Michael, he told them he was interested but there would be no need for Preacher's help until, and if, Ruiz actually called his father to testify.

Because Headley's testimony took most of the day, Judge Cavallo told Hart that she could begin her defense, if she had one, in the morning.

Hart thanked the judge and said that she was prepared right then to tell both the court and Michael that she *would* be calling Ruiz' father as her first and only defense witness.

When he got back to his office, Michael told Dina and Tim that he needed Preacher in the morning. "Have either of you heard from him?" When they said that they hadn't, Michael told them to find him.

The next morning, without having Preacher 'in pocket,' a term detectives use when they located someone they were looking for, Michael went over to the courthouse for the resumption of the trial.

True to her word, Deirdre Hart called Ruiz' father to the witness stand.

While he listened to the "bullshit alibi," Michael was praying for a miracle. Dina and Tim had no luck locating Preacher, so he needed all the help he could get to find him.

Without Preacher to put the lie to the alibi, Michael feared the jury might very well buy Mr. Ruiz' testimony. He was an elderly man, dressed in a suit, dress shirt, and tie that fit like he had gotten them from a Goodwill shop. His clean-shaven, weathered face carried the weight of all the years he worked in a factory to support his wife and son.

He was also a church goer and testified that he went to Saturday evening services on the night in question. He said that after the service he and his son had dinner in his apartment where they watched TV together until Mickey went to bed. His wife was away visiting relatives so "Mickey was sleeping over to keep me company," he said.

He testified that after Mickey went to bed around 11:30, he stayed up to watch the end of a movie. When he finally went to bed an hour later he said he walked past Mickey's room and "He was sound asleep."

Mr. Ruiz did a fine job. In fact it was so good that Michael cursed Preacher under his breath for the great prep job he did with him.

Before he began his cross-examination Michael asked the judge for a recess and for a conference with the defense attorneys. Judge Cavallo brought them all into his chambers and asked Michael what was going on.

Michael advised him of what Preacher told Dina and Tim. He also told the judge that he needed time to locate the witness and asked for an adjournment until the next day.

The judge looked at Deirdre Hart and asked if she was aware of the bogus alibi and the help from Preacher. Michael thought she would faint right where she was standing.

"Your honor, as an officer of the court, I tell you that I had no idea of any of this. However, with all due respect to Mr. Gioca, and his hearsay, we shouldn't just take this Preacher guy's word. If you permit him to testify I'll vigorously cross-examine him, and it will be up to the jury to decide."

Judge Cavallo said that he would give Michael time to locate Preacher, "But I'll only give you 'til this afternoon. If you're not ready to proceed by 3 p.m. you'll have to rest your case. I'm not keeping this jury here any longer than I have to."

Michael took what he could get from Cavallo and ran back to his office after the juries had been dismissed. They were told to return at 3 p.m.

When he got there Dina and Tim were waiting for him.

They had news and called the courtroom to fill in Michael. The court clerk told them that Michael asked for time to find his witness, which the judge gave him. "He just left here and is on his way back to his office."

"Guys please tell me you found Preacher," Michael said.

"Actually, Mike, we have," Tim replied.

"He's over in the holding pen in Brooklyn Criminal Court waiting to be arraigned on a new arrest," Dina told him.

"We had another ADA prepare a 'takeout order' and we're going to go get him and bring him here." A takeout order is a document by which the District Attorney asks the court to allow his office to assume custody of a prisoner for a limited period of time and for a specific purpose. Michael needed Preacher only for the afternoon during which he would testify in the trial against Mickey Ruiz.

Michael couldn't hold back his joy at what he had just heard. He let out a yell that could be heard several offices away. "Guys, I have to be back in court at 3, so please get him now so I can sort out this new arrest and prepare him to testify."

Within an hour Preacher was sitting in Michael's office. He had his handcuffs removed and Michael asked him straight out, "What the fuck happened?"

"Mr. Gioca, none of this was my fault. That inmate, Ike, who asked me to prep Ruiz' father when we was in jail together, came to my apartment yesterday. He said he was out on bail, and he asked me to do something for Ruiz that he couldn't do because he said he was busy."

"How did he know where you lived?

"I have no idea!"

"What did he ask you to do?"

"He said that Ruiz wanted me to go pick up his father this morning and drive him to the courthouse so he could testify. Ruiz and him couldn't possibly know that I had gone to you and told you everything. So I guess they still felt comfortable with me helping Ruiz."

Preacher then said, "When I told him I ain't got no car, he tells me that Ruiz left his car at a spot near his girlfriend's apartment, and he gives me the keys. He also told me that Ruiz wanted me to get the car last night, so I'd have it nearby to pick up his father first thing this morning."

"Did you go get the car?"

"I did, because I didn't want Ruiz to know that I was working with you. I wanted him to think I was still with him."

"What happened?"

"About five yesterday afternoon, I go and gets the car. As soon as I drive it one block, the cops pull me over. They says that the car was reported stolen and tell me to get outta the car. They start looking all over the front and back which is when they come up with a gun. They arrest me and charge me with the gun and with stealin' the car. I trys to explain that it's my friend's car, and he let me use it 'cause I got to do something for him. And I ain't have nothing to do with no gun."

"I even dropped your name, but the cops told me to tell it to my lawyer in court." That's why I was in Criminal Court when your people found me. 'Mr. G,' I was set up. Ruiz, and that scumbag inmate friend of his must have found out that I ratted. You gots to help me. I can't go back to jail. They'll kill me."

Michael told Preacher that he would definitely get him out from under the new case. "I know you've been set up," he said. "But as to that warrant case my offer to help depends on you getting on the witness stand and telling the jury the truth about that alibi."

Angrily Preacher said, "'Mr. G', I know all that, but I'm here to tell you that I'm ready to testify and I don't want nothing in return! That piece of shit Ruiz got me arrested this morning so fuck him. Let's go. I'm ready."

Michael took the time left to make sure that Preacher was in fact ready. Then he walked over to the courthouse and told Dina and Tim to bring him over and to stay with him in the DA's witness room until the court called.

Preacher testified and Ruiz' alibi was destroyed.

Both the prosecution and the defense rested their cases and Judge Cavallo ordered that summations were to begin at 9:30 the next morning.

The Headley jury deliberated for a day and a half before convicting him of the murder of Min Choi, the attempted murder of Sam Collins and the robbery of Eden Liquors.

The Ruiz jury took a day longer and convicted Ruiz only of the robbery.

After the jurors were discharged from jury service, Michael went to the jury room to ask about their verdict. They told him that because Ruiz was only the lookout they felt that he had no way of knowing that Headley and Cooper would shoot, so he shouldn't be held responsible for the execution of Choi and the attempted murder of Collins.

Michael didn't agree with the jury because that wasn't the law, but he could understand why they felt that way. To hold Ruiz responsible for a murder and an attempted murder that were not part of the robbery plan as he knew it was a leap that they were unwilling to make.

'At least they made the decision using their sense of fairness and not because of some interference by the Evil One,' Michael thought to himself as he left the jury room.

It wouldn't be until a couple of weeks later that Michael would learn that the jury had actually convicted Ruiz, *despite* considerable interference from Satan..

CHAPTER
SIXTY-FOUR

The day after the trial Michael was at his desk packing up the paperwork when he received a call from Lieutenant Alan Sullivan, the commanding officer of the 79th precinct detective squad. He was Greg Sanders' boss and supervisor.

After he congratulated Michael on the trial victories, they spoke about Greg and how proud he would have been that Headley and Ruiz were convicted. Michael told the lieutenant that he could not have done it without the work that Greg had put in.

"Lieutenant, he deserves a medal. And although it would be posthumous recognition, his family should have something that shows what a great detective he was. I'll be writing to the Police Commissioner to ask him to do just that."

"ADA Gioca, I agree one hundred percent. I'm sending a report to the PC laying out all of Greg's accomplishments and detailing the courage it took for him to go after one of his own. Not an easy thing, as you know, especially after the treatment he received from the job after he arrested that captain's son. Doing the right thing back then ultimately cost him his life."

"I'm happy to hear we feel the same way about Greg," Michael said.

"Me too. Now let me tell you the other reason I called you. Are you sitting down?"

Not knowing what was coming, Michael tentatively said that he was.

"When I got to my desk this morning, there was a message from a detective assigned to a Manhattan precinct to call him. So I called Det. Ronnie Taub and asked him why he called. Offering his condolences about Greg, he told me that the Manhattan DA's office was getting calls from people who saw photos of Headley in the morning newspapers' stories about the conviction."

"The press used photos taken back when Greg arrested Headley and did that perp walk to the car when he was taking him to criminal court. The people who called recognized Headley as the guy who robbed them at gunpoint a while back as they were eating dinner in an upper Manhattan restaurant in Det. Taub's precinct."

The lieutenant said that Taub told him that after getting the calls the Manhattan DA's office began reaching out to as many of the restaurant victims as they could find.

"So far they're all willing to view a line-up. The DA's office has asked Taub to conduct one with Headley. Taub said he'd keep me informed of the results. If there are ID's of Headley I'll let you know so you can use them when you prepare your sentencing statement for the Choi/Collins case."

Michael thanked the lieutenant.

When he hung up he just sat back in his chair and said out loud to his empty office, "You can't make this shit up."

Two days later Lt. Sullivan called and told Michael that Headley was picked out of the line-up by the victims of the restaurant robbery as one of the men who had robbed them. "Taub has charged him with multiple counts of armed robbery. He said that the Manhattan DA is going to the grand jury."

Two weeks later Michael was working on the sentencing recommendation for Headley and Ruiz when Dina knocked on his door.

"Michael, do you have a minute?" she asked. "There's something you need to know about that mess with Ruiz, Preacher, and that inmate Ike, whose full name is Isaiah Engels. It might have some impact on that recommendation you're preparing for Ruiz' sentencing."

Michael said, "Dina, sit and tell me what you've got."

"That first day when Preacher told Tim and me his story, he mentioned Ike. At that point I had no idea if you would use Preacher at trial because we didn't know if Ruiz would use his father's alibi. However, if it turned out otherwise, I wanted to be sure that the parts of Preacher's story that we could verify, checked out."

"So the first thing I did was to check to see if Isaiah Engels had actually been in jail with Ruiz and Preacher.. I reached out to a contact of mine in the city corrections department and asked him to look into it for me. Two days later he called and told me that he found Ruiz' and Preacher's names, but no one with the name Isaiah Engels was in their system or had been. I asked him to play with the spelling of both names, Isaiah and Engels, which he did. He came up with nothing. "He's never been one of our inmates, my guy told me."

"So I then called New York State Corrections and the Federal Bureau of Prisons and asked them to check. I got the same response. They had no Isaiah Engels and have never had anyone with that name."

"Michael, Preacher was so on the money with what he told us that it's hard to believe he made up some random guy and stuck him in his story. It just makes no sense. I don't know what all that means, and I can't explain why I feel this way, but it's a bit scary. I'll leave you to your work now, but I thought you should know." Dina said.

After he heard the account of Dina's investigation, a very strange feeling came over him. *'She might not be able to explain or understand what happened,'* Michael thought to himself. *'But my gut is telling me why Dina couldn't find Isaiah Engels.'*

He called Preacher, who Michael had moved to a location outside the city.

"Preach, It's Mike Gioca. How are you?"

"I'm good Mr. Gioca. Is there anything wrong? I hope there's no issue with that warrant case you helped me with?" he asked.

"No issue at all. I'm calling for something else. I want to ask you about that inmate Ike.'

Now frightened, Preacher stammered and asked, "Wha...what about him? Did he find out where you moved me?"

"No, no. I want you to think back to what he looked like. Can you do that?"

"Yeah, why?"

"Was there anything unusual about his face?"

"Now that you mention it, there was. He had this real ugly mark, like a mole or something on his left cheek. I even asked him about it one time. He said it didn't hurt. He said it was a mark he's had since he came into being. 'Mr. G' that's a strange way to say that it's a birthmark, don't you think?"

"No Preacher. Not for *HIM*."

PART FOUR

CHAPTER

SIXTY-FIVE

"It seems as if we haven't been here for months," Michael said to Monsignor Romano as they were shown to 'their table' by Emilio.

Romano laughed. "Mike, that's because it *has* been months since we were here last," he said.

"Wow! You're right. Choi, Collins, Headley, Ruiz, they're all I've been thinking about for well over a year."

"Except for a few phone calls, I've ignored you, my kids, and my dad. And I haven't checked on Kathy Baer for so long I have no idea if she's still rehabbing or if she's a free woman."

Michael really missed her.

The comment came out so easily he hoped that Romano hadn't picked up on it because he wasn't ready to admit it publicly, and didn't know how she felt about him.

Mihael was happy that Romano changed the subject. However through dinner all Michael thought about was Kathy Baer. He knew what he would do when he got home.

"Michael, with me you had no choice. Lately I haven't been around for you to intentionally ignore," Romano said with a laugh.

The monsignor had recently returned to Brooklyn after spending ten days living in a motel in Stormville, New York, home to Green Haven Correctional Facility. The monsignor was called to the prison because of a problem with inmate Patrick Patron, the defendant that Michael convicted for the murder of Firefighter Louis Amato.

According to the warden, Patrick was acting very strangely for some time. He was examined and treated by the prison psychiatrist, as well as by outside shrinks. No one could help him.

Having had experience in the past with this type of behavior by an inmate, Jimmy Davis, who also was convicted by Michael for the murder of off-duty police officer Robbie Thomas, the warden called Monsignor Romano.

As with Jimmy Davis, after sitting and talking to Patrick Patron, it was clear to Romano that Patrick was possessed by the *Evil One*. The monsignor would need to perform an exorcism.

Over nine long days, the rite of exorcism was performed by Romano, with no success. Finally, on the last day, Romano broke through, and the demon was expelled.

In his soft spoken Haitian accent, Patron professed to Romano that he was not a murderer. He said that he was overcome by an evil force which he could not control, and he would never forgive himself for causing Louis Amato's death.

He thanked the monsignor and asked if he would hear his confession. When Romano performed the rite of Reconciliation and forgiven Patrick's sins, the inmate vowed to become a regular attendee at the weekly Catholic Mass conducted by the prison's Catholic chaplain.

When he left the prison Romano knew that with his help, God had saved the young man. He was confident that when Patron completed his sentence and walked out of Green Haven, he would not be the same Patrick Patron who had walked in.

Romano was exhausted when he returned to Brooklyn. That night with Michael in *Emilio's* was the first night he felt rested enough to have dinner outside of his apartment. Coincidentally the sentencing of Headley and Ruiz for the Eden Liquors convictions took place earlier that afternoon.

"You can catch up with everyone tomorrow," Romano said to Michael. "Tonight is a celebration,"

"Now tell me about the sentencing," the monsignor said as Emilio poured two glasses of Michael's favorite *Nero d'Avola.*

"Before I get to the sentencing, I need to tell you about Isaiah Engels," Michael said.

He told Romano all about the inmate who in reality was the *Evil One,* then got to the sentencing.

"Headley was sentenced to thirty-three and a half years to life for the murder of Choi, the robbery of Eden Liquors, and the attempted murder of Collins. And Ruiz was sentenced to eight and a third to twenty-five years for the robbery only. Remember the jury let him off the hook for the murder and the shooting of Collins because he was only the lookout."

"But Headley has more trouble to deal with in Manhattan," Michael continued. "While we were waiting for the judge to take the bench for the sentencing, Headley's attorney told me that he was indicted in Manhattan for that restaurant robbery. He said that Headley had an offer from the DA to plead guilty, and in return the DA would recommend to the Manhattan judge that he run the sentence concurrently with whatever sentence Headley received in Brooklyn."

The lawyer couldn't believe it when Headley turned it down and insisted on going to trial. He said, "Mike, my client is an arrogant prick.'"

"Sal I'm certain he'll get convicted in Manhattan because multiple people have identified him, and he's not going to get any help from the *Evil One.* That ship has sailed. And when he is sentenced over there, the judge should pile on the years and not give him any break at all."

(Seven months later, Michael learned that Headley was convicted of the restaurant robberies and received eight consecutive sentences of twelve and a half to twenty-five years, all of which would also run consecutively to his Brooklyn sentence. Former police officer Bobby Headley would be in prison for the rest of his life.)

"One other happy note," Michael said. "While you were gone, the NYPD bestowed its highest service award, the Medal of Honor, posthumously on Greg Sanders. It was a wonderful ceremony. Greg's family was at Police Headquarters, and in his speech before he handed the award to Greg's mom and dad, the PC called him a hero. What a great day."

"Okay, now that you're up to date, can we eat? I'm starving."

Romano smiled and called Emilio over to the table.

"Emilio, please tell the chef that this is a night of celebration for us and I'm leaving the choices of antipasto, pasta, and meat to him," he said. "My friend *Michele* is starving so be generous."

"*Monsignore, lasci fare a me.* Leave it to me," Emilio told him. "You won't be disappointed."

After the spectacular meal Michael drove Romano to the monsignor's apartment. Before the monsignor got out of the car Michael said, "After what we went through with this case, let's hope for some down time."

"Michael, I'm praying for just that," Romano replied. "But as you are well aware, we have no control over our adversary. I'm sure *HE* felt great after Sabar was acquitted in the Coney Island case, but now that you beat him in the Eden Liquors case we have to be prepared for *HIS* revenge. So, stay vigilant and be careful."

When Romano left the car, Michael checked the time. The first thing he wanted to when he got home was call Kathy Baer.

CHAPTER
SIXTY-SIX

Michael felt terrible when he realized that Kathy had been asleep when he called. After an apology he quickly learned that she had completed her rehab and had been cleared to go back to work. "I'm not allowed in the field yet. Just desk duty," she told him. "And no need to apologize, I'm happy that you called."

"Kathy, that's great news."

"Let me make it up to you, " Michael asked. "Would you like to have dinner with me Saturday night? A friend of mine has opened a new restaurant in Long Island City and he's been bugging me to come see it and taste his great food!"

"I told him that I was on trial, and I promised that when I was done I'd stop by. I also told him that I'd be the judge of the quality of the food. What do you say? Want to join me on Saturday?"

Kathy laughed at Michael's lame joke and said, "I'd love to. Thank you."

When Kathy said yes, to his invitation, Michael was ecstatic. He hoped that this would be the start of a serious relationship.

"I'll pick you up at seven. I'm told it's a very nice place, and casual. Just thought you'd want to know that."

"Thanks for letting me know. I'm looking forward to it," Kathy said.

"I probably should have led with this; I hope you like Spanish food?"

When Kathy told him she did, Michael added, " Great! I hear it's authentic. His chef is American, but he was trained in Madrid. Looking forward to seeing you."

When he hung up he sat back in his chair and asked himself, *"Why do you feel like some high school kid asking the prettiest girl in class to the school dance?"* Michael knew the answer, but he couldn't admit it to himself.

The Saturday night dinner at *Sala* went better than Michael hoped. His friend Julio treated Kathy and him like royalty and insisted on making dinner selections for them. He didn't disappoint. At the end of the night over espresso and dessert, Michael told Julio, *"Now* you can tell people that your food is great! This was as delicious a meal as I have ever had."

Julio thanked him but quickly turned to Kathy and asked for her opinion. "I must confess something," she began, "When Michael asked me if I liked Spanish food, I told a little white lie, I said that I did. The truth is I've never eaten Spanish food before tonight. Boy am I happy I agreed to this date. The food was spectacular. Thank you."

Julio had not outwardly reacted when Kathy called the night a 'date.' But when he glanced at Michael he could see his longtime friend was surprised and very pleased by her use of the word. What Michael didn't know until this moment was that Kathy appeared to have feelings for him as well. But now he had evidence that she did.

In addition to her considering the night a 'date,' all through dinner, Kathy was effusive in complimenting him on his winning the Eden Liquors case. She told him, "I knew you'd be back after that Sabar loss. You're too good to let one defeat get to you. And *this* win was important for, not only the Choi and Collins families, but also for the NYPD and the city."

Since they met, Kathy was always supportive, but she wasn't

necessarily someone who went overboard with praise. Hearing her 'date' comment, feeling her warmth during dinner, told him his feelings for her were right on the money.

"I was hoping that what I began to feel about you wasn't only one way, because I didn't want to get hurt," Kathy said when they arrived at her apartment building. "After tonight I know that's not the case. "Thank you. The evening was terrific," Kathy said before she leaned over and kissed him.

"Mr. Gioca, you're a gentleman and it's way past my bedtime. Next time I'll have you up for a night cap." With that Kathy left Michael's car, but not before she had captured his heart.

At dinner Kathy told Michael that Sabar's trial for the hotel arson was scheduled to begin in "A couple of months." She said that she was looking forward to testifying so the 'bastard,' as she called Sabar, would be that much closer to a prison cell. Michael feared that with Kathy settling in at work and preparing for the trial, she wouldn't have a lot of free time until after she testified.

After their kiss in his car, Michael was anxious to see Kathy again, but as expected, her days and nights were occupied by trial prep and resting after long days back at the fire marshal's office.

She wanted to make certain that there were no lingering aftereffects from either her injury or her rehab work that would hinder her ability to testify or adversely affect its quality.

They talked on the phone but agreed that they wouldn't see each other until after she completed her time on the witness stand.

With no new cases, Michael stayed busy with Rackets Division work to keep up the façade of working for the Brooklyn District Attorney's Office. He made himself available to the ADA's in his division for conferences on their open investigations, and dispensed advice to those who were on trial.

Then, one day while packing up his briefcase to cut out early so he could hit the gym before the post-work crowd got there, he received a call from Romano.

"Sal, I'm just about to leave for the day and go to the gym, can this call wait until after my workout?" Michael asked.

"The discussion we need to have can wait, but my news is too good for me to wait until later. Are you sitting down?"

"I am now," Michael answered.

CHAPTER
SIXTY-SEVEN

"Caldwell just received word from your lawyer," Romano began, "Monroe Wilkins withdrew the civil suit Christine Miller filed against you. That case is over, Michael!"

"The attorney said he believed that because of the great job you did at the deposition, Wilkins had no choice. Apparently, their entire case was predicated on you screwing up under his questioning. And when you didn't, he was left with nothing other than Christine Miller.

"The lawyer told Caldwell that Wilkins would not have survived a motion to dismiss with her as his only witness. So, he saved himself the embarrassment and pulled the plug. Congratulations Michael!"

Gioca was speechless. He had beaten the *Evil One* yet again.

"Sal, that's great news," he finally said. "But *HE* won't just sit back and take the loss. I'm concerned about revenge. Can we talk when I'm done in the gym? The workout will give me time to think."

"Michael, call me when you get home. That will give me time to discuss this with Caldwell, and to pray for some guidance."

Throughout the gym session, all Michael could think of was

Satan's revenge, and his family. He decided that before he called Romano, when he got home he would call his father, his sister, and his sons. He had to figure out some way to put them on alert without causing them to panic.

After some quick thinking, he decided to handle it the way he had in a similar circumstance several years before he began to work for Caldwell.

Michael had prosecuted a mobster who was angry with him for having a young, female ADA act in his stead at the mobster's sentencing. She had never been involved in a case of that importance, so Michael decided to give her the experience of representing the prosecution to simply remind the judge that the mobster pled guilty, and that the agreed upon sentence was six to eighteen years. The court appearance went smoothly and was uneventful. Subsequently, the mobster was sent back to city jail to await transfer to state prison.

Two weeks after the sentencing, a detective assigned to the DA's office, George Moore, called Michael who was in his office working on trial prep for a case he was about to start.

"Mike, you better get up here. Someone wants to kill you," was the detective's message when Michael answered his call.

'Up here,' was the detective's office located one floor above Michael's. When he walked in he saw a nondescript young man sitting in a chair with his hands in cuffs. Michael sat down and before he could say a word the detective pointed to him and said to the guy in handcuffs, "Matty, tell this gentleman, what you just told me."

"There's a guy in jail with me who wants Michael Gioca dead," Matty said.

"Do you know who I am?" Michael asked.

"I guess you're some big shot cop who works with George," Matty answered.

"No, I'm Gioca. Now tell me who wants me dead and why."

"The guy's name is Mikey Misto. You supposedly prosecuted him for a murder and you let some lady ADA handle his sentence. He was pissed. Not because of the time he got, but because you disrespected him by having a broad sentence him."

"He's got a contract out on your life, and I was gonna take it, 'cause I'm gettin' out soon, and I needed the cash. But when I found out that the target was an assistant district attorney, I didn't want any part of it."

Michael shook his head in disbelief. "You gotta be shitting me," he said.

"I ain't lying. After I turned him down he had some guys visit him who looked like real hitters. You can check it out."

George did and the two "hitters" Matty had mentioned were just that. They had long records for witness intimidation, bribery, and assault. Matty was telling the truth.

When Michael went to the DA to inform him of the contract on his life, Price ordered that he be guarded by the DA's detectives around the clock until an arrest or the threat had been resolved in some other way.

George advised Michael that because he was living with his father following his divorce, his dad would have protection as well. As for his sons and his sister, their addresses were not public knowledge, so they were safe.

However, to be certain, it was decided to 'flag' the license plate numbers on their cars with the state Department of Motor Vehicles. Notorious for rampant corruption in the DMV, the concern was that someone could bribe a clerk to search the agency's computer to locate their addresses. The 'flag' would then pop up at the DA's office and George and his people could take measures to protect Michael's sister and sons.

To alert Pam and the boys to the steps that had been taken, but careful not to frighten them, Michael had a family meeting at his dad's home. He soft peddled the potential threat but made sure that they understood that until further notice they all had to be wary of their surroundings and those around them.

After all that preparation and caution, Misto was transferred to state prison. But before he left the city jail, Matty later told George, "Mikey called off the contract. He said that he didn't want to risk the heat that would definitely come down on him if an ADA was hit."

The threat was resolved and life for the Gioca family went back to normal.

When Michael returned from the gym he called his father, then his sister, and finally, his sons. He told them he needed to have a family meeting as soon as possible. They were all concerned thinking that Michael was in some kind of imminent trouble. He told them they shouldn't worry, and would explain everything when he saw them. They were all available the next night, so he set the meeting for 7pm.

Because he was now working for Caldwell, and not the District Attorney, there would be no detective investigators to provide security, as there had been the last time Michael went through something like this. He, therefore, had to find another way to protect his family from the ultimate mobster.

His next call was to Romano. That 'other way' was found.

"Michael, I just finished talking with Caldwell," the monsignor said. "He's concerned about you and your family's safety. He wants to have agents with you for at least the next few weeks. He also said that he'd make sure that your father, sister, and sons have protection as well. He wants to begin the protection tonight, and I agree."

Michael breathed a sigh of relief. '*Federal agents watching over them was a gift from heaven,*' he thought.

"Sal, I'll take it. I want to alert my family to what's going on. But I won't tell them where the threat is coming from. I'll make up a story similar to something that happened to me several years back with a wiseguy who wanted me killed. I put the family on alert without going into details. They understood then, and I'm sure they will now."

"I'm meeting with them tomorrow night, so have Caldwell tell his men to be as inconspicuous as possible until I speak to my crew. This way they won't be spooked if they see a strange guy or two hovering around them."

"Okay I'll let Caldwell know," Romano replied. "I'll be praying for this to be over very quickly."

"Monsignor, this is Satan we're dealing with. How will we ever know when it's over. To use a well-worn cliché, 'revenge is a dish best served cold,'" Michael said.

"Mike, I've been thinking about that. And to use another cliché, 'we'll know it when we see it.'"

"One other thing. Please stop by my office tomorrow before you meet with your family. I have something that I want you to give to them that I believe will be additional protection from the *Evil One*."

"Padre, it's getting late and I'm hungry. I'm going to make a sandwich, then I'm going to bed. I'll see you at your office around six tomorrow evening. *Buona notte.*"

CHAPTER
SIXTY-EIGHT

At seven o'clock the next night Michael's family gathered in his father's home to hear what he wanted to tell them. As planned, he was purposefully vague. He told them that similar to the incident a few years before, he had gotten word of a possible threat against him. It arose from a case he had handled. He down-played the seriousness of it, and said, "Like the last time, I'm certain it'll be resolved quickly. Until it is you'll have police protection, which will be unobtrusive. You won't know they're there, but trust me, they will be. Just live your lives like nothing is out of the ordinary."

Michael was surprised that he hadn't gotten any push back. Everyone, including his father, who Michael expected would give him the most trouble with this, just nodded and said that they understood.

He then had to finesse why he would give each of them a St. Christopher medallion.

The medals were what Romano wanted Michael's family to have as "additional protection" from the *Evil One*.

"Sal, St. Christopher medals?" Michael asked when the

monsignor handed them to him. "Isn't St. Christopher the patron saint of travelers? What's that got to do with my family?"

"Michael, we are all on a journey through life," the monsignor answered.

"Those medals have been blessed by the Holy Father. I've had them since my last trip to Rome several years ago and I can't think of 'travelers through life' more in need of protection right now than your family."

Michael looked puzzled. "I'm going to soft pedal this threat," he said. "So how do I explain why I'm giving them each a St. Christopher medal?"

"Tell them it's a gift from me from my last trip to the Vatican. You told me how much they admire and respect me, so they won't question it. And if you add that I always want them to be safe, so they should keep St. Christopher with them as they go about their daily lives, that should do the trick."

Michael did what Romano suggested, and it worked. His family couldn't have been more thankful and appreciative of the "Wonderful and thoughtful gift from the Monsignor," as his sister Pam said.

Two weeks passed without incident. Michael checked in regularly with the men Caldwell had assigned to his family and he also called his dad, sister, and his sons. However, so as not to alarm them with a call every day, his calls were irregularly regular.

On Wednesday morning of the third week the protection had been in place, Michael was summoned to Romano's office. Thinking the worst, he checked in with his dad, his sister, and his sons, before he left his apartment. Everyone was fine. Relieved, but now very curious, Michael set out for Red Hook.

As started his car, he checked his rearview mirror for the car driven by his ever present agent bodyguards. Neither they nor their car was where it had been every day for nearly three weeks. Concerned, Michael drove directly to Romano's building, checking his mirror all the way.

When he walked up to the monsignor's office, his bodyguards were standing outside the door. "We wanted to say goodbye and wish you good luck," they both said as they each held out a hand to shake with Michael.

Puzzled, he asked, "Guys, what's going on?"

Neither agent answered. One pointed to Romano's office door and said, "Mr. Gioca, the monsignor is inside waiting for you. He'll explain." Both agents then walked away.

"Good morning Sal," Michael said as he sat down in front of Romano's desk. Romano didn't acknowledge him. It was then that Michael realized that the monsignor was praying. After a minute or two, Romano finally returned Michael's greeting.

"What's happening?" Michael asked. "The agents who had been with me for the last three weeks weren't at my apartment this morning. They were here, and both just said goodbye and wished me good luck."

"Michael, Caldwell has called off the protection details."

Michael was upset at the news. He wanted to know how he would protect his family. "I have no way to hire security for them," he said, "And I can't go to DA Price and ask for detectives to watch over them. Sal, Caldwell has to reconsider. I can't leave them open to what *HE* might do to get back at me for beating *HIM* in that civil case."

"There is no need for you to worry," was Romano's response. "We believe that last night *HE* extracted *HIS* revenge for that case, and it wasn't on anyone connected to you."

"Monroe Wilkins was murdered," Romano told him.

Michael was speechless. He sat there in a state of shock for what seemed like an eternity. Finally he broke his silence with "Are you fucking kidding me?"

"Michael, no one is safe from the *Evil One*. Wilkins was secure when he got Sabar off the hook for the Coney Island murder, and that security would continue as long as he had that civil suit going.

But we believe that once Wilkins decided to withdraw the lawsuit Satan was using to defame and humiliate you so you would lose your law license, he was marked for death."

"Michael, you know, Satan does not like to lose."

"Sal, how did you and Caldwell come to that conclusion so quickly?"

"A witness at the scene of the murder placed *HIM* there," Romano answered.

"Please explain."

"What the police know at this point comes from Wilkins' wife and one of his neighbors."

"His wife told detectives that Wilkins received a call from someone he said was the father of a prospective client. The father told Wilkins that he was on his way to his home to bring him retainer money. Wilkins told his wife that he was in Brooklyn Supreme Court that morning with another client, when a man approached him. This man, she told the cops, was waiting for his son's case to be called."

"Wilkins told his wife that the man asked to speak to him outside the courtroom. When they were in the corridor the man told Wilkins that it was fortuitous that he was in the courtroom. He said that he saw Wilkins in court during the Sabar trial and was impressed by his skill. And since his twenty-year-old son had yet to retain an attorney the man wanted Wilkins to represent him."

"According to his wife, Wilkins said he agreed to take the case but wanted a retainer from the father before he filed papers with the court announcing his representation of the young man. The father told Wilkins that he would have the money that night and asked if he could bring it to Wilkins at his home. When the call came in Wilkins told his wife that the man had arrived, and he was going outside to get his money."

"Before heading upstairs to their bedroom Wilkins' wife looked out the front window of their home and saw her husband sitting in the front passenger seat of a car with the door open, talking to the driver. She began to climb the stairs when she heard several shots."

"Did she see anything that puts *HIM* there?" Michael asked.

"No. But Wilkins' next door neighbor also heard the shots. He looked out from his front door and saw two men walking away from the passenger side of a car that was double parked in front of the Wilkins' home. The door was open so the interior light in the car was on. The two men passed right in front of the neighbor's home, and he got a good look at the one closest to him. He told the cops that he would be able to identify the guy."

"Now here's the key, Michael. Because the interior of the car was lit the neighbor got a look at the driver. He said he wouldn't be able to identify him, but he did see the left side of the man's face, which, in his words, had 'this weird mark, like a tumor almost.'"

"Michael, with the description of the devil's mark on the driver's face, coupled with who was murdered after the withdrawal of the lawsuit against you, logic dictates that it was the *Evil One* who had Wilkins murdered."

As Michael was about to respond, Romano interrupted.

"There's one more thing. Caldwell checked with the courthouse, and there were no cases on the calendar in the courtroom, where Wilkins had appeared and met this man, in which a twenty-year-old had been indicted for murder. *HE* set up Wilkins with that retainer payment story and had two of *HIS* flunkies there to kill him."

"Monsignor, I'm ready to get started," Michael said. "Has Caldwell spoken to Price about me taking the case?"

"Mike, it's all set. I was told to tell you that Tommy Schwartz from Brooklyn South Homicide has the case. Apparently, you two know each other. He's waiting for your call."

"Thanks Sal. We do. But it's odd that Tommy was assigned to this case. There must be an organized crime component because he's the best they have when the mob is involved. Do you know of any OC angle?"

"Michael, I've told you everything I know," Romano replied.

"Okay, I'll reach out to him, and I'll keep you posted. I have a feeling this is going to be quite a ride."

"I'm sure you're right. So keep that St. Christopher with you so it's a safe ride."

CHAPTER
SIXTY-NINE

Michael met Tommy Schwartz at noon in *Lenny's Pizzeria* on 86th Street in the Bensonhurst section of Brooklyn. The restaurant was several blocks away from where Monroe Wilkins' had lived and was murdered.

"Mike we ain't gonna be able to eat this great pie much longer, *Lenny's* is closing for good," Schwartz said as he and Michael dug into their margherita pizza slices. The two law enforcement veterans spent many nights, while working together on cases, eating in *Lenny's.*

"Tommy do you remember we came here after we interviewed that informant in the skull case. We were so happy to get that evidence. We ordered and ate one entire pie and drank a bottle of wine the owner let us bring in. I couldn't sleep at all that night."

"Yeah, but it was worth it. We were starving from not eatin' all day working to turn that scumbag who led us right to Mikey Misto. Of course you paid the price for convicting him, with that murder contract he put out on you. But all's well that ends well."

Tommy Schwartz was the detective who brought the case to Michael. They worked several murder cases together, all convictions, when Tommy walked into Michael's office with what would turn out to be the Misto case.

At that early stage the case was nothing more than a cold case involving a missing boyfriend and a skull which had been discovered by a man who had hooked the plastic bag that contained it, while fishing in a Brooklyn creek.

When the skull was found there was nothing that the police or medical examiner could use to identify it. So it was buried in an unmarked grave on Hart Island in New York's East River, where the city buries unidentified bodies, or, as in this case unidentified body parts, in unmarked graves. The New York City Medical Examiner's office, however, kept records of the burial sites in the event evidence was later uncovered that could lead to an identification of the remains.

Tommy was notified by a federal agent friend of his that he had a defendant who was arrested on gun trafficking charges and was facing a long prison sentence. When the agent began to talk to the defendant, he immediately told him that he had information about an unsolved homicide that was committed several years before, hoping that his info could help him reduce his potential sentence. The agent called Tommy who worked homicide cases and asked if he wanted to speak to the defendant.

Tommy and Michael had a long conversation with him and were able to get enough information about the homicide and the identity of the person whose skull was recovered by the fisherman in that Brooklyn creek to open a murder investigation.

The story of the homicide was out of a bad horror movie or a very successful TV series about the mob, depending on your taste in entertainment.

The skull belonged to an ex-convict from Brooklyn, named Carlos Ortega, who was murdered by his girlfriend's brother, Mikey Misto.

His sister had complained to Misto that her boyfriend was abusive to her when Misto asked her about a bruise he saw under her eye. She begged him not to do anything because after speaking to her boyfriend, they worked things out, and the abuse stopped.

Nevertheless, Misto went crazy when he heard all that and wanted to kill the boyfriend that day. Because his sister continued to plead with him to leave Ortega alone he lied to her and said that he wouldn't touch the guy.

Misto bided his time but never dismissed the idea of killing Ortega for what he did to his sister.

Several weeks later Misto called his sister to check on her. She told him that all was well. Misto told her he was happy for her and Ortega, so much so that he talked to a friend of his about offering Ortega a job in his car repair shop. This made his sister very happy because she knew that a good part of Ortega's anger stemmed from not being employed.

Misto told her to let Ortega know that he would pick him up the next day and drive him to his friend's shop so they could meet. "It's sort of a job interview, sis. So tell Carlos to dress well," Misto said.

The next day Misto pulled up to his sister's apartment where they were waiting. He assured her that he would have Ortega back before dinner. Ortega got into the back seat of the car which was being driven by Tommy Schwartz' defendant/informant, Mario Renna.

Misto asked Renna to drive because he needed help with what he intended to do to Ortega. "Mario, this fuck ain't ever gonna hurt my sister again," Misto told him.

Misto was a soldier in the Colombo crime family, which Renna aspired to become one day. So hoping that Misto would put in a good word with the family for him, he readily agreed to help.

The three men set out on the Belt Parkway, a highway that runs along the southern coast of Brooklyn, parallel to the Atlantic Ocean, for the 'job interview.' When they got to an area of the highway where only trees, woods, and thick shrubbery lined both sides, Renna announced that there was something wrong with the car.

He pulled off the highway onto a side area that was particularly thick with vegetation of all kinds. Carrying on the charade, Renna lifted the hood of the car and pretended to look at the engine. He did that so as not to arouse the suspicion of any passing police, and Ortega. Misto then announced to Ortega that he was getting out of the car to stretch his legs. Once outside he pulled a gun and ordered Ortega out of the backseat.

With Renna still pretending to check the engine, Misto walked Ortega at gunpoint into the thick woods. After a couple of minutes, Renna heard two shots.

Expecting Misto to come out of the woods quickly, he closed the hood of the car and waited, and waited, and waited. Now concerned, Renna started to walk into the woods, but didn't get very far. He was attacked by Ortega, who had two bullet holes in his chest.

Ortega grabbed Renna and begged for help, but only managed to knock Renna to the ground and fall on top of him. Renna struggled to get Ortega off him, as Misto came out of the woods armed with a large piece of wood. Misto then beat Ortega over his head with the wood until he stopped moving.

"The fuckin' guy wouldn't die," Misto said to Renna as he rolled Ortega off him. "I shot him twice in his chest and he started to run. I had no idea where he was until I heard you two fighting. It's a good thing that wood was here. If I shot him again someone in a passing car might have heard."

With Ortega dead, their plan was to bury him in that remote area. However they forgot to bring shovels.

So they searched around the area, which was also a dumping ground for wrecked and abandoned cars and found old car tires strewn about the woods. They covered Ortega's body with the tires and planned to go back the next day to bury him.

As it turned out, they didn't return to the scene for well over two weeks. And when they uncovered the body they saw that it was in the advanced stages of decomposition, with maggots and other insects crawling all over it. Not wanting to touch it, they covered the body with the tires again and left it there, where it would decompose completely.

Two years later Misto heard that a real estate developer had purchased the land where they buried the body under the tires. The developer's plan was to build a shopping mall on the site.

Not wanting to risk the body, or what remained of it, from being found, Misto and Renna went back to dispose of it.

All that was left of the body of Carlos Ortega was his skeleton.

To dispose of the head, Misto broke it off the spinal cord and placed it in a plastic bag, which he tossed into a nearby creek. That was the creek where years later the fisherman would find it and notify the police.

Misto and Renna placed the remaining bones into black garbage bags which they left in several dumpsters all around Bensonhurst.

The first step in Michael and Tommy's investigation was the search for a missing persons report for Carlos Ortega.

Although Renna had told them about Ortega's murder and the way he and Misto had disposed of the skull and bones, an official NYPD report confirming that Ortega was indeed missing, would corroborate Renna's story. It would also give them the name of the relative or friend who reported Ortega missing. That information would become a crucial factor in solving the case and convicting Misto.

They found a missing persons report for Carlos Ortega, which had been filed by his brother Justo, just after he disappeared.

The next thing Michael and Tommy did was search NYPD records for the recovery of a skull in that area of the Brooklyn creek where it was found.

Once they found the report, they went to the medical examiner's office and found the location of the grave in the ME's records. Now an exhumation order signed by a judge was necessary to have the skull removed from its unmarked grave on Hart Island. This required

Tommy to contact Ortega's brother Justo to get his permission for the exhumation, which was necessary before a judge would allow it.

When Justo was told what Michael and Tommy learned about his brother's disappearance and why they needed his consent to exhume what was likely his brother's skull, Justo broke down.

"After all these years perhaps me and my family will be able to bury my brother, and have closure and peace," he said to them.

He readily gave his consent for the exhumation. The day a judge signed the order, Michael arranged for the medical examiner's personnel to be at the gravesite to accept the skull after it was dug up.

At his office when the medical examiner looked at the skull, he determined the only means to an identification were the teeth that still remained in the mouth. None of the front teeth were there because Renna said that when Misto broke the head off the spine, he punched out the front teeth to avoid any one using them to identify the body. What he didn't account for were the back teeth.

Tommy had the idea of searching Ortega's criminal record for any prison time he might have done. He found that he had served several stints in New York's prison system, and during one, Ortega had dental work. Tommy was able to get the dental records from the prison and with the expertise of a forensic dentist brought in by the medical examiner, the skull was definitively identified as that of Carlos Ortega.

With Renna's testimony, and with the dental records identification, Michael had enough evidence to present to a grand jury.

But Tommy Schwartz didn't stop there. He went back to Ortega's brother and asked if there was anything he could remember about Carlos' disappearance, or its aftermath, that might help him make the case against Misto stronger.

There was. Justo had called Misto's sister a day or two after Carlos disappeared to ask if she heard from or saw him. That's when she told him about the so-called job interview.

Justo called Misto to ask if he knew where Carlos had gone after the interview. On a tape recording of the call made by the brother, Misto said that after the interview he dropped off Ortega somewhere in Bushwick, the neighborhood where he was living with Misto's sister but had no idea where he went from there.

This seemingly innocuous recording proved to be golden when Tommy played it for Michael.

"Tommy, this is an admission that Misto had contact with Ortega the day he disappeared and corroborates Renna's story about the bogus job interview Misto used to get Ortega into his car. We got the son of a bitch. When I finish up in the grand jury and secure an indictment, you can have the pleasure of putting the cuffs on him."

Misto was indicted and rather than go to trial and risk a life sentence, he pled guilty, and with that young female Assistant DA standing in for Michael at the sentencing, received fifteen years in prison. Gioca and Schwartz had done it one more time. Another Brooklyn bad guy, this time a Colombo soldier, was taken off the streets and would spend the prime of his life behind bars.

Now here they were paired up once again, this time, unbeknownst to Tommy, the adversary was more formidable than even a member of the Mafia.

More out of curiosity than important to know, Michael asked, "Tommy, is there something about this case that's connected to organized crime that I'm not seeing?"

"I'm asking because that's your expertise. If this were an ordinary murder, it could have been assigned to a precinct detective, and not Brooklyn South Homicide's mob expert."

"Mike, I'm surprised you're asking that. You're the Chief of Rackets. Isn't a mob angle the reason for you to be on this case?" Tommy replied."

Not being able to answer truthfully, Michael just shrugged his shoulders.

Tommy said, "Wow, you *don't* know. The guy that was murdered,

Wilkins. He was a mob lawyer. He represented lots of other people, but he was well known for standing up for the 'bent noses.' Maybe he pissed off one of them and he had to go."

"The possibility of this being a mob hit is why we are on it. If it ain't a hit and just a robbery gone bad, we're still the best they got, and we'll catch the mutts who did this."

Michael nodded in agreement.

'You're right Tommy. No matter who pulled the trigger, we'll get them and convict them. But the mutt who is behind this murder, we'll never catch,' Michael thought to himself as Tommy ordered two more slices of pizza.

By the time they had finished their meal, the two law men had come up with a starting point for the investigation into the murder of Monroe Wilkins.

CHAPTER
SEVENTY

The next day, Tommy picked up Michael from his office. They were headed to Bensonhurst, and a hardware store on 86th Street, several blocks from *Lenny's Pizzeria*.

Tali's Hardware was owned by Jimmy Taliferro, Monroe Wilkin's neighbor who had heard the shooting, and afterwards, saw the two shooters walk away from a double parked car past his home. He later learned that his neighbor Monroe Wilkins had been sitting in that car when he was shot.

Taliferro was able to see one of the two men well enough to describe him to the detectives at the scene, and later to work with a police artist. The resultant sketch would later become the turning point in the trial of the shooters.

That sketch and what Taliferro had seen the night of the murder, were why Michael and Tommy needed to talk to him that morning.

"Mike, this guy can make the case for us. If he IDs even one of the shooters, I'll use that information to get the other one." Tommy said as he drove to *Tali's*.

Taliferro also saw the driver of the car that Wilkins was sitting in when he was shot. However, his description was very general except for the mark on the left side of the driver's face. When Tommy heard it, he dismissed the description as useless, but it was of primary interest to Michael.

Michael and Tommy walked into *Tali's*, identified themselves and asked the young man behind the counter if his boss was around. Taliferro must have heard the exchange because within seconds he came out from the rear of the store and asked if he could help.

When Tommy told him that they were there to discuss the Wilkins' murder, Taliferro was visibly shaken. In a whisper, he said. "Let's go into the back," as he pointed to a door behind the counter. "That's my office."

"Mr. Taliferro, we're here to ask you some questions about what you saw the night your neighbor was shot and killed," Michael began. "We won't take up much of your time but it's important that you give us your full attention. You seemed a bit shaken a few moments ago when we told you why we were here. Is everything alright?"

Tommy added that they wanted to hear exactly what he saw that led to him being able to assist the sketch artist.

At the mention of the sketch, Taliferro nearly collapsed. He began to shake and reached for his desk chair. He pulled it toward him and sat to compose himself.

"Sir, has something happened since the night of the shooting,?" Michael asked.

Taliferro looked at him with fear in eyes and said "Mr. Gioca I'm afraid I can't help you. Now you and the detective need to leave."

Michael calmed Taliferro down by telling him that they were only there to ask him some questions. "I understand the shock of seeing your neighbor shot to death is something that can shake you to your core. But we're just at the beginning of this investigation and you can point us in the right direction. I'm not asking you to view a line-up or to testify, I'm asking you to just talk to us. This visit, and what you tell us will remain confidential. Will you help us?"

Taliferro, now more relaxed, nodded in the affirmative.

"Jimmy... may I call you Jimmy," Tommy asked. Taliferro nodded and answered "Yes."

"Clearly something has happened since the shooting that has scared you. Am I right?" Another nod from Taliferro.

"Why don't we start there," Tommy said.

"We know from the reports that you heard the shots and saw two men walk away from the car and past your home. Right?"

"Yeah, that's right," Taliferro answered.

"We also know that you were able to see one of the men so well that you sat with a police artist and helped him compose this sketch," Tommy said as he showed the drawing to him. Taliferro nodded.

"Okay, good. Have you ever seen him or his buddy before that night?"

Taliferro answered that he hadn't.

"But I've seen him since that night," he volunteered. That surprised both Tommy and Michael.

"Is that why you're so afraid," Michael asked.

When Taliferro nodded that it was, Michael asked, "Tell us what happened."

He said that a couple of days after the shooting, someone who he thought was a customer, came into his store. "When I came out from the back to help the customer, I recognized him right away. It was that guy," Taliferro said, pointing to the sketch that Tommy was holding.

"What happened?" Tommy asked.

"Nothing. That's what has me so spooked. When I came out to help, he just stared at me. He said not one word, but he didn't have to. I knew that he was telling me to keep my mouth shut. After what seemed like an hour, but was only a minute or two, he walked to the door, opened it, and looked back at me before he left."

Did you happen to see what he did or where he went when he left the store?" Tommy asked.

"Yes I did. He got into a car that was double parked right out front. I couldn't see the driver, but the car sure looked like the one that Wilkins was sitting in the night he got shot. I got a pretty good look at it when it pulled off after the shooting. But I'm sorry I can't tell you anything about the make or model, just that it was a dark color, and"... Taliferro hesitated before saying, "It had the word BENSONHURST in a decal on the rear window, just like the car the guy in the sketch got into when he left my store."

"Thank you, Mr. Taliferro," Michael said. "You've been very helpful. If we need to speak to you again, one of us will be in touch."

Michael and Tommy handed him their business cards and told him they were always available, so he shouldn't hesitate to reach out to one or both of them if he remembered anything else.

"I don't think you'll see that guy from the sketch ever again," Tommy added, hoping to allay his fear. "But if you do, or if anyone else noses around for information or tries to scare you, call 911 and me immediately."

Taliferro shook their hands before they left and told them that he felt much better after their talk.

"I hope you get the guys who did this to Monroe. He was a good neighbor," he added, as they walked out the door.

When they got into the car, Tommy turned to Michael and said, "A Bensonhurst decal? You have to be shitting me. Why not just put a decal that says, *Mafia* on the rear window. What geniuses!"

"I see why the bosses put us on this. This has all the makings of an OC hit," he added.

"You mark my words, Mike, we're gonna find that the story of paying Wilkins a retainer fee was nothing more than the way to lure him out into the open so the two hitters could gun him down."

Tommy was correct, of course. Michael knew that Caldwell had already discovered there was no criminal case on which Wilkins could be retained. *HE* used that story to draw the attorney out in the open.

Tommy continued, "The street was dark and quiet, so no witnesses were likely to be around. Perfect for a hit. But when they saw that there was a 'looky Lou,' Mr. Taliferro, they made a visit to his store to scare the shit out of him, and to intimidate him into keeping his mouth shut."

"And now with the info that it was the car with the Bensonhurst decal from the murder scene that left after the visit to Taliferro... to my mind it's which family do they belong to? Not, 'Is the mob responsible?'"

CHAPTER
SEVENTY-ONE

The murder of prominent lawyer Monroe Wilkins and the subsequent investigation was the talk of Wilkins' Brooklyn neighborhood. It was a story that appeared in New York's tabloids for weeks and in his neighborhood's local newspapers every day for months.

Monroe Wilkins and his wife Abby were long time residents of their neighborhood and were active in civic organizations and their church.

Abby, a deacon in the First Baptist Church of South Brooklyn, was a prominent figure in local politics as well. The city councilman who represented their neighborhood was a member of their church, and Abby had the ear of the new mayor, having served on his election campaign committee.

Because of her connections she was kept apprised of the progress of the investigation by Tommy, his boss, and Michael. Unfortunately there wasn't much to tell. The investigation hit a dead end after Michael and Tommy's visit to *Tali's Hardware*.

Tommy had gone into the streets and spoken to every informant he knew hoping to put a name to the person in the sketch. He came up empty. No one had any idea who the guy in the sketch was, or if they knew, they weren't saying.

As days turned into weeks, and weeks into months, with no arrest, Abby Wilkins didn't give up. She remained persistent and ever hopeful that it would one day pay off.

To that end, since the murder, she attended every precinct council meeting, every civic association meeting, and even addressed her church's congregation, asking for help in finding the killers of her husband.

Tommy remained the assigned detective and spent as much time as his caseload allowed to beat the bushes looking for a break in the case. But crime did not stop, and the amount of time he could devote to finding Monroe Wilkins' killer became less and less. He had new cases to work on, with new victims' families looking for answers and arrests in the crimes against their loved ones.

Michael did his part by having Caldwell get Price to allow him to add Dina Mitchell and Tim Clark to the investigation. He felt that new sets of eyes and ears out on the street might break the log jam that was the Wilkins case.

It bothered him that every day that passed with no arrest, gave the *Evil One* cause for celebration.

Over dinner with Romano one evening Michael even asked the monsignor to pray for a break that would lead to the killers.

"Sal, if there was any time that we could use St. Jude's help, it's now," Michael said. "This seemingly hopeless cause is right in his wheelhouse. He's come through for me in the past when things seemed bleak, and now with both of us praying to him he should get the message that much quicker," Michael said jokingly, but meaning every word.

"Michael, you've come a long way from the early days of us working together. As I have repeatedly said, you have allies in this battle and it's apparent that you have come to realize that. Using the power of prayer will defeat *HIM* every time. I'm with you."

The next day the monsignor began a novena, which in the

Catholic religion is a petition for a divine favor and dedicated it to St. Jude. For nine days, Romano prayed to the saint asking for the break in the Wilkins case that Michael needed.

As for Michael, for those same nine days he attended the daily 8 a.m. Mass at St. Charles Borromeo praying for the same result.

Tommy, with Dina and Tim as reinforcements, took a different tact. They returned to the beginning of the investigation and re-traced all the ground that Tommy and Michael had covered.

They went back to Wilkins' neighborhood and canvassed the residents again.

They even returned to *Tali's* and spoke to Taliferro hoping that the passage of time did something to help him recall more than what he had originally told investigators.

Despite their efforts, they came up empty.

When they reported that to Michael he didn't react as they expected. He wasn't despondent, he was hopeful and confident that it was only a matter of time before his and Romano's prayers would be answered.

Two days later they were.

Two uniformed cops in the 68th precinct where Wilkins lived and was murdered, made a drug arrest of a street thug they knew as Marco.

Michael would soon learn that St. Jude had delivered for him once again.

Marco Antonelli was a constant pain in the ass for the cops in the precinct, all of whom knew him well. Marco had turned every one of his past arrests into 'a federal case,' as the saying goes. He would quote the law and criminal procedure to the arresting officers, as he threatened to 'sue their asses off.' His patented phrase, which he would spout as they formally booked him was, 'I'll have your jobs for this.'

On the day of his latest arrest, he was put into the precinct holding cell which was located in the 68 detective squad room. He had become a regular in that cell due to his long arrest record for mostly petty crimes, with the occasional serious drug arrest thrown in. This arrest was one of those. And, like every other time he was an occupant of the cell, he hadn't gone in quietly.

He began to mouth off at the arresting officers, telling them that they had no idea what they were doing because they had arrested him for possession of drugs for which he had a prescription.

When the cops paid him no mind, he changed his tactics and began to ridicule the detectives who were at their desks in the squad room.

They too ignored him until he turned his attention to the sketch of Monroe Wilkins' killer that Jimmy Taliferro provided the information for. The sketch was hanging on the squad room wall for many months since the murder.

Pointing to the sketch he taunted the detectives and asked, "Why haven't you guys arrested Joe Beef yet?" He began to laugh and continued, "When are you guys gonna get him?"

Marco had gotten the attention of every police officer and detective in the room.

He was taken out of the cell and brought to an interrogation room. A detective who responded to the scene the night of the Wilkins murder, and who was familiar with the case, asked him what he knew about it.

Marco repeated what he said when he was in the cell and added that the guy in the sketch was a drug dealer he knew on the street as "Joe Beef."

Tommy Schwartz was called at home and told of the development. He rushed to the precinct and sat down to question Marco more thoroughly. Marco told him that "Beef" whose real name was Joseph Comforto, and his partner in the drug business, Frank "Frankie Sap" Sapino, "Killed that lawyer Wilkins."

Marco then told Tommy the motive for the murder.

It was 3 am when Tommy called Michael.

Sound asleep, Michael thought the sound of his cell phone ringing was part of a dream. When it continued to ring, and ring, and ring, he finally realized that it wasn't. He shook himself awake, then struggled to locate it on his nightstand. When he finally found it and answered, what Tommy told him caused him to literally jump out of bed. Michael was now fully awake.

"Tom, I'll shower and be there in an hour. Don't let that guy go," he said.

"Mike, he ain't goin' nowhere. Be careful drivin'. I'll see you when you get here," Tommy replied.

CHAPTER
SEVENTY-TWO

"I ain't talkin' until I get a deal," Marco told Michael after the prosecutor introduced himself and told him what he wanted to talk about.

"Your cops got me for possession of drugs that I got a prescription for. When I tried to show them, they didn't want to hear nothin'. So Mr. DA, if you want to hear somethin', tell me you're gonna dismiss this arrest. You ain't gonna be disappointed with what I got to tell you."

Before he continued with Marco, Michael checked with the arresting officers. They told him that they were in the process of checking Marco's story about the drugs being prescribed, when he "Started shooting his mouth off about the guy in the sketch." While the detectives had him in the interrogation room we were able to reach his doctor. He was prescribed those pills."

Michael was pleased to hear that. He would now sound magnanimous when he told Marco that he quashed the arrest.

When Michael told him that it was, Marco remarked, "Those cops are dumb as shit for not believing me." He thanked Michael and said, "Now I'll tell you everything."

Marco told Michael that about a week before Wilkins was murdered, he was in a neighborhood bar with a few friends. "Beef and Sap came in and sat right next to me at the bar. I know them from the neighborhood. They're hooked up."

When Michael asked him to explain, Marco said, "They're made guys. Gambino family."

"After a couple of drinks," Marco said, "Beef and Sap started to complain about some lawyer. They said that he had represented one of the guys in their crew on a drug sale case in Brooklyn federal court. Mr. DA, the guy apparently fucked up royally. He made some big mistake in the trial and their friend was convicted. Because he had a record, their friend went away for fifteen years. They were pissed."

Marco went on to say that Beef and Sap said they wanted to whack the lawyer to teach guys like him a lesson. "They said that no one fucks with the Gambino family."

"Just then," Marco continued, "A strange looking dude, who I ain't ever seen before, was sittin' near them at the bar. He walked over to them. He must have heard what they was talking about because he told them that he knew how to get done what they wanted to get done."

"He says, 'I can help you with that piece of work. I know who you're talking about. I hate his fuckin' guts.'"

"Mr. G, I'm sittin' right there, and I hear him tell Beef and Sap that he could get the lawyer to meet him on the street somewhere quiet, with them nearby. And while he was talkin' to him, Beef and Sap could go up to the lawyer and do the job."

"What happened next," Michael asked.

"Unbelievably, Beef and Sap said that they was in."

"They had never met this guy before, and they was ok with him settin' up a hit for them? That's fuckin' weird. They must of hated that lawyer to agree right then and there without checking out who this guy was. Made guys are supposed to be sharper than that."

"They talked a bit more but that was away from me so I couldn't hear what they was sayin'. Then the guy left and Beef and Sap came back to where I was sittin'. I says to them that they must be fuckin' crazy to just go along with that guy, 'he could be a fed or a cop.'"

"Beef looked at me and said, 'Nah, there's somethin' about the guy that told us we could trust him.' Sap nodded. He must have felt the same way. I says, 'Okay, I hope yous are right.' They both then said that I should keep my mouth shut if I know what's good for me."

Marco continued, "A few days after that, I'm in another bar in the neighborhood and who walks in, Beef and Sap. Boy they was like struttin'. I don't say anything cause I don't want no trouble from them. They may think I'm too nosy if I start askin' questions. But 'Mr. G' I know that something had gone down, and they was happy about it."

"Next thing I know, the bartender is pouring champagne for everybody in the place. When he gives me a glass I ask who it's from. He points to Sap and Beef. Now I goes over to them and Sap, without me sayin' nothin', says 'That lawyer motherfucker is lookin' at heaven right now.' He and Beef give each other a high-five and Beef says 'Wait 'til Chucky hears what we done for him. He's gonna be smilin' big time.' 'Mr. G,' Chucky is the guy from their crew whose case that lawyer fucked up," Marco said.

"Marco, you said the guy who talked to Beef and Sap in that first bar was strange looking. What did you mean by that?" Michael asked.

"He was a tall white guy with close cropped hair like one of those brotherhood guys in the joint. He had this mark on the left side of his face that I thought was a tattoo. Them Aryan guys have tats all over. But then I got a closer look. It was some kind of mole. Like a small tumor or some shit. It made me sick to look at it."

When Marco was finished, Michael and Tommy stepped out of the room. "So the boss' instincts and my instincts were correct. This was a mob hit," Tommy said.

Michael, his mind elsewhere, absently nodded in agreement. The description of the guy at the first bar had confirmed what he, Caldwell, and Romano expected. The *Evil One* was the true instigator and facilitator of the murder of Monroe Wilkins.

With Michael lost in thought, thinking, '*Do I have enough to beat HIM?*', Tommy interrupted. "Mike, what's up? You worried that we ain't got enough to go to the grand jury? I ain't gonna stop looking for witnesses if that's what you're worried about. This ain't the strongest case, but I promise that it'll get better now that I know who did it."

"Tom, we have just the bare minimum. I'll go to the grand jury with what I have, but you have to do what you just said. I need more if we want to convict these assholes. Work with Dina and Tim and get it for me."

"And Mike," Tommy said, "I'm not gonna stop until I get that piece of shit who set Wilkins up. We don't know a lot about him but trust me I'll get that fuck."

Michael just smiled. He didn't say anything because he didn't want to distract Tommy from his task of finding the additional witnesses he needed. And he certainly didn't want to discourage him by letting him know that the 'piece of shit' who set up Wilkins would never be found.

Before letting Marco leave the precinct, Tommy told him that he'd pick him up in a couple of days and bring him to the grand jury. Michael warned him to say nothing about what he told them. They reminded him that neither Beef nor Sap would hesitate for a second to kill him to keep him from testifying.

"They killed a lawyer who they believe got one of their friends convicted. Think what they'll do to you to keep themselves from spending the rest of their lives in prison," Michael said.

Marco, visibly shaken at the thought, said, "Don't worry 'Mr. G,' I ain't sayin' nothin'."

Two days later, based on Marco's testimony alone, the grand jury returned an indictment against Joseph Comforto and Frank Sapino charging them with the murder of Monroe Wilkins.

The next day, armed with a grand jury warrant for his arrest, Tommy, Dina and Tim found Frankie Sap at home. When they knocked on his door he answered dressed only in a bathrobe even though it was mid-afternoon. When Tommy told him he was under arrest for the Wilkins murder, he began to loudly argue that they had the wrong guy.

Tommy told him to "Shut up and get dressed." As they entered Sap's bedroom, Tommy was surprised by what he saw. Lying on Sap's bed was a young man totally naked and fast asleep. It appeared that the arrest team had interrupted an afternoon tryst between Sap and the young man.

"Listen detective, you got to forget what you saw in here," Sap said tilting his head toward the now totally awake young man. "The guys in my crew can't know anything about this."

Tommy knew the deal. An openly gay wiseguy was as rare as hen's teeth. If the Gambinos found out about Sap's sexual orientation he'd be lucky to just be thrown out of the family.

"Sapino, your secret is safe with me. But if you give me any trouble I'll call the Don himself to let him know all about your boyfriend," Tommy said.

He turned to the now awake young man and said, "Kid get the fuck outta here. And if I were you I'd never come back to this neighborhood. If his boys find out about you, the cops and the ME are gonna have to scrape you off the sidewalk. His *goombas* in the family ain't gonna take the chance that you'd spread it around that Frankie Sap was your boyfriend. It don't look good for their image."

The young man just nodded and began to get dressed. Tommy told him to leave after he had taken Sap out to their car so Dina and Tim wouldn't find out about Sap's afternoon delight.

Two hours after Sapino was arrested, Tommy and three detectives from his squad executed a grand jury arrest warrant for Joseph Comforto. They found him walking on 86th Street near *Lenny's Pizza*. When they had him in their car and told him why he was being arrested, he said to no detective in particular, "How much time do you think I'll get for this?"

Tommy immediately noted his statement, and would later testify to the 'confession,' as Michael would characterize it to the jury, at Beef's trial.

That evening in the 68 detective squad two line-ups were conducted by Michael. One with fill-ins who looked like Frankie Sap, and the other with fill-ins who looked like Joe Beef.

The first person to view the line-ups was Marco. In seconds he identified both Beef and Sap as the men who had talked to the guy with the mole, and the guys who had bought champagne for the crowded bar after they killed the lawyer.

Next to view the line-ups was Jimmy Taliferro. Michael had him first view the line-up with Frank Sapino. Taliferro took his time, looked at each of the six men carefully and finally said that he didn't recognize anyone from the night of the shooting.

He was asked to look at the line-up with Joe "Beef" Comforto standing in the third position from Taliferro's left. Without hesitation he said, "It's number three."

When Michael asked where he had seen him before, Taliferro answered "He's the guy who walked away from the car after Monroe Wilkins was shot and passed right in front of my house. He's the guy in the sketch."

CHAPTER
SEVENTY-THREE

Late in the afternoon of the next day, Michael stood before Brooklyn Supreme Court Judge Morgan J. Owens and asked that both Beef and Sap be held without bail. The arraignment of the two defendants took just ten minutes to complete as neither Beef's lawyer, Joel Horowitz, nor Sap's attorney, Dean Miller, had contested Michael's bail request.

Both attorney's told Judge Owens that they would file bail reduction motions in three weeks when they were more familiar with the facts of the case. The judge set a date one month later for argument on their motion and for any other pre-trial matters that needed to be disposed of before he set a trial date.

That evening Michael met Romano for dinner at *Emilio's* where he brought the monsignor up to date on the status of the case over dishes of rigatoni Bolognese and a bottle of Chianti *Riserva*.

"Michael, are you sure you have enough to convict those two" Romano had asked.

"Sal you're getting good at this case evaluation business, "Michael responded. "The answer is that I don't. I went to the grand jury because I needed to make sure that they were held in custody. If they hadn't been I was concerned that *HE* and the Gambinos would have sent them somewhere I wouldn't be able to find them. Now Tommy Schwartz has enough time to make good on his promise to make the case stronger. I also have Dina and Tim working with him. That's a formidable team that I have a lot of confidence in. I'm sure that by the time I pick a jury, this will be a very strong case."

"But there is something I need from you and Caldwell. My case right now is Marco and Jimmy Taliferro. In the unlikely event Tommy fails to come up with additional evidence, I'll have to go to trial using their testimony. So I need to make sure that they stay safe. I'd like Caldwell to provide protection for them just as he did for me and my family when Wilkins withdrew the civil case. It'll probably be a few months before we start jury selection, which I know is a long time, but the peace of mind I'll have knowing Marco and Taliferro are safe is worth it. I won't have that as a distraction as I build this case into a winner."

'Wow! You certainly are confident in Detective Schwartz' ability," Romano said.

"Sal, I've worked with him in the past and he's never let me down. And, with Dina and Tim, my confidence is well placed. But I need a failsafe, and Marco and Taliferro are it. Please get Caldwell to keep them safe and secure."

Romano promised Michael that he'd have an answer from Caldwell by the next day.

When Emilio brought them espresso and two cannoli's , it gave Michael an opportunity to ask Romano what was going on with Sabar's arson case in Manhattan. He had tried to reach Kathy Baer several times with no luck. And his voicemail messages and texts went unanswered. He was concerned.

"Michael, Caldwell told me that the case has been delayed indefinitely until Sabar secured a new attorney. As you know Monroe Wilkins was his lawyer and with his death Sabar asked for time to hire someone new. My understanding is that if he is unable to do so, the court will assign a lawyer to represent him at trial."

Michael listened and nodded.

"But you knew there would be a delay because you're investigating the murder of the defense lawyer from that case," Romano said. "What you really want to know is why you haven't been able to reach Kathy. Am I right?"

Michael pretended not to hear the question as he took the last bite of his pastry. "Okay, you know me too well," he finally said. "Yes, what's up with her? Has she been in contact with you?"

"Of course not! She doesn't know I exist. But Caldwell has heard from the prosecutors in Manhattan that the delay was fortuitous because it gave Kathy time to go home to her parents. Apparently her mom took ill, and her dad couldn't take care of her, so Kathy went to help out her dad and care for her mom.

When Michael heard that he felt awful. He had been so busy and distracted that he hadn't followed up on her calls to him.

The next day he called the fire marshal's office and asked Kathy's boss for her parent's contact information.

"I understand she's home with her parents and I just want to find out how her mom is doing," he said when Kathy's boss hesitated before giving Michael the information.

Kathy answered on the second ring. Michael said he was sorry for not returning her calls and texts, and she was happy to finally have a chance to speak to him.

"Michael, after my dad told me about my mom, she was the only thing on my mind. My dad couldn't care for her so I packed a bag and came home. I've been so busy with cooking, cleaning, and taking care of mom and dad that when I went to bed each night I was asleep before my head hit the pillow."

"Kathy, I need to apologize. I should have responded to your messages and done what I did this morning, contact the fire marshal's office to find out what was going on."

"After our little pact to keep our distance while you were busy with the trial, I took it very seriously," Michael said.

"When Wilkins was murdered," Kathy said, "And my trial was postponed, I figured you had been assigned to his murder. I didn't want to bother you," Kathy replied. 'Then my dad called, and I rushed home."

"Okay, we're both feeling guilty." Michael said. "Now let's forget it. How is your mom?"

They talked for the next hour. She brought him up to speed on her mom's illness and he did the same on the Wilkins case. Before hanging up they both re-committed to their promise of not bothering each other, with one change. They agreed to talk at least once a week until after both completed their respective trial responsibilities.

After the call Dina and Tim walked into Michael's office and found him smiling from ear to ear. When Dina started to ask him what made him so happy, Michael waved her off as his cell phone began to ring.

"That's great news," Michael said to the caller. "I'll talk to Taliferro and Marco and let them know what's happening."

Michael told one of his white lies to Dina and Tim to explain the call he received. The caller was Romano who relayed the news that Caldwell agreed to provide protection for Marco and Taliferro.

Romano also told him that Caldwell wanted Michael to tell anyone who asked, including Tommy, Dina, and Tim, that the protective details would be manned by cops from the NYPD Intelligence Division. And that DA Price had secured their services in an agreement with the police commissioner.

Saying that it would be Intelligence Division cops, who weren't very well known to the rank and file, would provide the necessary cover for Caldwell's agents.

"Wow! How did you pull that off?" Dina asked.

Michael told them Caldwell's lie, and added his own, "I contacted the PC myself and called in a favor," he answered.

'Now," Michael continued, "You guys, and Tommy, have to beat the bushes and find me the additional evidence he's so certain is out there."

When Dina and Tim left Michael's office his first call was to Jimmy Taliferro. Michael explained that for the foreseeable future Jimmy and his family would have cops watching over them "Just as a precaution." He explained that they would be as unobtrusive as possible but the final call on how they deployed themselves would be up to them.

Taliferro was extremely happy with the arrangement.

"Mr. Gioca, you know how much I want to help so those murderers will be caught for killing Monroe, but I was worried about my and my family's safety. I'm a big movie and TV fan and I've seen plenty of films and shows where the Mafia has taken steps to eliminate witnesses, even threatening to kill a witness' family to discourage him from testifying. What you've just told me is a relief. Thank you. And don't worry, whatever the cops tell us to do, we'll do."

One down and one to go. Michael wasn't sure that Marco would be so amenable to the protection arrangement.

And he was right.

"I ain't havin' no cops watching everything I do," Marco told him.

"I can take care of myself. I been around wiseguys all my life. I know how they think, and how they act, and I got lots of friends who'll take care of me. So I'll be okay. No need to worry about me 'Mr. G.'"

Michael didn't take no for an answer. But no matter how much he tried to get through to Marco, he was stonewalled. Finally he said, "Listen, we'll do it your way for now. But if anything happens to change your mind, I want you to promise that you'll reach out to me so I can take care of you."

Marco didn't answer.

Michael then said, "Marco, I want to hear you tell me that you promise you'll do as I say. If you don't, I promise you that I'll get a judge to sign a material witness order and I'll have the cops scoop you up and lock you in civil jail, where material witnesses are held, until you have to testify."

"Okay, okay, I fuckin' promise," Marco reluctantly said.

CHAPTER
SEVENTY-FOUR

With his only two witnesses secured, Michael spent the next month preparing for what he expected would be a knock down, dragged out, brawl of a trial.

The hearing on bail for Beef and Sap was contentious, with their lawyers arguing that the prosecution had barely enough to indict their clients, let alone prove their guilt beyond a reasonable doubt. Judge Owens listened and had some troublesome comments for Michael about his evidence being shaky, but in the end ruled against the defendants and ordered that they remain in jail with no bail.

Seemingly to compensate the defendants for his ruling, at the end of the hearing Judge Owens set a trial date for six weeks later. "This way your clients will have their day in court sooner rather than later," he told both defense attorneys.

Before he adjourned for the day, there was one additional issue the judge addressed with them.

"I have been informed by Mr. Gioca, that the prosecution has a statement, made by Mr. Comforto that implicates both him and Mr. Sapino in the murder, which he wants to introduce into evidence against Comforto. As you know under the law that statement cannot be introduced against Mr. Sapino. Therefore we'll select two juries. Each will hear all the evidence, but only the Comforto jury will hear that statement," the judge explained.

"If there are no objections to proceeding that way, I'll see you all in six weeks?" Judge Owens said. When no objections were raised, court was adjourned for the day.

The pressure was now on Michael and his team to change the quality of the case from shaky to rock solid.

Tommy, Dina, and Tim had been out on the streets of Benson-hurst and neighboring Bay Ridge in an effort to do just that. They rousted mob wannabes and hit the clubs and bars in an effort to uncover anyone who Tommy was certain knew all about the murder of Monroe Wilkins.

However, just as they experienced in the days they worked the streets looking for witnesses in the Choi murder, Dina and Tim returned each day with nothing to show for their work.

As for Tommy, he still maintained that a break was around the corner and wasn't discouraged at the lack of success locating additional evidence. "I know it's out there," he would say to Michael every night when they talked. "Time is getting short Mike, I know that, but I'm not gonna stop until I have something."

With the start of the trial two weeks away, and with no progress made finding additional witnesses or evidence, Michael knew he had to begin to prepare Marco and Taliferro for their testimony. Prep would be easy because their testimony was not complicated. Cross-examination 'Would be a bitch,' he said to himself as telephoned Caldwell's people who were guarding Taliferro.

"Please let him know that I need him in my office tomorrow around noon so I can begin to prep him for trial," Michael told one of the agents assigned to the Taliferro's detail.

"Don't worry Mr. Gioca, we'll have him there," the agent replied.

It was lunchtime and Michael had made up his mind that he would get out to take a walk and pick up a sandwich at the *Queen* restaurant on Court Street, not far from his office. He knew that with the amount of work ahead of him in the next ten days or so, leaving his desk, even for a cup of coffee, would be next to impossible.

As he put on his overcoat his office phone and his cell phone rang. *'Shit, something's wrong,'* he said to himself as he reached for his cell. It was Kevin Richardson, the agent in charge of the detail guarding Taliferro.

"Mr. Gioca, that's us on your office phone. No need to answer it," the agent said.

"Kevin, what's going on? Has something happened to Taliferro or his family?"

When the agent answered "Yes," Michael's heart sank. He sat down and asked for all the details.

That morning, minutes after Michael called to ask that Taliferro be brought into his office the next day, a delivery van from *Gehenna Chemicals* arrived at *Tali's Hardware.* It belonged to the company that supplied the store with hydrochloric acid and other chemicals used in contracting and construction work.

Taliferro had the required New York City permit to sell the acid, which has strong corrosive properties. His customers used it to remove tough industrial and household stains, to clean badly discolored bathroom tile, toilet bowls, and other porcelain surfaces.

Because of its properties, the acid was packaged in glass jars with a red warning label which cautioned the user, *'Any contact with human skin causes severe acid burns which must be treated immediately by medical professionals. Acid resistant gloves need to be worn when working with this product.'*

Agent Richardson told Michael that Taliferro was not expecting the acid delivery for a few days and was surprised when the driver rolled the cases into the store. The driver showed Taliferro the packing slip and invoice bearing that day's date when he questioned the delivery. "I'm just the delivery guy," the driver said to him. "If you got a problem, call my company."

After a discussion, Taliferro conceded that he might have confused the date and accepted the delivery. However, he told the driver to let his boss know that in the future he wanted a "Day's warning that the acid was being delivered. I got to make shelf room for this stuff. It's too dangerous to just keep around the store."

After Taliferro signed for the cases of acid, the delivery man told him, "Don't worry I'll let *her* know what you said," as he quickly left the store.

What the delivery man said caused Taliferro to watch him as he got into his van and pulled off. When Richardson asked Taliferro if anything was wrong, he told the agent, "That company must have changed managers. The delivery guy referred to his boss as "her." I been dealing with a guy named Chic for well over a year now. That must be why the delivery came early. New people need to catch up on schedules and such."

Richardson didn't think anything of it and watched as Taliferro took the jars of acid to the rear of the store where he began to load them onto a high shelf. As he placed the last jar from the first of the two cases, Richardson heard a horrific scream. When he ran back to where Taliferro was working he saw him writhing on the floor, with his hands covering his face. His screams intensified with each passing second.

When the agent kneeled down next to Taliferro, he noticed that one of the jars of acid lay empty next to him. Clearly the jar somehow opened up and the acid spilled out covering Taliferro's face. And because he used his hands to rub and cover his face, Richardson could see that the flesh on them was eaten away.

Emergency medical personnel responded very quickly to the agent's call and carefully transferred Taliferro to the nearest hospital for triage. From there he was taken to Manhattan and admitted to the Cornell University Hospital burn unit.

"Agent Richardson, is Taliferro dead?" Michael asked.

"No sir. His burns are severe, but he's alive. I'm told that he's in an induced coma and will be for quite some time. They want him to remain still to encourage his body to heal somewhat before they could even think of skin grafting."

"Is his family okay?" Michael asked next.

"Yes. His family is with us here at the hospital. And other than suffering from the trauma of knowing how badly hurt Jimmy is, they are unharmed."

Michael asked Richardson to repeat what Taliferro told him regarding the delivery driver referring to his boss as female. Richardson did. Michael asked for the name of the company that delivered the acid. Richardson read the name off the invoice that Taliferro signed.

Michael asked one final question, "Kevin, did you get a good look at the delivery guy?"

"Mike, I'm sorry to say that I didn't. When Taliferro was talking to him, his back was to me. But from what I could see when he first came into the store, other than his blue denim uniform with the company name on the back of the jacket, and the protective mask I assume he wore because he was delivering chemicals, there was nothing distinctive about him."

"Okay thanks Kevin. Please keep me posted as to Jimmy's condition."

Michael hung up and just shook his head in despair. What Richardson told him about the delivery driver gave him a sick feeling. He didn't have definitive proof yet, but his gut had become an excellent indicator when it came to dealing with the *Evil One*.

He couldn't let this development stop him. He still had a trial to conduct.

Michael called Dina and Tim to his office. He told them about Taliferro and asked them to reach out to Tommy.

"Have him find Marco and bring him in. If he can't do it, you guys go and get him. I lost one half of my case today. I must make sure I don't lose it all."

Ten minutes later they returned and told Michael that Tommy would get Marco.

Then Dina spoke up. "Michael, something bothered me when you told us about the delivery of the acid being early, and the delivery guy saying his boss was a woman. So I called Taliferro's bookkeeper and asked her for the name of the company that supplied *Tali's* with the acid. She checked her records and told me that the company is *Metropolitan Chemical Supply, Inc.* That is not the name on that invoice Agent Richardson read from."

"Then I called *Metropolitan* and found out that they did *not* deliver to *Tali's* this morning. They have a delivery scheduled for that store in two days, just as Taliferro told the agent.... And, they have no women delivery dispatchers, or women sales managers, nor any women working in the back office of their company."

"I did one more thing. I googled that name *Gehenna Chemicals* and found no listing for it. So I checked with the city Department of Environmental Protection to see if they had that company listed as an authorized seller and distributor of hydrochloric acid.... They never heard of *Gehenna Chemicals*."

"Michael, the Gambinos got to Taliferro," Dina said.

"We've underestimated how important Joe Beef and Frankie Sap are to them, and how much they want this case to disappear. How could we have done that?" she angrily asked.

"Dina, calm down," Tim told her. "We'll redouble our efforts to find more evidence. I'm a believer, like Tommy, that there are people out in that neighborhood who know what happened and why. We have a little less than two weeks. So we're not out of time yet."

Michael said nothing during Dina's outburst. What she found out had confirmed the feeling in his gut that the Gambino family was not behind this atrocity. *HE* was.

CHAPTER
SEVENTY-FIVE

"Sal, *HE* has devastated not only the Wilkins family, but the Taliferro family as well. That's a means to *HIS* end: destroy families and family life, and Brooklyn as we know it, collapses!" Michael said as he and Romano were sitting in the monsignor's Red Hook office late that afternoon.

Michael was there to bring Romano up to speed on everything that happened to Taliferro, and to let him know who he believed was behind it all.

"Please thank Caldwell for the protection he provided to Taliferro and his family," Michael said. "And let him know that I believe that Satan is responsible for Jimmy Taliferro being in a coma for the foreseeable future."

"Michael, I will do that. "But I'm not only going to tell Caldwell that *you believe* it was the *Evil One* who did this to Taliferro, I'm going to tell him that it *was HIM*!"

"And in addition to everything else that points to *HIM* do you know what clinched it for me?"

Michael responded with a shake of his head.

"The name of the company that delivered the sabotaged jar of acid, *Gehenna Chemicals.*"

Michael had no clue as to what the monsignor was saying and the look on his face reflected that.

"Michael, *Gehenna* is the Hebrew word for HELL!"

"That acid was delivered by a company named for the place of unquenchable fire. *HE* wanted to make sure we knew who was responsible for the burning of Jimmy Taliferro."

Michael didn't think the depression he was experiencing since he learned of Taliferro's horrific injuries could have gotten any deeper, but he was wrong. After hearing what Romano had just told him, Michael had the feeling that he was drowning without a lifeguard or life preserver in sight.

Romano asked Michael to have dinner with him after their meeting, but he declined. He had to get back to his office to talk with Marco. Tommy located him and called Michael just before his meeting with the monsignor started, to let him know they were on the way.

And even if he didn't have Tommy and Marco waiting for him, in the mood he was in, *Emilio's* fabulous food would have been wasted on him. So from his car on the way back to the DA's office Michael decided to make a call to a longtime friend, who had acted as a sounding board for him during troubled times in the past.

Jimmy Kennedy was a retired NYPD detective who worked with Michael a decade before on a case in which two of Kennedy's fellow officers were gunned down. They became good friends who stayed in touch even though Kennedy lived several hours away from Brooklyn in upstate New York.

After he retired from the NYPD, Kennedy became a successful private investigator. He worked for most of the attorneys who practiced criminal law in the county where he lived and in the surrounding jurisdictions. And, with a gentle nudge from his wife and her friends, Kennedy became a prison minister.

For the past two decades he mentored and counseled both federal and state inmates. Kennedy's strong Catholic faith and his commitment to instill in them the idea that they should never despair and never give up, made him the perfect person for Michael to talk to.

When Michael told Kennedy his predicament, the former cop gave him a piece of advice that would ultimately pay off.

"Mike, Go back to the one sure thing you have, Marco," he said. "Knowing these street guys the way that I do, I'll bet he doesn't even realize that he has more to give you. And you must have faith in your ability to get it out of him. Once you do, the floodgates will open. You'll have more evidence than you ever thought was out there."

"And one last thing," Kennedy said, "I'll say a prayer to St. Jude for you."

As a result of that short ten minute call, Michael's confidence, which had been waning, was renewed and restored. He thanked his friend and said, "Jimmy, *when* you win that bet, dinner is on me."

When Michael got back to his office, Tommy and Marco were waiting. He stopped to buy coffee for the three of them. He knew that it would be a long night. He had a lot of work to do with the witness.

On the drive to the office, Tommy brought Marco up to date on the incident involving Taliferro. But instead of being frightened, Marco became more determined to testify against Beef and Sap.

"'Mr. G,' Tommy told me what happened. I want you to know that they don't scare me. I don't care that they're mafia. To me they're just drug dealing scumbags. It ain't right what they did to that lawyer, and it certainly wasn't right to send some fuck to have acid spill on a guy's face. I'm ready to work. So let's do it."

For the next two hours Michael took Marco through that first night in the bar where Beef and Sap were approached by the guy who said he could help them get Wilkins.

He then went through the champagne party in the second bar where they celebrated the Wilkins murder. Michael pressed him for details and asked him to think hard about anyone who was there who he hadn't mentioned, and "Who might be able to help us."

When questioned by Michael, Marco never deviated, even slightly, from the story he first told Tommy, then repeated for Michael, and testified to in the grand jury. But he hadn't come up with anything or anyone new.

However, during a break in the prep session to eat dinner, Marco spontaneously mentioned a name that neither Michael nor Tommy had ever heard before.

"Man, Jackie Sira is gonna miss those two motherfuckers when they go away," he mused, shaking his head as he took a bite of his pizza slice.

Both Michael and Tommy reacted instantly.

"Who is Jackie Sira?" Tommy asked. And before Marco could answer, Michael asked "Was he in the bar when Beef and Sap toasted the murder?"

With his mouth full of pizza, Marco nodded.

After he swallowed he said, "Even though he didn't really like them, Jackie Sira was one of Beef and Sap's best customers. He bought drugs off them for years. He even bailed them out one time when they ran out of product, and set them up with some connect he knew on Wall St. But one time when he had asked them to front him some drugs until he had got paid, they told him to go fuck himself. 'No credit,' they said. He never forgot that but had continued to cop off them because they were nearby."

"And yeah," he continued, "Sira was there when they was braggin' about killin' the lawyer," answering Michael's question.

"When they cracked open the champagne and toasted the murder, Sira took a glass, but he didn't drink anything. He just walked out of the place."

Michael and Tommy looked at each other. Both had the same thought.

"Where can I find this guy?" Tommy asked.

Marco told him where Sira worked and where he hung out.

When Michael finished with Marco for the evening he tried again to get him to agree to protection. He used what happened to Taliferro

424   FALLEN ANGEL - A TRUE CRIME FANTASY - BOOK 2

as an example of why it was the smart move, but Marco wouldn't budge. He said that he knew the streets better than "Some guy who owns a hardware store," and again told Michael not to worry.

Before Tommy left to drive Marco home, he said to Michael, "I know what you want me to do. I'll have Sira here sometime tomorrow."

Michael nodded and thanked him. "Tommy be careful," he said.

CHAPTER
SEVENTY-SIX

Jackie Sira worked as a runner and messenger for a brokerage firm in Manhattan's financial district. His work hours were from 9 a.m. to 5 p.m. , which gave him lots of free time in the evening, most of which he spent getting high.

He would begin his nightly partying after work at a bar near his office. In between tequila shots and beers, he and his fellow runners and messengers would toke up in an alley next to the bar with the weed and coke they bought from a supplier who worked with them.

When the drugs were finished Sira would go home and search out his neighborhood suppliers, Joe Beef and Frankie Sap. After scoring from them he would pick up food and go home to eat and top off his high.

Not having time to consult the NYPD's computer for a possible mugshot of Sira, Tommy only had Marco's general description of him as he waited in his car outside Sira's apartment. But when the tall, nearly emaciated, bleary eyed individual emerged from the apartment building at 8 a.m. and began walking toward the nearby subway station, Tommy had no trouble identifying him as Jackie Sira.

In his car, Tommy followed alongside Sira as he walked, and just as he was about to enter the subway station he got out and stopped him. At first Sira played dumb when Tommy told him why he needed to speak to him.

"I don't know no Joe Beef or Frankie Sap," he said.

Tommy told him he knew that Sira was at the champagne celebration for the murder of an innocent attorney, and "Like a good street thug you said nothing to the police about what you knew. But Beef and Sap don't know that. So when I put word out that you were talking to me, or somebody sees us since we're talking here out in the open, you think the bent noses the Gambinos send to pick you up to teach you a lesson are gonna believe it when you say you didn't rat?"

Sira began to shake and stutter. Tommy calmed him down and talked him into his car.

"Jackie, I promise that if you talk to me no one will know. And if you give me what we think you can and help the DA's office, they'll find you a new place to live and, if you want, they'll help you get a new job where the wiseguys won't find you."

"And besides, from what I hear, you hate those two pricks. So you'd be helping yourself and the neighborhood by getting them off the street."

Sira listened carefully before he finally said, "Okay I'll go with you, but you gotta call my boss and tell him something that will get me out of work today."

As Tommy drove to Michael's office, he called him and told him he was on his way in with Sira. Tommy also told Michael that he would need to call Sira's job.

Michael couldn't be happier. He said he'd deal with Sira's work situation when they got there because he'd need more info from Sira so his story to the boss would be plausible.

"Tom, ask Sira if he wants something to eat. And while I'm at it, do you want me to order breakfast for you?"

When Tommy and Sira walked into the office, Michael had two egg and cheese bagel sandwiches and coffee waiting for them.

After they ate, Michael got right down to business. He first assured Sira that what Tommy told him about a new place to live and work would be done, assuming he told them the truth about what he knew concerning Beef and Sap and the murder of Monroe Wilkins. "And you agree to testify at trial, if I need you."

"But if you lie to me, or you fuck us in any way, I'll make you regret it. I know all about the drugs, and you getting high nearly every day, which I'm sure your boss would not be happy to hear. There are a million guys who can do your job, and it won't be hard for your boss to find a replacement when he fires you. Am I clear?"

"Mr. G, I'm here ain't I? If I wasn't gonna tell you the truth I would have told your detective to go fuck himself and gotten on that subway this morning. What do you want to know?"

Jackie Sira spent the next hour telling Michael everything he knew about Beef and Sap and all that he knew about them killing Wilkins.

"I've known those two for a few years," he began. "I know they're hooked up with the Gambino family and they're drug dealers. I been buying coke and weed from them since we was first introduced by some guy I used to hang with."

He went on to tell Michael that over the years he got to know Beef and Sap pretty well and spent time with them most weekends.

"They trusted me so much that when I found out that they ran out of product one summer, a couple of years back, they asked me if I knew anyone from where I work that would sell them a supply until they could re-up. I hooked them up with the supplier I know over on Wall Street. They said they was very grateful, but they were full of shit."

"A week or so after they scored with the connect I got them, I needed them to front me some coke because I had no money. I blew my last paycheck on insurance for my car and wouldn't get paid again for a week. When I asked them for the drugs, I expected there would be no problem since I helped them out. But I got shit from them. They said they don't give credit and told me 'it's cash or nothin.'"

Sira said that he didn't make a big deal of their refusal because of who they were, and because he needed them to sell him dope when he had the money.

"Things went back to how they were before they refused to help me out and I started hanging with them again. But I never forgot what they done to me."

"One night not that long ago, we was in this bar in Bay Ridge, and they started to talk about their friend Chucky. He was one of their crew who got jammed up by the feds and was convicted of trafficking coke. They was pissed because they said that Chucky's lawyer made some big mistake at the trial which is what got him convicted. Both of them was high so they was doin' a lot of talkin' about how they was gonna take the lawyer out because of what he done. They said they wanted to send a message that you don't fuck with the Gambinos."

"After that night I hadn't seen either of them for a couple of weeks. Then one night I'm in another bar and the two of them walk in with bottles of champagne. The place was pretty crowded, but they was able to clear out a good sized space at the bar. They told the bartender to open the bottles and they started giving out the champagne. They was braggin' about having killed someone. I had no idea who it was until both Beef and Sap came up to me and said, 'We told you. That fuckin' lawyer ain't gonna fuck up no more. He's lookin' up at heaven.' At that point I was so disgusted over how stupid they were, braggin' to the whole bar, I just walked out. I didn't even have a sip of the champagne."

"Did you know who they were talking about?" Michael asked.

"Of course. It was the guy who had fucked up Chucky's case. They did what they said they would do. And when I heard about the murder the next day and saw it in the papers, I says to myself that it was a good thing that I left because I didn't want to be there if someone who heard what they were sayin' called the cops."

Michael then asked, "Jackie, do you remember who else was in that bar the night of the champagne party who could help us?"

"Wow, there were lots of people in the bar, but I don't think there are many, if any, who would help you. Beef and Sap didn't hide the fact that they were made guys, and no one is gonna want to fuck with the mob."

Then Sira said, "Marco Antonelli was in there and he had a glass of champagne in his hand when I left. He musta heard what they was saying. He's always getting arrested and if you help him out he may help you to help himself."

Not wanting to let on that Marco was the source for getting Sira, Michael just nodded and pretended to write Antonelli's name on a legal pad. Sira, then came through again.

"Ah, there is another guy," he began, "But he's been pretty tight with Beef and Sap for a while now. I know the guy from where he works on Wall Street. He's a broker and he lives in our neighborhood. His name is Sonny Alonzo."

"Why would he help us if he's tight with Beef and Sap?" Tommy asked.

"Cause he's in big trouble. He been buying dope from Beef and Sap and lately he's been selling it to the people he works with. He's making good money and has steady drug suppliers. A few days ago Alonzo got caught dealing in the men's room where he works. Security took him out of the building, and I heard he was arrested. Maybe you can get the DA in Manhattan to go easy on him in return for him helping you?"

Michael thanked Sira for the information and reiterated that unless he said something about how he had spent his morning, no one would know he cooperated until he testified in court.

"One last thing, Jackie. Stay out of trouble. No more getting high. Figure out some other way to pass your free time. Because if you're arrested, or worse, because of the drugs, you're no good to me and the deal is off. Do you understand?"

"Okay Mr. G. But now you got to call over to my job and smooth this over with my boss. If I walk in there now I'll be three hours late. He'll have my ass. And until you get me another, I need this job to eat and pay my rent. Michael asked Sira some questions about the job and his boss, then made the call.

Michael told Sira's boss that he had been mistakenly named as a witness in a case he was investigating and the police picked him up so he could be questioned. "It turns out that Jackie wasn't even at the scene of the crime that afternoon because he was working for you. Someone gave us bad information."

Sira's boss told Michael that he was just happy that Sira was not sick or injured and that he had no issue with him cooperating with the DA's office. Michael thanked him for understanding. "I'm going to have a police detective drop Jackie off at work in about thirty minutes. I'm sorry if we disturbed your operation over there."

Before he left the office Michael told Sira that he'd have him back for a prep session just before he was needed to testify. "I won't let you go on the stand cold. You'll be prepared for anything the defense lawyers can throw at you. Okay?"

"Don't worry Mr. G. I want to get out of that neighborhood where I live, and I really need a new job. I won't fuck this up," Sira said as he and Tommy left the office.

SEVENTY-SEVEN

Locating Sonny Alonzo was not a problem. Getting him to cooperate was another story entirely.

Michael started by using the information he got from Jackie Sira that Alonzo was a stock broker. In New York State brokers are required to be licensed in order to buy and sell stocks, bonds, and other securities. Michael contacted a former colleague from the DA's office who left and went to work for FINRA, the Financial Industry Regulatory Authority, and asked about Alonzo. His colleague provided a full dossier on Alonzo which included his home and business addresses, his work and cell phone numbers, and a photograph.

With one call to the cell number, Michael arranged to have Alonzo meet him at his office that evening after he completed his workday.

"Do I need my lawyer?" Alonzo asked.

"You're not in any trouble so the choice is yours Mr. Alonzo," Michael answered.

At 6 p.m. the security officer manning the DA's office reception desk called Michael to let him know that Alonzo arrived. Michael told the officer to have him come up to his office.

A few minutes later, Tommy Schwartz, who met Alonzo at the elevator, escorted him into Michael's office.

From the outset, Alonzo was belligerent. "What the fuck do you want with me?" were the first words he uttered even before Michael began to speak.

When Michael told him why he was asked to come in, Alonzo exploded. "Are you fuckin' crazy? I don't know any Joe Beef or Frankie Sap, but if I did I wouldn't rat on mobsters. It ain't good for my health."

"If you don't know them, why are you telling me they're mobsters?" Michael asked.

"Mr. Alonzo, I'm not a fool, " he continued. "I know, and you know, who Joe Beef and Frankie Sap are. And I know that you know, all about the lawyer they killed as revenge for the mistake they claim he made that got their boy Chucky convicted. So let's stop with the theatrics and the bullshit."

"You got a problem. We know that," Tommy chimed in. "We can help you with it, if you help us. *Capisce?*"

"Mr. Alonzo, not only are you in danger of going to jail for dealing drugs in your office, you're going to lose your license to trade. My contact at FINRA tells me they're just waiting for you to get convicted and then you'll never work in securities again," Michael added.

"So if you want to continue to earn legitimate money, I can help you. But you have to cut the shit and talk to me about Beef and Sap."

After a few minutes, Alonzo finally began calming down and reluctantly agreed to cooperate.

He told Michael that he knew Beef and Sap because they all lived in the same neighborhood on the Bensonhurst/Bay Ridge border in Brooklyn.

"They were selling drugs from before they became made men in the Gambino family. And I've been a customer of theirs for years.".

"They know that I'm a straight up guy who they can trust and who would never rat on them. So over the years they regaled me with stories of the heists they did for the family and the other jobs they were asked to do. Quite frankly Mr. Gioca, I've always felt that they were more into bragging about their business than they should have been."

"Recently they've been talking about how one of their crew, some guy named Chucky. He was convicted of drug dealing because his lawyer fucked up, and now Chucky's going to spend the next ten years in prison."

"A few weeks ago, I was with them in a bar called *Turquoise* in the neighborhood and they told me that they were going to get his lawyer for what he did. At that time they didn't yet know how they would get to him but when they did they said that they were going to kill him."

Alonzo went on to say that weeks later he was in the bar where Beef and Sap had the champagne celebration for killing the lawyer.

"I was curious, so I asked them how they managed to get to him. They told me about a guy who was sitting near them in a bar one night when they were talking about doing the killing. He came up to them and told them he overheard their conversation and could help."

"They told me this guy somehow knew the lawyer and he told them that it would be no problem for him to set it up to get the lawyer out in the open so they could do the job. They told me it all worked out. The guy did what he said he could do, and they shot and killed the lawyer right in front of his own house."

"As I told you before, they are too loose lipped and careless, so I asked them if this guy would keep his mouth shut about the murder. Sap answered and said that he and Beef were concerned about it, but after the shooting they never saw the guy again."

"They told me that they went over to where the guy said he lived and worked to make sure he would keep quiet, only to discover that no one knew who they were asking about." Sap added, "The guy's a ghost, which is good for us."

Once Michael secured a commitment from him that he'd testify at trial, he told Alonzo that he'd call the Manhattan District Attorney and work out a deal so Alonzo wouldn't lose his broker's license and would avoid a criminal conviction.

"Stay away from anyone in your neighborhood who may have a connection to Beef and Sap. And I know that you're smart enough to keep this meeting tonight to yourself. Also, stop whatever dealing you've been doing at your office. If you're arrested again I won't be able to help you and my first call will be to FINRA and your deal will be gone."

Alonzo said, "Mr. Gioca, I'm not stupid. Of course I'm going to keep my mouth shut. Besides, with Beef and Sap in jail, I have no drugs to sell. When you need me again, just call."

It was a productive few days of case building for Michael. Jimmy Kennedy's advice paid off. Going back to interrogate Marco led to Sira and Alonzo. He was now much more confident that he would win the case even though he wouldn't have Jimmy Taliferro.

Michael spent the remainder of his trial prep time with the technical witnesses, the police, the medical examiner, and the necessary body ID witness, Mrs. Abby Wilkins. When he was done prepping them he was satisfied that he had constructed a strong case. Then late Friday afternoon, two days before jury selection was scheduled to begin, Michael's case got even stronger.

He was packing up to go home, where he had intended to spend the weekend working on jury selection questions and preparing his opening statement, when his office phone rang. The number in the caller ID was not familiar to him but he picked it up hoping that there was no crisis he would have to deal with that would take away from his preparation time.

The call did turn out to be something that would take away from Michael's weekend prep time, but it was a welcome distraction. He had a new contact to talk to, and if things went well, an addition to his witness list.

CHAPTER

SEVENTY-EIGHT

Gennaro "Gerry the Killer" Peluso sat in Michael's office early Saturday morning eating one of the egg and cheese breakfast sandwiches that Tommy Schwartz brought in for himself, Michael, their potential new witness, and the correction officers who escorted Peluso from the Brooklyn House of Detention.

During trial prep later that morning Michael asked Peluso why he was called "Gerry the Killer." Fearing that the nickname was earned because Peluso had done a murder, or two, or three, or more, his answer surprised even Michael who felt that he had heard everything. "They call me that because I kill cats!" Hearing that, Michael made a note to make sure he kept animal lovers off the jury if he decided to use Peluso as a witness.

Gerry Peluso was sitting in his four by eight steel barred accommodation because he violated the parole he was on for over a year, when a new cell mate was brought in "From another cell block, about a week ago," he said.

The moment Peluso saw Joe "Beef" Comforto, he immediately recognized him as a partner, along with Frankie "Sap" Sapino, in a drug dealing operation in his neighborhood where they all lived. A few years back, he bought drugs from Beef when Peluso's regular dealer was not around.

Gerry also knew that Beef was a made man in the Gambino family who regularly carried a .9mm automatic, the same caliber gun that fired the bullet that killed Monroe Wilkins.

Beef hadn't recognized Peluso right away and barely said a word to him for the first couple of days they were cell mates. One afternoon that all changed. To Peluso, it seemed that a light went on in Beef's head because after they returned to the cell from lunch one afternoon, Beef approached him and said, "Don't I know you from the neighborhood?"

When Peluso reminded him that he once bought drugs from him, Beef seemed to relax, and from that point he talked Peluso's ear off.

Peluso told Michael that he heard through the prison grapevine that a mob lawyer was killed near where Peluso lived, but he had no idea Beef and Sap were the murderers until Beef told him all about it.

"Beef told me," Peluso continued, "That the lawyer fucked up their buddy's case and that he and Sap decided to kill him to send a message."

"He also told me about a guy who heard him and Sap talking in a bar about killing the lawyer. The guy approached them and said that he knew that lawyer named Wilkins. The guy told them that he was also looking for a way to get back at the lawyer and that he could set him up so Beef and Sap could kill him."

Peluso said that Beef told him the guy had come through. He got the lawyer to a spot right outside the lawyer's house, and he and Sap murdered him.

"He said, 'I hope the fucking worms are eating him right now.'"

Michael asked, "Gerry, are you telling me that just because Beef suddenly recognized you from the neighborhood, he opened up and told you everything? Or did he have another motive?"

"I guess that's why you're behind that desk and I'm sittin' in the Brooklyn House. You're a smart guy. Beef told me all that because he wants me to lie for him in court."

"I'm confused," Michael said. "Please explain."

"Beef wants me to contact his lawyer," Peluso said, "And tell him that when I was in jail on the charge for which I'm now on parole, I heard an inmate talkin' about some lawyer named Wilkins who the inmate wanted killed. He told me to say that the reason was because the lawyer had fucked up the inmate's case for which he paid a retainer and most of the fee."

"If I testified in his trial to what I heard, it would put doubt in the minds of the jurors. His lawyer told him that would get him out from under the murder case."

Peluso went on to say that he asked Beef what the DA had on him and Sap. "Beef said that they had a .9mm bullet that had been recovered from the dead guy's body and 'a scumbag named Marco.'"

"The bullet was a problem because everyone knew that he carried a nine, and there wasn't anything he could do about it. 'But', he said, 'Marco was another story.'"

"He asked me when I was gettin' out. I lied and told him that I expected to hit the street in a few weeks. He was thrilled. He asked me to kill Marco when I got out. He said if I did that for him there was a lot of money in it for me. The Gambinos would be grateful, and I'd have the family's protection from then on."

"That's all good stuff, Gerry. But I know you're not telling me all that out of the goodness of your heart. What are you looking for in return for testifying against Joe Beef?" Michael asked.

"I want to go home. I know you can smooth over the parole violation and get me the fuck out of the Brooklyn House."

"Gerry, I just met you. How do I know I can trust you to cooperate and testify?"

"Mr. G I'm a street guy so I know you want a guarantee. If I was in your shoes that's what I would want. So here's my proposition, you leave me inside until I testify. When I do what I said I'd do, *then* you get me out. This way you have your guarantee. Cause if I was stupid enough to fuck you, all you got to do is forget my parole officer's number and I'm stuck until I serve my time."

Michael was feeling a lot better about putting Peluso on the witness stand. *'He's a shrewd guy and he's smart,'* Michael thought to himself. *'He knows I can't turn him down after giving me the guarantee I was looking for. He's going to make a great witness.'*

"Gerry, we have a deal."

"Only one thing," Gerry said, "Until you get me out, I want you to get me moved to the witness security unit. This way I won't have some 'accident' which will take me out of the picture."

Michael agreed to have Peluso moved and then told him to stay out of trouble. "I'll have you back here to prep you for your testimony the night before you take the witness stand."

It was noon when Michael went back to his apartment. He made himself a sandwich and got down to work on his jury selection questions.

By 5 p.m. he had prepared the questions he needed to ask. With street guys like Marco, Jackie Sira, Sonny Alonzo, and Gerry Peluso, it was important to make sure that anyone who would sit on the jury understood that they didn't have to like the witnesses or agree with their lifestyles, they simply had to believe their testimony. Michael would make sure to hammer that point home as much as the court and the defense attorneys would allow.

Also, with the specter of organized crime hovering over the case, he had to identify those who would be intimidated by that. He didn't want jurors who would be fearful of convicting Beef and Sap even if he proved the case beyond a reasonable doubt. But he had to walk a fine line in his questioning. He couldn't come right out and alert a prospective juror to Beef and Sap's membership in the Gambino family, so he had to ask around the topic in such a way that the prospective jurors would get the message and hopefully be candid if they had reservations about sitting on such a case. He needed the jurors to voice their feelings so he could use his challenges wisely.

Satisfied that he crafted questions that would give him the information about each juror that would allow him to make an informed choice as to whether they should be challenged or not, he moved on to his opening statement.

As he was thinking of how to begin, his cell phone rang. When he saw that it was his father calling he realized that it was some time since he last checked in with his dad and his sons.

"We're all concerned about you, Michael," his dad said. "Michael Jr. and Kevin have been calling me to see if I'd heard from you. Having had those guards following them weeks back, they're worried that something has happened to you. And, quite frankly, I was worried as well. I know you're busy, your case is in the papers almost every day, but you need to give yourself a break once in a while. When you do, a call to your kids, and to me, would be greatly appreciated."

"Dad, you're right. I'm sorry. This case has had lots of problems and I've been so focused on solving them that I have neglected the people that I love the most. I'll call the kids when we're done. But I'm all right. In fact today was a very good day. The case has come together nicely after a disastrous beginning. I'm confident that I'm going to get these guys for killing that lawyer and destroying his family."

When he hung up with this dad, Michael called his sons. He spoke with them for well over thirty minutes and assured them that he was okay. He also promised to take them away for a weekend once the trial was over.

And just to finish off with his family, Michael called his sister Pam and caught up with her.

It was 2 a.m. Sunday morning, when Michael looked up from his legal pad, on which he wrote his opening statement. Surprised at the time, he decided to put his first draft aside and get some sleep.

Bright and early Sunday morning Michael dressed in his running clothes and ran to St. Charles for the 7 a.m. Mass. After Mass he ran another two miles and got home just in time for a call from Monsignor Romano.

Much like with his family Michael had been out of touch with the monsignor since their last talk. "Michael, I don't mean to bother you," he said, "But you know Caldwell. He wants an update on how the case is going and how you think the trial will proceed. Do you have time to meet me for lunch? We can talk then."

Michael told Romano that he needed to finish up his opening so he couldn't meet for lunch. "How about an early dinner?," he asked.

They agreed to meet at *Emilio's* at 5 p.m.

"I'll fill you in on everything," Michael said. "That will give me an opportunity to review the case once more before we start tomorrow."

CHAPTER
SEVENTY-NINE

As usual, dinner was delicious. Emilio had outdone himself. His Sunday sauce, as he called it, was perfect and the meatballs that accompanied the spaghetti were "Like my grandma's," Michael told him.

Michael only had one glass of wine, so he nursed it as he brought Romano up to date on everything that happened since their last talk.

"Mike, I'm pleased you didn't give up. You were so down the last time we met that I prayed you'd find a way. Talking to your friend Jimmy Kennedy was a genius move. But don't underestimate the *Evil One*. *HE* could spring something on you just when it will do the most harm."

"Sal after all this time, I'm ready for whatever *HE* throws at me. It's why I've put this case together in the way that I have. If *HE* screws around with my witnesses I can withstand it. And I've made sure that the physical evidence has been secured where *HE* can't get to it. That .9mm bullet is crucial because a witness is going to tell the jury that Joe Beef regularly carried a .9mm pistol and admitted to him that the bullet recovered from Wilkins' body damages his case."

"Then there's the sketch of Beef drawn from the description

Jimmy Taliferro gave to a police artist. Sal, the sketch is such a good likeness of Beef that it could be a photograph. Right now I can't think of a way to get it into evidence because Taliferro is out as a witness. But you never know, one of the defense attorneys can make a mistake and give me an opening to introduce it. *HE* won't like it if that happens, which is why I have it safe and secured."

"Mike, Caldwell will be pleased that you have things in such good shape. Now let's skip the espresso. You need to get home to relax and have a good night's sleep."

The next day Michael was up at dawn. He ran a couple of miles in order to think and go over his jury selection strategy. When he arrived at the courthouse at 10 a.m. Judge Owens had the prospective jurors all waiting in the corridor outside his courtroom.

After preliminary matters were dispensed with, jury selection began at 10:30. By 4 p.m. that afternoon ten jurors were selected for the Comforto jury. Judge Owens told everyone to return the next day at 9:30 a.m. when jury selection would resume.

After the prospective jurors filed out of his courtroom, the judge told the attorneys that he hoped that they would have both juries selected by the close of business the next day even if that meant that they would have to stay a little later.

"My plan is to have opening statements on Wednesday morning at 10 a.m. so please be guided by that. And Mr. Gioca you should be prepared to call your first witness when we're done with the openings."

When Michael got back to his office he called in Dina Mitchell and Tim Clark. When they arrived he telephoned Tommy Schwartz and had him on speaker. Michael went over the schedule that Judge Owens had laid out and gave them assignments for notifying the police witnesses and medical examiner when they would be needed in court. And as for Marco, Sira and Alonzo, to make sure that they were transported to the courthouse when he needed them.

He would take care of arranging for Gerry Peluso to be brought to his office for additional prep the day before he would testify. On that day he would be produced in the courthouse by the corrections department.

When that was settled, Michael called Abby Wilkins and brought her up to date on the status of jury selection. He also asked her to be in his office at 8 a.m. on Wednesday morning.

"Mrs. Wilkins, you're going to be my first witness. You won't need a great deal of rehearsal because your testimony will be limited to answering questions about your husband and your identification of his body at the city morgue. However, because you've never been in this situation before, I still want to prepare you for what you'll likely encounter as a witness in a murder trial. So if you would please be in my office on Wednesday morning around eight, that will give me enough time to do what I need to do and to answer any questions you might have."

"Mr. Gioca, thank you for all you're doing for me and my family," Abby Wilkins told him. "We have the utmost confidence in you and your ability. I'll see you Wednesday morning."

By 6 p.m. the next day, the two juries and alternates for the trial of Joseph "Joe Beef" Comforto and Frank "Frankie Sap " Sapino were selected.

And by noon on Wednesday, Michael and the two defense attorneys had delivered their opening statements.

"Call your first witness," Judge Owens said to Michael.

Abby Wilkins was escorted into the courtroom and took the witness stand. As Michael expected, Abby's testimony went before the jury without a hitch.

In most criminal trials the jury can see and hear from the victim. In a murder case the jury will only get to 'know' the victim through witnesses. Here that was Abby Wilkins. Earlier, in his office, Michael prepared Abby to testify in a way that would bring her late husband 'into' the courtroom. And she was masterful.

When Michael asked about the last time she saw him alive, she began to weep. And when he asked about her visit to the city morgue, she had a difficult time getting the words out. Her testimony regarding the identification of her deceased husband was mournful and touching, just as Michael hoped it would be.

For the remainder of that day, and for the next two days, police officers, detectives, crime scene experts, ballistics technicians, and the medical examiner testified to the dry, but necessary nuts and bolts of the prosecution's case.

After the weekend, Michael would begin to call the witnesses who he once characterized for Romano as "Right out of a fiction writer's drunken fantasy." Nevertheless he was confident that their testimony would seal the fate of Joe Beef and Frankie Sap.

He would lead off this part of his case with Marco Antonelli.

On Saturday afternoon, Tommy Schwartz picked up Marco from the safe house that Michael had convinced Caldwell he needed to rent after the acid incident with Taliferro. It took some doing, but as the trial got closer, Michael finally convinced Marco that staying there was good for his health.

Over breakfast and lunch, Michael went over the questions that he would ask Marco on direct examination for the prosecution's case.

Then came the tough part. Michael was brutal with Marco when he worked on preparing him for cross examination. During Michael's questioning Marco got angry and belligerent. But after some time he finally got the point and handled Michael's cutting questions like a pro.

By 7 p.m. they were done. Marco looked and felt wrung out.

His comment at the end of the day-long prep session was, "You're a prick, Mr. G. But I say that affectionately. Damn, I don't ever want to have you against me. EVER! But now I'm ready for anything those pricks throw at me. Thanks."

"Relax tomorrow and get a good night's sleep," Michael told him. "Tommy will pick you up on Monday morning and bring you to the courthouse. If you have any questions or any problems between now and then, you have my number, and you also have Tommy's number, so don't hesitate to use them."

On Monday morning Marco was a star. In the direct case he testified to everything he told Michael and Tommy about Beef and Sap. And he was strong and consistent on cross-examination. But when Sap's lawyer, Dean Miller pursued a certain line of questioning when he cross-examined him, Marco added something.

Miller was pressing Marco on how well he knew his client. The point he was attempting to make was that Marco lied when he told the jury that Sap confided in him about the murder, because he and Sap didn't really know each other very well.

But Miller went too far. He asked Marco, "Mr. Antonelli, isn't it a fact that despite you telling these jurors that you and my client were close, you and him never shared any secrets or any confidences?"

Marco answered, "That's not correct. We were very close, and we did share a secret."

Instead of leaving the answer alone, Miller violated the first rule of cross-examination: never ask a question that you don't know the answer to. "Oh really," he said. "Tell this jury what that so-called secret was."

"Counselor, your client is in the closet. He's gay, and many times when we've been alone he would ask me to let him blow me!"

The jury and the courtroom spectators erupted. Miller was so stunned by the answer that he didn't hear the rest of it. "And if I had said no, he would have killed me," Marco added.

When Michael looked over at Miller's co-counsel, Joel Horowitz, he had his head buried in his hands. Miller sat down. The damage to his client was done.

Michael announced that he had no redirect questions for the witness and Marco Antonelli was excused from the witness stand.

After court, the rest of Michael's day and night was spent preparing Jackie Sira for his testimony the next day. Dina and Tim were given the task of picking up Sira from the home he was staying in outside the city. Michael wanted to place him in another Caldwell safe house, but Sira told him that he had a cousin who lived in New Jersey and would rather stay there until he completed his testimony.

Michael was uncertain about agreeing to this arrangement because he had no idea who, if any, of Sira's friends and acquaintances were aware that he had a cousin who lived out of state. But he agreed after Sira assured him that just his immediate family knew where his cousin lived, and only they would know he was staying there.

When the prep session was completed Sira asked Michael how he should dress for court. Michael told him to "Wear what you would wear to church." Sira nodded and told Michael that he'd see him in the morning.

When Dina and Tim arrived with Sira, Dina went into Michael's office to alert him that they were there. But the look on her face told Michael that something was not right.

"Dina, what's up? Is Sira okay?" Michael asked.

"Physically he's fine. I'll leave the rest to you to determine if Sira is okay."

Now concerned, Michael told her to bring him into the office. As soon as Sira walked in Michael saw what was troubling Dina.

"Are you fucking kidding me!" was his reaction to how Sira was dressed. The six foot-two, skinny, blonde haired Jackie Sira was wearing a lime green suit! It consisted of a short waiter's type jacket and the skinniest pants Michael had ever seen. The pant legs appeared to have been painted on him. To finish off the outfit, he wore a white, ruffled-front shirt, and a dark green cowboy-type necktie. And, if that wasn't shocking enough, Sira had gelled his short, straight hair and wore it standing straight up. It looked as if he had stuck his finger into an electric socket.

Careful not to be overly critical lest Sira get angry and refuse to testify, Michael said, "Jackie, I told you to wear what you would to church." Sira looked at him with a puzzled expression and said, "This *IS* what I wear to church."

Michael shook his head, shrugged his shoulders, and said, "Let's go to court."

Sira didn't disappoint. His testimony was what Michael expected after completing the prep session the two had the night before.

However, what Michael had not expected was the manner in which Sira answered his questions.

Michael started the examination by asking Sira, "What is your name?"

Sira answered but when he did so he looked at the jury, grabbed his crotch and shook it as he answered, "Jackie Sira."

Michael was shocked. The jurors were shocked and the spectators in the gallery laughed.

Thinking that it was just a bit of nervousness that Sira would shake off as he continued his testimony, Michael asked question two. Sira once again grabbed his crotch and shook it when he answered.

When this continued for the next four questions, Michael asked the judge for a short recess, which Judge Owens granted with a big smile on his face. As Sira came down from the witness stand, Michael saw that the jurors were having difficulty suppressing they're amusement, while the spectator gallery was in hysterics.

Michael took Sira into the corridor outside the courtroom, looked at him and before he could say anything, Sira asked, "What? What did I do?"

When he told him Michael was astonished by Jackie's reaction. It was clear that Sira had no idea what he was doing. He truly didn't realize he was grabbing and shaking his crotch as he answered the questions.

Michael calmed Sira down and told him that when he resumed the witness stand, he was to sit with his hands on the arms of the chair and not let go of them until finished with all the questions. Sira nodded, said "Okay," and the two headed back inside the courtroom. As he was walking to the prosecution table, Michael thought to himself, *'Just another day in Brooklyn.'*

Michael completed his examination of Sira, who didn't once

move his hands off the arms of the witness chair. And Horowitz and Miller, try as they did, could not shake Jackie's story.

When the cross-examinations were done, Jackie came down from the witness stand and said goodbye to the jurors who couldn't stop smiling. Michael had snatched victory from the jaws of defeat.

Judge Owens adjourned for lunch and as the jurors filed out of the jury box, Michael watched them. They all kept the Sira produced smile on their faces, and some even looked at Michael and nodded.

CHAPTER
EIGHTY

Tim Clark was tasked with driving Sira home to New Jersey, so Dina was alone in Michael's office when he returned from court.

"Where is Alonzo?" Michael asked when he saw that the next witness he expected to call was not there.

"I don't know," Dina answered. "I spoke to him last night and told him to be here at noon. I even made it earlier than you said you needed him, thinking that he's the type of guy who is never on time. And I was right."

"Dina, call the police precinct where Alonzo lives and have them send a car to his home," Michael said. "If he's there, have them call me and I'll talk to him. If he's not, we need to call his office to see if he went to work. If he's there you can go pick him up."

"And if he's not in either place, then what?" Dina asked.

"I'll just have to buy some time," Michael said.

"I can't get Peluso here from the Brooklyn House in time to fill in so, I'll just explain to the court that I need a continuance until the morning. The trial has been moving along very well, so I don't think Judge Owens will be difficult about it."

Alonzo was nowhere to be found. None of his neighbors had seen him that morning, and his boss told Dina that Alonzo hadn't reported for work, nor had he called in to say that he wouldn't be there.

Michael had no choice but to ask Judge Owens for an adjournment of the trial. The judge was not pleased with his request, but he nevertheless granted Michael a continuance until 10 a.m. the next day.

While Dina, Tim Clark, Tommy Schwartz, and several of his detective colleagues searched for Sonny Alonzo, Michael contacted the Brooklyn House of Detention and asked that Gerry Peluso be brought to his office. If Alonzo was not found, Michael needed to be prepared to call Peluso as his next witness.

He spent the rest of the afternoon and part of the evening prepping Peluso for his testimony. Because what he had to tell the jury concerned Joe Beef and the statements he made to Peluso, only Beef's jury would be permitted to hear them. Nonetheless, Peluso had to be ready to handle Beef's attorney's cross-examination. His testimony would be crucial to the outcome of the case.

When Peluso was taken back to his cell that night he was more than ready to do battle with Joel Horowitz.

Michael was so focused on Peluso that he lost track of the time. When he looked at his watch he saw that it was 10 p.m. His first thought was how hungry he was, but that was quickly replaced by the realization that he had not heard from anyone who was looking for Alonzo.

He called Tommy Schwartz. The report he received was discouraging. Tommy told him they exhausted every means at their disposal to find Alonzo and came up empty. He also told Michael that he had posted police cars with two cops outside Alonzo's home and his office. "If he tries to sneak into either place tonight, we'll get him," Tommy said.

Michael told Tommy that he would be in his office for another hour or so and to call him with any developments. While he waited Michael called the *Queen* restaurant and ordered his dinner.

The veal parmigiana hero he ordered looked delicious, but Michael couldn't enjoy it thinking about the so far unsuccessful search for Sammy Alonzo.

At midnight Tommy called Michael, who had remained in his office, to tell him that they still hadn't located Alonzo.

"Mike, we've hit every place he's been known to frequent. We've canvassed his neighbors, and no one has seen him since last night. We've called local hospitals to see if he was brought in either sick or injured, with no luck. We even called the morgue. Luckily they didn't have either a Sonny Alonzo or a John Doe who fit his description. We're out of ideas and gonna call it a night. But we are gonna keep the radio cars on at his home and office all night. If I hear anything, do you want me to call and wake you?"

"Absolutely. Tommy, if they get him I want him in my office, no matter what the time is, and I'll meet them there," Michael replied.

"Okay. Get some sleep Mike. You have a full day in court tomorrow."

"Tommy, let's hope you're right."

After a fitful sleep, Michael was up before dawn. He went out on a run to clear his mind and to burn off some of the anxiety that had been building up since he found out that Alonzo was missing. He was at his desk at 7 a.m. when Tommy called him with the bad news.

"Alonzo did not return home and he never showed up at his office," he told Michael. "We'll keep looking but it don't look good, Mike. He's either dead or someone got to him and warned him about testifying."

"Tommy, my money is on the latter. He's the only one of the witnesses who didn't want to hear anything about protection. And look where we are. Even Marco ultimately agreed to stay in the safe house. Against my better judgment I didn't get a material witness order for him so we would have been able to force him to stay safe. I listened to his bullshit about needing to work and needing to be allowed to sleep in his own bed for his sanity."

"Well I hope you're right. If he's not dead he'll turn up," Tommy said.

"Yeah let's hope that when he does we still have a trial going on. Tommy I have Peluso testifying this morning then you're up next. So check in with Dina or Tim during the morning so you'll know when I need you."

Gerry Peluso took the witness stand at 10:15 and captured the Joe Beef jury's full attention with his Bensonhurst street personality and lingo until Judge Owens called for a lunch break at 1 p.m.

During his testimony he not only gave the jurors an inside look at life among inmates in the Brooklyn House, he also provided them with a look at life on the street among the denizens of his Brooklyn neighborhood.

His conversations with Joe Beef in the Brooklyn House of Detention had the jury mesmerized as he told the story of their becoming reacquainted, of Beef asking Peluso to lie under oath for him, and finally of Beef asking him to kill Marco Antonelli, with the promised payoff being that the mob would forever be his friend and protector.

When Michael finished his direct examination, Joel Horowitz did his best to destroy Peluso's credibility with his cross-examination. He surprised Michael with its quality and the toughness he exhibited when Peluso tried to avoid a direct answer to some of his difficult questions. Overall Horowitz did well by his client, however, Peluso did even better for the prosecution's case. He held up and never wavered from the most important parts of his testimony against Beef.

During the lunch break Michael learned that Alonzo still had not been located , so he told Tommy to be in his office at 1 p.m. to go over his testimony. Michael also called Judge Owens to let him know that the only witness he would have for the afternoon was Tommy Schwartz.

Because the majority of his testimony concerned only Joe Beef and the statement he made when he was arrested, the judge asked Michael to begin his examination of Schwartz with the questions that both juries were permitted to hear. After he completed that portion of his direct examination, the Beef jury was excused and testimony continued as to evidence against Sap alone.

When Sap's lawyer was done with his cross-examination the judge excused the Sap jury for the day and the trial continued with only the Beef jury in the courtroom.

Michael picked up the questioning and asked Tommy about his arrest of Joe Beef. Tommy told the jury that when took Beef into custody he told him what he was being arrested for and charged with. "Then without me saying anything else, Comforto asked, 'How much time do you think I'll get for this? Do you think I can get a deal? Maybe do only five to ten years?'"

Tommy testified that he told Beef that he or his lawyer would have to speak to the DA's office because Tommy had no authority to offer any deals.

Ideally Michael, at this point, would have loved to ask Tommy additional questions in order to get the police sketch of Beef before the jury. However, there was no legal way for him to do that. Jerry Taliferro would have had to testify in order to lay the proper foundation before it could be moved into evidence. He was the source of the drawing and therefore was the only person who could authenticate it and testify to what the sketch represented.

Therefore, Michael announced that he had no additional questions for Tommy.

It was now Horowitz' turn to question Det. Schwartz.

And while he had done a fine job questioning Sonny Peluso, his performance with Tommy on the witness stand left much to be desired.

Horowitz began by questioning Tommy about the quality of his investigation. He asked him when he became involved and mocked the fact that his client was not arrested until many months after the murder.

Now, because he was either incompetent, had forgotten that a sketch had been drawn which looked just like his client, or because he knew that Taliferro had been taken out as a witness, Horowitz asked, "The delay in arresting my client was because you had no witnesses to this shooting, isn't that correct detective?"

When Tommy heard the question he turned to Michael and silently asked with his look, 'Should I answer this question?' Michael read the look perfectly and gave him a slight nod. Tommy answered, "No counselor, that's not correct. There was a witness who supplied a description of one of the killers to the police and assisted a police artist in drawing a sketch of the man he saw."

Horowitz exploded when Tommy answered. He asked the judge to strike the answer from the court record and to admonish the jury to disregard it.

Michael asked the judge for a sidebar conference out of the hearing of the jury before he ruled on Horowitz' motions.

Judge Owens called the attorneys to the bench and in whispered tones asked Michael what his position was on Horowitz' requests.

"Your honor I believe you should deny them. *He* opened the door to Det. Schwartz' answers."

"Well before trial," Michael continued, "I gave Mr. Horowitz all the evidence, documents, police reports, photos, *and* the sketch. So he knew there was a witness. And he knew that the witness had been rendered unavailable to me. He was trying to take advantage of that, and he stepped on his dick doing it."

"Since he opened the door," Michael argued, "I should now be permitted to ask Det. Schwartz everything he knows about that witness and the sketch, and once I lay a proper foundation it should be admitted into evidence."

Horowitz was beside himself with anger. So much so that his colleague Dean Miller had to calm him down. "Your honor, what Mr.

Gioca just said is insulting and outrageous. In all the years I have been practicing law I have never attempted to improperly manipulate the court as he has just accused me. I demand an apology and I repeat my motions regarding the detective's testimony."

Judge Owens, having listened to both attorneys, asked Horowitz, "Is Gioca correct? Did he give you everything, including the sketch?"

When Horowitz answered that Gioca *had* provided the material, the judge said, "Then I agree with him. You did open the door to additional questioning of the detective on this subject, and to that sketch being admitted into evidence."

Judge Owens continued, "Mr. Horowitz, we don't know each other but from what I've seen, I think you were trying to take advantage of Gioca losing a witness. And given the background of your client, and Miller's client, it ain't too hard to conclude that they or their friends had something to do with that poor man having his face burned off. Now get back to your table and ask your questions."

A thoroughly defeated Horowitz asked a few nonsensical questions and sat down.

Michael then buried him and his client.

He had Tommy tell the jury all about what the witness said he saw the night of the killing. He explained that he had gotten a good look at one of the killers, and as a result, he was able to assist a police artist in drawing a sketch of one of the two men he saw walking away from the car where Monroe Wilkins was shot and killed.

Michael, over Horowitz' objection, which was overruled by the judge, then handed the sketch to Tommy. "Do you recognize that, Det. Schwartz?" he asked.

Tommy answered that he did. "It's the sketch of one of the men the witness said he saw walk away from the car where the deceased was shot." Michael offered the sketch into evidence and announced that he had no further questions of Tommy.

Instead of leaving a bad situation alone, Horowitz made it worse by asking Tommy a series of questions about the sketch. In response to one of the questions Tommy was able to offer his opinion that the person depicted in the sketch, "Looks just like your client."

With that answer the observers in the courtroom gallery erupted. As the judge attempted to restore order, Michael turned to the spectator section. When he did, he noticed a strange looking man rise from his seat in the last row of the gallery and leave the courtroom shaking his head. A gesture Michael interpreted as an expression of disgust.

Later, when the court day ended, Michael asked a court officer about the man. All the officer could remember about him was the "Strange looking mark or welt on the left side of his face."

After Tommy concluded his testimony, Judge Owens asked Michael if he had any additional witnesses. Michael told him, "I have no more for today. However, I may have an additional witness tomorrow morning. However, if that witness is unavailable, your honor, I'll just rest my case."

Before dismissing the juries, Judge Owens told both Horowitz and Miller at a bench conference to "Be ready with your respective defenses, if you have any. If you have no witnesses or evidence to present, I'll send the juries home and we'll have summations the next day."

The judge dismissed the two juries for the day and told them to report back to the courthouse at 9:30 the next morning. With that the court was adjourned.

When Michael got back to his office, Tommy, Dina, and Tim were waiting for him.

"We've located Alonzo," Dina told him. "But you're not going to like what I have to tell you. He's going to testify for the defense."

EIGHTY-ONE

I n court the next day, Michael informed the judge that the witness he intended to call was suddenly unavailable, "Because, your honor, he is about to testify for the defendants."

Surprised at the development, Judge Owens asked Michael what he intended to do. Having no additional witnesses, Michael rested his case.

Following motions by both defense attorneys in which they asked the court to dismiss the case on purely legal grounds, which Judge Owens denied, Horowitz called Sonny Alonzo to the witness stand.

With both juries in the courtroom, Alonzo began his testimony by telling them all about his education, and that he was a licensed stockbroker who worked at the Wall Street brokerage firm of Hynes and Cibella.

He testified that he was a close friend of both defendants and knew nothing of any plans for them to kill Monroe Wilkins. "If they had intended to do something like that they definitely would have told me," he said.

He went on to say that on the night of the Wilkins murder, he had dinner in a Bay Ridge restaurant with Beef and Sap and after dinner the three went to a club where they spent the rest of the night.

He testified that because he had a lot to drink, "Joe and Frankie drove me home. When I got into my apartment I checked the clock next to my bed and saw that it was 4 a.m."

Alonzo ended his testimony saying that he had no clue who killed that lawyer.

Dean Miller asked Alonzo a few questions which allowed him to repeat his story of the night in question.

Before Michael began his cross-examination of Alonzo, Judge Owens asked that the juries be taken out of the courtroom. "I have a legal matter that I need to discuss with attorneys," he told the jurors. "This won't take long. Then we'll bring you back in."

With the juries out of the courtroom, the judge asked Michael if he wanted to make a motion to strike Alonzo's testimony. "That was an alibi for which I don't believe the defense gave you notice as required by law," Judge Owens said. "Mr. Gioca you can make a motion to strike, if you see fit, I'll then hear the defense on the matter and I'll make my decision. It's your call."

Michael had no intention of asking the judge to strike Alonzo's testimony. It was true that he hadn't been given alibi notice as required, but he wanted to play a tape recording he had of Alonzo talking about the defendants killing Wilkins, and he needed Alonzo on the witness stand to do that. What Alonzo said on that tape recording was so explosive, Michael was certain that it would put the final nail in the coffins of Joe Beef and Frankie Sap.

"Your honor," Michael began, "I appreciate the court's position, but I do not want Mr. Alonzo's testimony stricken. I want to get right into the cross-examination so I can show the jury what a liar the witness actually is."

Alonzo resumed the witness stand and the juries were brought back into the courtroom. Michael started his cross-examination slowly, asking Alonzo simple easy questions designed to lull him into a false sense of security. Then he lowered the boom.

"Mr. Alonzo, do you remember speaking to me and Det. Schwartz about the defendants and their role in the murder of Monroe Wilkins," Michael asked.

"I remember talking to you but I didn't give you anything that could help you, if I remember correctly," Alonzo answered.

Michael then asked if he recalled telling him and Tommy that he knew that Beef and Sap wanted to kill Wilkins because he 'screwed up' their friend's case and got him convicted.

"No," was his answer.

"Do you remember telling us that the night of the murder you were in a bar, and Beef and Sap were there celebrating it?" Alonzo didn't answer, he just shrugged.

"In fact," Michael continued, "Didn't you tell us that they toasted the murder of Wilkins that night with two bottles of champagne they opened in the place?"

Again, Alonzo just shrugged.

"And, Mr. Alonzo, didn't you tell Det. Schwartz and me that both Beef and Sap told you that night that they killed the lawyer? You said the words they used were 'He's looking up at heaven right now.'"

Alonzo finally answered, "I don't remember any of that."

Michael then played Alonzo's tape recorded statement. The jury sat open- mouthed as they listened to Alonzo contradict everything he had testified to under oath during his direct and cross-examination.

As the tape played Michael glanced over to the defense table. He saw that Horowitz and Miller were in a deep discussion. And it appeared to Michael that they were asking each other if either had known about the tape recording.

Because Alonzo was not his witness, Michael had not turned over a copy of the tape to the defense attorneys. So it was possible that they were learning about its existence and its content as Michael played it for the jury. "They seemed to be completely surprised when I played the recording," Michael later told Tommy.

'Is it possible that Alonzo never told them he had been recorded?' Michael asked himself as he watched the two attorneys sit uncomfortably while hearing Alonzo completely refute what he had testified to.

At the conclusion of Michael's cross, both Horowitz and Miller told the judge that they had no additional questions for Alonzo, and no additional witnesses for the defense.

With that announcement, the man with the strange mark or welt on the left side of his face, who had been in the courtroom the day before, once again stormed out.

It didn't take long for the Beef jury to convict him.

The next day, within two hours of the conclusion of summations and the judge's charge on the law, the jury returned a verdict of guilty.

The Sap jury took a bit longer, but just after lunch that same day, they too returned a verdict and convicted Sap as well.

Abby Wilkins was in the courtroom for summations and waited around for the "Guilty verdicts I'm sure will come in just a few hours," she told Michael.

She was so pleased that through her tears she thanked Michael and told him that if he ever decided to run for political office, she would work tirelessly for his election.

What Abby said brought to mind what Louis Amato Sr. had told him after the verdict in the murder case in which Louis Jr. was the victim. As he had done with Mr. Amato, Michael just thanked Abby and told her that he was happy he could provide some closure after the horror she was living through since Monroe was murdered.

After telling Abby that he'd be in touch with her when it was time for Beef and Sap to be sentenced, he walked back to his office. And in what had now become a regular practice for him, he said a silent prayer. Michael thanked the Lord for having given him the strength to yet again beat the *Evil One*.

CHAPTER
EIGHTY-TWO

Dina Mitchell and Tim Clark were waiting for Michael when he got back to his office. Both congratulated him on the victory, but something in their demeanor told Michael they had news.

"What's happened?" Michael asked as he poured himself and them a glass of scotch to celebrate his wins.

"Mike, it's Sonny Alonzo," Tim said.

Michael thought they were going to ask him for the authority to arrest Alonzo for perjury after he clearly lied under oath at the trial. "I'll think about arresting Alonzo tomorrow. Right now I want to enjoy this drink," he said.

"You won't be able to arrest him," Dina interjected. "The cops found him dead this morning."

"They think it was an overdose/suicide because he was found with a needle in his arm. But Tommy told me he doesn't buy that because the guy didn't leave a note."

"Mike, it looks like a mob hit," Tim said. "Tommy thinks, and I have to agree, that they weren't too happy with his performance on the stand and this was their revenge."

Michael didn't agree with him. But he couldn't tell Tim and Dina that his gut was telling him that it was neither a suicide nor a mob hit. It was the *Evil One*.

'*Alonzo didn't perform the way HE expected, both Beef and Sap were convicted, and HE wasn't happy,*' Michael thought to himself after Dina and Tim left.

A few days later Michael's gut feeling was confirmed.

Tommy Schwartz called him with news about Alonzo's death.

"Mike, we found something when we did a search of Alonzo's apartment that confirms what I thought all along: the Gambinos were mad at Alonzo and they had him whacked."

"Alonzo kept a diary! And in it he wrote something to you about his flipping on us. If you're not busy I'm gonna come down there and let you read it for yourself. Maybe you can make some sense of what he wrote."

Michael told Tommy he'd be waiting.

The diary entry Tommy referred to was written by Alonzo sometime after he testified for the defense. The content provided Michael with an explanation of why Alonzo went missing in the days leading up to his appearance in court, and why he flipped to the defense. It also confirmed something that Michael was thinking while the tape was playing during Alonzo's cross-examination.

"I'm sorry Mr. G," it began. "I couldn't resist that man. It was like he had somehow possessed me. He wanted me to testify for the defense and I had no way of fighting him."

"One night after work, a few days before I was supposed to testify in your case, I was approached from behind by some guy as I was going into my apartment building. He called my name and told me not to turn around. The way he sounded I froze. He warned me against testifying for you. I turned to tell him to go fuck himself and there was no one there. He just disappeared."

"The next day I come home and my doorman has a package for me. When I opened it there was a bloody cow's tongue in the box with a note attached that read, 'You're next.'"

"That package was followed the next day by another which was delivered to my office. This one was different. It contained a sum of cash and another note. It said, 'There's more where this came from, just keep your mouth shut. Meet me at the Seaport on South Street if you want the cash.'"

"I was pissed, but I was scared too, so I went to the seaport and waited under the overhead highway at the foot of South Street. A guy pulled up in a car and got out. He was wearing a Covid mask. He approached and told me that the Gambinos would be very grateful if I testify *for* Beef and Sap. He then handed me an envelope that contained ten thousand dollars. And before he left he said to me, 'Don't fuck us. You'll be sorry if you do.'"

"The guy got back in his car and as it pulled away I saw a decal across the car's back window that read "BENSONHURST."

"I didn't see the guy who first approached me at my apartment building, but he did talk to me. This guy at the seaport sounded just like him."

"Mr. G, as I said, I just couldn't resist him. It was like he had somehow hypnotized me. He wanted me to testify for the defense, and I had no way of fighting him."

"But I had a plan. And I want you to know what it was and why I did it."

"To make sure that things would turn out the way they did with my testimony, I never told the defense attorneys, when they prepared me, that you had a tape recording of my statement where I implicated Beef and Sap in the murder."

"Because the tape contradicted everything they prepped me to say, I knew that you would use it to convict them."

"I'm sure they'll kill me for doing that, and if you're reading this I'm probably dead already. But fuck them! They're gonna spend the rest of their lives in prison, and I'm happy to have sent them there."

The diary entry ended with, "I'm sorry. Please don't hate me."

When Michael finished reading Tommy said to him, "What the hell does he mean that he couldn't resist the guy and that he felt he was possessed?"

"Mike this guy was a fucking nut job. And I don't believe one word of that shit."

"It's a good thing that he didn't testify for us!"

Michael didn't react to Tommy's comments. He thought to himself, '*No Tom, he wasn't nuts. He WAS possessed! But in the end, he DID testify for us.*'

Four weeks after the verdict Abby Wilkins sat quietly in Judge Owens' courtroom and awaited the sentencing of Joe "Beef" Comforto and Frank "Frankie Sap" Sapino. In New York State the law affords a family member of the victim the right to address the court to make what is called 'a victim impact statement.'

When Michael told that to Abby several weeks before, she asked that he speak on her behalf. When he had finished Judge Owens sentenced both Joe Beef and Frankie Sap to the maximum that the law allowed, twenty five years to life in prison.

As the judge said those words, Michael heard some commotion behind him in the spectator gallery. When he turned to see what it was, he saw the same man who had left the courtroom in disgust after Tommy Schwartz' devastating testimony about the sketch, and who had stormed out of the courtroom when Michael finished with the cross-examination of Sonny Alonzo, arguing with a court officer.

The judge heard the commotion and ordered that the man be escorted out.

Michael simply smiled and said a silent prayer of thanks.

EPILOGUE

That night after the sentencing, Michael sat with Monsignor Romano in *Emilio's*. The monsignor invited him to dinner to celebrate another victory over the *Evil One*.

"*Salute*," Romano said as he toasted Michael with his friend's favorite *Nero d'Avola*.

"Michael, Caldwell wanted to be here but he was called over to Manhattan for a conference with the Mayor, the PC, the fire commissioner, the administrative judge of the state supreme court, DA Price, and the district attorney of Manhattan. Something big's going on," Romano said.

"He sent his congratulations, however, and told me to let you know that you've earned it, so the government is springing for a vacation for you. Pick anywhere you want to go and it'll be arranged. And you're free to invite someone as your guest."

Michael immediately thought of Kathy Baer and realized that despite their agreement to stay in touch, it had been months since they had last spoken. They had exchanged texts early in the investigation of Monroe Wilkins' murder when the prosecution of Sabar for the hotel arson was put on hold while the defendant retained another attorney.

He made up his mind to call her as soon as he got back to his apartment. He wanted to catch up on what was going on with her trial and to ask her about taking vacation time from the fire department so she could accompany him on his holiday.

Over their main course, Michael told Romano all about the sentencing and Alonzo's diary entry.

"Sal, after reading that diary, there is no doubt that *HE* was responsible for Alonzo flipping on us. And when he didn't deliver on the witness stand, *the Evil One* punished him and made it appear to be a mob hit."

"Wilkins, Taliferro, and now Alonzo. That's three families *HE's* destroyed with this case alone, " Michael said. "Since *HIS* arrival *HE* has inflicted plenty of damage. Yet Brooklyn is still thriving. *HE* won't beat us! But when will *HE* realize that, and move on?"

Before he could answer, Romano's cell phone rang. He looked at the number and told Michael, "It's Caldwell."

For the next fifteen minutes, the monsignor said nothing as he listened to his boss.

"I understand, John," he finally said. "We're still in the restaurant, but we've finished our meal. I'll let him know and we'll see you in a few minutes."

"Michael, Caldwell apologized for interrupting our celebration but we need to meet him at his office. He wants to talk to you. It's urgent."

When Michael and the monsignor walked into the office Caldwell was behind his desk with a glass of whiskey in front of him. He told them to sit and asked if they cared to join him in a drink. Both Michael and Romano declined the offer.

"Michael. Let me begin by congratulating you on another job well done," Caldwell said. "That was a particularly difficult and demanding case, and as usual you handled it brilliantly. You make us all look good every time you defeat *HIM*. And I'm about to ask you to do it again."

Both Michael and Romano looked puzzled. "I believe I speak for the monsignor as well as myself," Michael said, "Neither of us has heard about anything new that *HE's* responsible for or anything you guys think *HE might* be responsible for. I'm pretty sure if that was the case Sal would have told me about it over dinner."

"You're right Michael. There's nothing new. It's something from *HIS* past that you're needed for."

"I've just come from a high-level meeting where it was decided that you would be taking over the prosecution of Ricky Sabar for the arson murders that occurred when he and the *Evil One* set fire to *The Calla Hotel* in Manhattan."

"Murders?" Michael asked. "I thought the only person who died in that incident was Alex Gazis. Are you saying someone died in addition to the fire marshal?"

"Yes. A woman named Pamela Totone, who was staying at the hotel on a visit to the city, was injured in the fire and taken to Mt. Sinai Hospital. She was elderly and had several pre-existing medical conditions that prevented her from recovering. A week ago she died from her injuries. The medical examiner performed an autopsy and classified her death as a homicide. His opinion is that the injuries she suffered in the fire were the contributing causes to her death."

"So what does that have to do with me?" Michael asked.

"The woman, as it turns out, was the second cousin of Manhattan Supreme Court Judge Laura Becca, the wife of Manhattan District Attorney Sean Myles. Judge Becca had no idea her cousin was in town, and of course knew nothing of her being injured in the fire. It seems that Ms. Totone lived alone and was estranged from her family. Only after her death did the investigators at the ME's office discover the relationship the deceased had with Judge Becca and notified her."

"The judge told her boss, the administrative judge for Manhattan, who in turn notified the judge presiding over the Sabar murder case and the District Attorney. When Sabar's new attorney, Lewis Cohen, was notified of all this by the trial judge, Cohen moved for a change of venue for Sabar's trial."

The administrative judge for the entire city granted Cohen's motion and administratively moved the case to Brooklyn. Camille Giordano, the judge before whom Sabar's Coney Island murder case was tried, was assigned to this case.

DA Price was informed of the move, and because of his connection to Sabar, Price reached out to Caldwell, who agreed to take over the case.

"Michael, you're going to get another shot at convicting that scumbag Sabar. I'm assigning the trial to you. The matter of *The People of the State of New York v. Ricky Sabar* will be on Judge Giordano's trial calendar next week. Good luck."

'*Maybe I will have that drink,*' Michael thought to himself.

ACKNOWLEDGMENTS

Fallen Angel is book 2 of a project that has been in the making for more than 30 years. The crimes described in the book all took place in Brooklyn during that time. I prosecuted these crimes along with the great detectives of the New York City Police Department, and the dedicated and extremely talented Detective Investigators and Assistant District Attorneys of the Brooklyn District Attorney's Office led by District Attorney Charles "Joe" Hynes. I call the book a "True Crime Fantasy "because some of the circumstances described in the investigation and trial of the cases, as well as the names of the characters, are fiction and were written to fit the overarching theme—the battle between Michael Gioca and Satan. Good versus Evil.

I could not have written *Fallen Angel* without the support, constant encouragement, and artistic assistance of my brilliant and talented wife, Lenor Romano, a talented designer and artist in her own right. Her contributions were invaluable. Lenor, I will always love you.

I also have to acknowledge and thank my friend and editor Dr. Sheldon Shuch, Ph.D., who teaches teachers how to teach and readers how to read and loves a good story well told. He watched over my story telling and grammar with the keen eye of a literature professor. Thank you Shelly for your support, guidance, honesty, and friendship.

Lastly, I want to thank Stephanie Larkin at Red Penguin Books who listened to my idea and had the interest, curiosity, and faith, to give me the opportunity to write it. Without the hard work and dedication, of her and her team, the story of *Fallen Angel* would not have been told.

Michael Vecchione

ABOUT THE AUTHOR

Michael Vecchione is the former Chief of the Homicide Bureau, Chief of Trials, and Chief of the Rackets Division in the Brooklyn District Attorney's Office, topping off a legal career of over 40 years, 30 of those as a prosecutor. In 2007 he was awarded the Thomas E. Dewey Medal as prosecutor of the year. He has co-authored four non-fiction, true crime books. *Fallen Angel* is his first solo project and is a work of fiction based on true events from his career as a prosecutor. He is a frequent contributor to true crime television productions and podcasts. He has served as an adjunct professor at St. John's University College of Professional Studies and as an adjunct professor of law at St. John's University School of Law, Brooklyn Law School, and The Maurice A. Deane School of Law at Hofstra University. He lives in Long Island City, New York, with his wife, Lenor Romano.